Praise for
Whiskey & Charlie

"A sharp, perceptive novel about family and forgiveness, *Whiskey & Charlie* will stay with me for a very long time."

—Christina Baker Kline, #1 *New York Times* bestselling author
of *Orphan Train*

"*Whiskey & Charlie* is a sharply observed family drama, which is affecting and ultimately uplifting without being sentimental. A finely crafted novel that keeps us reading because we care about the characters. It's a terrific book."

—Graeme Simsion, *New York Times* bestselling author of
The Rosie Project and *The Rosie Effect*

"Roiling with heart *and* soul, *Whiskey & Charlie* is a cleverly written journey through the maze of family relationships. What happens when an ordinary family is blindsided by an extraordinary tragedy? We should all have families like this. With her talent for nailing honest emotions, Annabel Smith draws you into her tale with a deft hand. By the end, you'll long to call your siblings and repair any petty squabbles. Here, brotherly love—with all its warts—is a bond that can be bent but never broken."

—Mary Hogan, author of *Two Sisters*

"*Whiskey & Charlie* is a clever, beautifully written book that pulls at the heartstrings and adeptly intertwines past and present."

—Lori Nelson Spielman, author of *The Life List*

WHISKEY
&
CHARLIE

ANNABEL SMITH

Published by Sourcebooks Landmark, an imprint of Sourcebooks, Inc.
P.O. Box 4410, Naperville, Illinois 60567-4410
(630) 961-3900
Fax: (630) 961-2168
www.sourcebooks.com

Originally published as *Whisky Charlie Foxtrot* in 2012 in Australia by Fremantle Press.

Library of Congress Cataloging-in-Publication Data

Smith, Annabel.
  Whiskey and Charlie / Annabel Smith.
     pages ; cm
  (softcover : acid-free paper) 1. Twin brothers—Fiction. 2. Sibling rivalry—Fiction. 3. Domestic fiction. I. Title.
  PR9619.4.S6W48 2015
  823'.92—dc23
                    2014044574

Printed and bound in the United States of America.
VP 10 9 8 7 6 5 4 3 2 1

For Duckers

CONTENTS

* * *

Sitting beside him in the hospital, Charlie is thinking that if Whiskey dies, he won't know which songs to choose for his funeral. Whiskey is his only brother; more than that, his twin: Alpha, the first born—the brightest star in the constellation, the person Charlie has loved and hated, pushed and pulled against all his life. Whiskey lies in a hospital bed in a maze of wires and tubes that connect him to the machines that help him breathe, keep his heart beating. He cannot move or speak, and his only brother no longer knows him.

But this is no place to begin; in fact, this may very well be the end.

ALPHA

Looking back, Charlie Ferns thinks it began when they were nine years old, the year his mother's sister Audrey moved to Australia. It was a Saturday morning, just like any other, when she came over to tell them. Charlie's father was playing squash; Whiskey, who was still William then, was upstairs. He was supposed to be practicing his trombone, but he was rebuilding his Scalextric track instead. Charlie knew this because he had gone upstairs to get his *Star Wars* figurines, and he had seen William kneeling on their bedroom floor with all the pieces of track out of the box, his trombone in the corner, still inside its case.

"Don't tell Mum," William said. Charlie shrugged. He knew his mother would work it out soon enough when she didn't hear William sliding up and down his scales. She was sharp like that. But on this particular day, his mother was distracted by what his aunt was saying.

Charlie wasn't listening at first. He was absorbed in orchestrating a furious light saber battle between Luke Skywalker and Darth Vader. It wasn't until he realized that his aunt was doing all the talking, that his mother wasn't saying anything at all, that Charlie began to take notice. You see, his mother usually kept up her part in a conversation. *Vivacious*, that's what people said about her, and although Charlie didn't know what this meant exactly, he knew it had something to do with her talking and laughing a lot. Her silence was a bad sign. It usually meant one of two things: one, Charlie or

William or, worse still, both of them had *gone too far*, or two, she had *a bone to pick* with their father.

"Your mother's upset, boys," their dad would say when their mother went silent on him, and they would leave the room, knowing an almighty argument was on the horizon.

"The calm before the storm," their father had joked to them once about their mother's silences, and they had laughed, guiltily, not really understanding, but knowing their mother would not find this joke funny. Charlie had never known his mother to go silent on anyone else. He stayed where he was, crouched on the floor beside the armchair, but he stopped the battle between *the forces of good and evil* and began to listen.

"I want to leave England, start all over again," his aunt was saying. "I want to go somewhere where people don't know me as Bob's widow, where they don't feel sorry for me or give me the cold shoulder because they blame me for his death. I want to go somewhere where nobody will even know what happened unless I tell them myself."

Charlie realized that both his aunt and his mother had forgotten he was there. None of the grown-ups ever talked about Uncle Bob's death when Charlie and William were around. They wouldn't have known anything at all if William hadn't overheard his mother on the phone, talking to her best friend, Suzanne. Bob had committed suicide, their mother told Suzanne, because Audrey confronted him about the other woman.

"Which other woman?" William had asked, but their mother had glared at him with such intensity that he had let it drop.

When they had asked their father about it later, he had snorted.

"Other woman?" he said. "That's a laugh. Other *women*, more like it."

This comment had left the boys no closer to understanding why it had happened, but their father did at least explain that *committing suicide* meant that Uncle Bob had killed himself, and he even told them how, explaining about the rope and his neck breaking before their mother overheard the conversation and stopped him by saying, "Could you *occasionally* engage your brain before opening your mouth?"

Charlie stayed absolutely still, thinking he might at last be able to solve the riddle of his uncle's death, and he felt a thrill go through him that he would be the one who found it out. He couldn't wait to tell William.

"You can understand that, can't you, Elaine?"

Audrey waited for her sister to answer, and in the silence, Charlie realized that his mother was crying. They had one of those shiny tablecloths you didn't have to wash—you could wipe it with a sponge—and Charlie could see his mother's tears sliding off her chin and dripping onto it, *plip, plip*.

"I'm not even forty yet," his aunt said, "but I feel like here my life's already over."

This comment was so surprising that Charlie forgot about his mum crying, or finding out the secret about Uncle Bob's death. Of course Charlie knew that Audrey was his mother's older sister. He had never known how much older, but if he had to guess, he would have said twenty years at least. In fact, Audrey seemed so much older that Charlie tended to think of her as his mother's mother, rather than as her sister. This thought was partly left over from when he was younger and hadn't been able to understand why other people had two grandmothers and he had only one. For a while he had pretended Audrey was his grandmother and not his aunt. He knew better now, of course, knew perfectly well that his mother's mother was dead, that she had died when he was three weeks old, and that's why he couldn't remember her at all. But his idea that Audrey was older had gotten stuck in his mind.

Once, his mother had shown Charlie a photo from Audrey's wedding, and Charlie could not believe the woman in the white dress in the center could possibly be his aunt. For some time afterward, he had tried to look for that skinny, pretty girl inside his aunt's soft and shapeless face, but he had never seen it, and after a while, he had forgotten to look. But he had asked his mother once how Audrey got so old. His mother had sighed, one of those big, long sighs she always gave when she talked about her sister.

"She's had a very hard life, Charlie."

To Charlie, a hard life was being a beggar, like in *Oliver Twist*, or your whole family sleeping in one bed, like in *Charlie and the Chocolate Factory*. He did not understand how two people who lived in a big house with a golden retriever could have a hard life. Besides, he had heard his mother say lots of times how lucky Audrey was.

"You're too young to understand this now, Charlie, but it's been a great disappointment to Audrey, not being able to have children..." She trailed off. Charlie looked at her. She seemed to be looking at something in the mirror. "And then the cancer," she said, but she was not really talking to Charlie; she seemed to have forgotten he was there. "She was really very young to have a mastectomy," she added, to no one in particular.

Charlie put his Matchbox Ferrari on top of his mother's dressing table and made a revving sound. He didn't want to talk about that. His mother had explained it to him before they went to see Audrey in the hospital, and it gave him a tummyache to think about it.

"Why else?" he asked.

"Why else what?"

Charlie revved the car impatiently. "Why else is she so old?"

"Well, I don't know, Charlie, isn't that enough? But I don't suppose Bob's behavior has helped."

"Why?" Charlie asked. "What did Uncle Bob do?"

"Oh, Charlie, you wear me out with your questions," she said, suddenly coming to, and she started tidying the dressing table, which meant the conversation was over.

So Charlie had asked his dad, which was what he always did when his mother's explanations didn't satisfy him.

"Did Uncle Bob make Auntie Audrey old?" he asked.

"Who told you that?"

"Mum."

His dad looked like he was about to laugh. "I suppose you could explain it like that."

"But *how* did he?"

"How did he? I suppose by being unfaithful. I think that's what your mother means."

"What's 'unfaithful'?"

"Well now, I suspect your mother might give me a thrashing if I told you that, boy. Nice try though, Charlie, nice try."

Unfaithful. It had sounded like something important, the way he had said it. Charlie had turned the word over in his mind. Faithful is what everyone always said about his granddad's dog, Tartan, because he always lay down at Granddad's feet and went every-where with him, even sometimes on the tractor. But why would Audrey want Bob to lie down at her feet? Charlie hadn't been able to make sense of it, and William, who was smart with those sorts of things, hadn't been able to work it out either.

Thinking about it again, Charlie lost the thread of the conversa-tion at the kitchen table. By the time he'd thought it all through, his mum had stopped crying.

"Australia! What an adventure, Audrey," she said as she put the teacups in the dishwasher. "I suppose we'll have to come out and see you there one day."

× × ×

"Alpha and Omega," she said when she explained it to the boys. Sometimes their mother spoke like that—bits of other languages, odd lines from plays she had read. Their father said this was because she had a brain but she didn't really get to use it, that it just boggled away inside her head and sometimes funny things came out. She said to Charlie and William that *Alpha* meant the beginning and

Omega was the end, and that for Audrey, moving to Australia was the end of one chapter and the beginning of another.

As well as being a new beginning for herself, in a way, Audrey's Omega was also Charlie's Alpha. Because before she left for Australia, she bought all of them lavish presents, the kinds of things they would never have bought for themselves. She took Elaine up to London to see *Cats*, a musical they both had on cassette tape and had wanted to see for years, and she bought their father a crystal brandy decanter.

But best of all, she bought Charlie and William the walkie-talkies, which were the beginning of everything.

* * *

The first day you do not even experience as a day. There are only minutes knotted into hours in which everything you usually do is forgotten, in which even eating and sleeping are of no importance whatsoever.

They sit in the waiting room, Charlie and his mother Elaine, Rosa and Juliet and Aunt Audrey. There are other people who come and are sent away again—Whiskey's friends perhaps, or colleagues, but afterward, Charlie does not recall who they were. Sometimes he dozes, sitting upright in one of the hard plastic chairs, and when he wakes, he cannot remember where he is or what he is doing there. He looks around, and possibly it is the smell that reminds him, or the expression on Rosa's face: he is at the hospital, waiting to find out whether his brother will live.

By the time Charlie had reached the hospital, Whiskey was already in surgery. Charlie cannot see him while he is being operated on, none of them can; all they can do is sit and wait for a doctor to emerge with a progress report. Charlie does not know how long they have been waiting. There is a clock in the waiting room, but the movement of its hands has no meaning for him.

So far, what they know is this: Whiskey is in a coma. He has a fractured skull, a punctured lung, a broken arm and broken ribs, and one of his feet has been crushed. Charlie has no idea of the implications of most of the items on this list of injuries. He attempts to picture Whiskey's foot. He pictures his own foot, the bones whose names he memorized for his human biology exams in high school and has long since forgotten. "Crushed," the doctor had said. Other things have been broken, but Whiskey's foot has been crushed. It sounds so much worse. The word *broken* somehow holds the promise of something that can be fixed—taped or glued or pinned back together. But *crushed* sounds beyond repair. Charlie pictures tiny fragments of bone all mixed together, an impossible puzzle. He thinks about gangrene, about amputation, briefly tries to imagine Whiskey with a prosthetic foot, and then just as quickly tries to wipe the image from his mind. He wonders about the impact of this injury on Whiskey's surfing and snowboarding. Then he realizes that he doesn't even know whether Whiskey still goes surfing. He thinks about asking Rosa, but when he looks over, she is crying.

x x x

When at last a doctor comes out to talk to them, it becomes abundantly clear that Whiskey's foot is the very least of his problems. The doctor explains that, during the accident, Whiskey received a blow to the head that caused bruising to his brain, a leaking of the blood vessels that resulted in the brain swelling.

"Unlike other tissues," the doctor says, "the brain has no room for swelling. It is trapped inside the cage of the skull. The lack of space causes a rise in intracranial pressure, leading to a decrease in blood flow, which in turn impacts on the ability of the brain cells to eliminate toxins."

Juliet puts her hand inside Charlie's. He tries to think of something to say to her, something positive and reassuring, but nothing comes to him.

While Charlie has been worrying about crushed bones, a neurosurgeon has been repairing the damaged blood vessels in Whiskey's brain, inserting a monitor to track the pressure and a device called a shunt to drain off the excess fluid.

Charlie remembers seeing a documentary in which a "trapdoor" was cut into a patient's skull to create more space and prevent further damage from the swelling following a head injury. In the same documentary, part of a brain deemed damaged beyond repair was cut away to increase the chance of recovery for the undamaged parts. Charlie supposes they should feel grateful Whiskey has not been subjected to such treatments. He takes it as a sign that things are not as bad as they might be.

That is until he sees Whiskey. For the person whose bed they are eventually led to could be anyone. At least one third of his body is cased in plaster, and most of his head is obscured by bandages. What Charlie can see of his face is so bruised and swollen that no features are recognizable. Worst of all, everywhere Charlie looks are tubes and wires connecting the body to machines, transporting substances in and out, measuring who knows what. Charlie cannot believe that this wrecked and wasted creature could possibly be his brother. No matter how hard he looks, he cannot find anything of Whiskey in that hospital bed. He stares and stares, and then he rushes to the bathroom and vomits so violently he bursts the blood vessels in his eyes.

BRAVO

Charlie's next-door neighbor Alison taught him the words to "Eye of the Tiger" while she helped him make his costume for the play. Alison was thirteen and knew the words to all the songs on the charts. She was good at things like that. It was also an undisputed fact in the village that Alison was the best at costumes. She proved it by winning first prize every year at the Rose Queen Fete.

The year she moved to Everton, she had dressed up as a Rubik's Cube. The rest of the kids paraded through the village in costumes that had been cobbled together the night before. They were ghosts with eyeholes chopped out of old sheets; cats with cardboard ears and ripped stockings for tails; miniature brides in communion dresses, wearing veils cut from curtain netting. The Rubik's Cube caused a sensation and established Alison's reputation.

The idea for the pharaoh costume had come from a picture in Alison's encyclopedia. According to the picture, the pharaohs didn't wear much in the way of clothing. Charlie supposed this was on account of it being so hot in Egypt. All he was wearing was a towel wrapped around his waist. But he had a magnificent headdress and a golden collar, and when he put them on, Charlie truly felt like a king.

"That towel used to be a nappy," William said when he saw the outfit. Their mum said it wasn't true, that diapers were square and the costume was wonderful, and anyway, she had given all their diapers to Auntie Sue when their cousin Hayley was born. Alison said that William was jealous because Charlie had a better part in the play. Charlie thought hard about this. William was better at soccer, better at telling jokes, better at yo-yoing and marbles. When he added it up, William was better at anything Charlie could think of. It was something quite new for William to be jealous of him, and Charlie found that he liked the idea of it.

Besides, he deserved a good part this year. Last Christmas, when they performed the Nativity play, Charlie had been given the part of an angel. He had asked if he and Timothy could be shepherds instead, but Miss Carty-Salmon had said there were already too many shepherds and that the boys should be honored to play the angels.

"But the angels are girls' parts," Timothy said.

"If you took the time to read the Bible, Timothy, I think you would find that the angels were men."

"Well then, why do they have girls' names?"

Charlie's mother had told the boys it was bad manners to talk back to a teacher. Timothy had obviously been given different advice. In the end, it made no difference to Miss Carty-Salmon, but Charlie thought Timothy was right. Gabriel was a girl's name, and if they were supposed to be boys, why did they have to wear costumes that looked like dresses?

This year the play was a shortened version of the musical *Joseph and the Amazing Technicolor Dreamcoat*, adapted by their teacher, the beautiful Miss Parker. All term they had been practicing "Any Dream Will Do," and Miss Parker, who had been to London to see the show, said they sang it even better than the real cast. The main part was Joseph, but the pharaoh was the second best part, and Charlie had spent weeks practicing his lines, shouting, "Throw him in jail!" until his mother said if he wasn't careful, he would wear out the words.

The night before, Charlie was so excited he couldn't get to sleep. He couldn't wait for his mum to see that there was something he was good at; that for once, William wouldn't be the first, the best, the fastest. But on the morning of the play, their mother had a migraine. Their father had a big job to finish. So Aunt Audrey came to watch the play in their mother's place. Charlie was bitterly disappointed.

But as it turned out, Aunt Audrey was a far better audience member than their mother had ever been. She shrieked with laughter at all the jokes, started all the other mums and dads clapping along to "Any Dream Will Do," and, best of all, when Charlie stepped forward to take his bow, she stood up out of her chair and shouted, "Bravo! Bravo!" Charlie thought he had never been so happy. *Bravo*, he said to himself as he went to sleep that night. *Bravo* was the word that meant there was something Charlie could do better, and he held on to it like it was a life buoy.

× × ×

The night before she left for Australia, Aunt Audrey came around to say good-bye. She told the boys she had a special going-away surprise for them, which they couldn't have now, but which would be waiting for them when they got home from school the next day.

Charlie and William ran all the way from the bus stop the next afternoon, rushed out of breath into the house to find their mother sitting in the armchair with Audrey's dog, Barnaby, at her feet.

"Are we looking after him," William shrieked, "until he can go to Australia?"

Their mother smiled and shook her head. "We're going to keep him."

"Forever?"

She nodded.

"Does Dad know?"

She nodded again. William and Charlie threw down their schoolbags and did their Zulu warrior dance twice, slapping their thighs and beating their chests before dropping onto the carpet to roll around and bury their faces in Barnaby's fur.

"Let's call him Bravo," Charlie said.

"No," said William, "let's call him Tomahawk."

"His name's Barnaby," their mum said. "You can't change a dog's name."

Barnaby was a golden retriever with velvet ears, and his name was engraved on a silver tag that hung from his collar. He held his right paw in the air when his tummy was rubbed, would fetch a stick or a ball no matter how far it was thrown, stood on his hind legs with his front paws on the bench when the boys were putting food in his bowl. He had a leash, but they never used it; they let him run ahead through the fields behind their house, let him get so far away they could hardly see him, and then they sang out his name to call him back.

"Baaaar-na-beeee!" William would call.

Braaaa-vo! Charlie would silently correct him.

× × ×

They had been looking after Barnaby for three months when he was hit by a car. Charlie was walking him that day, and Barnaby was racing ahead as he always did, crossing the High Street, when the car came around the corner from Tempsford Hill. Charlie saw the car clip Barnaby from behind, heard him yelp, watched the car slow and then speed up again. He ran to where Barnaby was lying, panting, his fur already soaked with blood; he knelt down and pulled the dog onto his lap, screaming and screaming until someone came out of the pub to see what the commotion was.

Then they were in Mary Partridge's car on the way to the vet, Charlie in the back holding Barnaby, stroking his head, begging him not to die, while his blood seeped onto the backseat, Mary Partridge behind the wheel, crying so hard she could barely see the road in front of her.

The vet came out to the car to carry the dog inside.

"Hit and run," Mary said to him. "What a crying shame."

"What's his name?" the vet asked.

"Bravo," Charlie said. "His name's Bravo. Is he going to die?"

"We'll see what we can do."

Mary sat with Charlie in the waiting room and held his hand until his mother arrived, and then all three of them sat, and the waiting went on and on.

When the vet opened the door to the examination room, Bravo was lying on the metal bench with his eyes closed, breathing slowly. Charlie stood beside him and stroked his ears and said his name, over and over, so he wouldn't have to listen to what the vet was saying to his mother. When they came over to the bench, Charlie's mother put her arm around him, and Charlie held his breath.

"One of his hind legs is broken," the vet said, "but otherwise the damage isn't too bad. He's badly bruised, but that'll heal. We can have a go at pinning the leg—he'll never run like he used to, but he'll get by." The vet paused. "There's a small chance of gangrene setting in, in which case we'd have to amputate. Your mother thinks we should give it a go, but she said it's up to you."

The whole time the vet was talking, Charlie had been stroking Bravo's ears, looking at his dry black nose, his whiskers twitching. He had thought Bravo would die on the road where the car hit him. He had thought Bravo would bleed to death in the back of Mary's car. He had sat for a long time on a hard chair, waiting for the vet to come out and tell them Bravo had died on that cold metal table while they were trying to put him back together. He had wondered how on earth they would tell Aunt Audrey.

He couldn't believe it was only a broken leg. He was so relieved he couldn't speak. Even if they had to cut it off, it would be all right. Three legs were enough; Charlie had only two, and he found it plenty. He was laughing or crying, or laughing and crying; it didn't matter which. Bravo would still be there, wagging his tail, pushing his wet snout into their hands when they got home from school. He'd still be able to catch a ball and hold a stick in his mouth and gulp his dinner down in five seconds flat. Broken leg or not, he'd still be their very own dog, their Bravo.

CHARLIE

F or a long time, Charlie had wished he wasn't called Charlie. In his school class alone, there were three other boys with the same name. His mother, who loved the royal family, who years later would cry uncontrollably when Princess Diana died, said it was a fine name, a strong name, the name of the Prince of Wales, the man who would be King of England. Their father said Prince Charles was a pompous, jug-eared fool, but your name was your name, and once you had it, you were stuck with it.

But Charlie knew that wasn't true. After all, it was only a few months ago that Bravo used to be called Barnaby, and no one ever called him that name now. And if a dog could have a new name, then why couldn't he? The name Charlie had chosen for himself was Steve, after Steve McQueen, with whom Charlie had been obsessed ever since he and his dad had watched *The Great Escape* one Saturday afternoon when his mother was at the theater.

It was Buddy who made Charlie change his mind about his name. Buddy had lived next door to Charlie's parents when they were first married, and he was stationed on the air base at Chicksands. Until Buddy came to visit them, Americans had existed for Charlie and William only on television. They were enthralled by Buddy, by his accent, by his strange habit of eating with his fork in his right hand, the way he said, "Aw, c'mon, guys," or "You betcha!" No one had ever called them *guys* before.

Since Audrey bought them the walkie-talkies, the boys had put away their LEGO space station and their Playmobil fort, their *Star Wars* figurines, and their Scalextric. Instead, they played at being cops and robbers, private detectives, or secret agents. They used phrases they had heard in films and on television, words they didn't even understand, but had used so often in their games they had come to have a real meaning. They said, "Do you read me?" and "Get the hell out of there!" They said, "Meet me at the southwest exit at eighteen hundred hours." They said "roger" and "niner" and "over and out." They said these things without embarrassment, with that nine-year-old conviction that they were saying all the right things in exactly the way they should be said. But when Buddy overheard them, he started to laugh.

"LAPD, twenty-six hundred!" Buddy repeated, slapping his leg as he laughed. "What the hell kind of crap are you guys spouting into those damn things?"

So Buddy had taught them the two-way radio alphabet. And that was how Charlie found out that his name was a useful one, that it stood for something. That it was the third letter of the NATO phonetic alphabet, established in 1955 and approved by the International Civil Aviation Organization. It had represented the letter *C* to the U.S. Navy, the British Army, the RAF, and, best of all, it had been used on board the aircraft in the Dambusters raid.

William was put out that his name wasn't part of the phonetic alphabet. To compensate, he started calling himself Whiskey. Their father, whom they had always called Dad, became Papa. Their mother, of course, remained simply Mum, and Bravo, lucky Bravo, was spared a second name change, since his name was already part of the alphabet.

Knowing the alphabet made the walkie-talkie games even better, though William could never remember the whole thing and would make up his own words under pressure, saying silly things like *Mouse* instead of *Mike* and *Lulu* instead of *Lima*. Charlie never corrected him, but he remembered the words William could not, learned to recite the two-way alphabet backward as well as front ways, and his command of it, his place in it, was one small thing he had that his brother did not.

* * *

Charlie goes to the hospital first thing. He wants to be in and out before his mother arrives, dreads the thought of having to talk to her about the situation or, worse still, talk around it. Easier to avoid her altogether. Rosa will be there, of course; she hasn't left yet, as far as Charlie knows.

Standing outside Whiskey's room, Charlie sees her through the glass pane of the door. She is sitting with her head bowed, as close to the bed as she can get. Charlie thinks she must have fallen asleep, opens the door gently so as not to startle her, but she looks up at once and speaks without greeting him. Charlie knows then she has been awake all night, thinking, wanting to talk, waiting for someone to come.

"This is not the way he want to die," she says. Her Spanish accent, somehow thicker in a whisper, makes what Rosa is saying sound even worse than it already is.

Charlie flinches at the word *die*, the word no one else in his family will say. He doesn't know if he believes that Whiskey can hear them, but he doesn't want to stand right next to him and talk about him as though he's already gone. He pulls Rosa away from the bed.

"You mustn't think like that, Rosa," he whispers. "You know what the doctors said. There's a good chance he'll recover."

"Fifty-fifty, they said," Rosa insists. "That means good chance of dying."

"Well," Charlie says lamely, "that's the worst-case scenario."

"Do you think so, Charlie? I think worst case is for months he stays alive like this, for years he lives, these machines doing the things he used do for himself. Worst case is he wakes up with brain damage, and the Whiskey we know is gone." Her Spanish accent, somehow thicker in a whisper, makes what Rosa is saying sound even worse than it already is.

Charlie sits down in one of the hard hospital chairs. It is less than twenty-four hours since he received the phone call from his mother, and in those hours, his only thought has been that Whiskey must not die. He must not die because he, Charlie, needs more time. He and Whiskey have not been friends, have not talked or laughed together for months, years. But he had never thought it would end like this. They're still young, only thirty-two; there should be forty or fifty years, at least, for them to sort out their differences. He had always thought there would be time.

Now he sees that there might be things worse than Whiskey dying, that they might have all the time in the world and it wouldn't make any difference.

"He want to die in that crazy car, or jumping out of airplane," Rosa says.

Charlie thinks that if Rosa hadn't come along, Whiskey would have died like Elvis, of booze and drugs and too many cheeseburgers, although knowing Whiskey, they would have been hundred-dollar cheeseburgers made of Japanese beef from calves that had been massaged with milk. He doesn't say this to Rosa. She is sitting with her palms up in her lap, and he notices for the first time how small her hands are. He wants to give her something.

"You're right," he says eventually. "Whiskey's always been a daredevil, even when we were little kids. Once, when we were about six or seven, he dressed up in his Superman suit and jumped out of a tree in our driveway with a rope tied around him. He probably would have broken his neck, but the rope got caught under his armpit, and he dislocated his arm instead."

"He never tell me that," she says.

Charlie smiles at the memory. He had almost forgotten it himself.

DELTA

Charlie found out about *Delta of Venus* on the first day of term because it was Whiskey's friend, Grainger, who owned the book. But he didn't actually read any of it until a couple of weeks later, by which time every boy in the school was talking about it. Grainger had been on holiday to France and claimed to have bought the book from a kiosk, an ordinary kiosk, selling newspapers and chewing gum and cigarettes. It was a well-known fact that France was a land of sex maniacs, that you could buy things there that you couldn't possibly get your hands on in England, and there were plenty of other boys who'd come back from holidays with dirty French comics. But Grainger's book was different. For starters, there were no pictures. In theory, when you read something dirty, you could make up your own pictures. But some of the scenes described in Grainger's book were beyond Charlie's imagination; he could find no place for them within his own concept of sex.

Not that he would have called himself an expert. At the age of fifteen, sex was one of those subjects you pretended to know everything about while knowing almost nothing. If you asked questions, you were exposed, tainted with the word *virgin*, and would never live it down. Finding out more without risking exposure, that was the challenge.

Charlie had no sexual experience of his own to speak of, except for a fumbled kiss with Michelle Perry in a cupboard at a party, during a game of spin the bottle. Other boys had come out of the same cupboard with different girls and much better stories to tell. Tom Costello had put his hand up Louise Barker's skirt, Chris Lennox had felt Claire Corbell's breasts, and, allegedly, Charlotte Graham had put her hand down Joel Orton's pants.

Would things have been different if it was Charlie who had ended up in the cupboard with Charlotte Graham? Would she have put her hand down Charlie's trousers—down anyone's trousers? Or did Joel possess some skill that Charlie had not yet mastered? Could Charlie have touched Michelle's breasts if he had tried? How did you know if a girl would or wouldn't? How could you change her mind?

These were the questions that plagued Charlie, questions he could not ask and could not find the answers to: not in the encyclopedias and medical books at the library, not in their father's awkward and incomprehensible talk about *the birds and the bees*, not in the explanation they had been given in health education by the dried-up, flat-chested Miss Pennacombe, who, it was agreed, could not possibly ever have had sex herself and therefore could have nothing to teach them. Certainly her interminable description of the sperm fertilizing the egg had done nothing to help Charlie decipher the dirty jokes he heard, though he always laughed anyway, hoping he was laughing at the right moment.

He thought he understood the mechanics of it, the what-goes-where. But that, to Charlie, was not sex. Sex was what he had seen in the dirty magazines boys at school had pilfered from older brothers or stolen from newsstands. Or, at least, that was what Charlie had thought, until he read what was inside Grainger's book.

Delta of Venus. That was the title. Nobody knew what it meant exactly; no one could have used the words in a sentence, but they were passed from boy to boy, muttered and snickered over until they came to represent everything you needed to know about sex and didn't know how to find out. Very few people had actually seen the book. Apparently, it had a very sexy cover: a picture of a naked woman, but not like a centerfold, more *arty*, so you couldn't see her face. In fact, you couldn't even be sure which part of her body you were looking at, though you had a pretty fair idea. After the first week, no one got to see the book at all, apart from Grainger's close friends, Whiskey included, who confirmed for Charlie that the rumors about the cover were true.

All the other boys ever saw were the photocopies. Grainger made the photocopies at his dad's office on a Saturday morning, and at school on Monday, you could buy them for twenty pence a page. You couldn't choose which parts you wanted; it was the luck of the draw. But according to Grainger, who claimed to have read the whole book, there wasn't a page that wasn't dirty, so it really didn't matter which one you got.

The first week, he made twenty copies, and he'd sold them all before lunchtime on Monday. The following Saturday, he made a hundred copies, and he put the price up to fifty pence. It didn't matter if you'd paid twenty pence the week before; fifty pence was the new price, take it or leave it. You weren't allowed to show them to anyone else or swap them, and anyone who tried to make their own copies wouldn't be sold any more. Those were the rules. No one argued. Everybody wanted the photocopies, and Grainger was the only one who had them. They were shocking and disgusting, and he got rid of a hundred in two days. With the help of Whiskey and his friend Joel, he sold them before school and after school, between classes, at recess and at lunch, in the bathrooms and behind the bike shed and on the school bus. Even when he made one hundred fifty copies, there still weren't enough to go around.

Charlie did not have to pay for the photocopies, because Whiskey got them for free, as many as he wanted. Charlie had mixed feelings about this setup. On the one hand, he was relieved that he did not have to buy the copies himself. Once he had read a few, he knew there was something wrong about them, something that made him feel guilty and shameful. Charlie suspected he was not the only one who felt this way. He noticed that though everyone was talking about the photocopies, no one actually talked about what was in them. You bought them, put them in your bag, and took them home, and when you came to school the next day, you said "I got the baron and the little girls" or "I got the woman and the dog." But you didn't talk about the things you read.

The story of the man who pulled the corpse of a naked woman out of a river and then had sex with her dead body was disgusting to Charlie, but when he read it, his penis got so hard it was almost painful. There were sentences he read over and over again until they got stuck in his mind and he couldn't close them out. Charlie had rubbed himself raw over the story of the Cuban and the nymphomaniac, and for days afterward, one sentence went around and around inside his head. On the bus and in his math class and at the dinner table it would come to him unbidden—*She was moist and trembling, opening her legs and trying to climb over him*—and it took all of Charlie's willpower and concentration to control his erections.

There was nothing you could say about that. So you didn't talk about the stories with your friends; you didn't talk to anyone about them. Even when he got the copies from Whiskey, Charlie couldn't meet his eye. The thought of buying them at school, like the other boys had to, was unbearable. He was sure that if he had to make that transaction, in front of other people, every one of them would know what he was thinking, what he did alone in bed at night once the light was off. So he was grateful to Whiskey for sparing him that humiliation.

At the same time, he resented him for once again being at the center of something that Charlie was on the outside of. For although it was Grainger's book, Grainger was part of Whiskey's gang, which meant that in the eyes of everyone at school, Whiskey was as much a part of it as Grainger himself. Whiskey had seen the book, knew the story about where it had come from, was helping Grainger to sell the copies—it might as well have been his own book. Whereas

Charlie, as always, was on the sidelines, hadn't so much as glimpsed the book, didn't even have the gumption to buy his own copies, but had to get them secondhand from his brother, and for that, Charlie hated him. For he knew this book was just the beginning, that in sex, as in sport, Whiskey would be Charlie's superior: he would go further faster, and Charlie would be left behind, as he had always been since the day they were born.

× × ×

Delta of Venus dominated Charlie's life, all their lives, for a little more than four weeks. In the fifth week, Whiskey, Grainger, and Joel were caught selling the copies in the science-block bathroom, and the jig was up. The book was confiscated, presumed destroyed; the boys were hit with a cane and suspended, and the proceeds of their sales, which totaled almost two hundred pounds, were donated to the Salvation Army. The situation was evidently too scandalous to be handled by a woman—the special assembly, for the boys only, was addressed not by their headmistress, Mrs. Aster, but by the deputy headmaster, who also happened to be the head of religious education. There was barely a boy in the school who wasn't implicated, and the hall had never been so still or silent, two hundred fifty pairs of eyes trained resolutely on the ancient woodblock floor as Mr. Daniels spoke of his *shock and disgust* over the confiscated materials and his *disappointment at the lack of moral fiber* evidenced by this incident.

The assembly lasted less than ten minutes, long enough for Whiskey, Grainger, and Joel to be made an example of, long enough for the same fate to be threatened to any boy caught in possession of such filth.

"The shit's going to hit the fan," Whiskey joked to Charlie on the way home, but Charlie knew that Whiskey feared their mother's reaction more than any punishment meted out at school. To be caned was not a humiliation but a badge of honor, a sign that you'd been outrageously rebellious, and, as such, earned you the respect of the other boys. As for the suspension, Whiskey looked upon it more as a reward than a punishment.

Though the boys knew their mother must have had a telephone call from the school, she was ominously silent when they arrived home. They slunk off to their rooms, assuming she was waiting for their dad to come in from work before she made her move. But at dinnertime, she still said nothing, only glared at Whiskey, and at Charlie as well, as though he too was implicated, though she could not have had evidence of that. Or could she? Charlie prayed that she hadn't found his photocopies wedged beneath his mattress.

It wasn't until Whiskey attempted to excuse himself that she finally spoke.

"Sit down, William," she said in a low voice. "What have you got to say for yourself?"

Whiskey shrugged, keeping his eyes on the table.

"Look at me when I'm speaking to you."

Whiskey looked up but said nothing, knowing from experience that whatever he said would only make matters worse.

She looked at their father. "Bill, do you have something to say to your son?"

This surprised Charlie. Their mother was the disciplinarian; that was the accepted order of things. These were obviously deemed to be special circumstances, as they had been at school: a man-to-man matter. But Charlie could see that his father was unprepared, stuck for words.

"Not one of your better ideas, Whiskey boy," he said eventually.

Their mother stared at him expectantly, waiting for him to go on. He let out a sigh, appeared to be thinking hard, and then he began nodding his head; something had come to him.

"Certainly very entrepreneurial though, I'll give you that."

Charlie cringed.

His mother exploded.

"That's right, Bill, encourage him; that's the idea! Your fifteen-year-old son is producing and distributing pornography, and you tell him he's entrepreneurial! For pity's sake, is there anything at all between your ears?"

"All right, Elaine, calm down. I was just trying to have a joke. Whiskey knows he's done the wrong thing; I don't think we need to labor the point."

"Labor the point?" She laughed then, a sharp, abrupt sound like the bark of a dog that has been unexpectedly shut outside. "No, you're right, of course. We shouldn't *labor the point*. Better to make a joke of it, give him a pat on the back, and with any luck, he'll leave school at sixteen to become a pimp. Is that what you want?"

Charlie was shocked to hear his mother use the word *pimp*. He sneaked a look at Whiskey, but Whiskey wouldn't meet his eye.

"Don't be ridiculous, Elaine, you're overreacting."

"Overreacting? Do you have any idea how many times I've had William's headmistress on the phone this term? He can't stay out of trouble for five minutes. I'm at the end of my rope!"

Bill coughed. "Well, perhaps you're right. But the boy's already been punished. I don't think there's any need for us to get heavy-handed as well."

Their mother snorted. "One week off school! You call that a punishment?" She turned her attention to Whiskey. Charlie did not often feel sorry for his brother, but he felt sorry for him then.

"There'll be no bike riding, no skateboarding, no television, no Atari. No phone calls, no hanging around at the shopping center, no listening to your records. And you won't be seeing your partners in crime, that's a certainty."

Whiskey was flattened. "What am I supposed to do then?"

"There are plenty of ways you can make yourself useful around the house. I can give you a list so long you won't have time to scratch yourself. And woe betide you if you defy me, William, because I'll find out, believe me, and then you'll really know the meaning of the word 'punishment.'"

× × ×

By the time Whiskey got back to school, the whole thing had blown over. Once the book was gone, the source cut off, the fever subsided. When people stopped talking about them, the photocopies lost their currency; Charlie gave up reading them, left them for weeks under his mattress, eventually threw them away.

Sex became once again about the girls you knew and how far you could go with them. As in the American movies they watched, progress was measured in *bases*. Since they had never played baseball, and no one knew the rules, there was some confusion about exactly what happened at each base. First base was kissing, that much was generally agreed. But to Charlie, even first base was a gray area. Because as everybody knew, there were two kinds of kissing.

There was the kind of kissing that took place during a game of spin the bottle, in which you were shut in a darkened cupboard with a girl you may or may not fancy (and who may or may not fancy you, although this was considered largely irrelevant) and you had thirty seconds to locate her mouth and work your tongue inside it. To Charlie's mind, this kind of kissing had more in common with pin the tail on the donkey than with baseball, and he did not know if it counted as first base.

He suspected that first base meant the kind of kissing that happened at junior high parties, where no one played spin the bottle anymore, but people somehow paired off anyway, the kind of kissing where you locked lips with a girl and didn't come up for air until you had attempted to touch every square inch of her body with your roaming hands. The second kind of kissing Charlie had seen plenty of but had never participated in himself, which meant, depending on one's definition, he had never even gotten to first base.

Second base had to do with breasts, tits, jugs, knockers, baps, or whatever else you might call them. A lot of the girls in Charlie's grade didn't seem to have much to offer in that department, at least not compared to the women in the magazines Charlie had seen. But if he had to touch a girl's breasts to progress to the next base, he was prepared to do so, even if the girl in question was as flat as a pancake.

By the end of junior high second base seemed to have been so widely achieved that it wasn't worth discussing anymore. A lot of boys claimed to have gotten to third base, some even farther, while Charlie was still stuck on first. According to reports, there were plenty of girls who'd let you touch their breasts or even slide your hand up their skirt. But Charlie always seemed to end up with the frigid girls, girls like Alice Brown, who had kept her lips clamped shut when he kissed her, so he couldn't get his tongue in her mouth, or Susan Wilkes, who had gripped his wrists while they kissed, so he couldn't touch her body at all.

Whiskey, of course, had already made it to third base. He had made out with Louise Barker at a party, and then gone out with her for about three weeks, before dropping her because she wouldn't "go all the way." What he failed to take into account was that when you dropped a girl because she wouldn't go far enough, she would want to get back at you. And the best way to do that was to make out with someone you knew and go much farther with that person, maybe even all the way, and then to make sure you found out about it. If she really wanted to get back at you, she'd make out with one of your best friends or, better still, your twin brother. Which is how Charlie, in a surprise twist of fate, managed to cover three bases in one night.

It happened like this. There was a party at Tom Costello's house in the first week of the summer holidays. Because Tom's brother was sixteen, there was beer at the party, which meant that by nine o'clock, everyone was making out with someone. Charlie was in

WHISKEY & CHARLIE • 31

the kitchen, swigging his beer as though he loved the taste of it, when Louise's friend Claire came over.

"Charlie! Where've you been? I've been looking for you!" She said this playfully, as if they were good friends having a joke together, which confused Charlie, because although he knew Claire by name, he had never actually spoken to her before.

"Louise wants you," she said conspiratorially.

"Louise Barker?"

Claire rolled her eyes. "Of course Louise Barker. Who else would it be? You know she's mad on you."

Charlie couldn't make sense of this conversation. He thought he must be drunk. "But Louise went out with Whiskey."

"Whiskey!" Claire scoffed. "Louise *hates* Whiskey. You're the one she likes. That's why she asked me to come and find you. She wants to talk to you."

"Where is she?"

"She's upstairs," Claire said, "in the first bedroom on the left. She's waiting for you." And then she took the beer can out of Charlie's hand and gave him a little push toward the stairs.

Charlie went upstairs slowly, trying to work things out in his head. It couldn't be true that Louise liked him, when only a week ago she'd been so into Whiskey. Probably she wanted to talk to him about Whiskey, see if there was any chance of them getting back together, ask Charlie to put in a word for her. But if that was all, why did she have to send Claire to find him? Why couldn't she come and talk to him herself? Perhaps Claire was setting Charlie up; perhaps Louise was upstairs with some other boy, or she wasn't upstairs at all and the whole thing was a wild-goose chase designed to expose Charlie's desperation. But what if Claire was telling the truth and this was Charlie's big chance to make some progress on the bases? Charlie knew it was a long shot, but it was this last thought that propelled him up the stairs and into the first bedroom on the left.

The room must have belonged to Tom's little sister; everything in sight was pink, except for Louise, who was sitting on the bed on top of a Flower Fairies duvet cover.

"Hello, Charlie," she said. "I've been waiting for you."

So that much at least was true. Charlie smiled, or perhaps grimaced, unsure of how to proceed.

"You'd better shut the door," she said and patted the bed enticingly. Charlie sat down.

"You look exactly like him," Louise said, staring at Charlie in a way that made him feel even more uncomfortable.

"We're identical," Charlie said awkwardly. He hated it when people commented on how alike he and Whiskey were. He especially didn't want to talk about it with Louise. But Louise continued to study him.

"I think Whiskey's a little taller," she said thoughtfully.

It was true, but Charlie was hardly about to admit it. He wanted to get off the topic of Whiskey altogether.

"Claire said you wanted to talk about something."

"Well, we can talk anytime. Wouldn't you rather kiss me?" Louise said. And then she leaned forward unexpectedly and pressed her mouth against his. Charlie had a moment's hesitation. It didn't seem right to start kissing without a little more chitchat. And given that Louise had just broken up with Whiskey, Charlie probably shouldn't be kissing her at all. But she smelt like fruit salad, and her mouth was so warm and soft that Charlie couldn't help himself. He leaned in closer to her, but she pulled away to look at him again.

"It's so weird kissing you," she said. "I feel like I'm still kissing Whiskey."

There they were, back to Whiskey already. But then Louise pulled his face into hers as though nothing else mattered, and side by side in that pink and sparkly room, they kissed until Charlie couldn't tell where his mouth ended and Louise's began. Without knowing how they got there, Charlie found that they were lying down on the bed, and getting to second base happened so quickly he barely had time to take it in. Even the fact that he couldn't undo Louise's bra didn't slow them; she sat up and took it off herself, and though she had hardly any breasts to speak of, her perfect pink nipples were as soft as her mouth, and Charlie found that her breast size didn't matter at all. They were pressed thigh to thigh, hip to hip, and Charlie had the biggest erection of his life.

When Louise looked at her watch and said, "Imagine if Whiskey knew what we were doing," Charlie knew something was wrong, but when she undid his belt and put her hand inside his boxer shorts, he didn't care, he didn't care. The feeling of Louise's hand wrapped around his penis was so intense, so consuming, that he didn't even care when the door opened and he saw Whiskey standing there, with Claire behind him.

"Don't stop, it doesn't matter," Charlie groaned, feeling himself only seconds from ejaculating. But as soon as the door was closed, Louise pulled her hand away and, seeing the look on her face, Charlie understood what he had taken part in.

It had all been for Whiskey. Louise wasn't interested in Charlie at all. Now that Whiskey had caught her with Charlie, caught her going farther than she had with him, Charlie might as well have not existed. She didn't even look at him while she put on her bra and straightened her clothes. Charlie didn't care that he'd been set up, that Louise had used him. Those twenty minutes he had spent with her had been the best twenty minutes of his entire life. What he couldn't stand was that this moment, this triumph, was not his own. That even when he had overtaken Whiskey, it was Whiskey who had helped him to do it, so the triumph, as always, was Whiskey's.

ECHO

I n the lead-up to their departure from England, Charlie had convinced himself that somehow, in Australia, where everything was upside down, there would be some kind of role reversal in which suddenly he, Charlie, would become the popular one, the funny one, the one everyone remembered, and Whiskey would be the one left on the sidelines. Part of him knew it was nothing but wishful thinking, but another part of him clung to it. It was what pulled him through those months before they left England, months in which most of his childhood was donated to charity and what was left was packed into cardboard boxes, ballast for the ship that would take them to Melbourne.

× × ×

The *Spirit of the Deep* sailed from Southampton on a September day so glorious it made Charlie's father wonder out loud why they were leaving.

"It's like this every day in Australia," their mother reminded them, but it did not make them feel any better as they stood on the deck, watching England slide away.

"Let's go and find our room—get settled before dinner," their mother suggested.

"They're not rooms, Elaine. They're cabins," Charlie's father said.

The stairwells and walkways were crowded with people, all heading in the same direction. Charlie traipsed behind his parents, thinking of the *Titanic*, wondering how they would ever find their way back to the deck if the ship were to sink.

"We must be beneath the waterline now," Charlie's father said excitedly when they reached C deck.

"One more floor to go!" their mother said in her fake cheerful voice.

"One more *deck*, Elaine, one more deck."

"I thought only the luggage was underwater," Charlie muttered to Whiskey.

"And the animals." Whiskey smirked.

"Here we are!" their mother said at last, opening the cabin door.

Charlie peered inside. There were two sets of bunk beds separated by a miniature washbasin, and a tiny wardrobe between the end of the beds and the door. Charlie doubted whether there was enough space for all four of them to stand up simultaneously.

Their father ducked through the door, closely followed by Whiskey. "Port or starboard, Whiskey?" he said, gesturing to the bunks.

"Which is which?" Whiskey asked, climbing up a little ladder to claim one of the top bunks.

"Hell if I know!"

"I didn't realize the windows would be covered up," Charlie's mother said, sitting on one of the bottom bunks.

"Portholes," Bill corrected her.

"Since when do you know so much about boats?"

"It's a ship, Elaine, not a boat."

"Why couldn't we fly to Melbourne, like normal people?" Whiskey said.

"This is the experience of a lifetime," their mother said, as if she was quoting the brochure, but she did not sound entirely convinced.

There was a knock at the door. A man in a burgundy uniform stepped into the already overcrowded cabin. "I'm your steward, Sanju," he said, smiling. "I'm here to make your journey comfortable, so please don't hesitate to ask me if there's anything you need: sheets or towels, a cup of tea or coffee. I have a little galley halfway along this corridor. You'll find me there most of the time. Do you have any questions so far?"

"How many passengers are on board, Sanju?" Charlie's father asked immediately. Charlie couldn't remember the last time he had seen his father so excited.

"Two thousand three hundred, sir, give or take a few."

"Where's the bathroom?" Charlie asked. He didn't need to go to the bathroom, but he didn't think he could stand to spend another minute crammed inside that cabin. He'd had enough of his family already. He wondered if it was possible to develop instantaneous claustrophobia.

× × ×

Charlie was woken by the ship's PA system, belting out a jaunty hornpipe. The cabin was pitch-black.

"Why are they playing that bloody music in the middle of the night?" Charlie heard his father say from the bunk below.

Charlie turned on his reading light, looked at his watch. "It's six o'clock," he said.

"Why are they waking us up so early?" Whiskey groaned.

Whiskey, like their mother, was not a morning person.

"Breakfast, I suppose," Bill said, already wide-awake, rolling out of bed and standing up, his face appearing suddenly next to Charlie.

"Why would we want to eat breakfast at six o'clock?"

"Well, there's two thousand people, aren't there? We can't all have breakfast at once. Someone has to be in the first sitting," Bill said cheerfully.

"Why us?" Whiskey complained.

"Because we're in the cheap seats, boys. That's the way the mop flops. Now up you get. It takes so bloody long to get there—if we don't look lively, all the bacon will be gone."

Charlie slid down from his bunk, landing in the suitcase his dad had dragged out from beneath the bottom bunk.

"Watch out, Charlie!"

"Shhh," his mother said, clamping the miniature pillow over her head.

Charlie clambered out of the suitcase, struggled into jeans and a T-shirt in the cramped space at the end of his bunk.

"I wonder what the weather's going to be like," Bill said, rummaging through his suitcase.

"It's a cruise, Dad. It's sunny every day," Whiskey said sarcastically, pulling on yesterday's clothes without getting out of his bunk.

"What about Mum?" Charlie asked when they had finished shuffling around each other.

"She'll live," Bill said.

× × ×

"Where do you think we are, then?" Whiskey asked his dad when they went out on the promenade deck after breakfast.

"We'd be somewhere along the French coast, I suppose, heading for the Bay of Biscay."

"I didn't realize it would be so cold," Charlie said.

"That Atlantic breeze is certainly nippy," Bill said.

"I wish I'd brought my sweater up."

"Well, go down and get it."

"I can't be bothered," Charlie said. "It takes too long."

"You're right about that," his father said. "By the time you get back, the sun will be out, and you won't need it anymore. It'd be handy if we could communicate with your mother—get her to bring us something warm—if she ever emerges."

"Maybe they'll let you use the PA system," Whiskey joked.

"We could do with your old walkie-talkies," their dad suggested.

"Do we even have them anymore?" Whiskey asked Charlie.

"I doubt it," Charlie said. "I don't remember packing them, anyway."

"Your mum probably threw them out years ago, knowing her."

"Bummer," Whiskey said. "They would have been great." He made a crackling sound, held an imaginary walkie-talkie to his mouth. *"Deck to cabin Delta 12. Sweater required urgently, over."*

Charlie laughed, crackled back. *"Delta 12 to deck. Can you repeat that command? Over."*

"Sweater," Whiskey said. *"Sierra—Whiskey—Echo—Apple—"*

"Alpha," Charlie corrected him.

"Whatever." Whiskey shrugged. *"Sierra—Whiskey—Echo—Alpha. What's 'T'?"*

"Tango." Charlie didn't even have to think about it.

"Tango—Echo." Whiskey stopped again.

"Romeo," Charlie finished for him.

"SWEATER. Roger that. Over and out!"

They laughed.

Bill looked mystified. "I never did understand how you boys managed to remember that gibberish."

× × ×

It did not take many days for Charlie and Whiskey to exhaust the ship's entertainments: at fifteen, they were too old for the children's activities and too young for the adults'. Once the novelty had worn off, Charlie grew tired of swimming, and of table tennis, which Whiskey almost always won. They had watched *Ferris Bueller's Day Off* in the ship's cinema so many times that they could quote entire scenes verbatim. They had even worked their way through the board games in the lounge, Yahtzee, Monopoly, and Guess Who?, games they had long since outgrown but that filled a few hours in which they had nothing better to do.

Charlie tracked their progress on a map so small that their entire journey was barely longer than his index finger. Through the blue-black reaches of the Atlantic they crawled, following the coast of Portugal as it curved toward the Mediterranean Sea, through the

Strait of Gibraltar and south of Sicily to Crete, where they spent the day. Then there was the slow and eerie journey through the narrow Suez Canal into the Red Sea, a day in Djibouti, and then at last into the Indian Ocean.

From Djibouti to Perth, Western Australia, took a whole week, seven long days in which there was nothing to see from the promenade deck except water and sky, water and sky, and if it weren't for the huge waves, slapping relentlessly against the hull of the ship, Charlie would have sworn they weren't moving at all. The deck was bare, the dining room empty; everyone was seasick, sweating and moaning in their cabins until the whole ship smelled of vomit and disinfectant. Charlie found himself curiously immune to the rough seas, wandering the stairwells and walkways alone, wondering if they would ever see land again.

One day SanJu took pity on him and led him off for an unofficial tour of the bridge.

"Ask how deep it is," their father said from his bunk when he found out where Charlie was going. Even in the midst of his seasickness, he was still collecting facts about the voyage.

Charlie could have spent all day in the control room. He was fascinated by the navigational instruments, the vast panel of buttons and switches and levers, the screens that flashed and beeped constantly, continually updating their speed, their latitude and longitude, the temperature of the air outside, and the surface temperature of the water, the direction and speed of the wind. When Charlie asked about the depth, the first officer showed him the echo sounder equipment, explained how it sent a beam of sound through the water to the ocean floor and gauged the distance by the time it took the echo of that sound to return.

"Tell your dad," he said, "that the deepest part of the Indian Ocean is the Java Trench, four and a half miles deep, give or take a few feet."

× × ×

Lying in his bunk that night, listening to the drone of the engine, Charlie remembered something his history teacher, Mr. Carr, had said on the first day of the school term the year before.

"Battle of Hastings, what was the date?" he had asked before they had even opened their notebooks. Hands had gone up cautiously, dreading the outcome; surely they weren't getting tested on the first day of term.

"Henry the Eighth's wives: What were their names? How did he get rid of them?" Hands went up; hands went down.

"Who. Thinks. That. Makes. History?"

There was a sigh of relief. All hands went down. Not a test—a rhetorical question. In fact, not even a question but a paragraph, each word a separate sentence, with the same meaning: *how little you know.* Mr. Carr rolled the blackboard down to reveal the quote he had written there, read it aloud to make sure no one missed it: *"History is nothing more than the thin thread of what is remembered, stretched out over the ocean of what has been forgotten."*

"Until you understand that," Mr. Carr said, "you'll never be a historian."

Charlie had written it down, because he was that kind of student, and on that ship, so far out to sea that there was not a single thing on the horizon in any direction, he remembered it and understood it for the first time. And as they crossed the Tropic of Capricorn, Charlie became a historian of his own life. Surrounded by twenty-eight million square miles of water, Charlie spun the thread of what he wanted to remember and discarded the rest. Into the endless ocean went all the things he wanted to forget, right back to the moment of his birth, so afterward he would refuse to allow himself to remember the fact that defined him—that it was Whiskey who was born first. Over the side of the ship he threw the runner-up rosette he had been wearing for fifteen years, imagined it sinking to the depths, spinning slowly in the great darkness until it reached the ocean floor, miles below.

The ship was a no-man's-land. It was neither the past, nor the future, no longer England, and not yet Australia, but a buffer zone between the two—exactly the place for Charlie to effect his transformation. Lost at sea, he found himself, the all new Charlie Ferns: rebel, daredevil, joker.

× × ×

Due to an administrative glitch, Charlie was placed in the grade below Whiskey at their new school in Melbourne, so their mother went early with them on the first day to straighten things out. They were ushered in to see Mr. Balzarelli, whom the secretary called the principal and their mother referred to as the headmaster. Balzarelli was a short, balding man who was overfamiliar with their mother and not nearly apologetic enough for the mistake that had been made. His excuse was that they had never had twins at the school before and that the secretary, who was *not the shiniest apple on the tree*, had been confused by the paperwork. He winked at their mother as he said this, but their mother, who had been more tense than usual since they arrived in Australia, did not look impressed. Balzarelli changed tack then, saying that though they were now definitely in the same year, they had been assigned to different homerooms. He explained that they always separated siblings in order to promote a bit of *healthy competition* on sports days and the like. Whiskey rolled his eyes at this; their mother said nothing. There was a brief, awkward silence, and then outside the office, Charlie heard a siren wail.

"Thar she blows," Balzarelli said with visible relief, and he stood up to shake their mother's hand.

× × ×

"Mum gave Balls-of-Jelly a hard time, didn't she?" Whiskey asked when they caught up after the first two classes.

"What?"

"The principal, Balzarelli."

Charlie laughed.

"What was your homeroom like?" Whiskey asked.

"It was okay," Charlie said. He had always gone to a school where he knew at least half the students in his grade, and he had felt awkward and self-conscious through every minute of his first two hours at this new school.

"How was yours?" he asked Whiskey.

"The usual crap," Whiskey said, as though he started new schools all the time, as though he were some hardened serial expellee. "They made me stand up and introduce myself."

"Did they ask you why you moved to Australia?"

"Yep." Whiskey laughed. "I told them it was because my dad was having an affair."

"You're such a dick, Whiskey. Why did you say that?"

"What did you want me to say? *My dad got offered a great job; it was a momentous step in his thrilling career as a boilermaker and an exciting opportunity for our whole family.* I'm sure no one wants to hear that crap. So who's your homeroom teacher?" he asked, changing the subject.

"Mrs. Blighty," Charlie said sullenly.

"What does she teach?"

"She's the librarian. Why? Who's yours?"

"Miss Kemp. She's the phys ed teacher."

Charlie noticed he said *phys ed*, not PE, which was what they'd always called it before. Charlie made a mental note to add to his collection: elastic bands were *lackies*, sunglasses were *sunnies*, phys ed was *PE*.

"Apparently she's a lemon," Whiskey added.

"What's a lemon?" Charlie asked.

"A lezzo, a dyke—that's what they call it."

"Who told you that?"

"A guy in my homeroom. Asked if I wanted to go up to the football field at lunchtime, kick a footy around with his mates."

"They play soccer?" Charlie asked hopefully.

"Aussie Rules."

"But we don't know how to play Aussie Rules."

Whiskey shrugged again. "Soon find out. Are you in?"

"Okay," Charlie said. He hadn't had any better offers.

× × ×

The lessons were easy enough. The hard part was knowing what to say, when to say it, and who to say it to. The hard part was thinking you spoke the same language and finding out you didn't. The bell was a *siren*, break time was *recess*, when you went swimming you did not wear trunks but long shorts called *boardies*. People had different names. The girls were called Narelle and Charlene and Kerrilee, names Charlie had never heard of. And the boys—who were not called boys but guys—had names from American soap operas: Brett and Todd and Shane. Even the food was different. There were no lunch ladies serving greasy cafeteria food and mashed potatoes. There was an outdoor cafeteria where you chose your own lunch and ate it where you pleased—standing up, sitting down, lying on the football field if it took your fancy—no one cared. There were bread rolls smothered in melted cheese and deep-fried sausages coated in breadcrumbs affectionately known as *crumbed dicks*. There were licorice straps, which you bought less to eat than to attract the attention of the girls, by using the straps to whip the backs of their legs.

After the first few days, Whiskey and Charlie no longer spent recess or lunch together. Whiskey had made friends with the football players and the kids who smoked cigarettes—*smokes*—in the bushes on the far side of the football field. Charlie stayed in the quadrangle, hanging around with a guy from his homeroom called Marco and a gang of Marco's friends. Charlie did not feel that he had anything in common with Marco's friends particularly, but he felt more at ease with them than he did on the field with Whiskey's mates. And if Marco's friends didn't go out of their way to make him welcome, neither did they do anything to indicate they wanted to get rid of him, which was a good enough reason to stick around, Charlie supposed.

By the end of their third week at the school, people Charlie didn't recognize were greeting him between classes, shouting *yo, dude* and *hey, man* at him and occasionally offering him high fives in the corridors, which he declined to accept. They had been at the school for four weeks when one of the prefects accosted Charlie in the bathroom, saying, "Whoa, man, Whiskey never told me he had a little brother. Shit, you are the spitting image. What grade are you in?"

"I'm in tenth grade, same as him," Charlie said. "We're twins," he added through gritted teeth. And there it was. The part of his life he thought he had discarded in the depths of the Indian Ocean, echoing back at him from the seabed.

Charlie had been kidding himself, thinking things could be different in Australia. Whiskey was a character. He possessed a quality Charlie had missed out on, a quality that made people want to be around him. He was Whiskey Ferns, fresh off the boat, and Charlie bet there wasn't a single student in the school who didn't know his name.

× × ×

One story went like this: aged twelve, Whiskey had stolen a bottle of scotch from his parents' liquor cabinet, slugged at it through math and biology, and then in final period, while his classmates were conjugating Latin verbs, Whiskey had gone to the bathroom and vomited his guts up, passed out right there on the stall floor, come around hours later to find himself alone in the dark, locked in the school overnight. Another version had Whiskey drinking the booze at home while his parents were out, stealing his mother's car and driving it into a tree.

Whiskey had ripped jeans, high-top Airwalk sneakers, which you couldn't even buy in Australia, a flattop like Ice out of *Top Gun*. People wanted to hear stories about him, tell stories about him. He had come from England a month ago, without a past, without a history, and if there were no stories to tell, they would make them up themselves, pass them around until they became accepted truths. Whiskey never confirmed or denied any of the rumors that circulated about him, worked on the theory that any publicity was good publicity. So there was no one to verify the stories except Charlie. And Charlie didn't count.

It didn't matter that William had been called Whiskey since he was nine years old; it didn't matter that the stories couldn't be true because their mother didn't even have a car of her own in England and she always tipped down the sink any whiskey that came into the house because she said their father liked it too much and couldn't be trusted with it. If Charlie had said, "Whiskey's just his walkie-talkie name from when we were kids," everyone would have thought it was Charlie who was lying.

Even after hours of sitting beside Whiskey, Charlie can't bring himself to really look at his brother. At first, he angles his chair to the foot of the bed so that Whiskey's bloody, bandaged head is out of his line of sight and all he can see is the pristine plaster cast on Whiskey's foot, which allows him to pretend that Whiskey's injuries are in the realm of the ordinary. Later, Charlie looks at the machinery keeping his brother alive. He watches with a certain fascination the IV bags hanging by Whiskey's bed. He does not know the exact contents of the bags, but the sight of those fluids making their journey through their transparent tubes and into Whiskey's body, the process of watching them emptied and eventually replaced, bring Charlie comfort, make him feel that somehow healing must be taking place.

In addition to the IV tubes, Whiskey is hooked to an array of wires that are monitoring his vital signs. All the information transmitted through these wires is displayed on a small screen next to Whiskey's bed. Charlie stares at this screen for a long time. He does not know what the lines and colors mean, but he finds them soothing, like watching television late at night with the sound turned down.

Whiskey's right arm is in a plaster cast to the elbow. On the left arm—taking its place between the tubes and wires—is a blood pressure cuff. Charlie remembers having his tonsils removed when he was eight or nine years old, needing to have his blood pressure taken again and again after he came around from the anesthetic. He remembers the nurses putting on the Velcro cuff, inflating it with the black pump that looked exactly like the one on his bicycle horn. He remembers the tightening sensation, like pins and needles, and then the feeling of release. Whiskey's cuff is left on permanently. Every so often, a machine kicks on and automatically inflates it, displaying the results on the monitor. Over and over, Charlie watches the cuff inflate and deflate again, but when the results appear on the screen, he looks away. He has never understood blood pressure, doesn't know what a normal reading is for a person in good health, let alone someone in Whiskey's condition. He would rather not know.

× × ×

Charlie is relieved when Rosa returns that afternoon.

"Did you sleep?" he asks.

"Your mother made me to take a tablet."

Charlie nods. He doesn't know what to say.

"What kind of music does he like?" he asks suddenly, in the yawning silence.

"You think we should play music in here? Do you think that would help?"

"I don't know, maybe. But it was more that I was wondering. I didn't know… I wanted to know."

Rosa nods, thinking. "He likes a lot of old things. The Beatles, the Rolling Stones," she says after a while. She pulls up a chair on the other side of the bed, holds on to Whiskey's good hand, the one without the cast. "He has some records, you know, original ones." She thinks for a minute. "And he loves that guy with the big suit. What is his name?"

Charlie shakes his head.

"You would know him, Charlie; it makes me crazy, that electric music."

"Electronic," Charlie corrects out of habit.

"I'm too tired to speak perfect English today, Charlie."

"Sorry, Rosa. I don't know why I said that."

"Don't be sorry. Usually I like it, you know that; I want to get better. But today I'm too tired for it." She looks at Whiskey then, and Charlie remembers himself, gets up to leave. He is at the door when Rosa looks up again.

"You want to look through the records?" she asks.

Charlie nods. "I'd like that."

"You can play some, if you want. Go there now. I will be here all night anyway." She rummages in her handbag for the keys. "Take Whiskey's car."

Charlie hesitates.

"Come on, Charlie," she says. "Whiskey knows you hate it. It does not suit you one bit. It will make him laugh to think of you driving it."

Charlie takes the keys.

x x x

It's probably a good ten-minute drive from the hospital to Whiskey and Rosa's place, but that afternoon, Charlie makes it in six. It might be because there's not much traffic at that time of day, but it probably has more to do with the fact that Charlie breaks the speed limit all the way there, runs every yellow light into red. He would never drive his own car so recklessly, but sitting behind the wheel of Whiskey's car, he finds there is no other way to drive it. It has something to do with the position of the seat, the angle of the windshield. For the first time, Charlie has a sense of what made Whiskey buy a car like this. He has never understood it before; has been blinded by his embarrassment over the ridiculous price tag, the personalized license plate. If he had driven it himself, he might have seen it differently. But Whiskey had never offered, and Charlie had never asked.

x x x

It's too quiet at Whiskey and Rosa's. Charlie feels afraid to disturb things, as though Whiskey is already dead and his home, his belongings, have moved into the realm of the sacred. He shakes off the thought, goes into the kitchen to make himself a cup of tea. He has never been alone in this house before, has to rummage to find cups, tea bags, sugar.

While the kettle's boiling, he goes into the living room to look for Whiskey's records. But there are no records there, only CDs, mostly greatest hits albums—Santana, Fleetwood Mac, the Eagles—which must belong to Rosa. Charlie has an urge to lie on the voluminous couch, kick off his shoes, and go to sleep.

Instead he makes his tea and takes it into the other part of the house, the other wing, he supposes it would be called. He hasn't been here for so long—the last time must have been the cocktail party Whiskey organized for Rosa's thirtieth, almost two years earlier—he's forgotten how enormous the house is. It's far too big for the two of them, but as Charlie knows, when they bought it, they'd imagined they would fill it in no time.

At least three, Rosa had told Juliet in the beginning, maybe even four.

Since he made his decision, Charlie has tried not to think about these things. He and Juliet had talked about it endlessly at the time, and they had both felt the same: Whiskey and Rosa hadn't known each other long enough, and Whiskey was fickle; their marriage couldn't last. Charlie was doing them a favor by saying no. Charlie had communicated his decision not to Whiskey, but to Rosa, in a letter. He knew it was cowardly, but he was afraid that face-to-face, Rosa would work on him, wear him down, change his mind. After the letter was sent, the subject was never raised again. Neither Whiskey nor Rosa ever questioned Charlie about his reasons, and if his mother or father knew, they never spoke of it to him. As far as he knew, Rosa had never mentioned it to Juliet. Charlie and Juliet did not discuss it either; they had agreed on this, that they had to be resolute; there was no point rehashing it again and again, doubting themselves, wondering if they had done the right thing. They had made the decision that seemed best at the time, and they had to leave it behind them.

But there, in Whiskey and Rosa's house, Charlie is struck by the thought that though he and Juliet had tried to be objective, tried to look at it from every angle, he had never imagined how Whiskey and Rosa would feel, rattling around in their five bedrooms and two living rooms, every doorway a reminder of what they couldn't have.

Charlie takes his tea into the room that was to have been the kids' playroom. Whiskey jokingly calls it his "man room." He had done it up a year or so earlier, had talked about it once at their mother's, but Charlie hadn't listened. Instead, he had created his own image of Whiskey's man room, furnished it with clichés—a corner bar, a pool table, a trophy cabinet, and a *Sports Illustrated* calendar—and then joked with Juliet about it, mocked Whiskey for being so puerile.

Puerile. Charlie thinks about the word. His mother, who must be one of the only people in the world who still remembers the Latin she learned at school, has told him it comes from *puer*, the Latin word for *boy*. In English, it has a negative connotation, but all it really means is boyish. *And what is so wrong with Whiskey being boyish?* Charlie wonders now. *There are worse things a person could be, self-righteous being one of them.*

As it turns out, the room is nothing like Charlie has imagined. There is no sporting memorabilia, no rifles on the walls or high-backed leather chairs. There is a vast desk and a bookcase covering an entire wall, a big comfortable-looking armchair, and a record player—a brand-new Technics, Charlie notices—on top of a shelving unit built to hold records. Charlie immediately feels envious of this setup, thinking of his own meager record collection, his secondhand turntable.

He sits down on the floor and begins to flip through the records. Rosa's "guy with the big suit" turns out to be David Byrne; Whiskey has everything by Talking Heads, and some later, solo stuff Charlie has never heard. Awed by the size of the collection, Charlie drags the armchair over to face the shelves, sits down for a closer examination. Whiskey has hundreds of records, most of which are in pristine condition, all stored in plastic sleeves and alphabetized. Bob Dylan and Benny Goodman, Django Reinhardt and De La Soul, Stevie Wonder and the White Stripes. Looking through his brother's records for the first time in more than ten years, Charlie finds everything from the ultrahip (Disposable Heroes of Hiphoprisy) to the truly ridiculous (Hall & Oates), and within those circles of vinyl, Charlie learns things about Whiskey he has never known.

Listening to Sonic Youth's "Teenage Riot," Charlie remembers Whiskey being in a band once, when they were about nineteen. The band was called Silent Revolution, a name they had thought brilliantly ironic and incisive at the time. Whiskey was the drummer. The guitarist and bass player were two brothers with Afros, Dominic and Will. Mostly when they got together, they smoked dope and drank cask wine out of old jars with the labels peeled off, while they speculated on what image should go on the cover of their first album, whether they should tour the United States or Japan first, etc. Once, when Charlie had gone to watch them jam, Will had suggested a "brother wrestle." *Me and Dom against you and Whiskey.* Charlie had pretended he thought Will was joking. Now he wishes he had gone for the brother wrestle. Better to wrestle together against someone else than to wrestle against each other.

FOXTROT

According to the lecture that was delivered in a special assembly on the first day of term, the beginning of eleventh grade was the time to focus on academic goals and to begin thinking seriously about life beyond high school. From the students' perspective, they'd been expected to focus on academic goals ever since they started high school, and as for life beyond school, they were about as capable of thinking seriously about that as they were of imagining life on Mars.

For the girls, there was something far more pressing than exams to think about in first term: the school prom. Within a week of being back at school, Charlie had seen the girls in his homeroom excitedly showing each other pictures of dresses in magazines, had heard them agonizing over skirt length and fabric color, lowering their voices, presumably to discuss whose bow tie and cummerbund might be matched to their dress.

The official line was that the guys couldn't care less about the school prom. Jokes about potential partners might be made, but all suggestions were resoundingly rejected, backed up by the vehement declaration *I haven't even thought about it.* In truth, it had been on Charlie's mind ever since he heard the girls discussing it. The problem was, all the students were expected to attend the prom with a partner. And even though, technically speaking, girls could invite boys to the prom, in reality, they never did. It was the boys who did the asking and the girls who had the luxury of accepting or declining the invitations. Charlie wished it was the other way around. He was no good at those sorts of things. To help with the process, he had compiled a mental list. At the top of the list was Sasha Piper, a girl he would never even think of actually inviting, but who would be the girl he would choose if he was in one of those American movies where the school dork becomes popular over-night and is suddenly pursued by the beautiful blond cheerleader type who previously did not even know his name. Not that Charlie considered himself the school dork. Still, he had enough social awareness to know he was not in Sasha Piper's league. Probably, Charlie thought, Sasha was at the top of every eleventh-grade boy's wish list, but none of them would have the guts to ask her, and she would end up going to the prom with a boy from twelfth grade.

Next on Charlie's list was Shantelle Simpson, the girl who sat in front of him in math and occasionally shared a joke with him, a girl he would ask if fate threw him an unexpected opportunity, even though, in all likelihood, she would say no. Then there was Melissa Capelli, his biology partner, who was shy but pretty and would possibly say yes if he timed it right. His last resort was Bronwyn Chambers, a girl from his homeroom who he didn't fancy in the slightest but who he suspected had fancied him since he started at the school, a nice girl, although a little on the chunky side with unfortunate frizzy black hair, very unlikely to get any better offers and, therefore, almost guaranteed to say yes.

Charlie did not know if his friends had such lists. He would not ask, but he bet that Whiskey did not have a list of four, of whom one was an impossibility and one extremely unlikely. He would most definitely not have a last resort. He would not need to. It would be simple for someone like Whiskey. He would ask one of the pretty, popular girls, and she would say yes. He wouldn't have to agonize over it as Charlie was.

The way Charlie saw it, timing was everything. If you asked too early, the pretty girls would be waiting to see if they might get any better offers. They would tell you they wanted to think about it, and then you would be in limbo. You might be lucky, and no one they liked more might ask them, in which case they would come back to you with a halfhearted yes. On the other hand, they might keep you in suspense for a few weeks and end up saying no, during which time your third and even fourth choice might have been snapped up. In this regard, the efficiency of the school grapevine was both a blessing and a curse. If you were rejected, you would rather it wasn't common knowledge. But it was helpful in keeping abreast of who had asked whom, who had accepted or declined in order to assess the market, to judge the best time to make your move.

x x x

Though there was a student committee for the school prom, the teachers, as always, had the last word, and it was the teachers who had decided that in order to *set the right tone* and avoid *too much bumping and grinding* later in the evening, as Mrs. Gill apparently put it at the meeting, there would be an hour of ballroom dancing before the DJ arrived to play the music the students wanted to hear. Of course, none of the students knew how to ballroom dance, so it was arranged that twice a week, throughout first term, they would learn ballroom dancing instead of their usual phys ed activities.

It was widely known that Mr. Baxter had represented the state in ballroom dancing, but the teachers were apparently smart enough to realize that the students would not have taken one of their own teachers seriously. So outside instructors were brought in, a young guy who was introduced to them as Mr. Randall, and a very beautiful, voluptuous woman who was not introduced. Charlie did not know about the girls, but none of his friends wanted to learn ballroom dancing. They thought ballroom dancing was for sissies and would rather have been playing sport. Mr. Randall seemed to sense this and took control as soon as their phys ed teacher had left the room.

"You can call me Mr. Randall, if you want," he said. "But I would rather you called me Mr. Bond…James Bond." He said this with just the right amount of drama, and there was laughter all around.

"Of course, if you're going to call me a ridiculous name, you'll want to know the reason why. So I'll tell you. How many of you think ballroom dancing is only for gay men?"

There was snickering and muttering through the gym, though no one spoke.

"How many of you boys think that by taking part in a ballroom dancing class you're in danger of becoming gay?" He paused knowingly. "Last question: How many of you are wondering if I'm gay?"

Surprised laughter followed this question.

Mr. Randall smiled. "If you want to know that, the best person to ask would be my wife, Carmel." Here he gestured toward the woman he had arrived with. She gave a curtsy and a small twirl, just enough to show a bit of leg and reassure all present that Mr. Randall, or Mr. Bond, or whatever you wanted to call him, was most definitely not gay. There was laughter, applause, a wolf whistle from the back of the gym.

"'That's all well and good, but why James Bond?' I hear you asking. Well, let me ask you this. Who else but James Bond can wrestle a giant on top of a train *and* charm a lady without appearing to even try? Does anyone look better in a tuxedo? Do you think James Bond knows how to dance? You bet he does. So, for the purposes of these classes, not only am *I* James Bond, but I encourage each of you gentlemen to think of yourselves as James Bond also. Ladies, if you wish, you may call your partner Mr. Bond. Or, if you feel daring, you may like to call him James. I'll leave that up to you. Now on your feet; let's dance."

Everyone stood up, considerably more enthusiastic than they had been when they arrived at the gym. The James Bond speech had won them all over. Charlie could see he wasn't the only one who had benefited from imagining himself as sharply dressed and debonair, even if, in reality, they were all sweaty and pimply with two left feet. He hoped his partner would call him Mr. Bond.

Week one was the jive. The boys stood on one side of the room behind James Bond, the girls behind Carmel on the other.

> *Rock step, triple step, triple step*
> *Rock step, triple step, triple step*

Over and over again they repeated the movements, girls on one side, boys on the other. Once they had gotten the hang of it by themselves, it was time to have a go with a partner. Partners were assigned by height, with no consideration whatsoever given to social status. Which meant that in some cases, the prettiest girls were paired up with nerds from the chess club, weirdos who stayed after school to play Dungeons & Dragons; the good-looking boys with girls who had braces and the wrong hairstyles, who spent their lunchtimes in the library. In these oddly matched pairs, neither partner felt comfortable. One inevitably felt embarrassed and unworthy, the other simply embarrassed. They did not know how to talk to each other. In some cases, they had never even said hello.

Charlie's assigned partner was Anneliese Spellman. Anneliese was widely acknowledged to be one of the prettiest girls at school; the year before, she had been a finalist in the *Seventeen* Covergirl competition. She had been photographed at the beach in a low-cut top and short shorts, and Charlie, who considered himself a legs man, had torn her photograph out of a copy of the magazine he had found in the dentist's waiting room. Anneliese also happened to be the girl Whiskey had been hanging around with that term and who was to become, if you listened to gossip, the latest notch on Whiskey's proverbial bedpost.

Two places down the line from Charlie, Whiskey's assigned partner was Karen Sand, the deputy library prefect. Charlie tried not to notice, but Whiskey caught his eye, gestured to himself and Karen, and then to Charlie and Anneliese, raising his eyebrows as if to say *Clearly there's been a mistake here.* Whiskey gave the universal gesture for *let's swap partners*. Karen looked at the floor. Charlie nodded his assent. What else could he do?

"You're only a bit shorter," Whiskey said as he came over. Charlie hated it when Whiskey made reference to their height difference. He found it a particularly annoying quirk that they were identical in every way, except for Whiskey being slightly taller. Charlie told himself he must still be growing, that eventually he would catch up with Whiskey.

"James Bond won't notice," Whiskey said, taking Anneliese's hand. "He hasn't got X-ray vision."

But apparently James Bond did have X-ray vision. Because when the music began, he was suddenly beside them. Without a word, he took Anneliese's hand out of Whiskey's and replaced it in Charlie's. Then he took Karen's hand in his own.

"May I have this dance?" he asked her, bowing graciously.

"You may sit and reflect on your ill manners," he said to Whiskey, gesturing toward the bench that ran along the side of the gym.

Whiskey's face colored. Charlie looked away from him and away from Anneliese too. He concentrated on his feet and hoped his palms weren't too sweaty. He could not think of a word to say.

At home that night, Whiskey said he'd rather be doing algebra than ballroom dancing, that Randall was the biggest turkey he'd ever met and must have paid a minx like Carmel to marry him. Neither he nor Charlie mentioned the failed partner swap.

x x x

In week two, they waltzed. *One* two three, *one* two three, rise and fall, rise and fall. Charlie spent most of the lesson counting under his breath. He felt awkward about the strange triangle he and Anneliese were part of, which made it difficult to concentrate on the steps they were learning. Charlie didn't know if Anneliese was counting the beats in her own head, but she made no attempt at conversation either. He found himself wishing Whiskey's scheme had been successful, thought how much more comfortable he would have felt dancing with Karen.

In week three, they learned the cha-cha. Their first Latin dance. According to Mr. Randall, it was all in the hips.

> *One, two, cha cha cha*
> *One, two, cha cha cha*

Charlie noticed that Anneliese seemed to pick up the steps more quickly than he did, that when it came to dancing, she seemed to be something of a natural. Though Charlie did not consider himself anything more than average when it came to sport, at least when he was playing soccer or cricket, his arms and legs seemed to go mostly where he needed them to be, without him having to think about it too much. Ballroom dancing was a different proposition entirely. Suddenly none of his limbs seemed willing to do what he asked of them, and certainly not all at the same time. Often Charlie found himself stepping left when he had meant to step right, back when he wanted to go forward, turning in the wrong direction, moving too late or too early. And on the rare occasions when he managed to get control over his feet, inevitably his arms were all wrong—his elbows too slack or too rigid, his grip on Anneliese too tight or too loose.

"Are you wrestling a bear?" Mr. Randall asked him once, adjusting Charlie's arms.

"She's not your prisoner!" he said on another occasion, loosening Charlie's grip on Anneliese's shoulder.

The week of the samba, Anneliese came home from school with Whiskey for the first time. She was sitting on the couch watching *Full House* with Whiskey when Charlie got home from Marco's.

"You know Anneliese," Whiskey said dryly, without looking up from the television.

"Hey, Anneliese," Charlie said uncertainly.

"Hey, Charlie." She smiled at him for the first time. She was still in her school uniform, her hair in a ponytail, and Charlie thought she looked about as pretty as a girl could get. *Lucky Whiskey*, he thought to himself as he dragged his bag down the hallway to start on his homework.

× × ×

The fourth dance they learned was the fox-trot.

"Who knows the story of *Fantastic Mr. Fox*?" Randall asked them before he showed them the steps.

Charlie raised his hand. When he was younger, it had been one of his favorite books.

"What about *Chicken Little*?" Randall asked. More hands went up.

"What's the fox always trying to do in these stories?"

"Eat the chickens?" one of the girls suggested.

"Exactly! And that's what this dance is all about—stealing chickens. We've got to be cunning as foxes, quick and fast and light on our feet. Otherwise we won't be getting any dinner."

Charlie didn't know what it was about the fox-trot, but it was during that class that he began to feel he was at last getting the hang of ballroom dancing, gaining control of his elbows and hips, hands and feet, finally beginning to lead Anneliese instead of the other way around.

That same week, Anneliese started saying hello to him when she saw him around the school, although Charlie did not know if this was because of the dancing or because of whatever was going on between her and Whiskey. The week of the fox-trot was also the week when some of the guys started asking girls to the prom. As expected, Sasha Piper got snapped up pretty sharpish, by the student body president no less, and Charlie's second choice, Shantelle Simpson, wasn't far behind, also poached by a twelfth grader. So much for Charlie's list. Still, there was plenty of time left, and Charlie thought it would be a few weeks yet before most of the guys made their moves.

× × ×

In week five, after they had learned the salsa, Mr. Randall announced that since they were progressing so well, it had been decided—by the teachers, presumably—that there would be a demonstration at the prom, for which couples would be chosen to perform one of the five dances they had learned. Charlie was surprised to find he was thinking more about the ballroom dancing demonstration than about how and when he might invite Melissa to the prom. Once he and Anneliese had gotten over their initial awkwardness, Charlie had started to enjoy dancing with her. Now, instead of embarrassed apologies, they laughed together when they made a mistake, sometimes shared a joke with each other or a bit of gossip they had heard around the school.

The couples chosen for the demonstration were announced in week six. Charlie and Anneliese were selected as one of the couples for the fox-trot. Anneliese gave Charlie a hug when the announcement was made.

"We did it, Charlie!" she said excitedly, giving him one of her beautiful smiles. Charlie felt himself redden. He was pleased that he and Anneliese had been chosen. He thought they had earned it. He did not know why he felt guilty about it, as though he had done something underhanded by dancing to the best of his ability, by wanting to be chosen.

× × ×

Later that week, Charlie was lying on his bed, underlining key quotes from one of his English literature books, when Anneliese poked her head into his room.

"Hey," she said. "Have you got a minute?"

Charlie sat up.

"Hey, Anneliese."

Anneliese had been to their house a few times by then, but she had never been into Charlie's room before. He looked around to see if there was anything he might be embarrassed for her to see, kicked a pair of boxer shorts—cleanliness unknown—under his bed.

"Sure, come in," he said.

"What are you reading?" she asked.

"*Heart of Darkness*," Charlie said, holding it up. "Have you read it?"

"'The horror, the horror!'" she said, clutching her throat.

They laughed.

"Where's Whiskey?"

"He's downstairs. I wanted to see if maybe we could…if you wanted to…if you didn't mind, we could maybe…you know… practice the dance."

Charlie couldn't believe it. Anneliese Spellman was in his bedroom, asking him to dance. Sure, it wasn't slow dancing to "Never Tear Us Apart" in a darkened room, but it was probably as close to that as Charlie was ever going to get. So why was he hesitating?

"I got the music from Mr. Randall," she said uncertainly, showing him a tape. "But if you're busy, that's okay…"

Charlie made up his mind. "No, no, you're right," he said, virtually jumping off the bed. "It's a good idea to practice. Mr. Kurtz isn't going anywhere." They laughed again. "Do you think there's enough room in here?" he asked, shoving his schoolbag into the wardrobe. He hoped she would say yes. He didn't want to go downstairs and practice in the family room, where they ran the risk of his mum or dad coming home from work and wanting to watch, not to mention Whiskey.

"Plenty of room," Anneliese said. She put the tape in his stereo and pressed Play.

Dancing with Anneliese alone in his bedroom was completely different from dancing with her in the gym, along with forty other students and Mr. Randall, with his adjustments and wisecracks. Undistracted by anyone else, Charlie was suddenly acutely aware of how close he was to Anneliese, the places where his body met hers. He could smell her hair. They bumped and shuffled around the room, and he couldn't concentrate on the steps at all.

"That was our worst time ever!" Anneliese said when the music finally stopped.

"Maybe there's not enough room," Charlie suggested apologetically.

Anneliese looked around. "It's not that. It just feels different here. We'll get used to it. Do you want to try again?" She rewound the tape.

The second time, Charlie pretended he was dancing with someone else. He did not allow himself to look at Anneliese's face or to think about his hand on her shoulder; he thought instead about his feet, his posture, his elbows and wrists, tried to remember everything Mr. Randall had ever told them. They were doing brilliantly until Charlie looked up and saw Whiskey standing in the doorway, smirking at them.

"Gold medal, guys," he said sarcastically. "Lovely."

Charlie and Anneliese broke apart. Nat King Cole carried on singing "The Lady's in Love with You." Charlie wondered how long Whiskey had been watching them. He had an urge to apologize. But Anneliese beat him to it.

"Go away, Whiskey. It's embarrassing," she said coyly. And then she shut the door in his face.

"Shall we try again?" she asked Charlie, unruffled.

Charlie thought she might be the most wonderful girl he'd ever known.

The second time Anneliese came into his room to ask him to practice, she shut the door before they began. "Rehearsals are closed to the public," she said, and Charlie laughed conspiratorially.

The following week she didn't come over to their house at all. Charlie missed her. Dancing with her at school was not the same as having her all to himself at home, however brief and illusory it might be. In their Friday class, he asked her hesitantly if they might have a chance to practice the following week.

Anneliese looked uncomfortable. "I can't come over next week," she said. "I've got too many assignments."

Charlie thought she and Whiskey must have had a fight. Whiskey hadn't mentioned it, but he never talked to Charlie about those kinds of things. Usually Charlie heard them from someone else, most often Marco, who had a keen ear for gossip. If they had fought, Whiskey didn't seem bothered by it. He had been his usual self that week. But then, he always was. Girls were around for a while, and then they were not, but it never seemed to be Whiskey who was left crying. Charlie wasn't sorry things hadn't worked out between Whiskey and Anneliese. But he hoped Anneliese wasn't wasting any tears over Whiskey.

× × ×

Later that week, Charlie heard from Marco that Whiskey had asked Anneliese to the prom and she'd turned him down, saying she was going with someone else.

"Who?" Charlie asked Marco, trying to keep his voice casual.

"I thought you might know that," Marco said pointedly.

"How would I know? Whiskey never tells me anything."

"Don't come the raw prawn with me, mate," Marco said. "I'm in your phys ed class, remember? I've seen you two dancing together. I thought you might have beaten Whiskey to the punch."

"As if," Charlie said.

"They say all's fair in love and war, mate. I wouldn't blame you if you did."

"Well, I didn't," Charlie said emphatically.

Marco put his hands up. "Point taken. It's your business. But if I thought it, you can bet Whiskey has."

"Thanks for the heads up, Marco."

Sure enough, when Charlie got home, Whiskey was waiting for him, lying on his back on Charlie's bed, legs crossed, arms behind his head.

"Well, you've really done that dickhead Randall proud," he said without even looking at Charlie.

"How's that?" Charlie asked warily, putting down his schoolbag.

"You've got the most cunning fox-trot going, Charlie. You certainly know how to steal another man's chicken."

"I don't know what you're talking about, Whiskey."

Whiskey nodded slowly. "So what really happens after she shuts the door and puts on the music?"

"We practice the dance."

"Bullshit, Charlie!" Whiskey sat up suddenly, slammed the side of his fist against the wall. "When did you ask her?"

"Ask her what?"

"Don't screw around with me, Charlie. I already know you asked her."

"I don't know what you're talking about."

"I'm talking about Anneliese, dickwad, and the fact that she's going to the prom with someone else. Ring any bells?"

"I don't know anything about it," Charlie repeated.

Whiskey looked at him hard. "So you're saying you haven't asked her?"

Charlie shook his head.

"You haven't hinted at it though?"

He shook his head again.

"But have you ever said anything that might have made her think you were going to ask her?"

"We've never talked about it."

"Never?"

"Never."

"So you're not planning to ask her?"

"Jesus, Whiskey, what is this? The Spanish Inquisition? I said no, didn't I?"

"Well, that's good," he said eventually. "That's good. Because we're decent men, aren't we, Charlie? We wouldn't take what belonged to each other, would we?"

She doesn't belong to you, Charlie thought, but he didn't say so. He only shook his head again, worn out by the conversation.

"Shake on it?"

Charlie sighed.

"I'm asking you to shake on it," Whiskey insisted, putting out his hand.

Charlie shook it impatiently. "There you go. Are we done now? Happy?"

"Close as I'll get," Whiskey said, getting up off the bed. "Close as I'll get."

× × ×

Needless to say, there were no more rehearsals with Anneliese. When Kelly Varga broke up with Todd Jackson that week, Whiskey asked Kelly to the prom. During their biology class, Melissa told Charlie she was going with Brett Speedman. Charlie didn't even care. Miserably, he asked Bronwyn, couldn't even bring himself to feel bad about how excited she was, bringing in a piece of fabric from her dress so he could match his accessories to hers, *if he wanted*. He heard, from Marco, predictably, that Anneliese was going to the prom with Todd. A neat swap.

He told himself that if he could get through the last week of term, things would settle down. Once the ballroom dancing was over, he would hardly ever see Anneliese, have no reason to speak to her, would stop thinking about her eventually. There was only the prom itself to be endured. One dance with her, less than five minutes, and it would all be over. Charlie thought he could do it.

But he hadn't counted on Anneliese, on her lipstick and the strands of hair curled against her neck. He hadn't counted on her strapless dress, on the fact that he would have to touch her bare shoulder with his left hand. It took him to pieces.

"You look beautiful," he said before he could stop himself.

"Not as good as Bronwyn though," she said cattily.

"Don't be like that, Anneliese, please. You must know I wanted to ask you."

"Then why didn't you, Charlie?"

"I couldn't, not after Whiskey had."

"But why not?"

"He's my brother, Anneliese."

"I don't see what difference that makes."

He felt despair. He didn't know if he had ever truly felt it before.

"It wouldn't be right. I can't explain it. I'm sorry."

Anneliese bit her lip and looked away from him. Charlie did not think about his heel-toe action or remembering to sway slightly on his chassés. The dance they had spent all term practicing no longer mattered. Whether Charlie danced poorly or perfectly made no difference now. He simply moved in time to the music, and Anneliese followed. He looked at her throat and her shoulders. He could smell her perfume. He tried to memorize its scent. Then the dance was over. Charlie bowed to Anneliese as they had been taught, and as he walked away from the first girl he had fallen in love with, to find the partner who had been his last resort, he wished Whiskey had never been born.

GOLF

Charlie was sixteen when his father, who'd had a bad back for years, finally took the advice of his chiropractor and gave up running in exchange for golf. Bill asked the boys if they were interested in caddying for him.

"Golf's an old farts' game," Whiskey said. "I wouldn't be seen dead on a golf course."

"I thought it would be a good way for you to earn some pocket money."

"Pocket money!" Whiskey was disgusted. "How old do you think we are?"

"Well, you're always complaining that you're broke."

"I'd rather stay broke," Whiskey said.

"I'll do it," Charlie said.

× × ×

Initially it was only the money Charlie was interested in, but as time went on, he found himself getting more and more interested in the game. He saw his father play with golfers good and bad, careful and indifferent, and he studied the shots, listened and remembered when he heard people say, "I should have used my 5-iron on that one."

He had been caddying for his dad for a few months when, one Saturday, the fourth member of their group didn't turn up.

"We'll play with three," one of the men said.

"We can't play with three, Greg; you know that," a man named John said. "We'll have to drop out."

Charlie's father had played with John before. Charlie remembered that he had been a stickler for the rules.

"What about your son, Bill? Why doesn't he join us?" Greg suggested.

"Charlie? He doesn't know one end of a golf club from the other."

"Dad!" Charlie protested.

"Don't be ridiculous," John said. "He's not a member. He's not signed in as a guest. He's not even appropriately attired."

Greg ignored him. "What do you think, Charlie?"

"I'll give it a go," Charlie said.

He found it awkward at first, harder than it looked, but after a few holes, he began to get a feel for it.

"You're doing pretty well, Charlie," Greg said. "Is this really the first time you've ever played? You're a natural."

"I taught him everything he knows," Bill joked.

By the end of the game, even John had come around. "You ought to sign up for a junior membership," he said enthusiastically, shaking Charlie's hand as they parted.

× × ×

Though he lamented the loss of his own personal caddy, Charlie's dad encouraged his interest, and before long, Charlie was on the driving range or the putting green whenever his dad wasn't using his clubs. For nine months he caddied for competitions and corporate golf days to save the money for his own clubs, a half set to begin with, secondhand, but good ones and true. Even when he had a full set, Charlie carried on caddying, using the money to pay for lessons.

Charlie got up early on Sunday mornings to work through math equations, label diagrams of human organs, and write essays on Shakespeare and Joseph Conrad so that Sunday afternoons he could go out and play eighteen holes. A couple afternoons a week, he went straight from school to the golf course, not even bothering to get changed, practicing his putting and driving with his school tie rolled up in his pocket. And on Saturdays, he played in the competition, putting in card after card until his handicap was down to thirteen.

Whiskey was a surfer. He got up at five a.m. most weekends to get a ride down the Peninsula or along the Ocean Road with some friends from school. Even with five-millimeter wet suits, booties, and hoods, they emerged from the water blue-lipped, and it took them the hour and a half back to Melbourne with the car heater on high to thaw out. Whiskey never showed the slightest interest in golf, until Charlie won a trophy for the most promising junior. After all, Whiskey was the sporty one, the athletic one. If anyone was going to be winning trophies, it should be him.

"Maybe I should give it a go myself," he said at Charlie's celebration dinner. He did not say, "There can't be much to it, if Charlie's winning trophies," but the words were there at the table all the same. Only their father did not notice.

"Charlie's bloody good," he said. "He's better than me, in fact, but you might be able to give him a run for his money, Whiskey."

Their mother frowned. "What about your surfing, William?" She was the only person who still called Whiskey William.

Whiskey shrugged. "The ocean's not going anywhere."

x x x

Charlie didn't want to play with Whiskey, didn't want to lend him his clubs so Whiskey could play with their dad.

He didn't want Whiskey hacking around the course with the clubs he'd saved up to buy. He had seen how Whiskey treated the things he borrowed—CDs stacked in piles without their cases, books with their covers bent back. If Whiskey wanted to play golf so badly, let him get a job and save up for his own clubs to ruin. Charlie wanted no part of it.

"You'd be better off sharing Dad's clubs, seeing as you're taller than me," he said when Whiskey asked him, knowing full well it was against the rules to play out of one bag.

Charlie thought that would be the end of it, but he underestimated their father, who, though he had the utmost respect for the rules of the game, had what he called a *healthy disregard* for the rules of the club.

"There's plenty there for both of us," he said.

So Whiskey started playing with their dad while Charlie made excuses, saying he had a test to study for, an essay to write. Their dad didn't notice Charlie's reticence. Before Whiskey had put in a single card, he was telling anyone who would listen that both his sons were golfers now, joking that if only he could persuade Elaine to take it up, they could form a family team.

Charlie knew playing with Whiskey would take all the pleasure out of it for him, and he managed to avoid it for almost two months, until their father signed the three of them up for a competition, with his friend Neil making up the foursome. Charlie thought about making another excuse, but he knew what Whiskey would think, didn't want to give him the satisfaction of saying, "Charlie's scared I'm going to beat him."

"What's Neil like, then?" Whiskey asked on the way to the club, already sizing up the competition.

"Well," their dad said, "he's good company, Neil. I like playing with him, but to be honest, he couldn't hit a cow's ass with a shovel."

Whiskey laughed. Charlie said nothing, thinking it unsportsmanlike of his dad to speak of his friend that way. But once they were on the course, Charlie saw that his dad was right.

Neil took a long time over his shots, seemed to plan them carefully enough, but once he stepped up to the tee, he went to pieces, shafting the ball as though it didn't matter to him which way it went. He made the same mistakes again and again, muttered to himself as he saw it, yet seemed incapable of correcting himself.

Their father was a different kettle of fish entirely. When anyone asked him how his golf was going, he always said *shithouse*, but in fact he played off a steady fourteen and, other than the odd bad day, was true to his handicap.

When he was younger, he'd been a first-rate forward, faster and more wiry than the rest of the team, unafraid of plowing headfirst into the tangle of legs that had so terrified Charlie when he had attempted to play rugby. Charlie remembered watching his dad standing mud-smeared on the side of the pitch while a gash in his eyebrow was stitched up, and then going back out to finish the game.

Whiskey took after their father. He had taken to golf the way he took to every sport he had ever tried. All those months of paddling out on his surfboard had given him the strength in his upper body to drive the ball a good long way, and his aim was good, his swing sure.

"He's not bad, is he, Charlie?" their dad asked at the third hole.

"Beginner's luck," Charlie wanted to say but stopped himself.

He was playing badly, allowing Whiskey's confidence to erode his own, so blind with envy that they were on the seventh hole before Charlie could see that Whiskey lost his edge once he was on the green. He lacked the concentration for putting, and though he could have mastered it if he practiced, there was no chance he would practice. Charlie realized that golf was too careful a game for Whiskey, that though his swing was better than Charlie's, golf required a focus and single-mindedness Whiskey did not possess and would not cultivate. Once he had seen this, Charlie knew Whiskey could not beat him.

When the game turned, Whiskey became a stranger to the rules, failing to count penalties, throwing his ball out of a bad lie, nudging it with his toe.

"I hope you're going to count that," Charlie said when he saw Whiskey dribbling the ball out of the rough as though he were on a soccer pitch.

Whiskey shrugged. "We're not playing for sheep stations."

Charlie had the urge to take a swing at him, to break Whiskey's nose on the end of his club. "It's only yourself you're cheating," he said.

They were on the eleventh hole when Whiskey finally lost his temper. Charlie had been playing steadily, making up what he'd lost earlier in the game. The better he played, the more agitated Whiskey became. When he teed off on the eleventh, he drove his first two balls straight into the lake. His face was dark when he took the shot for the third time. He stood for a long moment at the tee, and Charlie could see the tension in his shoulders, knew he wasn't going to make it. Whiskey didn't even wait for it to hit the water.

"Fuck it," he said, and he swung the putter hard against the side of the buggy. Charlie heard it crack, watched Whiskey fling it into the bushes and stalk off, leaving the buggy behind him.

Neil was the first to speak. "Well, golf's not for everyone," he said.

"No indeed," Charlie's father said. "Looks like it's back to just you and me, Charlie boy."

In the beginning there is no real plan. No one thinks it will last so long that they will need to make a roster. Rosa is there almost all the time, except for a few hours each day when Charlie's mother pries her out of the chair beside Whiskey's bed, takes her home, and puts her to bed with a sleeping tablet. Aunt Audrey makes sure Charlie's mother is also getting her sleep. And when Elaine's not there, Audrey keeps Rosa company herself.

Charlie has taken time off work so he and Juliet are free to come and go. On the third day, they are there early in the morning with Rosa and Charlie's mother. Later that afternoon, they return, the route through the hospital to Whiskey's ward already tiresomely familiar. But when Charlie looks through the window to Whiskey's room, the bed is empty.

"Don't panic," Juliet says quickly, seeing the empty bed for herself. "They've probably moved him to another room."

But Charlie can tell by the look on her face that she thinks the same as he does, that Whiskey has died while they've been gone, that his body has already been removed to make room for some other desperate case.

Juliet dashes to the nurses' station, but Charlie can't move. He sinks to the floor outside Whiskey's room. *It happened so quickly*, he thinks. *We should have been here. What were we thinking, going home to sleep?*

But then Juliet is back. "It's okay, Charlie, it's okay," she says as she rushes toward him, a nurse behind her.

"Your brother's gone for some tests," the nurse says kindly, helping Charlie into one of the chairs that line the corridor. She gives Charlie a plastic cup of water to drink. "Rosa's with him," she says. "Now that his condition's stabilized sufficiently, the neurosurgeon wanted some X-rays and scans run, to get some more information about the damage to his brain."

Charlie nods. "Just tests," he repeats, finding it difficult to let go of the thought that it is something far worse, that Whiskey is gone. He feels exhausted. It has only been three days, and already he feels like he can't take any more.

"How much longer?" he asks the nurse.

The nurse looks at her watch. "He hasn't been gone long," she says. "He'll be another couple of hours, at least. Perhaps you should go home and get some rest."

"How much longer in here, I mean."

"In ICU?"

She doesn't call it intensive care—none of the staff do. In the hospital, everyone is too busy to call things by their full names; there is an acronym for everything, Charlie has discovered.

"He'll be onto the neuro ward as soon as he's off life support," the nurse says. "That depends on how his other injuries heal. But this is the best place for him right now," she adds reassuringly. "We can monitor him for any change in status."

"No," Charlie says, frustrated at being misunderstood again. "How much longer in the hospital altogether?"

The nurse purses her lips. "I'm not really the best person to answer that," she says carefully. "You'd need to talk to the neurosurgeon." She hesitates. "But it's still early days. It's very difficult to predict things at this stage. We'll know a little bit more once these tests are done. Would you like me to have someone from neuro come and talk to you, after we get the results?"

Charlie shakes his head, closes his eyes.

"Thank you," he hears Juliet say. "We'll be fine now. We just had a fright."

"I'm sorry about that," the nurse says softly. Charlie thinks she is gone, but then he hears her speak again. "You're a good brother," she says. "He's lucky to have a family like you."

× × ×

It is Aunt Audrey's idea to start the journal. She comes across the idea on a website she has found, which contains homespun advice for families coping with coma, written by people who've experienced it for themselves.

"We can record what happens each day," Audrey suggests. "Any changes in Whiskey's condition, anything the medical staff tell us. That way we don't have to keep asking them the same questions over and over, and we won't feel like we've missed anything important when we're not here."

Charlie is glad his mother has her sister to support her. He likes the idea of the journal. He likes the idea of anything that will keep him occupied while he sits beside Whiskey, even if it is only the process of writing something down, reading over what someone else has written. He had used something similar when he worked as a seasonal employee in the camera section of a department store while he was still at college. The communications book was designed to allow the whole team to keep abreast of things that happened when they weren't there, in the interests of providing better customer service. It contained entries such as: *Mr. Ecker returned his SY220—lens not retracting again. No longer under warranty but will repair free of charge because same problem as before. Approved by TD.* Occasionally, when the store was quiet and the staff was bored, they resorted to the communications book to entertain themselves. *Mark, your wife came looking for you. I told her you had gone to lunch with Samantha from the lingerie department,* some card might write, or, *Josh sent home early due to excessive body odor.*

Charlie cannot imagine anyone writing such jokes in Whiskey's communications book. For the day on which Charlie went to the hospital and found Whiskey's bed empty, Elaine has recorded the tests he was sent for. *EEG, MRI,* she has written, using the acronyms the medical staff must have given her. Later, in a different pen, she has amended the entry with the full names of the tests: *electroencephalogram, magnetic resonance imaging scan.*

The very first entry reads, *Magdalena says rare for coma to last more than two weeks.* Charlie returns to this entry again and again. Of all the information recorded in the book, he finds this the hardest to absorb. In the state that Whiskey's in, two weeks seems an eternity. Though his brain swelling has gone down and his critical functions have stabilized—albeit with the help of machines—Whiskey seems barely alive. He hasn't opened his eyes since he was brought in after the accident, has made no response to stimuli of any kind. Charlie can hardly believe that a person can stay alive in this state for two whole weeks. And yet he wants to believe it. He needs to.

Which of the staff is Magdalena? Charlie wonders. He would like to talk to her about what his mother has written. But in these early days, the medical staff is a blur to Charlie. There seem to be dozens of them coming and going, and he finds it impossible to keep track of them. Many of them know his name long before he even recognizes their faces.

In the back of Whiskey's communications book, he starts to make a list, like the list of characters in a play. He begins by writing the names of everyone who comes into Whiskey's room. Over time, he adds their physical descriptions to jog his memory, and then their various roles in Whiskey's care. Through this process, he is eventually able to identify Whiskey's neurosurgeon, the members of the trauma team, to establish which of the staff are nurses, which are specialists of some kind. In making this list, Charlie comes to understand who to approach for different kinds of information. He gets to know which staff are the most patient, who will take the time to answer his questions—even those he has had answered before—to explain things in a language he can understand.

Charlie's list doesn't do Whiskey any good, of course. It doesn't stop Charlie's nightmares or the panic that rises in him from time to time when he allows himself to acknowledge the state Whiskey's in. But it gives Charlie something to do during the interminable hours of waiting for Whiskey to wake up. It gives him a tiny sliver of control in a situation in which almost everything is hopelessly beyond his control. And more importantly, most of the time, it keeps his thoughts from ranging into the territory he is so afraid to explore, from thinking about himself and Whiskey and how things ever went so wrong.

HOTEL

Charlie rented the storage space before he moved in with Kristy. They had known each other for only three months, but they were already sleeping together five nights out of seven, and it made no sense to pay rent on two places, especially when Charlie was between jobs. Even with a few creative storage solutions, Charlie could see it was out of the question to cram all his junk into Kristy's one-bedroom flat. He had fantasized about putting a price sticker on everything he owned and getting rid of it all at once in an "everything must go" garage sale, but he had been talked out of this option not only by his mother, but also Marco.

"What if things don't work out?" they said. Charlie couldn't imagine things not working out. Kristy was sharp and quick-witted, the first girl Charlie had ever gone out with whom he admired, and that made him feel like he was finally having a mature relationship. But he valued Marco's opinion, so he paid seventy-eight dollars a month to keep all his worldly goods in a glorified garage: a concrete space ten feet deep and eight feet wide, complete with a metal roller door. In fact, when he signed the contract, the larger units were on special, so he got two hundred fifty square feet for the price of one hundred fifty, and all he took with him to Kristy's was a suitcase full of clothes and a shoe box of CDs.

It didn't take Charlie long to work out that almost everything he thought he knew about Kristy was wrong. To begin with, there was only one way to do things, and that was her way, which was always better, neater, and more efficient than any method Charlie might use. Kristy never said this explicitly, but she made it clear by the way she scrutinized Charlie at certain tasks and then silently corrected his mistakes when he had finished. Her rules included:

- Always rinse clean dishes under a hot tap before leaving them to drain.
- Peg T-shirts under the arms, not by the shoulders.
- Make the bed as soon as you get out of it.
- Replace CDs in their cases immediately after playing.

In the beginning, Charlie made allowances for Kristy's behavior. The flat was small, and she wasn't used to sharing it; that was all. He made an effort to be extra tidy, thinking she'd get used to having him around. But she didn't get used to it. In fact, she got worse. They started to argue, and it was then that Charlie saw what she had managed to keep hidden before they lived together: Kristy was a sulker. If they disagreed about something, or if Charlie said something she didn't like, she would give him the silent treatment. She would switch on the television, ignoring his attempts at conversation or answering in monosyllables without looking at him, would go to bed without saying good night. Sometimes Charlie knew what had upset Kristy, but mostly he didn't. His role, he discovered, was to run through a potentially never-ending list of possible misdemeanors until he hit upon the cause of the sulk, and then to apologize profusely and commit to never making the same mistake again. Once he understood the rules of this game, Charlie made the decision that he didn't want to play.

The first time he didn't act the role, Charlie had been living with Kristy for a month and a half. It was a Saturday morning; they had read the paper, and Charlie had made an omelet, and then, without anything seeming to have happened, Kristy went into the bedroom and slammed the door. Charlie knew she would be lying on the bed, facing the wall, waiting for him to come in and ask her what was wrong. He finished washing the dishes, *without* rinsing, and then he grabbed his keys and jacket and went out.

He didn't know where he was going exactly; he just knew he needed to get out of the flat. He knew that things weren't going to work out with Kristy, that he wasn't in love with her, that he didn't even like her. He knew he should move out, but he didn't want to think about that. Breakups were to be avoided at all costs; that was one of Charlie's policies. It was a poor policy, he knew this, and it had served him badly in the past, in the countless months he had wasted in relationships that had long since shriveled and died. He knew he should have learned something from this, but he couldn't bear the drama of breakups, the torrent of feelings that were unleashed when relationships ended. They seemed to bring out the worst in people, converting even the consistently rational into the certifiably insane. Charlie had witnessed this transformation countless times, not only in his own relationships, but also in those of his friends. He thought about the Paul Simon song "50 Ways to Leave Your Lover." How simple they made it sound. Charlie wished he could do it that easily. Pack up what he came with and leave quietly, dropping the key in the mailbox on the way out. How he loved this fantasy, in which there was no room for the screaming of recriminations or the destruction of property. No crying fits, no counseling, no relationship autopsy, just a quiet exit. But even as he dreamed it, Charlie knew he wouldn't do it. He would do what he always did, which was to withdraw, bit by bit, until there was barely any part of him left in the relationship, at which point Kristy would break up with him.

The thought of this, the inevitability of it, depressed Charlie. He thought about seeing a movie to take his mind off things, but when he got to the Astor on Chapel Street, he kept walking, without stopping to look at the calendar posted on the door. He thought he might go and see Marco, see if he wanted to go to the park and throw the Frisbee around; it had been a while since they'd done that. But then Charlie remembered that his Frisbee was in storage and that Marco had a knockoff Frisbee, a Speedy Flying Disc, which was too light and therefore not speedy at all. He decided to drop into his storage unit and grab the Frisbee on the way to Marco's house.

He congratulated himself now on the wisdom of getting a storage unit that was only a ten-minute walk from the flat. When he made the decision, both Kristy and his mother said he would have been better off getting one in the outer suburbs and saving himself twenty dollars a month. But Charlie had thought he might want to pop into the unit now and again, and the last thing he wanted was to drive out to the boondocks just to pick up a book. As it happened, Charlie hadn't been back to the storage facility once. He'd gotten used to looking at Kristy's pictures on the wall, drying himself on her towels, drinking out of her chipped Snoopy cups, which she hadn't replaced because she didn't drink tea.

Now Charlie had a sudden hankering for his own things, a feeling of longing for the flat where he had lived quietly and happily on his own. He turned off Chapel onto Union Street, glad he had left the key to the unit on his key ring. Inside the storage facility, he remembered the day he had moved. How Whiskey, who had promised to help, had canceled that morning, so there had been only Marco, who had to leave at three to play soccer. There had been no time to organize the unit, sort things into some kind of logical order. Boxes and bookcases and tables and chairs came off the truck and went straight into the unit, stacked or balanced or wedged wherever they would fit. When the truck was empty, Charlie had rolled down the door and forgotten about the mess that lay behind it.

Rolling up the door, he remembered it. Switching on the light, he also remembered that he had ignored the golden rule of moving house: LABEL THE BOXES.

He had packed them carefully, working through a seventy-foot roll of bubble wrap in the process, but he hadn't written so much as a word on a single box. A detailed inventory was what Charlie was wishing for now, listing the exact contents of each and every box. Failing that, he wished he had at least had the sense to write something generally helpful such as *kitchenware* or *books*. Instead, he was faced with the task of picking his way through various items of household furniture and then sifting through twenty or more boxes in search of a plastic toy.

Charlie knew he ought to give up, that it could not possibly be worth the trouble, that he would be better off going to the toy shop and buying a new Frisbee, or seeing if Marco wanted to get a beer instead. But as his mum had always told him, Charlie had a pigheaded streak, a willful determination to finish what he had started, and that was what drove him to start shunting and shoving at his bed base, dragging and pushing it right out of the unit in order to create the space to go through the boxes.

In the first box, Charlie found his crockery and, tucked in the top, a lighter and a packet of Marlboro Lights. Charlie was not a smoker, not even a social smoker really, but from time to time he craved a cigarette, and he had always liked to keep a packet on hand for those moments. Charlie's mother said it was a disgusting habit that Charlie ought to give up, and Whiskey too while they were at it.

Kristy had been of the same school of thought. She said that even if Charlie didn't smoke inside the flat, when he smoked outside, he would bring it in on his clothes. So Charlie had given it up. In the weeks that he had lived with her, he hadn't missed it, but once he had the packet in his hand, he found himself wanting a cigarette, needing one. He was sure there must be a rule against smoking in a storage facility, thought he might have even seen a sign on the way in, but he lit the cigarette anyway, drew on it deeply. After six weeks without it, the nicotine made his head spin. He pictured his storage unit on fire, thought of the smoke and flames destroying not only his own belongings, but also those of other people, other families. He wondered if he should get insurance or if insurance was included in his rental fee. He made a mental note to find this out, knowing at the same time that he never would. He stubbed the cigarette out, ground it into the concrete floor to make sure it was dead.

The second box Charlie looked in held his cooking utensils— pots and pans, whisks and ladles and spatulas. Charlie loved cooking. He thought of Kristy's kitchen—the gas stove on which only two burners worked, the cramped workbench, the blunt knives and thin-bottomed pans to which everything stuck. Charlie realized he hated cooking in Kristy's flat; he hadn't cooked a good meal since he moved in.

In the third box, Charlie found his notebooks and pens, his Stanley knife and a roll of tape, a handful of markers held together with a rubber band. He forgot about the Frisbee. He decided to do what he should have done in the first place and label the boxes. It was cold in the unit, but Charlie was soon warm, shifting white goods and lamp stands and coffee tables to reach the boxes. He slit them open, made a rough inventory, taped them up, and wrote the contents on the side before stacking them against one wall of the unit. By the time he finished, it was five o'clock. Charlie had been in the unit for almost four hours. He felt sweaty and elated.

When he arrived home, Kristy was out of her sulk. She did not ask where Charlie had been, and Charlie did not tell her. Somehow in his absence, the conflict had been resolved, and Charlie felt ashamed of his earlier thoughts. He didn't want to leave her; that was foolish. He had to give it more time, allow things to settle, that was all.

× × ×

The next time they fought, Charlie went again to the storage unit, and by the third time, it had already become a habit. In the beginning, he went there on the pretext of looking for something, but he never brought anything back with him. Eventually he gave up the pretext. He just liked being there, found that the cold, concrete box felt like his own space in a way that Kristy's flat did not.

Over time, he made it more comfortable, dug his transistor radio out of a box and unwrapped the cushions for the couch so he had somewhere to sit. On his fifth or sixth visit, Charlie discovered that as well as a single lightbulb, the storage unit was fitted with an electrical outlet. He unwrapped his record player, his speakers, and his amp, and after a long search for a power strip, he plugged them in. He listened to the records he had loved as a child, seven-inch singles by Duran Duran, Adam and the Ants, and Michael Jackson that he had saved up his pocket money to buy. He listened to the records he had inherited from his mother's childhood—Bob Dylan, Roy Orbison, and the Everly Brothers. Then he listened to the albums he had bought in his late teens, when he should have moved on to CDs. He lay on his couch, inside a storage unit, listening to the Pixies and the Stone Roses and a dozen other bands who had long since disappeared into obscurity, and Charlie felt happy.

When Kristy nagged him, when she sulked and cried, ranted and raved, Charlie pictured himself in his storage unit, alone and at peace. He didn't always listen to records. He read books and flicked through his journals, spent an evening looking at old photos; sometimes he played his guitar. He had moved the fridge closer to the electrical outlet, and when he wasn't there, he left it plugged in so he could have a cold beer when he felt like it. When the weather got cooler, he plugged in his fan heater to warm up the space. He never told Kristy where he spent his time. He did not know what she thought, and he did not care.

When he was angry, he made a mental list of all the things he disliked about her. Then, when he had convinced himself he would have to leave, he backpedaled, made excuses for her by reminding himself of her difficult childhood, her sister's death, her father's drinking. He forced himself to remember what had attracted him to her in the beginning, the way she made him laugh with her sharp wit, the fact that she was so decisive, so certain about what she wanted from life. Eventually, when all the things he had liked about her became things he couldn't stand—when he finally admitted to himself that she was not just well organized but controlling, not emotional but neurotic, Charlie gave up, tried not to think about it at all.

One afternoon, a Sunday, Kristy was nagging him about cleaning the toaster.

"I've never heard of anyone cleaning a toaster," Charlie said. Her demands had gone from the reasonable to the absurd.

"But crumbs fall out every time I move it," she said.

"So don't move it." He had given up trying to please her, because no matter what he did, it was never enough.

"You're disgusting, Charlie."

"It's crumbs, Kristy. You could clean it every day, and crumbs would still fall out of it. It's a waste of time trying to clean it."

"Fine, that's fine. If you don't want to clean it, you don't have to clean it." She went into the kitchen and unplugged the toaster, and as Charlie watched, she pushed open the window and threw it out. Charlie heard the crash as the toaster hit the ground, two stories below. He looked at Kristy, her red face, her tight mouth. She wore an expression of triumph, as though she had beat him, won a round in some twisted game of her own devising. Charlie grabbed his keys and walked out the door.

"Where are you going?" she shrieked after him.

"I'm going to get another toaster," Charlie said.

"You liar!" she screeched, leaning over the railing into the stairwell. "Tell me where you're really going, you fucking liar!"

At the unit, Charlie did unpack his toaster, but when he went back to the flat at ten o'clock that night, he didn't take it with him. He was glad afterward that he hadn't bothered, because he found that he couldn't get in. Kristy had latched the door with the chain so he couldn't open it more than a couple of inches. Charlie banged on the door a few times, more out of frustration than out of any conviction that Kristy might change her mind. Sighing, he went downstairs and stood in the street, pondering his options.

It was too late to go to his parents', and if he went there, he'd have to go through the whole miserable story, which was out of the question tonight. He could go to Marco's, but there was nowhere for him to sleep except on the couch, and if he was going to sleep on a couch, he thought it might as well be his own. So he found himself once again back at his storage unit, looking through his boxes for his sleeping bag and a pillow. He even found himself a pillowcase, which was slightly damp and musty after three months in a box, but better than nothing. Walking back there, he had thought it would be like camping, the sort of makeshift arrangement he had loved as a boy. But when he was lying there in the dark, it was not like camping. There was no sense of fun or adventure. He was surrounded by storage units filled with other people's unwanted things, bits and pieces of lives they had lived and then packed away and forgotten, and he felt sad and ridiculous. He got out of his sleeping bag, switched on the light, and began to pack away his things. Back into boxes went his record player and amplifier, his books and records. He unplugged the fridge and took out the remaining beers, put away the fan heater and the power strip. It was two in the morning by the time he had returned his storage unit to its proper use.

He walked back to Kristy's flat and knocked on the door until he heard her get up.

"What do you want, Charlie?"

"I just want to get my things," he said calmly.

"It's two in the morning, Charlie. Can't it wait?"

"Let's get it over with, Kristy." He wasn't angry anymore, just tired, and she must have heard that in his voice. She opened the door. Charlie went into the bedroom, turned on the light, and dragged his suitcase out from under the bed. She stood in her pajamas, watching while he pulled his clothes off hangers and threw them into the case.

"Where have you been, Charlie?" she asked eventually. "Where do you go for all those hours when you leave the house?"

Charlie sighed. There had been a time when it had seemed important to keep it a secret from her, to preserve some part of his life that she couldn't criticize or try to improve, but it didn't matter now.

"I go to my storage unit," he said. "I go to my unit, and I drink beer and listen to records."

"For god's sake, Charlie," she said. "You can't expect me to believe that. Obviously you've got someone else. Do you go to her house? A hotel? You might as well tell me the truth. It doesn't make any difference now anyway."

Charlie laughed. He couldn't help it. It struck him as funny that he had told her the truth, and that truth was so absurd she couldn't believe him. He realized he couldn't be bothered to try to convince her he was telling the truth, that he could not begin to explain to her how he had come to spend several hours a week inside a concrete cubicle surrounded by the unwanted belongings of strangers. He could not explain it to himself.

"A hotel?" he said. He laughed again. "That's one way to describe it. The only thing that's missing is the room service."

He slid the key to Kristy's flat off his key ring and put it on the table, and then he walked out of the flat and closed the door. And as he walked down the stairs with his suitcase in one hand and his box of CDs in the other, he thought he had done Paul Simon proud.

INDIA

T he official job title was runner. Whiskey referred to the role as dogsbody or shit kicker. Charlie thought he could handle these names, at a push, but he drew the line at being called Girl Friday.

"It's just an expression," Whiskey said.

"The expression is *Man* Friday," Charlie said, "as in Daniel Defoe's *Robinson Crusoe*."

"For fuck's sake, don't be such a pedant, Charlie," Whiskey said good-naturedly. "Do you want the job or not?"

Whiskey was an advertising hotshot by then, working as a creative director for an agency called Mustard. The job on offer was working on an advertisement Whiskey had written, and Charlie didn't want it, but he needed it. His dad's affair and his parents' separation had come as a total shock. He'd used it as an excuse to quit his job setting up expos at the new exhibition center, which he hadn't liked anyway, and had mooched around his dingy flat, feeling depressed ever since. He didn't know what he wanted to do, couldn't stick at anything, owed money to his father and to Whiskey, to Kristy and to Marco, and he knew Whiskey was doing him a favor by offering him this job.

Besides, he and Whiskey had been getting on better since their parents split up. Whiskey was the first person Charlie called when he found out; he knew Whiskey was the only person in the world who would understand how he was feeling at that moment. Charlie thought working together on this job might be good for him and Whiskey, give them a chance to get closer again.

Whiskey promised him hard work, low glamour, and a fat paycheck, all of which turned out to be true. There was only one small fact Whiskey omitted to reveal—the advertisement was being shot in India.

At the age of twenty-five, Charlie was continually revising his mental list of *Places I Want to Go*. At that time, the list was topped by Canada, Antarctica, and Peru. India wasn't in the top ten; in fact, in the entire history of the list, it had never once made an appearance. If Charlie was going to go to Asia, it would be to Thailand or Indonesia, to lounge on the beach, drinking cocktails delivered to his hammock by beautiful girls in sarongs with delicate hands and flowers in their hair. It would most definitely not be to India, where, judging by what he'd seen on TV, every street was lined with beggars with severed limbs and people drank the same water they shat in. When he stopped to think about it, Charlie realized that India was not on his list of *Places I'll Go When I'm Older* or even *Places I'll Go When I've Been Everywhere Else*; that in fact, the only list India appeared on, a list where it occupied the number one position, was Charlie's list of *Places I Absolutely Never Ever Want to Go*.

So it was hard to fathom how, less than two weeks later, he came to be on an Air India flight to Mumbai, surrounded by the rest of the film crew, all of whom seemed to know a great deal more than Charlie about shooting advertisements in general and about this advertisement in particular. Charlie had no idea what a grip was, couldn't have explained the difference between a producer and a director, didn't know if a dolly was a piece of equipment or a member of the crew. More than that, Charlie was horrified to discover that the car they were shooting the advertisement for was constructed of a metal only marginally more hardy than aluminum foil and was widely known to crumple like a paper cup on impact.

It had been a long flight, but as soon as they arrived at the hotel, Charlie tracked down Whiskey and confronted him with what he'd heard about the car's safety record.

"The first lesson of advertising, Charlie," Whiskey said. "You don't have to believe in the product; you just have to make other people believe in it."

"But it's misleading," Charlie insisted.

"There's nothing misleading about it. We're not pretending the car will hold up well in an accident; all we're saying is that driving one will increase your chances of getting laid."

"You're encouraging people to buy a car that will endanger their lives. It's completely unethical."

"Grow up, Charlie," Whiskey said. "You don't make money out of ethics. So if your little lecture's over, I'd like to go to bed. We're due on set at seven."

× × ×

Charlie was not on set at seven. When the phone rang, he was still in his hotel room, working out how soon he could get out of India.

"Where the fuck are you?" Whiskey asked.

"I can't be part of this, Whiskey. I've changed my mind. I'm going home."

"Jesus Christ, Charlie, you've got to be kidding. I could name at least twenty people who would have killed for an opportunity like this, but I stuck my neck out and gave it to you. And now you're going to piss it up the wall, like you do with every decent chance you're given. What exactly is your problem?"

"I told you already. It's totally unethical. I don't want to be involved in it."

"I can't believe I'm listening to this shit. Since when did you become Mr. Holier-Than-Thou? Let me guess, you're also becoming a vegan."

"You can take the piss, Whiskey, but I know what's right."

"So what's your plan then, Charlie?"

"I'll get a flight back as soon as I can. End of story."

"Think again, little brother. If you fly home without doing the shoot, then you'll owe us for the flight and the deposit on your hotel room."

"Says who?"

"Says your contract."

"Bullshit."

"Bullshit nothing. Check the small print."

Whiskey was silent for a moment. Charlie wondered if he was bluffing.

"Do you know how much a flight to India will set you back?"

Charlie did not know, but he imagined it was a four-figure sum, a sum he could not afford to add to his already substantial debt.

"Still want to leave?" Whiskey asked. "Say the word. I can replace you within an hour."

Charlie drew a zigzag pattern on the letterhead stationery on the hotel's tiny desk.

"I haven't got all day, Charlie. I've got an ad to shoot, and believe it or not, your little tantrum is the least of my worries. Either you can get your ass on this set pronto, or I can send you a bill for two grand. It's up to you."

"All right," Charlie said eventually.

"All right, what?"

"I'll be there."

"Good," Whiskey said. "I'll expect you by eight." And he hung up.

In the taxi on the way to the film studio, Charlie made a decision. He would fulfill his contract. He would turn up on set and do whatever was required of him. He would get through these next couple weeks, collect his pay, fly home, and try to forget about the whole thing.

× × ×

As a runner, Charlie was at the bottom of the pecking order. The client, the creatives, the other crew members—anyone and everyone could make demands of him, but most of his instructions came from Susie, the assistant director. It soon became evident that Whiskey would be spending most of his time schmoozing the client, who was unusually particular and wanted to deal directly with the creatives, so Charlie thought it shouldn't be too difficult to keep out of Whiskey's way.

It wasn't a huge crew. People soon worked out that Charlie was Whiskey's twin brother. Charlie gritted his teeth through the usual round of initial responses: *You're like peas in a pod! How do people tell you apart?* He thought the difference should be fairly obvious when he was wearing shorts and T-shirts and Whiskey was never seen in anything more casual than pants and shirts, but people still managed to mistake him for his brother.

It was a disadvantage with the crew, being Whiskey's brother. It was not that Whiskey was disliked particularly—at least no more than any of the other creative directors they worked under—but there was a line drawn between the agency people and the rest of the crew, and Charlie sensed he made people uncomfortable, because they didn't know which side of that line he fell on. He tried to make it clear that he didn't expect any special treatment, but in those first few days, he knew he was on the outs.

Charlie decided he didn't care. He wasn't here to make friends. He had no desire to go out and explore Mumbai. He wanted to forget he was in India at all. Three nights in a row he went straight from the set to his hotel room and drank the minibar dry. Since they were double rooms, the hotel thoughtfully provided two rounds of each drink on their menu. Charlie started with the gin and vodka, moved on to scotch and bourbon, and finished with Baileys. He didn't like Baileys, but it didn't matter. By that stage, he would have drunk anything.

Looking at the pairs of bottles lined up on his bedside table, Charlie was reminded of the animals boarding Noah's Ark. He was watching cable TV with the sound turned down, and he remembered a song he used to sing at playgroup:

The animals went in two by two, hurrah! hurrah!
The animals went in two by two, hurrah! hurrah!
The animals went in two by two, the elephant and the
  kangaroo
And they all went into the ark, for to get out of the rain.

Once he was past the white spirits, he didn't bother with ice and mixers or even with a glass. He sat on the neutral hotel bedspread, wrapped in a fluffy white hotel towel, and as he flicked between channels with the remote control, he drained the little bottles in one go.

There would be no more conversations with Whiskey about their parents' separation, no more conversations about anything. He would not speak to Whiskey unless he absolutely had to, either there in India or back in Australia. The new phase in their relationship was already over. It had lasted less than two months.

× × ×

On the fourth day of shooting, Susie was in a flap.

"Johnno's in the hospital," she told Charlie. "Sick as a dog; they think it's dengue fever. We had to fly someone in last night to replace him. His name's Jason. Will you get him to sign these forms? He's a tall guy, dark hair."

Charlie took the forms over to the catering table where a few members of the crew were standing around, having their morning tea.

"Holy crap!" the new cameraman said. "I thought for a minute you were Whiskey."

Charlie put his hands up in mock surrender. "Not Whiskey," he said. "Just cursed with the same face. I'm Charlie."

"Jason," he said, shaking Charlie's hand and laughing. "I thought we were going to get busted for taking a long break. I downed my coffee in one go."

"Well, if in doubt, I'm the one who looks like a slob."

"I'll keep that in mind. You're not going to give us a motivational speech then?"

Charlie felt suddenly that everyone was watching him, waiting to hear how he would respond to Jason's question.

"God, no," Charlie said. "I hate Whiskey's little pep talks. I think he's full of shit, actually."

There was a pause. Charlie was sure everyone agreed with him, but no one dared to say so. He was hungover for the third day in a row, but still sharp enough to realize that two weeks of drinking alone, night after night, wasn't his best option. He wanted people to know where he stood.

"The better you know him, the worse he gets," he added.

There were a few laughs then, and Charlie felt the tension pass.

"Good for you," Susie said when the others had moved off.

Charlie wasn't sure what to make of her comment. Was it a good thing to badmouth your only brother in front of a group of strangers?

But it turned out Susie was right. After that incident, things changed with the rest of the crew. All of a sudden, Charlie was on their team, part of the gang, privy to their nicknames and in-jokes, included in their invitations.

× × ×

It didn't take Charlie long to work out where the term *runner* had come from. His job was to run errands—anything and everything that was needed to keep the shoot running smoothly and the client happy. He bought printer cartridges and makeup brushes, desk fans and ice buckets, sequins and gold trim, even a miniature plastic palm tree. He picked up and delivered film, ran call sheets from the office to the set, organized taxis to take the client, the talent, anywhere they needed to go. He made hundreds of cups of tea and coffee, ferried bottles of chilled water around the set endlessly. In the first few days, whenever he received a request, he asked, "When do you need it by?" But once he discovered the answer was always "Five minutes ago," he stopped asking.

The days on set were long and exhausting, but most nights when he finally finished, Charlie found he was too tired to sleep. He wasn't the only one. There was always someone who wanted to go out into Mumbai and try a restaurant or a bar, or failing that, he'd end up in someone's room, cutting up lemons on the bedside table with his Swiss Army Knife, ordering ice from room service to make another round of gin and tonics (Bombay Sapphire, of course).

It was not a terrible time. The work wasn't challenging, but there was a good buzz on the set, and at least he was busy. It was better than sitting around in his flat, worrying about money. Sometimes Charlie even felt like he was enjoying himself, and then he felt guilty. He had to remind himself that taking a stand would have made no difference. He was only a runner. If he'd walked off the job, the advertisement still would have been made.

× × ×

The advertisement they were shooting was for a car called a Pace. It was not a new car—it had already been released in parts of Asia, but it had been rebranded for its Australian release, as a way, Charlie supposed, of distancing itself from its appalling safety record. The Pace came in a variety of different colors named after exotic fruits. It was being marketed as the *funmobile* and was aimed at girls in their late teens buying their first car. The plot, if you could call it that, was a classic girl-meets-boy story, with a Bollywood twist. According to Whiskey, Bollywood was going to be the Next Big Thing.

In the advertisement, a blond, a redhead, and two brunettes jumped in and out of different-colored Paces at locations such as a beach, a nightclub, and a pool party. In less than one minute of footage, the girls appeared in nine different outfits, each of which was shorter, tighter, and more colorful than the last. Then the love interest appeared in a Pace of his own. Smoldering looks were exchanged, and a caption appeared on screen, saying *Your Pace or mine?* In the final scene, the brunettes and the redhead were squeezed together in the backseat of the cherry-colored model, while the blond and her new love kissed passionately in the front. Meanwhile, the Pace was surrounded by the entire cast of a Bollywood musical, singing and dancing their hearts out, and while fireworks exploded in the sky behind them, the final caption read: *Can you handle the Pace?*

The key talent, as it was called, had been cast in Australia: four rake-thin girls with names like Saskia and a male model called Hayden, who sported incredible biceps and a jaw that must have been designed with a set square. The rest of the talent was local, a selection of minor stars, chorus girls, and hopefuls from the Mumbai film industry. If life was fair, Charlie thought, every one of these beautiful Indian girls would become a star. They were slim and graceful with flawless skin, perfect teeth, and exemplary manners. Sometimes they waited hours for their scenes to be shot, changed outfits again and again, had their makeup reapplied countless times, performed the same silly dances over and over in the oppressive heat, and Charlie never heard them complaining. Every last one of them was polite and patient, thrilled to be working on an Australian advertisement, unlike the Australian models, who complained incessantly to anyone who would listen, about the facilities on location, the costumes, the heat, the food.

Charlie was mesmerized by the Indian girls. He fell in love with them collectively and worried that they would be persuaded by the advertisement to buy the Pace themselves. He wanted to warn them, every one of them, about the car's atrocious safety record, had to remind himself that none of these girls would be able to afford a car, that the Pace wasn't sold in India anyway.

x x x

Sometimes while they were shooting, Whiskey would call him over and say *Give this to Susie* or *The client wants an updated call sheet.* Charlie would pick up or deliver, the same as he did for anyone else on the set. Beyond that, he and Whiskey didn't talk at all. They did not discuss the client, the talent, the crew. Charlie managed to avoid socializing with Whiskey until the wrap party on their last night in Mumbai. He was at the bar with Susie and one of the other runners, a guy named Tex, when Whiskey came over.

"Great job, guys," Whiskey said, raising his glass to them, all charm now that the job was wrapped up.

Charlie did not raise his glass, would not meet his brother's eye, but Whiskey pressed on.

"How did he do?" he asked Susie jovially.

"He was bloody useless," Tex butted in. "He sat around on his bony bum making eyes at the dancers while I ran around like a blue-assed fly."

"Dream on, Tex," Susie said. "Charlie put you to shame, and you know it. I'd have him on my set anytime."

"You didn't have to say that," Charlie said when Whiskey was gone. "I don't care what he thinks."

"I don't care what he thinks either," Susie said. "I didn't say it for his benefit; I said it for yours. And I meant it. In fact, I've got a spot for you on a shoot back in Melbourne in a couple of weeks, if you're interested."

"Susie, Susie, you're breaking my heart; you haven't mentioned this to me," Tex said. "If I didn't know you batted for the other team, I'd think you had the hots for Charlie."

"I didn't ask you because I happen to know you're allergic to cats."

"What's that got to do with the price of tea in China?"

"It's a Whiskas ad," Susie said wryly.

"Ah, no thanks," Tex said. "I'll take these Indian babes any day."

Charlie laughed. "They certainly did make the shoot more bearable," he said.

"So how about it?" Susie asked him.

Charlie hesitated. "It's not one of Whiskey's, is it?"

Susie rolled her eyes. "Jesus, Charlie, give me some credit. I think I've seen enough on this shoot to know that you and Whiskey are no Torvill and Dean when it comes to working together."

Charlie nodded, thinking. He didn't have any better plans. He grinned at Susie.

"I like cats," he said.

*　*　*

Within five days of the accident, Whiskey's condition is deemed stable enough for a coma arousal program to begin. Charlie and Juliet are sitting with Whiskey the first time the therapists come. They introduce themselves as Angie and Fergal, and Charlie writes their names in the book as they wheel their trolley in.

"Should we come back later?" Juliet asks.

"You can stay and watch, if you want," Angie says. "We can show you a few techniques you can use yourself. A lot of family members like to take part in the therapy." She smiles encouragingly.

Charlie feels apprehensive. He doesn't know the first thing about coma arousal therapy. Surely it's not that simple. What if they do something wrong? It might do more harm than good. And there is something about Angie and Fergal that makes him uncomfortable. For starters, they're not wearing uniforms, and their appearance doesn't exactly scream professionalism. Angie is wearing colorful stockings and shoes with flowers on them, like a little girl, and Fergal has something of the mad scientist about him, with his thick-rimmed glasses and great mop of hair. But Charlie doesn't know how to say no to them. He will have to report their visit in the book. And what will Rosa and his mother think if they find out he refused to take part in the therapy?

Angie begins by explaining that ideally they attempt to engage each of the five senses as well as stimulating the patient through physical movement. In Whiskey's case, she says, his other injuries prevent any physical movement, and while he is being fed through a nasogastric tube, they won't be able to work on his sense of taste.

"We'll start with the sense of smell," Angie says, and Fergal takes the lid off a small glass bottle and holds it under Whiskey's nose.

"What's in there?" Juliet asks.

"Eucalyptus oil," Fergal tells her.

"Whiskey doesn't like the smell of eucalyptus oil," Charlie says, remembering how his mother used to put it on a handkerchief when she had a cold, and Whiskey used to complain about the stink.

"That can be a good thing," Angie says to Charlie. "We're looking for a grimacing response as an indicator that he's aware of the smell, and sometimes you're more likely to get a response with a smell the patient doesn't like. But we'll try all sorts of things—garlic, peppermint, spirits of ammonia. You might want to bring in some scents from home—perfumes or aftershaves he'd recognize, things like that."

Charlie doesn't know what aftershave Whiskey wears. He makes a note in the book to ask Rosa.

"Next we'll have a go at his sense of touch," Angie says. "Usually we'll work on a number of points on the body, but because of Whiskey's injuries, at this stage, we'll just focus on his right foot."

Fergal peels back the sheet from Whiskey's bed and begins to massage Whiskey's foot.

"Deep pressure massage is very effective," Angie says. "Also things like pinching and slapping can work."

"Won't that hurt him?" Juliet asks. Charlie is thinking the same thing. Surely Whiskey is already in enough discomfort without their adding to it.

"It's only a minor discomfort," Angie explains. "And in comatose patients, pain can be a helpful stimulus. But if you're not comfortable with that, you could try rubbing a loofah on the sole of his foot or even a scrubbing brush—something rough. The intensity of the sensation is important with the sense of touch."

Scrubbing brush/loofah, Charlie writes in the book, though he doesn't think he will bring one. He still hasn't really gotten used to even looking at Whiskey; he doesn't feel anywhere near ready to touch him. But he thinks perhaps Rosa or his mother might want to try it.

"Okay, now we're going to work on his visual perception."

Charlie is appalled when Fergal opens each of Whiskey's eyelids with his thumb and shines a penlight right into his eyes. Fergal explains that they are hoping to see the pupils constrict. Angie demonstrates this for Charlie and Juliet by holding open her own eyes while Fergal shines the penlight in her face. Charlie feels like he is back at school, taking part in some half-baked human biology experiment to test reflexes. *Next we'll start tapping each other's knees with hammers*, he thinks.

But what they do is even more ridiculous than that. To test Whiskey's auditory response, Fergal crashes two tin plates together, rings a bell, and then, after warning Charlie and Juliet to cover their ears, blows a piercing whistle right next to Whiskey's head. *It is worse than a science experiment*, Charlie thinks. *There is nothing scientific at all about what they are doing.* Charlie doesn't wait to hear Angie's explanation for Fergal's antics. He leaves the room and heads straight for the nurses' station, Juliet right behind him.

"You need to do something about that therapy right now," Charlie says to the nurse on duty, a woman called Robina Charlie has come to like.

Robina comes out from behind the counter. "What's the problem, Charlie?"

"Those two clowns in my brother's room are the problem," Charlie says, barely controlling his anger.

Robina looks at Juliet for clarification.

"Angie and Fergal," Juliet explains. "They're...banging on saucepans and things. It seems a bit...ad hoc."

"Ad hoc? It's total mayhem in there! Somebody needs to stop them, or I'll stop them myself."

"No, Charlie," Robina says firmly. "I want you to stay right here while I get this sorted out for you."

"I'm not losing my grip, am I, Jules?" Charlie asks desperately when Robina is gone. "Did what they were doing seem crazy to you? It's not me, is it?"

"Of course not," Juliet says, putting her arm around him. "It definitely wasn't what I expected."

"They're packing up for now," Robina says, coming back to them. "I've called one of the counselors to come down and have a chat with you about this."

"I don't need to speak to a counselor. As long as those two charlatans stay away from Whiskey, everything will be fine."

"They'll already be on their way now. Juliet can sit with Whiskey. You'll probably find a chat will do you good."

"I don't want to talk to anyone," Charlie insists.

"If I told you it could help Whiskey, would that change your mind?"

"How could it possibly help Whiskey? He's not even going to know about it."

"Robina's right, Charlie," Juliet says. "It can't do any harm."

Charlie's head is swimming. All the anger has gone out of him, and he feels suddenly weak, too tired to argue.

× × ×

The counselor they send is nothing like Charlie expects. He had envisaged a middle-aged woman with glasses and a floral shirt, a fake maternal vibe. Instead, he is introduced to a young Jamaican guy called Thomas, in jeans and a T-shirt.

"Can I call you Charlie?" Thomas asks, shaking his hand. He leads Charlie into one of the little waiting rooms, sits down in an armchair across from him, over a coffee table stacked with trashy magazines. *Stars Without Makeup*, Charlie reads on the cover of one magazine; *What Celebs Really Weigh!* promises another.

"Robina tells me you're upset about your brother's arousal therapy," Thomas says, coming straight to the point.

"It's a farce," Charlie says. "Whiskey's lying there all bandaged up, attached to every machine known to man, and they're behaving like a pair of monkeys who've escaped from the zoo. They could have given him a heart attack the way they were carrying on."

"How did that make you feel?"

Charlie snorts. "How do you think it made me feel? How would you feel if someone was doing that to your brother?"

It is a rhetorical question, but Thomas chooses not to take it that way.

"I suppose I'd feel worried, frightened even, a bit helpless. Is that how you felt?"

"No!" Charlie says vehemently. "I felt fucking angry, if you really want to know."

Even as he says it, he knows that Thomas is right. Underneath the anger he is shit-scared, feels more helpless than he's ever felt. But he isn't going to admit that. He looks down at the magazines, avoiding Thomas's eyes. *Bikini Bodies—Get in Shape for Summer*, one of the covers says. Then the words go blurry, and he realizes he is crying. Thirty-two years old, and he is blubbering like a baby in front of a complete stranger. Not since he was a child has he cried in front of another man, not even his own dad. He tries to pull himself together.

"Sorry," he says, still not looking at Thomas. Thomas hands him a tissue. Charlie blows his nose, wipes his eyes. "Sorry," he says again.

"No need to apologize," Thomas says, and he sits and waits until Charlie is done with his crying.

"It's totally normal to feel angry in this situation," Thomas says then. "It's a perfectly reasonable response to a situation that's so frightening, so beyond our control. It's instinctive for our protective mechanism to kick in when someone we love is under threat. Are you very close to Whiskey?"

Charlie nods, and then wonders who he's trying to fool. He shakes his head. "We used to be," he says and then stops. "We don't talk anymore," he tries, but he knows that's a cop-out too. "We've had a falling out," he admits eventually. "We haven't talked for a long time."

"Do you want to talk about that?"

Charlie shakes his head again. "Not really," he says. "Not now, anyway."

"Fair enough. We can talk about that some other time, if you change your mind. Right now, I want to come back to what happened this morning during Whiskey's therapy, if that's okay."

Charlie nods his assent.

"All of the staff here at the hospital, we're all on the same side, Charlie. We all want what's best for Whiskey, the same as you do. The surgeons, the nurses, the therapists—they're all working for the same goal. What they do might not always make sense to you, but every decision they make, they make with Whiskey's well-being in mind."

"But you didn't see them," Charlie protests.

"I've seen them working before," Thomas says. "If it makes you feel any better, you're not the only person to have reacted like this the first time they've seen Angie and Fergal in action. Their methods are unorthodox, I know that. But they're trained professionals, very well regarded in their field, and they've had a lot of success with their program, much higher than the success rates with conventional methods. Now if you're not ready to take part in Whiskey's therapy, that's okay. But you've got to let Angie and Fergal do their job," Thomas says. "You've got to trust them. And not only them—the whole team. You've got to let them do what they need to do to get Whiskey better."

"All right," Charlie says after a time. It makes sense to him, what Thomas is asking.

"Great." Thomas gives Charlie a card with his pager number on it. "If it gets too hard," he says, "you call me, okay? And we'll talk again."

Charlie puts the card in his pocket. "Thank you," he says. It feels inadequate. He is ashamed, not of crying, but of getting angry.

"I'm sorry—" he begins to say.

"No need for that, Charlie," Thomas says. "It's already forgotten."

And Charlie puts his apology away and pushes open the door to Whiskey's room.

JULIET

J uliet was Whiskey's girl first. Whiskey was earning a mint by
then, winning awards left, right, and center, going to parties in
penthouse apartments with models and actresses and TV produc-
ers, all of them shoveling cocaine up their noses by the bucket load.

Whiskey had offered to take Charlie to one of his parties. Marco
suggested that Whiskey might be trying to patch things up, to make
up for what had happened in India. Charlie knew better. He knew
his brother wanted only to show him that the world he lived in was
more glamorous than Charlie could imagine, that the people he
knew were richer, more beautiful, and more successful than anyone
Charlie might have the fortune to meet and that all these people
knew Whiskey by name; he was part of their world. He wanted
to show Charlie what a mistake he'd made in India by blowing the
chance to work for Whiskey again.

Charlie had no desire to socialize with Whiskey and his friends.
He wouldn't even have considered taking up his invitation if it
hadn't been for the fact that it was New Year's Eve, and out of his
own pigheaded stupidity, Charlie had found himself with nowhere
to go and nothing to do.

By September that year, Charlie had already had enough of all the
hype about Y2K. He had always found New Year's Eve overrated,
but never more so than this year. He wanted to slap people who used
the phrase *the dawn of a new millennium*; 2001 was the new millennium, anyway. He had turned down invitations to rent a beach house

in Byron Bay, to cruise the Murray River on a houseboat, to go to an outdoor concert at the Sidney Myer Music Bowl, a dance party, a masked ball, a twelve-course degustation dinner. When people asked Charlie how he planned to celebrate, he said he would be staying at home to watch the *Star Wars* trilogy. Those who believed that the so-called Millennium Bug was going to bring the entire planet grinding to a halt the minute the clock struck twelve told him his VCR wouldn't be working. Charlie said he would take his chances. He had been called, by various friends and acquaintances, a party pooper, a killjoy, a misery guts, a stick-in-the-mud, a freak. He had felt strangely smug about the choice he had made until he woke up on the morning of December thirty-first and felt inexplicably excited. It was the dawn of a new millennium! He wanted to celebrate. He made frantic phone calls. He couldn't get a flight to Byron or Adelaide. The ball, the dinner, the dance party, and the concert were all sold out. Every single one of Charlie's friends had tickets, costumes, limousines on order, magnums of champagne on ice. Charlie had his *Star Wars* box set and a packet of corn chips. It was not enough.

He rang Marco. "Can I come out with you tonight?"

"I thought you weren't going out. I thought you were boycotting the whole thing."

"I changed my mind," Charlie said. "Don't make me eat humble pie. Just tell me, can I or can't I?"

"Course you can."

"Won't it be sold out though? Everything's sold out."

"I can get you in—Robbie's one of the organizers."

"Tell me what you're doing again," Charlie said.

"You know what I'm doing. I'm going to a dance party at the Docklands. Alice Down the Rabbit Hole."

"That's *such* a gay name," Charlie said.

"It's a gay dance party. What do you expect?"

"Will there be men in pseudo cowboy outfits with their asses hanging out?"

"Hopefully," Marco said.

"I'll hate it, won't I?"

"Probably. There are heaps of things on though. Who else have you called?"

"Everyone I've ever met," Charlie said miserably.

"What about Whiskey? I bet he'll be doing something good."

"You must be joking." Since their return from Mumbai almost two years earlier, Charlie had barely seen Whiskey at all.

"Well, you've got Darth Vader or Whiskey. It's your choice."

× × ×

Whiskey did not sound overly excited to hear from Charlie, but he said he would *pull a few strings* to have Charlie's name added to the guest list of the party he was attending. Charlie suspected Whiskey had agreed to let him tag along only because it gave him the opportunity to show off his latest girlfriend. Juliet was a model, Whiskey told Charlie. He had met her on the set of an advertisement he was making for the Crown casino. This did not impress Charlie as it might have impressed someone else. All Whiskey's girlfriends were models. Or actresses. Or models who wanted to be actresses. Charlie had met some of them over the years. They all looked different but were essentially the same. One thing they all had in common was that they adored Whiskey, hung on his every word, which made Charlie feel ill.

Whiskey picked Charlie up in his convertible.

"Can we put the top up?" Charlie asked immediately. Whiskey always drove with the top down, even in the middle of winter. He wanted everyone to see him in the car, talking on his mobile phone, ignoring the beautiful girl who was sitting in the passenger seat beside him.

"Why do you want the top up?" Whiskey asked.

It was the kind of car everyone looked at—sleek and shiny, it reeked of money. As if that wasn't enough, the car was orange.

Burnt orange, Whiskey called it. Charlie thought the color was hideous. Whiskey liked it because it was the only model of that color in Australia. He thought of it as his signature color, his trademark, a symbol of his originality. Charlie thought of it as the worst kind of ostentatiousness, the height of mindless consumerism. He did not say this to Whiskey.

There was a time when he used to say those things, in the beginning, when he thought it might make a difference, that it might give Whiskey some kind of reality check. After India, he had realized it was too late. Whiskey had such a warped sense of his own importance that if Charlie told him how much he hated the car, he knew Whiskey would think he was jealous. So he saved his breath.

"It's too cold to have the top down," he said mildly.

"It's summer," Whiskey said.

"It's *Melbourne*," Charlie said.

"You're such a lightweight, Charlie," Whiskey said, getting out to unclip the roof.

Charlie ignored this. He felt much better when the roof was up. So what if people stared at the car? The windows were tinted; no one could see him and make the mistake of thinking he was part of the show.

"Where's Juliet?" he asked.

"She's meeting us there," Whiskey said. "She's the 'independent' type." When he said the word *independent*, he took his hands off the wheel to draw quotation marks in the air and accompanied this gesture with a smirk, which failed to conceal his annoyance.

Seeing this chink in his armor made Charlie feel warmer toward his brother. Whiskey had become more like a cardboard cutout than a real person, so Charlie found it increasingly difficult to think of him as someone who could be hurt or unhappy, who had the same ups and downs as everyone else. He had changed so much that Charlie found it hard now to believe that not so very long ago they had been friends, stranger still to think that once upon a time, when Whiskey was still William, Charlie had wished to be exactly like him. But in that brief moment when the mask slipped, Charlie remembered these things, felt a rush of affection for his brother.

"What's she like then?" Charlie asked.

"She's beautiful," Whiskey said. "She's the most beautiful girl you'll ever see."

The way he said it, Whiskey sounded almost angry, as though for the first time in his life he had found something he wanted that was beyond his reach. Charlie said nothing. All his brother's girls were beautiful: beautiful, shallow, and inane, the kind of girls who seemed less and less beautiful the longer you talked to them.

× × ×

Juliet, however, was not like Whiskey's other girls. She was a beauty; that part was true. But everything else about her was a surprise to Charlie, and also, it seemed, to Whiskey. To begin with, she didn't rush over as soon as they arrived, only smiled and waved and carried on talking to a pale, striking girl with dark hair and heavy eye makeup. Whiskey seemed uncertain for a moment how to proceed.

"Vodka?" he asked, recovering himself. At the bar, they drank in silence, Whiskey looking across at Juliet while trying to pretend he wasn't. When at last she did come over, he seemed awkward, short of words in a way Charlie had never seen him.

"Did you get here okay?" he asked finally, when the introductions had been made.

"Monique picked me up," she said.

This comment seemed to enrage Whiskey. "I thought you were going to walk," he said.

She shrugged.

"If you needed picking up, I could have picked you up myself."

"It's no big deal, Whiskey," she said.

He exhaled heavily.

It had been years since Charlie had seen Whiskey lose his temper. As he got older, he'd become more easygoing, and in his adult life he had cultivated this quality, made much of it with others so that it became something he was known for, along with his orange car. Now he glanced around the room, as if he was looking for something to hold on to, something to steady himself. Seeing someone he knew, he called out, waved his hand in a way that seemed desperate to Charlie.

"Marty! How are you?" he exclaimed, breaking away from Juliet, shedding his exasperation like a jacket, leaving her alone at the bar with Charlie.

"I hate riding in his car too," Charlie said. He didn't know what made him say it. It was an entirely inappropriate thing to say to his brother's girlfriend, whom he had only just met. To his surprise, she laughed, leaned closer to him, and said conspiratorially, "I never said a word, Charlie."

Charlie was struck by her extraordinarily low voice, the woody scent of her perfume, which was the kind of smell he did not usually like on women but seemed right for her. He tried to think of something else he could say that would make her laugh.

"Do you want another drink?" he asked instead. And then he asked her anything he could think of, anything to keep her talking, just to hear her voice and watch her lips move. And so he found out she hated modeling, that what she really wanted to do was write screenplays, that she had already written one in fact—the story of a young man who wanted to be a writer but thought he had to read everything everyone else had ever written before he could begin. She told him this story shyly, as though she was giving him a gift she was not sure he would like, and as she told it, Charlie found himself feeling glad Whiskey was so out of his depth with this girl, not because Charlie liked her himself, though of course that was part of it, but because she was much too good for his brother, too real and lovely for someone as empty as Whiskey had become.

"What about you, Charlie?" she asked suddenly, as if embarrassed by the story she had told. Usually Charlie didn't bother trying to explain his job to Whiskey's friends. He knew they would find it incomprehensible that someone would give up an opportunity in television to work at a local primary school. But his brief stint in TV had given Charlie none of the rewards his job at the school did. He had made five times as much money as a runner, but those enormous paychecks did not bring him the same happiness as seeing a student who had struggled for months learn to spell the word *because*. He told Juliet this as a kind of test.

"You're probably the only person in this room who does something meaningful for a living," she said.

She passed the test. Charlie thought about kissing her, pulled himself up. He had used his brother to get a party invitation, and now he was sitting at the bar, making eyes at his girlfriend. Whiskey did not deserve her, that was true, but she was still his girlfriend.

"Well, I shouldn't monopolize you all night," he said, standing up. Juliet smiled. Charlie had come across books containing phrases like "when she smiled she lit up the room." He had always thought of these lines as the worst kind of clichés, had said that their authors should be taken out and shot. But when Juliet smiled at him, he saw what those awful writers had meant, found there was no other way to describe it.

He made a halfhearted attempt to look for Whiskey then, but when he found him, Whiskey seemed even less interested in playing at brothers than Charlie was. So Charlie moved randomly about the party, trying not to notice where Juliet was, hoping she would come over and talk to him, promising himself that if she did, he would extricate himself as quickly as politeness allowed. Though he returned again and again to the bar, it seemed that his glass was always empty before the ice had even begun to melt. Alone in the bathroom, he thought again about kissing Juliet, said to himself, "She's your brother's girlfriend, for god's sake," realized he had spoken aloud, decided he must be drunk.

Midnight came and went. Charlie clinked glasses, shook the hands of men, and kissed the cheeks of women whose names he had forgotten the minute he was introduced. He snorted two lines of cocaine because he was offered it, and it seemed a possibility that in the circles he moved he might never be offered it again. He did not know what he should expect to feel, but it turned out to be nothing much of anything, except that his gums became numb and he felt the need to keep pressing his thumb against his teeth to make sure they were still there. He did become more talkative—found himself taking part in conversations he would ordinarily have avoided, held forth on the true nature of Tom Cruise's relationship with Nicole Kidman, expressed several other opinions he had not been aware he had.

When the cocaine wore off, Charlie remembered that he was drunk. He knew he should go home, but it was a long time since he had seen either his brother or Juliet, and the thought of working his way through the party to search for them was exhausting. He wanted to lie down, wandered down a corridor, sticking his head through doors until he found an empty room. The room he found was not a bedroom but a study, and there was nowhere for him to lie down, only an imposing leather desk chair, which looked uninviting, but on closer inspection turned out to be a deluxe model, fitted with a series of knobs and levers that raised and lowered the seat while altering the angle of the backrest. Charlie played around with the chair until he achieved a position in which he thought he might be able to sleep if only the light in the room was not so bright. Unfortunately, he couldn't find the light switch, though he had explored the room in a manner thorough enough to make Sherlock Holmes proud. He thought briefly that there should be a law against the fitting of light switches in positions that were not immediately obvious to the uninitiated.

Giving up on sleep, Charlie rolled his way along a bookcase that ran the length of one wall. He pulled out a copy of J. M. Coetzee's

Disgrace, which he'd been meaning to read. But when he opened the book, he found that the letters were not behaving as they ought to: familiar yet strange, they danced and jigged and spun before his eyes like the chorus line from *Riverdance*.

Charlie was holding the book in his lap when Juliet came into the room. He did not want to attempt standing up out of the chair, but he swiveled to face her.

"Whiskey's looking for you."

"Here I am," Charlie said.

She smiled. Truthfully, this time, he could not have said that it lit up the room, because the room was already far too bright. But it moved him just as it had when they were sitting at the bar.

"What are you reading?" she asked.

Charlie held up the book. He had forgotten which book he'd chosen.

"I couldn't stand that book," she said. "What do you think of it?"

Charlie tried to think of a sensible answer to such a perfectly reasonable question, but nothing came to him, so he told her the truth. "I can't read at the moment," he said.

She laughed in the dry, restrained way she had. Charlie thought she was ridiculously beautiful, and he had no idea what to do about it. Juliet went over to the desk, picked up a pen and a notepad.

"Do you want to give me your number?" she asked.

"My phone number?"

She laughed again. "What other number would I want?"

Charlie felt confused. He wondered if he had missed some essential component of this conversation. He was afraid for a moment that he would not be able to remember the number, but it came to him when he tried, all the digits in a sequence that seemed suddenly more meaningful because it was Juliet who was writing them down.

"Mobile?" she asked.

"I haven't quite caught up yet."

She smiled, putting the paper in her pocket, and then she leaned down and kissed him, not on his cheek or on his forehead, but his mouth, pressed her warm and perfectly shaped lips to his and held them there for a moment.

"I'll tell Whiskey you're here," she said, and then she walked away from him, stopping at the door to dim the light on the switch that was by the door in plain view.

× × ×

Charlie slept late the next day, was woken at two in the afternoon by Whiskey's phone call.

"I broke up with Juliet," he said.

Charlie felt groggy. He tried to think back over the events of the night before, wondered if his brother knew about the kiss, found he couldn't remember getting home.

"What happened?" he asked cautiously.

"Who knows?" Whiskey said. "It was her idea to end it. She said we had no connection or some crap like that. You know how it is with models. She's probably after someone with more money."

Charlie did not really know how it was with models, but from the little dealings he had had with them, he thought it entirely possible that the state of someone's bank balance could make or break a relationship. If Whiskey had been talking about any one of his other girlfriends, Charlie would have believed him. But not Juliet.

Though he had only just met her, though he barely knew her, Charlie felt certain Whiskey's financial status had had no impact on Juliet's feelings. But what Charlie thought didn't matter to Whiskey anyway. Whiskey was not waiting for Charlie's confirmation of his theory—he did not need agreement to continue; he was not that kind of conversationalist.

"She probably thinks she can do better. But she's not as perfect as she thinks she is. She seems pretty at first, but when you really look at her face, it's actually quite out of proportion."

Charlie thought of Juliet's face. Despite the state he had been in the night before, he had no trouble recalling it, and it did not seem to him to be the slightest bit out of proportion. In fact, he thought that if he had to make a template for a human face, hers would be the face he would choose. He did not remind his brother that less than twenty-four hours earlier he had described Juliet as the most beautiful girl you would ever meet. He tried to think of Whiskey as a person he liked and wished the best for, rather than as the brother he tolerated but could not respect.

"Are you upset?" he asked.

Whiskey snorted, as a horse snorts, through his lips as well as his nose. "There's plenty of fish in the sea," he said.

× × ×

After he hung up, Charlie tried to sort out his thoughts about Whiskey and Juliet, himself and Juliet, himself and Whiskey. Though he knew that cocaine did not have hallucinogenic properties, he could only conclude that what had happened with Juliet in the study had been exactly that, an elaborate hallucination—the lucid dreaming of a mind addled by vodka and whatever he had put up his nose.

He did not allow himself the luxury of even considering the other option: that Juliet had actually written down his phone number and then kissed him good-bye. He stuck with his theory until five o'clock, when the phone rang and he heard Juliet's low, melodic voice at the other end. She asked him to meet her for a drink in St. Kilda, and he tried on five shirts before he left the house, finally returning to the one he had begun with, ashamed of himself.

At the bar, he sat beside her in a booth, and she looked as perfect when he was tired and hungover as she had when he was high. He couldn't believe she might be interested in him.

"I'm so sorry about last night," Juliet said without preamble. "I've been feeling absolutely sick about it all day. I know you must think very badly of me, and I don't blame you if you do, but I wanted to at least try to explain."

Charlie had tried, earlier that day, to put the events of the previous night into some semblance of order, without much success. There were great gaping holes in his memory, whole chunks of time in which he had no idea who he had been with, what he had said or done.

"Which part, exactly, are you sorry for?" he asked Juliet.

She took a breath. "I'm sorry that we—that I—I'm sorry for what happened in the study. I know it was wrong, but I was angry with Whiskey. I was...drunk."

A memory came to Charlie then, of the night more than ten years earlier when he realized that Louise Barker's interest in him was purely for Whiskey's punishment. He was embarrassed that he had allowed himself to think that a girl like Juliet might be attracted to someone like him.

"You used me to get back at Whiskey," he said bitterly.

"I wasn't using you!" Juliet said. She looked as though she might cry.

"You kissed me because you were drunk and angry with Whiskey. That's what you just said."

"No," she said. "No." She gulped at her drink. "I kissed you because I...liked you. I *like* you," she corrected herself. "I allowed myself to do it because I was drunk and angry."

She kissed him because she liked him? Charlie wanted to ask her to repeat that statement, to clarify it.

"Why were you angry with Whiskey?" he asked instead.

Juliet shook her head. "There's no point in me telling you that," she said. "I don't want to come between you and Whiskey."

"Well, you needn't worry about that," Charlie said.

Juliet looked anguished. "Are you very close?" she asked.

"We're not close at all. I thought Whiskey would have told you we don't get along. I don't know if that makes you feel any better about what happened."

"That makes me feel worse," Juliet said. "I'd hate to be responsible for driving you further apart."

Charlie looked at her. What she was saying made sense, but he found that he didn't care. All he could think was that she must not leave, she must not leave.

"I should go now," she said, reading his mind.

Charlie put his hand on her wrist. "Don't go," he said. "We don't have to talk about Whiskey. But we're here now. Let's at least have a drink."

Juliet looked with embarrassment at her empty glass.

"I'll get you another one," Charlie offered. "What are you having?"

"Campari and orange juice."

Charlie went to the bar. He was almost certain that when he returned she would be gone; it took all his resolve not to keep looking back at her. But when he came back with the drinks, she was still there.

Charlie sat back down, tried to think of something neutral to say. "What did you think of the party?" he asked her.

"I'm tired of those parties, Charlie," she said. "I'm tired of that whole scene. It looks appealing from the outside, but when you live in it, it's empty; nothing means anything. That's why it was so good to talk to you. You live in the real world, where things matter. You do a job that makes a difference. That's the world I want to live in."

"Do you want me to see if I can get you a job?" Charlie asked lightly.

Juliet laughed. "You really do look exactly the same, don't you?" she said, studying Charlie. "I know that sounds silly. I mean, I've seen identical twins before, on television or in magazines, but it's different to meet two people and actually see that amazing similarity for yourself. It's uncanny."

Charlie had taken part in some version of this conversation more times than he could remember. Usually he found it extraordinarily tiresome to be examined like a creature in a laboratory, but it felt different now that it was Juliet who was performing the examination. It was wonderful, in fact, to have her eyes rest for so long on his face.

"You're a little thinner in the cheeks," she said, still looking at him.

"And somehow more handsome in a way that you can't put your finger on?" Charlie suggested.

She laughed again. She seemed to be thinking about whether to tell Charlie something.

"You wanted to know why I was angry with Whiskey," she said eventually.

Charlie nodded.

"When I first met Whiskey, he told me he wanted to give up advertising, do something for the community, maybe become a teacher. When he said that, I felt like we were at the same point in our lives, like we could understand each other. It took me a while to realize he didn't mean any of it, that he was totally caught up in advertising, that he'd never give it up. He just told me what he thought I wanted to hear. It wasn't until I met you last night that I realized the story he told me was your story, and I knew that the person I wanted to know wasn't Whiskey—it was you."

Charlie had thought that falling in love was a gradual process, that it happened suddenly only in Hollywood movies and airport bestsellers. He didn't know what to say to Juliet. He hadn't read his part in the script. He pushed all thoughts of Whiskey out of his mind, leaned over, and kissed her.

KILO

Juliet found the dog on a Saturday morning. She had gotten up early to go for a run, and when she opened the front door, he was huddled on the doorstep, so small and disheveled she thought at first he was a guinea pig. She shouted for Charlie, who was still in bed.

"What's the matter?" Charlie called, groggy with sleep.

"There's a guinea pig. It must have escaped from somewhere."

Charlie yawned. He didn't feel like getting up so early, but he remembered that Juliet was scared of guinea pigs. Not long after they met, she had told him about being bitten by a guinea pig when she was small. Charlie regularly forgot all sorts of important information, but for some reason, he remembered every detail of this story, even down to the guinea pig's name, which was Olive. He rolled out of bed and went to the door.

"It must belong to one of the kids in the neighborhood," Juliet said. She had tied her hair into a ponytail, which made her look younger than she was. She sounded panicked. Charlie kissed the back of her neck and then bent down to look at the animal.

"It's soaking wet."

Juliet disappeared and came back with a towel. "Use this," she said. "Poor little thing. It's probably been wandering around all night in the rain, trying to find its way home. It might belong to those children in the blue town house."

"We'll have to put it in a shoe box or something until we find out where it lives."

"You're not putting it in one of my shoe boxes."

"Why not? You've got at least a hundred," Charlie teased. "Surely you've got one to spare for this little fellow." But when he picked the creature up, he saw that it wasn't a guinea pig at all.

"It's a puppy," he said, "but he's not in very good shape." He held the little dog up for Juliet to see.

"Oh, Charlie, look at the poor thing. It looks half dead!" She burst into tears.

"Don't get upset," Charlie said. "It's probably just cold and hungry and a bit bewildered. It'll work itself out. Why don't you take it, and I'll see if I can get hold of a vet."

Charlie drove to the animal hospital in North Melbourne while Juliet held the dog on her lap. Charlie had a sudden sharp memory of sitting in the back of Mary Partridge's car, sick with anxiety, after Bravo had been hit by the car. He didn't say so to Juliet, but he didn't think the dog was going to make it. It was limp and trembling, with glazed eyes and matted fur, had barely lifted its head since they found it, hadn't even sniffed at the bowl of warm milk they put under its nose. Charlie put his hand on Juliet's shoulder.

"It'll be all right," he said. "Don't worry."

According to the vet, the puppy was some kind of spaniel, about seven weeks old, who had almost certainly been abandoned. He weighed just under a kilo—about two pounds, less than a bag of flour—which was about half the average weight for a healthy spaniel of that age. There were no broken bones or serious injuries, but he was in shock, as well as suffering from dehydration and hypothermia. He explained that there was no obligation for Charlie and Juliet to do anything more, that the animal hospital would clean him up, keep him warm, and try to get some food into him, and if he recovered, he would be put into the hospital's adoption program.

Charlie thanked the vet and put his arm around Juliet, who was still looking at the puppy.

"I think we should take him," she said suddenly. "He'd have a much better chance if we took him home. I could look after him. He probably just needs some love, doesn't he?" she asked the vet.

"It's probably true that a bit of nurturing would do him more good than anything we could administer here," the vet said cautiously. "But as I said before, there's no obligation."

"Oh, Charlie, let's take him. He'll probably die if we don't, and I'll feel awful."

"I know it's difficult," Charlie said, "but I think it's better to leave him here."

"Not better for him, the poor little thing."

"This is the animal hospital, Juliet. We're leaving him in the best hands. And I'm sure they'll find a good home for him. There's always lots of demand for puppies."

"But you heard what the vet said, Charlie. Our taking him home will give him a much better chance."

"I know you're upset, Juliet, but you don't go out and get a dog, just like that."

"Why not?"

"Why not?" He realized he should have seen this coming. "Getting a dog is something you have to think about carefully," he said.

"But he needs us, Charlie. He found us. Why leave him here when we can give him a good home ourselves? We've got a garden. There's nothing to think about."

Charlie coughed. This was not a conversation he wanted to have in front of the vet. To his relief, the vet seemed to realize where things were leading.

"Would you excuse me for a moment?" he said. "I need to check on something."

"Please, Charlie," Juliet said as soon as the vet had left the room. "Why don't you want to?"

"It's not that I don't want to." He felt around for the right words.

"I don't think we're really ready for a dog. We've never even talked about it before."

"What do you mean, not ready? It's not like having a baby, Charlie."

"Well, it's not so different," Charlie said. "It's a serious long-term commitment." He could not look at her as he said this.

"I'm ready for that kind of commitment, Charlie," Juliet said in the voice she used when she was about to cry.

Charlie knew she wasn't talking about the dog anymore. He looked out of the window. He thought of her earlier that morning, how animated she'd been about the guinea pig. He didn't want to make her cry.

"You know that he might not pull through, don't you?" he asked carefully.

Juliet nodded.

"You're sure you want to take him home anyway?"

She nodded again.

Charlie put his arm around her and kissed her forehead. "Let's go and find that vet then," he said.

× × ×

The vet said the dog might respond to Juliet's heartbeat, that it would remind him of his mother. So when they got home, Juliet made a sling out of a sarong, and for the rest of that day, she carried the dog around with her like a baby. She talked to him softly and stroked his head, and every hour she squirted warm milk into his mouth with a pipette the vet had given them. When he peed on her, Juliet took it as a positive sign. Charlie refrained from saying that wetting themselves was often the last thing people did before they died.

When they went to bed that night, Juliet tucked the dog into a cardboard box with a hot water bottle and an old sweater and put him on the floor next to her side of the bed. Despite her ministrations, the dog was still showing very few signs of life, and

Charlie felt sure they had found him too late, that the dog would die in the night. But Juliet got up three times to feed him, and in the morning, he was still hanging on. Juliet kept him in the sling all day on Sunday, and by that evening, he was starting to show signs of recovery. The glazed look had gone from his eyes, and he was sniffing at Juliet when she gave him the milk. By the time Charlie got home from work on Monday, the dog was looking considerably better. Juliet had bathed him, and he was lying on a towel in front of the heater to dry.

"He looks better now I've cleaned him up, doesn't he?" Juliet said.

Charlie knelt down to have a look at him. He was chestnut colored with a round face and floppy ears, and when Charlie put out his hand, he lifted his head and began to lick Charlie's fingers.

"He reminds me of an Ewok," Charlie said.

Juliet laughed. "He does look a bit like a bear," she said.

"It looks like your Florence Nightingale routine did the trick."

Juliet nodded. She looked so happy. Charlie put his arm around her. He didn't know what to feel. He hadn't wanted the dog to die, of course, but that didn't mean he wanted to keep him. Since they brought the puppy home, neither he nor Juliet had mentioned their dispute at the animal hospital, but it was still on Charlie's mind.

It had been difficult enough when Juliet had asked Charlie to move in with her. On the surface, the suggestion had seemed logical. But they had started talking about it when they'd been together for six months, and it had taken another six months for Charlie to actually make the move. He hadn't been attached to the house he officially lived in, nor to his housemates, whom he had found through the paper. And it was not that he had feared the loss of his independence; he knew Juliet respected his independence and valued her own.

Initially he had put his reluctance down to his experience with Kristy. He'd been burned, he had told himself, and it had made him wary. But Juliet hadn't accepted that explanation. She had said her house was much bigger than Kristy's flat, and they would still be able to have their own space, that Charlie wouldn't have to put anything into storage, that he could bring everything he owned with him and make the place his own. Her arguments made perfect sense. Charlie agreed with everything she said. But he still didn't want to move in with her. And eventually he realized his fears had nothing to do with Kristy, that what it boiled down to was that Charlie had no faith in his relationship with Juliet.

There was no question about his love for her. Charlie was smart enough to know that Juliet was the best thing that had ever happened to him. And that was the problem. It was too good to be true, and Charlie was sure it couldn't last—exactly like his own parents' marriage—that eventually Juliet Katrina Robertson would realize she was far too good for plain old Charlie Ferns.

Charlie couldn't see the point of moving in with her when it was only a matter of time before he would have to move out again. He thought their living together would accelerate the inevitable. And that having lived with her would only make things harder when he had to go back to a life without her. He didn't want to get used to opening the wardrobe and seeing her clothes hanging there. He didn't want to get used to the smell of her shampoo or the color of her toothbrush because he knew that one day he wouldn't have them anymore. One day Juliet's house would stop being his house. He would have given back the keys and would have to ring the doorbell when he went back to collect the things he had accidentally left behind when he moved out. Juliet would have put them in a plastic bag, as though she didn't want to touch them or look at them, and they would be waiting inside the front door when he arrived so there would be no need for him to go into the house.

And it would be the same with the dog. You couldn't divide up a dog the way you could with other belongings. The dog would have to go one way or the other. And Charlie already knew which way it would go. He loved dogs. He had loved Bravo, and he would love this little bearlike dog just as much, would treat him with fresh minced meat, walk him, and let him sleep on the bed, spend hours throwing a stick or a ball for him. And then Charlie would move out and leave him with Juliet in the house that was no longer his. But how could he begin to explain that to Juliet?

Charlie stroked the dog's head. "What are you going to call him then?" he asked Juliet. "You can't keep calling him your little bag of flour."

She laughed.

"You'd be better off calling him Kilo," Charlie suggested. "At least it rolls off the tongue a bit more smoothly."

Juliet poked him in the ribs. "Don't be horrible, Charlie," she said. "I don't want him to be permanently reminded of his ordeal. I thought I might call him Chester."

"Why Chester?" Charlie asked.

"He looks like a Chester to me." She tried it out. "Chester!" she called, and the dog lifted up his head to look at her.

"You see, he already knows his name."

"Chester it is then," Charlie said, and he reached down to rub his little snout.

* * *

It is the morning of the eighth day when Charlie is awakened by the phone before it is even light outside.

"What's happened?" he asks. A call at that time of day can mean only one thing.

"He's got a fever. They can't get his temperature down," his Aunt Audrey says.

"How bad is it?"

Juliet sits up in bed and turns on the bedside light.

"They're treating him now, but there's no change as yet. You should probably come."

"We'll be there in twenty."

"You can't die from a high temperature, can you?" Charlie asks when they are in the car. Juliet reaches over and squeezes his hand. Charlie takes this as a yes. He has to restrain himself from running a red light onto Dandenong Road.

Already Whiskey's coma has lasted longer than Charlie would have thought possible. He has never known a week to pass so slowly as the seven interminable days and nights they have lived through since Whiskey was hit by the car. But Charlie has kept himself going by reminding himself of what his mother has written in Whiskey's journal, that it is extremely rare for a coma to last more than two weeks. With every day that has passed, Charlie has told himself they are one day closer to Whiskey waking up.

He has comforted himself with the thought that if Whiskey was going to die, he would have already died by now, would surely have died right after the accident, when he was bleeding in so many places that they didn't know where to begin stitching him up, when the oxygen that should have been traveling through his bloodstream was hissing in and out of his chest cavity through the hole in his lung, when his brain was swelling, swelling, pressing against the bones of his skull.

Charlie has thought that now they have controlled the swelling, the bleeding, reset his bones, repaired his lung, the worst of the danger has passed. He has convinced himself that within weeks, Whiskey will be sitting up in his hospital bed, complaining about the food.

x x x

When Charlie and Juliet arrive at the hospital, Audrey is waiting for them in the foyer.

"Are they getting his temperature down?" Charlie asks as she hugs him.

"Not yet," she says as they wait for the elevator, "but they're doing everything they can."

"Why has it gone up so much?" Juliet asks. "Has he caught an infection?"

"They think there's been damage to the part of the brain called the hypothalamus. The doctor we spoke to said that usually, if you get too hot or too cold, the hypothalamus will get some other things happening in the body to bring the temperature back to normal, but when the hypothalamus is damaged, that cycle breaks down, and the body keeps getting hotter and hotter, or colder and colder, as the case may be."

"What can they do for him?"

"They've got him on a cooling blanket," Audrey says. "They pump iced water through it. That's the only way they can treat it, from the outside. It seems to need a bit of time to take effect."

"Is it"—Charlie struggles to find the words—"life-threatening?"

Audrey puts her arm around Charlie. "They won't say as much. But the way they've responded, it feels like it."

"How's Mum?"

"And Rosa?" Juliet adds.

"It's been quite the shock," Audrey admits. "I think they thought—we all thought—that things were under control. We didn't realize there were other things that could go wrong. This came out of nowhere."

They are at the intensive care ward by then, and she pauses, looks at Charlie seriously. "Try to be strong for them," she says. "I know it's just as hard for you. But we've got to try to keep ourselves together."

Walking up the ward, Charlie can see his mother and Rosa sitting on the chairs outside Whiskey's room.

"We're not allowed in there," Audrey tells him as they approach. "Any change?" she asks, sitting down next to her sister.

Elaine kisses Charlie hello, shakes her head. She looks terrible, Charlie thinks, worse even than after she saw Whiskey for the first time. Juliet sits down next to Rosa, takes her hand. Rosa doesn't even turn her head.

Charlie looks through the window to Whiskey's room. There are three staff inside, holding ice packs on Whiskey's legs and under his arms, adjusting the machine that pumps the water through the blanket on which Whiskey is lying. Whiskey's body is shaking so violently it frightens Charlie to watch. He turns away from the window, toward his family, and then, remembering what Audrey asked him, he turns the other way so his mother and Rosa won't see his face. When he trusts himself to speak, he turns back.

"He's shivering," he says. "That must be a good sign."

His mother registers his comment but appears to be too exhausted to respond. It is Audrey who answers.

"Apparently it's an involuntary response to the ice. In a healthy person, it would be a good sign, but in Whiskey's case, it doesn't mean anything."

Charlie sighs, sits down next to Juliet. They wait in silence until at last the doctor emerges.

"We've got it under control," she says cautiously. "The nurses are finishing up, and then you can go in and see him." She smiles wanly, as though the effort has drained her, and she walks away.

It crosses Charlie's mind that he should have thanked her, but he doesn't have the energy to get up and go after her. He closes his eyes, waits his turn to see his brother, who is still, for now, alive.

LIMA

As far as Charlie could remember, Whiskey had never shown any interest in marriage. While most people were content with the phrase *tying the knot*, Whiskey always referred to it as *putting on the world's smallest handcuffs*. When their mother's friends asked when Whiskey and Charlie might get married—a popular question, it seemed, for middle-aged parents to put to their friends—Charlie tried to avoid hearing what his mother said about himself, but he had heard her say that Whiskey was married to his work. It was true that since Whiskey had been working in advertising, he'd never had a girl-friend who lasted more than six months—and there had been quite a number who hadn't lasted anywhere near that long. In fact, the girls had been replaced so frequently, and Charlie had seen Whiskey so infrequently, that Charlie had rarely met the same girl twice.

Whiskey never went into the details of his relationships with Charlie, just as Charlie wouldn't have discussed his own relation-ships with Whiskey—even before Juliet—but from what Charlie could tell, Whiskey didn't really share his life with the girls he met. He didn't bring them to family gatherings or take them away for romantic weekends or even stay at home watching videos with them. When he was in their company, Whiskey seemed largely indifferent to them, and he never spoke of them when they weren't around. It seemed to Charlie that Whiskey thought of his girlfriends chiefly as accessories, decorative pieces to enhance his appearance at parties and industry events.

So it came as a great surprise to Charlie to find out that Whiskey had come back from Peru a married man—and an even greater surprise when he met Whiskey's wife.

× × ×

He met Rosa for the first time at his mother's place, the Sunday after Whiskey and Rosa got back from their honeymoon. The first thing Charlie noticed about Rosa was that she didn't look like Whiskey's other girlfriends. They had always been tall—although never taller than Whiskey, of course—dangerously thin, and perfectly groomed. Objectively, Charlie knew the girls were beautiful, but he had found their flawlessness contrived and banal. But Rosa looked real. She was what Charlie called short and Juliet called petite, with dark eyes and a mass of unruly black hair. She wore no makeup and was dressed rather conservatively in a black turtleneck and beige pants—not a side-split skirt or a plunging neckline in sight. She was neither glamorous nor beautiful, though later, when Charlie got to know her better, he saw that when she felt passionate about something, her face was full of expression, and there was something beautiful in her then.

They had been invited to their mother's place that day to *celebrate the marriage*. That's what Charlie's mother had told him on the phone, though Charlie knew his mother would not really be in any mood to celebrate the marriage. He knew exactly what she would be thinking: as if it wasn't bad enough that one of her sons refused to get married, despite the fact that he had a *perfectly lovely girlfriend*, her other son had to go and get married to a complete stranger in a city she had never heard of.

Though this was their first meeting, Rosa also seemed to know what his mother was thinking. Charlie was surprised to see that she did not shy away from it but tackled it head on before they had even sat down to eat.

"I'm sorry you were not at the wedding, Mrs. Ferns. Everything happen so quick. I know you must be disappointed, and I want to make it right. I told to Whiskey I want to have an Australian wedding, to share with his family also. As soon as we settle in, we start planning, and we like to hear your ideas. That is important for us."

Charlie's mother nodded, all the wind gone from her sails, and then there was no more tension between her and Rosa, only the usual tension between Whiskey and Charlie, which was always present at these rare family gatherings, though never acknowledged.

× × ×

In the space between finding out that Whiskey had gotten married and seeing him with his new wife, Charlie and Juliet had speculated endlessly on the reasons why he might have gotten married at such short notice to a Peruvian girl he hardly knew. It was not the kind of question Charlie could imagine ever asking Whiskey outright. At best, he thought, he might eventually hear a secondhand version from his mother, somewhat condensed and warped by her own impressions and opinions.

Charlie would never have guessed that Whiskey would choose as a wife the kind of person who would tell you the whole story the first time she met you. But that was exactly what happened.

Whiskey told the first part, the part that revealed nothing about himself. He had gone to Peru to shoot a soft-drink advertisement at Machu Picchu, he said, and when he arrived, he discovered the shoot had been pushed back because of delays in preproduction. Since he was stuck in Lima for three days, his agency arranged a driver and a tour guide for him. Rosa had shown him around, and everything else had unfolded from there.

At that point, Rosa interrupted him. "Unfolded?" she said. "We are not telling the story of a picnic table, are we?"

Charlie was startled to hear her mocking Whiskey so blatantly, but when he looked over, he saw that Whiskey was laughing.

Rosa shook her head. "You really are a very bad storyteller,

Whiskey," she scolded. "Don't you think your family would like to know what really happen?"

"Perhaps Whiskey thinks it's private," Charlie's mother suggested.

"Private!" Rosa sounded shocked. "Of course not. You are Whiskey's family."

Charlie saw his mother raise her eyebrows. He expected Whiskey to change the subject then, or explain that things might be different in his family than they were in Rosa's, but Whiskey was looking at her indulgently, waiting for her to go on.

"It is a good story," Rosa said, "and I will tell you how it really happen. Me and my brother have been paid to show Whiskey around, that part is true. However, Whiskey forgot to tell you the part where he was acting like a big shot, calling Miguel *driver* like he was in a James Bond movie." Rosa grinned at Whiskey as she said this and poked him in the ribs.

"The first thing he want to do is get some cigarettes, so we stop at a kiosk. He ask if we had Peter Stuyvesant in Peru," Rosa said, "and I told to him we did. Then he ask me to get him a packet. 'Soft pack, if they have them,' he said. Well, he had been in the car only a short time, but I already had enough of him. So I tell him, 'I am your guide, not your slave. Get your own cigarettes.'"

Charlie was astonished by Rosa's story. He looked at Whiskey, waiting for him to deny what Rosa had said, but Whiskey shrugged and admitted Rosa's story was true.

"I didn't quite understand the role of the guide," he said cheerfully. "Poor Rosa was a bit insulted. She had to put me in my place."

Charlie could hardly believe what he was hearing. The way he saw things, it was always Whiskey who was putting people in their place, never the other way around.

Rosa was nodding proudly. "I gave him the rules," she said. "I told to him to say please and thank you, and to say about my city plenty of nice things. I told to him if he could not think of any nice thing to say, it is better to say no things at all. In return, I told to him I will translate for him, make sure he does not get ripped off, and if he want, show him the real Lima, not just the places tourists go."

"Well," Charlie's mother said. "William's not usually that keen on following other people's rules."

"That is true, Mrs. Ferns," Rosa said. "I thought your son would fire me straightaway. But he accept my rules and say sorry like a gentleman."

Whiskey looked embarrassed by this.

"So that's the real story, is it?" Charlie's mother said. She looked amused.

"Oh no," Rosa said. "That is only the beginning. There is much more to tell. Once Whiskey had gotten over his bullshit, the three of us get along fine; we even start to like each other. But I was not planning to marry him, certainly not."

It didn't take long for Charlie to work out that *bullshit* was one of Rosa's favorite words, or that her lexicon of slang—picked up from years of working for American tourists—easily outdid his own. But at this first meeting, Charlie was surprised to hear a word like *bullshit* thrown in with her heavily accented English. He couldn't help noticing that the word raised his mother's eyebrows too, and he hoped she wouldn't hold it against Rosa.

Rosa went on with the story, saying that when the three days were up, Whiskey had gone to Machu Picchu, and she had thought no more of it until two weeks later, when someone from Whiskey's agency had contacted her to tell her he was back in Lima and wanted her to act as a guide for him again. Rosa said she already had a job lined up for the next four days, so she had recommended some other guides she knew. But Whiskey had refused the other guides.

"I was the only guide he want," she said, looking at Whiskey fondly. "So that night, when I had finish working, I go to Whiskey's hotel. When he came down to the lobby to meet me, I realize I was happy to see him, but of course, I do not let him know that.

"I told to him, 'If you want to see Lima, there are plenty of guides as good as me, better even. But if you want to see me, don't ask me to be your guide; ask me to go to dinner.'"

Juliet laughed. "You certainly know how to get straight to the point, Rosa," she said.

Rosa beamed at Juliet. "You are right," she said. "I don't like beating all around the bush."

"You can say that again," Whiskey said. "I think the word *forthright* was invented for Rosa." He was pretending to be gruff, but from the way he was looking at her, Charlie saw that that was exactly what Whiskey liked about Rosa, the way she stood up for herself, and stood up to him.

"Go on then," Whiskey said softly. "Tell them the rest."

Rosa told them that after that first dinner, they saw each other every night for a week, and when she wasn't working, they spent the days together too. The night before he was due to leave, Whiskey asked her to come back to Australia with him.

"He told to me he would buy me a return ticket, so if I do not like it, or if things do not work out with us, I can come back any time I want.

"But I refuse," Rosa said. "I told to him it is not fair for me to give up my job, my family, my home, to go to a place I have never seen with someone I know for less than two weeks. I told to him if I am going to risk everything, he has to risk some things too—he has to marry me."

That was on Thursday, Whiskey told them, becoming involved in the story again. On Friday, he met Rosa's mother to *ask for her hand*—Rosa had insisted on that. On Saturday morning, they bribed a local official into accepting the paperwork, which should have been submitted a month and a day in advance, and that afternoon, they were married, in a church of all places, though Whiskey hadn't set foot in a church in a good ten years. He did not understand a word of the service, but he ate the bread and drank the wine because Rosa said it was less complicated than admitting he was not a Catholic. On Sunday, he and Rosa flew to St. Barts for their hastily planned honeymoon, and two weeks later, they flew back to Australia.

"And here we are," Rosa said happily.

"Here we are," Whiskey echoed, putting his arm around her.

Seeing the way Whiskey doted on Rosa, watching him behave as Charlie had never seen him behave before, it struck Charlie that Rosa was the first woman Whiskey had ever really been in love with. And he began to see that Whiskey's decision was not so out of character as he had first thought, that Whiskey was, after all, a person who would throw a party at an hour's notice, drop everything for an impromptu snowboarding weekend, fly up to Noosa on an impulse to surprise a friend for his thirtieth—that his marriage to Rosa was perhaps not very surprising at all. What was more puzzling to Charlie, once he had met Rosa, was exactly what she saw in Whiskey.

She had mocked him for acting like a *big shot*, as she called it, had told him off for talking about money. ("It is such a boring topic," she had said when Whiskey told their mother the cost of their holiday in St. Barts.) She was a smart girl, Charlie thought, and she clearly found Whiskey's behavior idiotic in many of the same ways Charlie did. And yet, despite this, it was obvious that Rosa was as crazy about Whiskey as he was about her, that those aspects of Whiskey's character, which were so unbearable to Charlie, were endearing to Rosa.

"Perhaps she's just that sort of person," Juliet suggested when Charlie brought it up. "Maybe she looks for the good in people and doesn't worry about the rest."

"I look for the good in people," Charlie protested.

"Not in Whiskey," Juliet said sagely.

Charlie didn't want to get into that conversation. He had vowed never to tell Juliet the real reason he couldn't stand Whiskey.

"It's just a show he's putting on," he said decisively. "It won't last."

× × ×

A couple of weeks after the lunch, Charlie received a phone call from Rosa.

"I took your number from your mother," she said. "I hope you don't mind. I want to invite you and Juliet to lunch."

Charlie swallowed. Surely Whiskey had told her they didn't get along. And even if he hadn't, wouldn't she have seen it for herself that day at their mother's?

"It's very nice of you to call, Rosa," Charlie said carefully. "It's just that Whiskey and I don't really…socialize with each other."

"Yes, Charlie, I know all this," Rosa said quickly. "Whiskey told to me the same thing. But I have been thinking about it, Charlie, and because you have troubles with Whiskey, it does not mean you have to have troubles with me also, does it?"

"Well…" Charlie began, but he didn't get any further. He felt awkward about having to speak so directly about something every-one in his family understood but nobody mentioned. He couldn't think of a tactful way to explain to Rosa that in his experience, when two people didn't get on with each other, they inevitably didn't get on with each other's wives either.

"I would like to be straight with you, Charlie," Rosa said.

Charlie braced himself. Rosa had already been a great deal straighter about things than Charlie felt comfortable with. Unfortunately, he didn't have an opportunity to tell her this, because she'd already launched into a speech.

"You and Whiskey are brothers, Charlie," she began. "You are family, whether you like this or not. And your family is never going away. Always it is somebody's birthday or somebody's wedding, somebody is born or somebody dies, and there they are, hanging around like a bad smell. Sooner or later you have to see them, even if you do not want to. That is how it is with families, in Peru, in Australia, it make no difference. And now I am Whiskey's wife, I am part of your family also. And my feeling is, if we have to see each other, why don't we try to like each other as much as we can? Whatever happen between you and Whiskey is in the past. It has nothing to do with me. When I meet you at your mother's you seem like a decent person, and I like Juliet also. Whiskey is going away for the weekend, and I will be alone. So what do you think? Will you come and have lunch with me?"

Charlie did not know what surprised him more: the way she said such complicated things in such a matter-of-fact way, her use of the expression *hanging around like a bad smell*, or the fact that her twisted logic somehow made sense to him.

"Does Whiskey know you're calling me?" Charlie asked once he had managed to gather himself together.

"Whiskey and I do not keep secrets," Rosa said proudly.

"But what does he think of it?" Charlie persisted.

"He does not like it too much," she said reluctantly. "But he is my husband. He is not my boss. I make my own choices."

"I don't want to cause trouble between you and Whiskey."

"That is not for you to worry about, Charlie," Rosa said stubbornly. "There will not be any trouble, and if there is, it will be my own trouble. Now please tell to me that you come to lunch, or I start to think you are going to be a difficult brother."

Charlie heard the mischief in her voice. He laughed. "You're not going to take no for an answer, are you?"

It was Rosa's turn to laugh. "You are correct, Charlie. I can see you are begin to understand me."

"Okay, Rosa," Charlie said, wondering what on earth he was getting himself into.

× × ×

"Do you think she knows I went out with Whiskey first?" Juliet asked on their way there.

"God knows what Whiskey's told her," Charlie said grimly, already regretting the fact that he had agreed to this little get-together. "It's only lunch though," he said, trying to reassure himself as much as

Juliet. "We'll keep it as short as we can, and hopefully we can avoid any contentious subjects."

As it turned out, there was no chance at all of keeping it short. Rosa had chilled two bottles of wine and prepared three courses of traditional Peruvian dishes, and Charlie saw at once that after she had gone to so much trouble, they couldn't possibly leave early without insulting her, and he didn't want that. He resigned himself to being stuck there for several hours and having to wade through all manner of uncomfortable and awkward topics that she might see fit to dredge up.

But Rosa didn't say anything about Whiskey, and after a couple of glasses of wine, Charlie felt himself relaxing. Rosa told them about Peru, about her family, her first impressions of Australia. She wanted to know about their jobs, their social lives, Juliet's family.

"My goodness, Charlie, every time I look at you, I have to make a reminder to myself that you are not Whiskey," Rosa said as she cleared their plates after the main course. "It is crazy that you are so alike. My eyes still cannot believe it!"

For dessert she served churros, which were doughnuts shaped like heads of corn, coated in sugar and filled with caramel.

"What are you trying to do to us, Rosa?" Charlie asked. "If I eat another one of these, I'm sure I'll have to get carted out on a stretcher, but I can't help myself."

"That is good, Charlie," Rosa said. "I want to make you defenseless, because I have a favor to ask."

Charlie looked up, immediately tense. He knew what she was going to say. She wanted him to meet Whiskey and talk things over; she wanted the four of them to meet up and talk things over; she wanted them to resolve their differences, bury the hatchet, shake hands, make friends. This whole lunch had been moving toward it, and he hadn't noticed; he'd let his guard down. He could have kicked himself.

"I wonder if you will help me with my English," Rosa said, suddenly timid.

Charlie laughed with relief.

"What is funny?" Rosa asked.

"Oh, nothing," Charlie said, "nothing."

"Well, I know you are a teacher," Rosa said uncertainly. "But I am not asking for proper lessons. All I want is for you to talk with me and correct to me when I make a mistake."

Juliet frowned at Charlie. "I'm sure Charlie would be happy to help you, wouldn't you, Charlie?" she said.

"Of course, Rosa," he said, recovering himself. "But your English is already excellent."

Rosa shook her head. "Excellent is not enough," she said. "I want to be perfect."

"I'm at your service," Charlie said.

× × ×

"I think that went really well," Juliet said as they got into the car.

"It could have been worse," Charlie agreed.

"Oh, come on, Charlie!" she said. "You were having a good time. I could see that you were. You like her, don't you?"

Charlie had imagined that if Whiskey ever did get married, it would be to someone from the same glamorous, vacuous circles he moved in, someone Charlie would have nothing at all to say to. But Juliet was right.

"I do like her," he said reluctantly. "But I don't see what difference it makes whether we like her or not. We don't get on with Whiskey, and we're not going to be socializing with them."

"Speak for yourself, Charlie," Juliet said gently.

"All right then, if you want to split hairs. *I* don't like Whiskey, and *I* don't want to socialize with them."

"I know all that, Charlie. But think of the position she's in. She's a long way from home, and other than Whiskey, we're the only people she knows. I think she could use some friends."

"Well, she'll have to look elsewhere," Charlie said. "It's only going to make things more awkward if we become friends with her."

"That's only one way to look at it, Charlie."

Charlie rolled his eyes. "What's the other way then?"

"Don't you think there's a chance that our being friends with Rosa might improve your relationship with Whiskey?"

"The only way to change my relationship with Whiskey would be for him to become a decent human being."

"He can't be as bad as you make out, Charlie."

"He's worse, Juliet. You don't know the things about him that I know."

"Well, why don't you tell me then? What's he done to you that's so unforgivable?"

Not for the first time, Charlie contemplated telling Juliet what Whiskey had said to his mother about her when they first got together. It would certainly be easier for him if she understood. But he also knew how sensitive she was. There was no sense in hurting her to score points against Whiskey.

"You're better off not knowing," Charlie said.

Juliet turned away from him to look out the window.

"Look," Charlie said eventually, "if you want to see Rosa, if you feel that's what you need to do, go ahead. But don't ask me to get involved. I know you don't understand, but I can't do what you're asking. Can you accept that?"

"He's your brother," Juliet said. "It's your choice."

MIKE

Charlie was the first to receive his letter, a hand-addressed envelope with a Canadian stamp. He hardly ever got personal mail, and he had never been to Canada, didn't know anyone who lived there, couldn't even think of anyone who might be passing through. Yet it was addressed to him; there was no mistake.

He opened the envelope, unfolded four handwritten pages of that curly script peculiar to the French. The letter was from a Mike Lawrence, a man who claimed to be Charlie's brother, adopted at birth and brought up by French Canadian parents in Quebec. As he read the first page, Charlie thought someone was playing a prank on him, some absurd and elaborate joke. By the third page, Charlie thought the letter must be real, only meant for a different Charlie Ferns, some other poor sap with a long-lost brother he had never known about. But when he came to the end of the letter and took the photo out of the envelope, Charlie knew it was neither a joke nor a case of mistaken identity, for the man in the picture looked too much like him for there to be any doubt.

Charlie knew that all families had secrets: griefs and grievances left unspoken in the hope that they will one day be forgotten. Charlie had believed his family already had their share. But it seemed it was not enough that his parents didn't speak to each other, that he and Whiskey didn't speak to each other. Now there was something else: a lost sibling, a secret more than thirty years old, that even now, Charlie was sure, no one wanted told.

Charlie read the letter through three times, and then he folded it back into the envelope with the photo and threw it in the paper rack, a place he knew Juliet never looked. In the letter, the man called Mike, whom Charlie could not begin to think of as his brother, said he was also writing to Whiskey—though he called him William—and to their mother. But Charlie wasn't concerned about that. He was almost certain not one of them would mention it, that if they all trod carefully, they could creep past this mess.

What Charlie had not counted on was Rosa.

"Did you get your letter, Charlie?" she asked without preamble when she called him the following day.

"What letter?"

"Don't bullshit me, Charlie, the letter from your brother Michael."

"He's not my brother."

"Didn't you look at the photo?"

"Well, he looks like us, so what? That doesn't make him our brother."

"He is your brother, Charlie."

"You don't know that for sure, Rosa. There's no proof, whatever the photo suggests."

"It is true, Charlie. I spoke to Audrey."

"You what?"

"I telephoned your Auntie Audrey. She told to me the whole story."

"Jesus, Rosa, you had no right to do that. This is between me and Whiskey and our mother. It's up to us if we want to respond to these ridiculous letters."

"Oh, please, Charlie. Not one of you would have done a single thing. And this poor man would have been waiting and waiting to hear from you. Can you imagine how that would make him feel? Have you even thought about how much courage it would have taken to write those letters?"

"It's none of your business, Rosa. This is about *our* family. If we decide not to write to him, that's *our* choice."

Charlie hung up. He had never hung up on anyone in his life. His heart was racing. He found the envelope in the paper rack and tore the letter into small pieces, page by page.

× × ×

When Juliet came home, he was lying on the bed, reading her childhood copy of *Winnie-the-Pooh*.

"Are you okay?" she asked, touching the back of his neck.

"I'm fine." He forced a smile. "Why wouldn't I be?"

Juliet looked at him hard. "Rosa told me about the letter, Charlie."

"Fucking Rosa," he said. "I don't want to talk about that letter, okay?"

"Don't get angry, Charlie. Can I read it at least?"

"I threw it away."

Juliet got up to go to the trash.

"I tore it up and threw it in the trash can, Juliet. Can you leave it alone, please?"

"You tore it up?" Juliet sounded shocked. "Why on earth would you do that?"

Charlie said nothing.

Juliet sat back down. "I can't believe you weren't going to tell me this, Charlie."

"I was going to tell you. I needed some time, that's all."

"Are you going to write to him?"

"I haven't decided yet."

"You're not going to, are you?"

"Jesus, Juliet, not you as well. So what if I'm not? He's my brother. That makes it my decision. It's nothing to do with you, or with Rosa. It's between me and my family."

Juliet stood up. "I may not be your wife, Charlie, but I would have hoped that after all this time you might have come to think of me as part of your family."

She left the room, closing the door sharply behind her.

× × ×

A few days later, Audrey came to see him during recess at the school where he worked, something she had never done in all the years he had worked there, though she lived only streets away.

"I'm on my way to the shops," she said. "I thought you might want to come for a coffee."

"I can't," Charlie said. "I'm on yard duty." He had never been grateful for yard duty before.

"I'm sure someone will swap with you, won't they? Tell them it's a family emergency."

Charlie raised his eyebrows. He knew why Audrey had come, but he hadn't expected her to be so bald about it.

"I'd hardly call it an emergency," he said. "It's waited more than thirty years already."

"You must want to know, Charlie."

He smiled grimly. "I'll let you know if I do."

× × ×

According to the letter, Mike was an only child. The couple who came to be his parents was already in their midthirties when they adopted him and took him to live in Quebec. They were loving in a reserved sort of way, the letter said, a librarian and a civil servant who worked in the same jobs all their lives.

Mike had always known he was adopted; he had been told as soon as he was old enough to understand. When his adoptive parents first told him, they encouraged him to ask questions about his adoption, but he couldn't think of any questions then. At the age of seven, he couldn't imagine any life other than the one he was living, and he didn't want to try. When he was older, he began to wonder about his biological parents, and in particular, to wonder if somewhere in the world he had brothers and sisters. But by then, he felt that it was too late to ask. He loved his parents, and he didn't want to hurt them by making them feel that they weren't enough for him.

When he was twenty-seven, Mike had received a letter explaining that a change in the law now allowed adoptees to trace and contact their biological parents, if they wished. Mike's adopted father, Greg, was already dead, killed in a boating accident five years earlier. But it wasn't until his daughters were born that Mike decided to look for his biological parents.

It took him fourteen months to find them, Mike said in the letter, an endless paper trail through government departments in England, Canada, and finally Australia; fourteen months during which Mike worked all day as a graphic designer and made phone calls and searched Internet directories at night after the girls were fed and put to bed.

Even once he had found them all, knew their names and birthdays and even their addresses, he still didn't do anything about it. It wasn't until a year after his adoptive mother Gloria's death that he finally wrote the letters.

× × ×

Charlie tried hard not to think about Mike's letter. Neither Whiskey nor his mother had mentioned it, and he refused to discuss it with Juliet. But eventually his curiosity got the better of him, and he went around to see Audrey.

Charlie thought he knew as much about his parents' courtship as any child knows—which was barely anything. He and Whiskey had always been told that their parents had come from the same town, gone to the same school, that their father had had to wait until he got a job before they could get married. Now he didn't even know if that much was true.

Audrey told Charlie that when his mother was sixteen, she had taken up with a local boy named Harry Blower. He was very handsome, but it was said that his family mixed with the gypsies, and one of his brothers had been in jail. Audrey said she didn't know how her father found out, but it didn't take long—it was a small town, people knew each other's business.

"Dad was a hard man, but fair," Audrey said. "He wanted the best for us. Elaine was forbidden to see Harry, and Dad had her spend the summer working in his office, where he could keep an eye on her. She sulked her way through the summer, but when she went back to school that September, she started going out with your father. She seemed to be over Harry, back to her old self. She went out with your father all through her last year of school, and when he left school and got his boilermaking apprenticeship, he proposed to her."

Charlie felt better hearing this. He hadn't known about Harry, of course, but at least it hadn't all been lies.

"I have to admit, I was surprised when your mother accepted Bill's proposal," Audrey said carefully. "I always liked your dad, and he loved your mum; there was no doubt about that. But Elaine was a bright spark, a bit of a live wire, and I suppose I'd imagined she'd end up with someone a bit more..." She trailed off, looking at Charlie uncertainly.

"Don't worry, Audrey," Charlie said. "I'm not blind. I know he was no match for her. And besides, you know how I feel about him since they split up. Don't hold back on my account. This is what I'm here for. You might as well tell me everything."

"The wedding was planned for April," Audrey went on, and then one day in late March, she had arrived home from work to find Elaine in a state, waiting for her. Elaine had told Audrey she was pregnant, not by Bill but by Harry, whom she'd been seeing in secret all the time. Audrey winced as she said this, as though even decades later the memory of it was still painful to her.

"Your mother was hysterical, not because of the trouble she was in," she said, "but because when she'd told Harry, he'd said he didn't want anything to do with it, that he didn't love her, that he didn't want a wife or a baby.

"I was already married to Bob then," Audrey said, "but I was only twenty-one myself—I didn't know anything about the ways of the world. So I told Bob, and Bob told your mother to keep her mouth shut, marry your father, and no one would be any the wiser."

Audrey stopped again there, but Charlie motioned for her to go on.

"Your mother thought she would live at home and bring the baby up herself. But Dad soon put a stop to that. He said she could marry your father—if he'd still have her—or she could leave, because he wouldn't have her pregnant and unmarried in his house. It seems harsh, but you mustn't think badly of him, Charlie—things were different then. People didn't accept illegitimate children as they do now. There was no such thing as a single mum. My dad and your dad came to an arrangement. Your father agreed to marry your mother the next month, as planned. When she went into the hospital to have the baby, it would be put up for adoption, and people would be told it was premature, stillborn."

"It's like some shitty soap opera," Charlie said angrily.

"I know it must be hard for you to hear this, Charlie. I never dreamed I'd have to tell you. None of us did. We thought it was over and done with, thirty-three years ago."

"I wish it had been," Charlie said. "I wish this Mike character had had the sense to leave things alone. We could have done without him opening this can of worms."

"I'm sure it's normal to feel like that. But don't forget, Mike doesn't know the story behind his adoption. All he has is his birth certificate—a list of names and places. He doesn't know he's opening a can of worms. All he wants to do is find his family."

"Well, what if they don't want to be found?"

Audrey put her hand on his arm. "It's a shock for all of us, Charlie. I can understand it if you feel like you don't want to meet him. But you don't have to make a decision about it straight away. Take some time and have a think about it."

But Charlie didn't want to think about it. He didn't want to think about it, and he didn't want to talk about it—ever again, if he could help it.

He took what Audrey had told him and every thought and question that had arisen about his mother and father, his half brother—everything he knew and everything he didn't want to know—and he pushed it right out of his mind. He pretended the letter had never arrived. He did not allow himself to think about it at all. He worked so hard at it, he was sure he would have been successful if it weren't for Whiskey and Rosa. Because when it came to Mike Lawrence, Whiskey and Rosa apparently had their own ideas, in which Charlie's meticulously constructed denial had no part. They had their own schemes, their own plans, and there wasn't a single thing Charlie could do to stop them.

In films Charlie has seen, episodes of soap operas, coma victims lie peacefully in dimly lit rooms, the machinery required to keep them alive beeping discreetly beside them. There are tubes and wires, but somehow these celluloid coma patients manage to look exactly like the people they were before they slipped into unconsciousness. Whereas Whiskey is still unrecognizable, and though it has been two weeks since the accident, the medical staff never leaves him alone, except during the long, dead hours of the night watch. During the day, there is always someone wanting to interfere with Whiskey, to adjust him, to measure him, to administer something to him.

Take a ticket, Charlie feels like saying, every time a member of the medical team appears at the door. There are the regular ICU nurses who are always in and out—changing dressings and IV bags, emptying catheters, checking the monitors. There are Angie and Fergal, a physiotherapist named Grant, specialists of various kinds whom Charlie struggles to keep track of, even with his extensive list. Charlie knows he should feel grateful to these people, their efforts to treat Whiskey's injuries, to rouse him from his coma, but sometimes he resents them, wishes they would leave Whiskey alone.

Again and again, Charlie hears the medical staff use the term *secondary complications* to describe the various problems that might arise, either because Whiskey cannot move or because his brain can no longer be relied upon to control his bodily functions. It is only after the temperature scare that Charlie begins to comprehend the seriousness of these secondary complications, the very real threats they pose to Whiskey's life.

Gradually it becomes apparent that Whiskey is just as likely to die of something Charlie has previously thought of as minor—such as pneumonia—as he is of something major, such as organ failure. Whiskey is susceptible to deep vein thrombosis, bladder infections, deformities of the bones, joints, and muscles. Simply from lying in the same position day after day, he can develop pressure sores on his skin that can be difficult to heal. These pressure sores can become gangrenous, can lead—in extreme cases—to the amputation of limbs. Charlie had thought of gangrene as a thing of the past, a condition that existed only in the adventure stories of his boyhood, something that affected wounded soldiers in the field hospitals of World War I, injured explorers who ventured into uncharted territory in colonial times. He had imagined that in an age of sterilization, in a modern hospital equipped with gleaming instruments, trained staff, tried and tested pharmaceuticals, no one's life could be threatened by something as simple as a bedsore. But every day at the hospital, what he sees and hears begins to convince him otherwise.

Whiskey has been placed on a pressure relief air mattress to avoid the development of bedsores. He wears intermittent pneumatic compression stockings to prevent the formation of blood clots. The staff checks regularly for symptoms of pneumonia, and the physiotherapist comes every day.

"Regular physio makes recovery much easier if the patient regains consciousness," he tells Charlie.

Charlie likes Grant. He has unruly hair, muttonchops, a manner that suggests he knows how to have a good time when he's not working on life-threatening cases. He's the kind of person Charlie thinks he might have become friends with, under different circumstances, someone he might have invited out for a beer. But he says *if* the patient regains consciousness. Because Whiskey has now been in a coma for more than fourteen days, which means that statistically speaking, he has become more of an *if* case than a *when*.

Rosa has been asked to consider an operation in which Whiskey's nasogastric tube is replaced with what the medical staff call a G-tube—a gastronomy tube, which is inserted in an incision in the stomach. Charlie almost laughs when he hears the word *gastronomy*. He imagines the gastronomy Whiskey is used to enjoying—the oysters and white truffles, wagyu beef and Iranian caviar—all the delicacies he must have charged to his company credit card over the years, wining and dining corporate clients at Melbourne's finest restaurants.

The operation is recommended for patients who need a feeding tube for an extended period. It is a simple operation that will make Whiskey more comfortable, Rosa has been told. That is enough for her. But not for Charlie. He is suspicious of the term *extended period*. And in a short space of time, he has already come to the conclusion that in a case like Whiskey's, there is no such thing as a simple operation. For starters, the operation requires a general anesthetic. Almost everyone Charlie knows has, at one time or another, undergone a medical procedure that required a general anesthetic. In the past, it has never crossed Charlie's mind that in even the most routine of operations, something might go wrong, that a person might fall into that sickly sweet sleep and never wake up. But it is different for Whiskey. Charlie has had it explained to him more than once that being in a coma is not like being asleep, that, in fact, one of the characteristics of coma is a lack of sleep–wake cycles. But to Charlie, this is a medical technicality. As far as he is concerned, Whiskey might as well be asleep. Might an anesthetic not wrap him in another layer of unconsciousness, let him descend to the next level?

Charlie knows everyone thinks Rosa is suffering the most as a result of Whiskey's situation, closely followed by his mother. He suspects many people—especially Whiskey's friends—think it matters less to

Charlie because he didn't get on with Whiskey. No one understands that makes it matter more, that it is Charlie, in some ways, who has the most to lose by Whiskey dying.

Charlie wishes to be presented with a mathematical diagram in which Whiskey's increased comfort is measured against the risks of the G-tube operation. In the absence of this, he wishes for the opportunity to ask a few simple questions. But he doesn't even get that much. It is Rosa's decision, and as soon as it is made, the preparations for the operation begin. And then no one has time to talk to Charlie, to explain what he needs to know, to wait while he writes it down in Whiskey's journal. Everyone is too busy getting Whiskey ready. There is a brief flurry of activity, and then Whiskey is gone, wheeled away to the operating room, and Charlie is left with his questions in an empty room.

NOVEMBER

Whiskey was in a South Yarra side street around the corner from his office when the car hit him. A driver exiting a parking lot suffered a massive heart attack, careened across the road, mounted the curb, and slammed Whiskey against a wall. One moment Whiskey was on his way to get a coffee, the next he was unconscious on the pavement, his bones crushed, bleeding inside and out.

Charlie was walking down Swanston Street when his mother called to tell him about the accident. Thinking back on it, Charlie cannot remember exactly what his mother said; he remembers only that she used the phrase *critical condition*. He had heard this phrase many times before, but it had always been in relation to someone far removed from his own life. To hear it applied in the context of his own brother knocked the wind out of Charlie. What did he say to his mother? Did he swear or gasp or moan? He remembers looking at a sign outside a bookshop that said *Only 30 shopping days to Christmas!* The sign made no sense to him. He understood it was the last week of November, but in the space of that phone call from his mother, Christmas had become utterly irrelevant, nonsensical even, some exotic land he might never visit again.

These were the thoughts that ran through his head as he stood on the corner of Collins Street trying to hail a taxi. He remembers calling Juliet, but he does not remember what he said. He remembers that every taxi he saw was already occupied and that eventually he got on a tram for the Alfred Hospital. He remembers that on the tram he had the sense that people were staring at him. Was he crying?

× × ×

In the days that followed, Charlie felt overwhelmed by information and yet, at the same time, he felt he knew nothing, understood nothing. His brother was in a coma. But what was a coma? Charlie's head was filled with questions. He talked to the doctors and nurses, to Rosa and Juliet, his mother, their friends. He was told that Whiskey had a high chance of this, a low chance of that, he might be paralyzed or brain damaged or both, he may have the mental age of a child, be confined to a wheelchair or bedridden for the rest of his life. Charlie was offered expert opinions and hunches, facts and statistics, fears and prayers and miracle stories—a desperate hodgepodge of science and blind faith. He heard so many different things from so many different people that he couldn't keep it straight in his head.

There were the things he knew and wished he didn't, the things he didn't know and didn't want to, and then there were the things he needed to know and could not ask. He read an article in the local newspaper about the accident, though he knew nothing he read could tell him how to feel about what had happened, how to deal with those feelings. Charlie did not need a tin-pot journalist to tell him it was a *freak accident*. It was of no interest to him that local residents, business owners, and shoppers had expressed shock and heartfelt sympathy for the victims and their families. According to the article, Whiskey was *only at the beginning of a stellar career* in advertising and the car that took him down was a pewter 1991 Mazda 626. As he read this, Charlie came to understand that Whiskey's accident, which was, to him and his family, a very real tragedy, was being turned not into news, not even that, but entertainment.

Since neither Charlie's family nor the family of the man driving the car would talk to the journalist from the local paper, he had interviewed anyone who was willing to say anything at all. The owner of the café where Whiskey was headed that morning was reported to have said Whiskey's coffee of choice was a soy latte. And a café regular said she had seen Whiskey at the café many times and had always noticed him because he was so well dressed. Charlie wished he could find this woman, this woman who could say something so utterly inane in such a situation; he wished he could find her and slap her face. Instead, he cut the article out of the paper and burned it in the sink.

× × ×

When Charlie tried to imagine a car accident, it was always nighttime on a remote stretch of a dark freeway. He found it incomprehensible that such an accident could happen just off Chapel Street, in broad daylight, on an ordinary weekday morning, while less than a few hundred feet away, people were listening to CDs at the Virgin Megastore or trying on jeans at General Pants. Charlie thought of all the people who were in the vicinity of the accident on that day, how it might easily have been one of them who was hit by the car instead, how if Whiskey had stopped for a moment to make a phone call, slowed down to look at a window display, left his office ten seconds earlier or later, the car would have narrowly missed him.

The accident that had put Whiskey in a coma had also left the driver of the car dead. Charlie did not know whether it was the heart attack or the accident that killed the driver, or some combination of the two. It made no difference. What mattered was that it was not the driver's fault Whiskey was in a coma. It was no one's fault.

Sometimes Charlie wished there was someone to blame. He thought that if he had someone else to be angry with, he might be less angry with himself. He knew, of course, that he was not responsible for the state Whiskey was in. But he could not avoid the fact that he had made no attempt to repair his relationship with his only brother while he had the chance, that he had held a grudge against him long after he should have let it go.

All the times he had thought about the demise of his relationship with Whiskey, it had always been Whiskey's fault. In Charlie's version of events, any bad behavior on his part had always been justifiable as a response to a graver misdemeanor on Whiskey's part. But now that Whiskey was in a coma, it no longer mattered whether Whiskey had been a bad brother to Charlie. The moment that car hit him, Whiskey entered the realm of the blameless, a state in which he was responsible for nothing, and nothing could be held against him. Their relationship, or lack thereof, was now Charlie's responsibility entirely.

OSCAR

It was less than three weeks after Whiskey's accident when Juliet's nephew Oscar was rushed to the hospital with breathing problems.

"It's not a virus, Mummy," he had said to Juliet's sister, Genevieve, between sobs. "I'm actually dying."

It turned out to be just a severe case of croup, and he was back home in bed within hours, but Charlie was still upset when Genevieve rang and told them.

"First Whiskey, now Oscar. It feels like the last straw," Charlie said to Juliet.

"You really love him, don't you?" Juliet asked, touched by Charlie's response.

"He's my little buddy," Charlie said.

It had taken him a while to warm up to Oscar. When Juliet first started spending time with him, Charlie had kept clear. He loved the children he worked with at the school, but toddlers were a different story. Oscar could walk, but he couldn't run or throw and catch a ball, and though, allegedly, he could say a few words, Charlie couldn't understand a thing that came out of his mouth. Apart from birthday parties, which Charlie was expected to attend, looking after Oscar was Juliet's thing.

Then one Saturday, long before Whiskey's accident, Juliet had agreed to look after Oscar so Genevieve and her husband, Maurice, could choose the fixtures and fittings for their bathroom renovation. Genevieve had just dropped Oscar off and Juliet was making him some fairy bread when the phone rang.

"I completely forgot!" Charlie heard her say. "No, no, I'll be there in ten minutes."

"My dentist appointment," she said to Charlie when she hung up. "I can't believe I forgot it."

Charlie could believe it. Though she was extremely organized in other ways, Juliet dreaded going to the dentist and somehow always managed to forget her appointments.

"I have to go, Charlie. You'll be all right with Oscar for a couple of hours, won't you?"

"Me?" Charlie was shocked. "Can't you reschedule?"

"I've already rescheduled twice."

"Why can't you take him with you?"

"I'm going to be stuck in that horrible chair for over an hour. What's Oscar supposed to do for all that time?"

"You could take some books for him," Charlie had suggested hopefully.

"Don't be silly, Charlie. I can't possibly take him with me."

"Well, maybe we should ring Genevieve and ask her to come and get him."

"I don't want to do that. She only just dropped him off. They've got things to do today; that's why I took Oscar in the first place. All I'm asking you to do is look after him for a couple of hours. I don't know why you're making such a fuss about it."

"I'm meeting Marco," Charlie protested. They often caught up at the Windsor Castle, a pub that at one time had been their local and years on was still their favorite. They had a couple of pots of Tooheys pale ale and a counter meal, always the same: a rib eye for Charlie, medium rare, chicken parmigiana for Marco, crinkle-cut fries all around.

"You can take Oscar with you."

"To the pub?"

"Of course not. It's too smoky for a child in a pub. I'm sure you could find somewhere else to have lunch this once."

"What time will you be back?"

"I don't know. Around three, I suppose."

"That's more than three hours! What am I supposed to do with him for all that time?"

"Take him on the train," Juliet suggested. "Take him to the park. Take him to Marco's workshop, he'd love that. He likes tools, like Bob the Builder, don't you, sweetheart?" she said, giving Oscar a kiss on his sticky cheek.

"Who's Bob the Builder?" Charlie said, but she was already gone. He had forgotten to say good luck.

Charlie rang Marco. "Change of plans. I'm in charge of Juliet's nephew. We can't have lunch at the pub. It's too smoky, apparently."

"What about the beer garden?"

"Good idea," Charlie said, brightening.

× × ×

Charlie had held Oscar's hand as they walked down to the station. Juliet always chatted to Oscar, but Charlie couldn't think of anything to say. He was surprised when Oscar pointed at a Holden Commodore and asked, "Is that a Porsche?" Charlie hadn't realized how much his language had come on. He couldn't think of how to keep the conversation going. It was only later that he thought he could have asked Oscar if he liked cars, thought of telling him about Whiskey's convertible.

Charlie was relieved when they arrived at the station, and the process of letting Oscar press the buttons and put the coins in for the tickets consumed all their attention.

"It's a new train," Oscar said when it pulled into the station.

Charlie looked. Oscar was right. It was one of the new trains. Charlie sat down in a double seat halfway down the carriage. Oscar did not sit next to him.

"I want to sit near the doors," he said. They changed seats.

"The doors go like this," Oscar said, and he held his palms apart in the air and then moved them slowly together, making a *shhh* sound. When his two pinkies were touching, he brought his hands toward his chest. Ten seconds later, the doors closed in exactly the way Oscar had demonstrated.

"Can we go on the elascator?" Oscar asked.

"That's only in the city. We're not going to the city. We're only going as far as Windsor."

"How many stops?"

"One."

On the train, people looked at the two of them. Charlie supposed it was because he was fair and Oscar was dark, like Maurice. People could see at a glance that Charlie wasn't his father. Charlie wondered what they were thinking. He tried to wear an expression suggesting *kindly uncle*. Oscar demonstrated the action of the doors over and over again. Women smiled at him and then, less certainly, at Charlie.

"He's beautiful," one woman said. Charlie looked at Oscar's little round face, his dark eyes and long eyelashes. He looked like pictures Charlie had seen of the Dalai Lama as a child.

"How old is he?" the woman asked.

"Nearly two," Charlie said, trying to remember.

The woman frowned suspiciously. Charlie wondered if he might be wrong about the age. He was relieved to get off the train.

× × ×

Marco was already sitting in the garden with a beer when they arrived at the pub.

"Hello, young man," he said. He introduced himself and shook Oscar's hand.

Oscar did not seem to find this strange. He said his name and shook hands back. "We came on a new train," he said by way of conversation.

"A new train, eh? Did it go very fast?"

Oscar nodded.

"How old are you, Oscar?" Marco asked.

"He's two and a bit," Charlie tried.

"I was two," Oscar said, "but I turned into three."

"I thought you said he was a baby," Marco said to Charlie.

Charlie shrugged. "He's grown up a bit since I last spent time with him. Listen, what do you think about taking him to see your workshop later? I've got to keep him entertained all afternoon. Juliet said he might like it. He likes tools, apparently."

Marco checked with Oscar. "You like tools?" he asked.

Oscar nodded.

"I've got a lot of tools."

"Have you got an angle grinder?" He pronounced it *gwoinder*.

Charlie and Marco laughed. "That's a big word for a little guy," Marco said. "Do you go to preschool?"

Charlie noticed Marco was much better at talking to Oscar than he was.

"Not preschool. Kindy," Oscar corrected.

"And do you like kindy?"

Oscar looked at Marco and Charlie slyly. "I like it. But I tell Mummy that I don't."

"Why do you do that?"

Oscar looked at Marco as though he was stupid. "Because I want to stay at home and watch *The Wiggles*!"

"Who's your friend?" the barmaid, Emily, asked when she took their order.

"Oscar," Charlie said. "He's Juliet's nephew."

"And what's Oscar having?"

Charlie hadn't even thought about Oscar. He hadn't a clue what children ate.

"Chicken curry," Oscar said decisively. "I like chicken curry."

Emily giggled. "Eat a lot of curry, do you?"

"Sometimes it's too spicy for me," he admitted solemnly.

"What a character," Emily said, and Charlie felt strangely proud, as though he was responsible for Oscar's charm.

"We've got chicken pasta. Would that do?"

"Yum," Oscar said.

× × ×

After he had finished his arts degree, Marco had decided what he really wanted to do was make furniture. He said he was too old to do an apprenticeship and he liked the good life too much to work for two hundred dollars a week, so he took whatever jobs he could find—a bit of turning, a bit of carving, a bit of French polishing—until, after a few years, he had learned enough and saved enough to have a go at doing it on his own. He set up a workshop and made chairs and tables and beds, whatever people asked for. After a couple of years, one of his clients had asked him to make a new front door for his house. He had shown Marco a photo of an ornate door he had seen in Prague and asked if he could replicate it. The door was hundreds of years old, and Marco had spent several months aging the wood, carving it, copying every detail until the door he had made looked exactly like the door in the photo. After that, Marco was suddenly a specialist, and before long, all he made were doors. People paid over five thousand dollars and waited up to six months for some of them.

Charlie always liked going to Marco's workshop. He liked the smells of wood and varnish, the combination of chaos and order. Oscar seemed to like it too. He went over to the workbench to examine Marco's tools.

Marco sat him up on a stool so he could see better. "Do you know what this is?" he asked, holding up a screwdriver.

Oscar examined it carefully. "Phillips screwdriver." *Scwoodwoiver.*

Marco took it back. "Phillips head. He's right. Priceless. What about this one?"

Marco held up a tool Charlie would have described as a saw.

"Hacksaw," Oscar said without hesitating.

Marco whistled. "Are you going to be a carpenter when you grow up?"

"And a train driver," he said.

× × ×

The game of naming all the tools took a long time, and then Marco put on a bit of a show, did some sanding and sawing and boring for Oscar's entertainment. By the time Charlie got him home, it was after four.

"You've been gone for ages," Juliet said. "Why didn't you take your phone? I've been worried about you. Is he all right?" She picked Oscar up and gave him a kiss.

"He's perfectly all right," Charlie said, feeling slightly put out. "There's nothing to worry about. We had a great time, didn't we, Oscar?"

"We went to Marco's workshop," Oscar said. "He's got more more more tools than I've ever seen."

"Sounds like you boys had fun together," Juliet said, relieved.

"It wasn't as bad as you expected then," she said to Charlie once Oscar was playing with his toys in the family room.

"He's more grown up than I thought," Charlie said. "I didn't realize he could talk so much. He's amazing."

"He does seem to be quite advanced for a three-year-old, doesn't he?"

"I didn't realize he was three."

"We went to his third birthday party."

Charlie shrugged. "I couldn't remember how old he turned."

Juliet laughed. "Sometimes you're truly useless, Charlie."

"Rubbish," Charlie said, putting his arms around her. "You're just jealous because I'm his new favorite."

× × ×

After that, Charlie had tried to make sure he was around whenever Juliet looked after Oscar. He bought him toys, shoes with lights that flashed when he took a step, a T-shirt saying *Talk to My Agent*. Charlie took dozens of photos of him, wrote down the funny things Oscar said so he wouldn't forget them.

"I can't come over," he had said on the phone one day. "I've got chicken pops. I'm in quarantine."

Charlie cracked up when he told Juliet. He couldn't say *pox* but he could say *quarantine*.

Before long, Oscar's visits were established rituals. They would ride a couple stops on the train, go to a nearby park for running races—in which Charlie was under strict instructions from Juliet to let Oscar win two out of three—and then catch the train home again.

"Play dough now?" Oscar would ask after lunch, and they would roll out the dough on the kitchen bench and cut shapes out of it with cookie molds. And now and again, if Juliet was busy, they would go to Marco's workshop.

× × ×

"Shall we go and see Oscar?" Juliet suggested after Genevieve rang to tell them about the croup.

"Is it catching?" Charlie asked.

"Not for adults, I don't think."

"Let's get him a present, to cheer him up."

They stopped at a toy shop on the way, and Charlie picked out an enormous LEGO robot.

"That seems a little bit over the top," Juliet said when she saw the size of it. "I mean, I know he's sick, but…"

"He went to the *hospital*, Juliet," Charlie said defensively. "He deserves something special."

Oscar loved the robot. Charlie sat on the end of his bed for two hours, helping him build it.

"Look how big it is, Mummy!" Oscar shrieked excitedly when it was finished.

"You've perked up," Genevieve said. "Perhaps Uncle Charlie should have been a doctor, Oscar. What do you think?"

"Why?" Oscar asked.

"Well, you certainly seem to be feeling a lot better since he arrived."

"It was really Oscar who cheered me up," Charlie said, "isn't that right, Oscar?"

Oscar beamed.

× × ×

"You'd make a great dad, Charlie," Juliet said on the way home.

"I think one day a fortnight's enough for me at the moment," Charlie said lightly.

"That's true. But still. Don't you think about having kids of your own one day?"

"I can't really think about that right now, Juliet."

"I know you're thinking about Whiskey. And I am too. But for some reason, the accident's made me think about other things, kids and stuff. Have you found that?"

"I'm still trying to take it in."

"Has it made you wonder though," she said carefully, "about what Whiskey and Rosa asked us, about the decision we made?"

"We said we wouldn't talk about that."

"I know. But it feels different now. I've been thinking about it, haven't you?"

"No, Juliet," Charlie said. "I haven't and I don't want to. What's done is done."

But Charlie was lying when he said he hadn't been thinking about the decision they'd made. Since Whiskey's accident, it had been one of the things he had thought about most. Two years before, when Rosa broached the topic with them, things had seemed simpler, clearer. Rosa had told Charlie the facts. They had started trying to have children as soon as they were married. When nothing had happened after six months, they had gone for testing, which was how they had found out Whiskey was, as Rosa put it, shooting blanks.

Rosa said Whiskey's infertility was probably due to an accident he'd had when he was twelve. Charlie knew immediately which accident Rosa was referring to. Whiskey and his friend Joel had built a makeshift bike ramp up against an ancient piece of farm machinery in the abandoned yard behind their house. On the first run, the ramp had collapsed under Whiskey's weight, and he had ripped open his groin on the rough edge of the rusty old machine. Charlie hadn't seen Whiskey cry since they were very young boys. Whenever he fell out of something or crashed into something, when he broke something or cut something open, he staved off the pain by swearing, muttering every foul word he could think of until their mother or father loaded him into the car for the hospital. This time he didn't swear. He lay on his back groaning, and Charlie could see tears sliding across his face and running down the back of his collar. Seeing the mess and blood down below, Charlie had felt the pain in his own groin. Even Joel, who never knew when to shut up, was momentarily silenced. After they had stitched him up, the doctor said the accident might affect Whiskey's ability to have children. Charlie had hardly understood what he meant. They were still children themselves.

The details came later, via Juliet. Trying for children straightaway had been one of the conditions on which Rosa agreed to marry Whiskey. Already twenty-nine when they met, she had been thinking about having children for some time, and now that she had met Whiskey, she didn't want to wait.

This detail was one of the things that had bothered Charlie. Until he met Rosa, Whiskey had shown no interest in children. Charlie had thought he was too selfish for it, that he would be afraid it would cramp his style. It did not seem right to Charlie that Whiskey could have changed his mind so quickly.

To get married after two weeks' acquaintance was one thing. If it didn't work, Whiskey and Rosa could separate, never had to see each other again if they didn't want to. Financially speaking, Rosa would be slightly richer, Whiskey slightly poorer; emotionally speaking, they might both be more cynical, less likely to jump so quickly the next time, but otherwise intact. But children were something else. To have them or not to have them did not seem to Charlie to be a decision you should make in the throes of a whirlwind romance. It wasn't a choice you could make to please someone else. It was a decision that needed a lot of time and thought, that you had to make slowly and carefully, that you had to be sure of. Certainly this was how Charlie viewed the decision when it came to having children of his own.

Because Whiskey and Rosa had started trying for children so quickly, by the time they asked Charlie to be a sperm donor, they hadn't even been married for a year. True, this was longer than any of Whiskey's previous relationships had lasted, and from the little he saw of them, Whiskey did seem different with Rosa than he had been with girls in the past. But Charlie wasn't convinced the changes in Whiskey were permanent. Nine or ten months was no time at all. It didn't mean they would last the distance. It seemed far more likely to Charlie that within a few months, the luster would wear off Whiskey's relationship with Rosa, and he would revert to type, cheating on her with a cutout doll who would be impressed by his salary, his car.

The first thing Charlie did was have his own sperm tested. Even though he was almost certain it was the accident that had caused Whiskey's infertility, there was a tiny chance that something else had affected Whiskey, something that might also have affected Charlie. Getting the all clear felt complicated. It meant Charlie could have children of his own someday, when he wanted...if he wanted. But it also meant he had to make a decision about donating sperm to Whiskey and Rosa.

It would be, genetically speaking, exactly the same as Whiskey's sperm. The child would be like Whiskey. No one would ever need to know it had grown out of Charlie's cells. And that was the way Whiskey wanted it. He told Rosa he didn't want other people speculating about his ability to father children. He wouldn't even consider adoption. Which meant Charlie was their only hope.

Charlie had tried not to let that cloud his decision. He had tried to be unemotional about it, to keep his head clear of his heart. He had questioned whether Whiskey would make a good father. He had wondered if Whiskey could ever put someone else's needs before his own. He had asked himself if there was much chance of Whiskey's marriage to Rosa lasting. To each question, the answer had been no. And so in the end, no was the answer Charlie had given Rosa.

To Rosa's credit, she had not asked Charlie to justify his decision. It had never again been discussed, and Charlie had tried to forget about it. In the two years since, he had mostly been successful. But since Whiskey's accident, it had been on his mind again. Now Charlie felt that everything about the decision he made had been wrong. He was ashamed of the high moral ground he had taken, ashamed of the opportunity he had taken away from Whiskey, from Rosa.

Now he wondered what had given him the right to decide if Whiskey and Rosa were equipped to be parents, to judge them and their relationship. What arrogance he'd had, to think he might do any better at it himself. He had failed in the role of brother. It was not unreasonable to suppose he would do just as badly in the role of father. At the time, it had seemed to Charlie that he was doing everyone—Whiskey, Rosa, the child—a favor by preventing the advent of something that was doomed to failure.

But Whiskey and Rosa had not asked him to make a decision for them. They had asked for his help, for a gift only he could give. And he had refused.

* * *

Ever since the G-tube operation, Charlie has been avoiding the hospital. Initially he told himself that all the time he'd spent at the hospital had worn him out, that he needed a few days to regroup, recover his strength. But he finds that the longer he stays away, the less he wants to go back.

"It's awful, isn't it," Juliet says, "just waiting for something else to go wrong?"

But in fact, it is not the feeling that something might go wrong at any moment that frightens Charlie—it is the absence of that feeling.

In the first couple of weeks after the accident, when everything had been a matter of life and death, Charlie had been able to occupy himself with learning about coma, understanding the particulars of Whiskey's condition, finding his way around the hospital, getting to know the staff. There had been the surgical procedures required to stabilize Whiskey's condition, the endless testing, the medical emergencies—a constant flurry of activity, which had left Charlie with neither the time nor the energy to think beyond the immediate problems they were facing.

But the insertion of the G-tube seems to have marked a turning point. Charlie gets the impression that the medical staff are no longer expecting that Whiskey might die at any moment, but they are no longer expecting that he might wake from the coma either. Whiskey is still monitored constantly by the nurses in the intensive care unit;

the therapists still come daily. But the sense of anticipation that surrounded Whiskey seems to have ebbed away, leaving a gap. And it is into this gap that Charlie's thoughts flood, the thoughts he has, until then, managed to keep at bay.

And that is the real reason why he can no longer bear to be at the hospital, and, more importantly, why he can't bear to be left alone with Whiskey, not even for the five or ten minutes it takes Rosa or his mother to get a coffee or freshen up in the bathroom. Because Charlie can't stand to sit there beside Whiskey, asking himself the same question over and over again: Why didn't he accept Whiskey's apology when he had the chance?

PAPA

Charlie never thought of calling his brother anything other than Whiskey. But it had been a long time since he called his father Papa. After his father moved back to England, Charlie couldn't even bring himself to say Dad. If he had to speak about him to others, he referred to him as *my father*; otherwise, he called him Bill.

Charlie was twenty-five when his parents split up. At that stage, in his own relationship history, he'd never once made it past the one-year mark. He didn't know the first thing about commitment, about what it took to make a marriage work. But he had thought he understood his parents' peculiar dynamic. Even from a young age, it had been clear to Charlie that his father was more in love with his mother than she was with him. Over the years, Charlie had often thought his mother might one day leave his father. It had never crossed his mind that it might go the other way.

True, it had seemed slightly odd that Bill's two-week trip to England for his father's funeral had ended up lasting two months. But when Charlie's father said the will was not as straightforward as it had seemed, that his sister's husband was making things difficult, that he wanted to stay until the sale of the house went through, Charlie had no reason to disbelieve him. And as it turned out, the reasons he gave for staying were far less preposterous than the truth, which was that he had extended his trip because he had fallen in love.

"Your father's had a rush of shit to the brain," Charlie's mother had said when she told him and Whiskey.

Never in his life had Charlie heard his mother use such a crass expression. But when he heard the story, he couldn't blame her. Their father had confessed to the affair on the way back from the airport, explaining that he had wanted to be honest from the start but had thought it better to wait until they were face-to-face. Elaine had pulled into the emergency stopping lane on the Tullamarine Freeway, unloaded Bill's suitcase, and told him to get out of the car. As soon as she got home, she had arranged to have the locks changed, and then she had gone through the house, separating Bill's things from her own and throwing them into garbage bags, which she dumped on the front lawn.

Charlie's father had called him a few days later from his friend Neil's house where he was staying. He had said that Elaine had never really loved him and that he hadn't been happy for years. He'd said he didn't expect Charlie to understand but he felt he'd been given another chance with Terri, and if he didn't take it, he might regret it for the rest of his life. He had wanted to meet up with Charlie and Whiskey, to explain it properly, but they both felt the same—they didn't want to hear it. They were disgusted with their father, more disgusted still when the details filtered through from their father's sister in England, who was as appalled by the situation as they were.

It turned out that Terri had been their grandfather's home caregiver, whom Bill had met at his father's funeral and begun his affair with only days later. To make matters worse, Terri was years younger than Bill, only a year or two older than Whiskey and Charlie.

When Audrey heard about it, she'd said it was a midlife crisis, a response to the shock of his father's death, that Bill would never leave Elaine. But Audrey had been wrong. Charlie's father sorted out his belongings, packing those he wanted to take with him to England and getting rid of the rest. He had booked his ticket, closed his bank accounts, sold his car, and in a matter of weeks, he was gone.

Charlie's mother had said she should never have married him in the first place, and then that she wished she'd left him when she first thought about it, before they moved to Australia. It wasn't until Mike's letter came and Audrey told Charlie the story of how his parents' marriage began that his mother's comments made sense to Charlie.

Bill had been gone for years by then. He had sent a card every Christmas and on Charlie's birthday, and every once in a while, he had called Charlie. He was always drunk when he phoned—Charlie could hear it in his voice. Charlie didn't know if he called because he was drunk or if he got drunk in order to call. He didn't much care. He had nothing to say to his father. He answered Bill's questions in monosyllables, and when the silences became too long to bear, his father would make an excuse and hang up.

After the letter came from Mike, Charlie began to feel that he had been too hard on his father, that some of the things Bill had tried to tell him before he left for England might have been true. He thought about calling his father, making an effort to patch up their relationship. But then Whiskey had the accident, and everything changed.

× × ×

"Does Bill know?" Charlie asked his mother when he saw her at the hospital the day after the accident.

"I rang him this morning."

"When's he arriving?"

"He said he'll 'sit tight' for a day or so until there's a clearer… diagnosis."

"He said *what?*"

Elaine shook her head.

"Did you tell him how serious it was?"

She nodded.

"You told him Whiskey was in a coma?"

She nodded again.

"Does he know Whiskey might…?"

"I told him, Charlie. I told him everything we know."

"And he isn't coming?"

"He didn't say he wouldn't come. He just said he wanted to wait a day or two, see what happened."

"Jesus Christ," Charlie said. "What's wrong with him? It might all be over in a day or two, doesn't he understand that? Whiskey's his son!"

"I don't understand it any better than you do, Charlie. But he's not my husband anymore. I can't tell him what to do. If he doesn't have the sense to know he should be on a plane right now, it's not my place to tell him."

"Well, then I'll tell him," Charlie said. "This is no time to wait and see. Any normal person would be on the first flight out. I'll tell him whether he likes it or not."

✕ ✕ ✕

Bill wasn't home when Charlie called, but Charlie was so fired up he couldn't wait to say his piece; he delivered it to the answering machine, expletives and all. Afterward, he could barely remember what he had said, but whatever it was, it had the desired effect: Bill left his own message for Charlie the next morning, giving details of a flight arriving the following day. *Neil's meeting me, so you don't need to worry about picking me up,* the message said. Charlie couldn't believe Bill had thought it might be an option for Charlie to pick him up after the blasting Charlie had given him. He tried not to let the message irritate him. He knew he should focus on the positive—at least his father was coming.

The following morning, Charlie called from the hospital to confirm that his father's flight had arrived on schedule. Taking into account the time needed to pass through customs, collect his luggage, and drive through the city to the hospital, Charlie estimated his father should be there within two hours.

By the time Bill finally arrived, almost five hours after his plane landed, Charlie was incensed.

"Where the hell have you been?" he asked when he saw his father dithering around at the nurses' station.

"Charlie," Bill said, moving toward him awkwardly, as if unsure about whether to hug him.

Charlie stood rigid, and his father dropped back.

"I was absolutely shattered," Bill said apologetically. "I thought it would be better to have a few hours' shut-eye before I came down here."

"Better for who?" Charlie felt like knocking his father to the ground. *Your son could have died while you were catching up on sleep!* he wanted to shout, but he was so angry he couldn't speak.

"How's he doing?" Bill asked.

"What do you care?" Charlie asked. He hadn't seen his father for six years, and he walked away from him without even shaking his hand.

"Come on, Charlie," his father called after him. "Don't be like that. I've come all this way. I need to talk to you. I've got something to tell you."

But Charlie didn't look back. He didn't want to hear it.

He was angrier still when he learned from his mother that Bill had planned to stay only for a week.

"I don't believe it," Charlie said. "He stays in England for eight weeks for someone who's already dead, but when his son's at death's door, he can't even spare eight days."

"He implied that there was some reason why he couldn't stay, something important," Charlie's mother said.

"Some reason like what?" Charlie demanded. "He's retired, isn't he? He probably just sits around on his ass all day. What's all the rush about?"

"I don't know," Elaine said. "Something to do with Terri, I suppose. I didn't press him. It was obvious he didn't want to tell me. He seems to want to talk to you about something though, asked me when you'd be back."

"Well, here I am," Charlie said. "And where the hell's he? Catching up on sleep, I guess. Or maybe having a round of golf with Neil. Is he here to see Whiskey or not? What does he think this is, some kind of holiday, a chance to catch up with his old mates?"

Charlie's mother sighed. "It's none of my business, Charlie. We've been separated for six years. I'm not responsible for his behavior."

"But doesn't it make you angry?"

"I don't want to waste my energy being angry. Your father's the one who's going to have to live with the decisions he's made. Leave him to it. Being angry won't help William. That's what we've got to focus on right now."

Charlie knew his mother was right. But there was a relief in feeling angry, in having someone or something to rail against. And it took his mind off other things, off the endless, shifting calculation of Whiskey's chances of survival.

He held out on his father for two days. On the third day, he agreed to have a coffee with him at the hospital cafeteria.

"I'm glad we've got a chance to talk," Bill said gratefully as they sat down. "I was starting to think I wasn't going to catch up with you at all."

"It's not my fault you're only staying for a week," Charlie said.

Bill put his hands up, as if to defend himself. "I know you're angry about that, Charlie, but there's a reason for it, believe me. That's why I've been wanting to talk to you."

"It better be good."

"I hope you'll think it's good."

Charlie waited.

Bill cleared his throat. "I didn't want to tell you this on the phone. But Terri and I have been wanting to have a child. We've been, well…trying, for some time—a few years actually—and it's finally…well, it's finally happened."

Charlie thought he must have misinterpreted his father's speech.

"That's right, we've had a baby—a little girl, I should say. You and Whiskey have a half sister," his father said, smiling uneasily.

Charlie found this news utterly ridiculous. He felt vaguely disgusted, embarrassed for his father, a man in his fifties behaving like some young newlywed. He wouldn't even entertain the thought that his father's new daughter was related to him. He could not think of any suitable response to his father's news.

"Jessica. Her name's Jessica. Three weeks old. That's why I can't stay, Charlie boy. Terri needs me."

"What about Whiskey?" Charlie asked. "What if he needs you?"

Bill swallowed. "That's why I'm here. But I need to think about Jessica now too."

"Well, I feel sorry for her," Charlie said. "I feel sorry for her and sorry for Whiskey and sorry for myself. Because you're a fucking pathetic excuse for a father. I don't even know why you bothered to come."

Charlie stood up. As far as he was concerned, the conversation was over. But his father had other ideas.

"Well, that's rich coming from you, Charlie," he said. "Jesus. Maybe I could have been a better dad. But you haven't exactly been the world's best brother, have you? This sounds to me like the pot calling the kettle black."

"You don't know what you're talking about," Charlie said. "You've got no idea what's been going on here. I've been with Whiskey night and day."

"So I've heard. And we all know what's behind that—your guilty conscience. Your mother told me you and Whiskey hadn't patched things up before the accident. I imagine you're feeling pretty bad about that. But don't take it out on me."

"Fuck you," Charlie said. "Fuck you, Bill."

QUEBEC

After Whiskey and Rosa had made their preposterous plans for Mike's visit, Charlie had not been able to avoid thinking about his half brother. But in the days following Whiskey's accident, in his anger over his father's arrival and departure, Charlie had forgotten about Mike completely.

He and Juliet were at Whiskey and Rosa's when the call came. It was the day Whiskey's coma arousal program commenced, the day of Charlie's first counseling session with Thomas. Juliet said their being at the hospital would do Rosa more harm than good, with Charlie in the state he was. So they had tried to make themselves useful by going over to Whiskey and Rosa's, tipping away cartons of milk that had turned sour, sorting the mail, paying bills with the American Express card Rosa had given them, and washing the clothes in Rosa's laundry basket, which already smelled of the hospital. They did these things to keep themselves busy and so that when Rosa came home from the hospital to knock herself out with a sleeping pill, there would be nothing else for her to think about.

The red light was flashing on the answering machine, and Juliet had been listening to the messages, because she knew Rosa wouldn't; writing down the names and numbers of the people who called, knowing someone would have to call them back eventually.

Though their voice mail still said *You've called Whiskey and Rosa*, all the messages were for Rosa. Mostly they were people who'd worked with Whiskey on one job or another, who'd heard the news through the advertising grapevine. Usually they didn't know Rosa, so they began by explaining who they were before going on to say how they'd heard the news, how sorry they were, what a horrible tragedy it was, etc. Charlie thought these people were brave to ring up and leave these awkward messages, but he found it tiring listening to them, and sometimes he thought about turning the machine off.

When the answering machine picked up Mike's call, and he began by saying, "Hi, Whiskey," both Charlie and Juliet looked up from what they were doing.

"I'm wondering where you and Rosa are... I'm wondering if you've changed your mind."

In hindsight, Charlie thought he should have realized as soon as he heard the Canadian accent, but Whiskey had worked on a lot of international jobs, and quite a few of the messages had been from overseas. Besides, at that stage, Mike was the furthest thing from Charlie's mind.

Charlie was certain that everyone must have heard about the accident by then. He could not imagine how anyone acquainted with Whiskey and Rosa could not know. If there was someone who did not know, he did not want to be the one to have to tell them. He looked at Juliet desperately.

She pressed the speaker button. "Hello?"

"Rosa?" the voice asked.

"This is Juliet."

"Juliet? Charlie's wife?"

"Not wife," she corrected. "Who's calling?"

"Juliet, it's Mike, from Canada."

"Mike!" Juliet looked at Charlie, appalled. "Where are you?"

"We're at the airport. Whiskey and Rosa were supposed to pick us up. We've been waiting over an hour, and they're not answering their cell phones. I thought perhaps—you'd all...you'd changed your minds about...meeting us."

Juliet took a breath. "No," she said. "It's not that, of course not. It's just that..." She looked at Charlie for help. "I'll come and pick you up," she said. "I'll explain then. I'll be there in forty minutes. Where are you waiting?"

Charlie had made no secret of the fact that he hadn't wanted Mike to come. If it had been up to him, he would have said thanks but no thanks, best wishes and good-bye. Unfortunately, Whiskey and Rosa had other ideas. They had argued that Mike had a right to know who his family was, that they wanted to meet him. After a great deal of debate, they had said they would be inviting him and his daughters to stay with them for a month over Christmas, with or without Charlie's blessing. Now they were here, and Whiskey and Rosa were not available to play host.

"They can't stay," Charlie said, as soon as Juliet hung up the phone.

But even as he said it, Charlie understood that they couldn't turn around and go straight back to Canada. They needed to sleep, for starters. Their flights would have to be changed. Until arrangements could be made, they would have to be accommodated.

"We could find them a hotel," he suggested.

"I don't think we should do that, Charlie," Juliet said quietly. "This poor guy's flown all the way from Canada to meet his two brothers, and he's about to find out one of them is in a coma. He'll be in a state of shock. And what about the little girls? The least we can do is offer them a place to stay."

Charlie put his face in his hands.

"I know it's hard, Charlie," Juliet said. "It's a terrible situation. But try to imagine how they're going to be feeling. I don't want to make things worse for them than they already are. We'll send them off as soon as we can. But for a few days, I think we should help them, if we can."

Charlie nodded.

Juliet squeezed his hand. "I know this isn't easy for you."

"We'll have to let Rosa know."

Juliet pulled a face. Rosa was barely eating or sleeping as it was. They were all concerned about her.

"I'll tell Rosa," Charlie said, standing up. "You take Whiskey's car to the airport. That'll give me some time to get my head around it."

Juliet held him tight for a moment. "Good luck."

× × ×

To Charlie's surprise, Rosa suggested that Mike and the girls should stay the month, as planned. Charlie had expected her to be upset by the situation, to say she couldn't cope, that she didn't want to know about it.

"He has come all this way," was what she said. "We might as well to make the best of it."

"But what on earth is he going to do?"

"He can show the girls around, come in to see Whiskey. I don't know. Maybe it can help Whiskey."

The notion that a visit from his long-lost half brother might bring Whiskey out of his coma was laughable to Charlie, like something out of a B-grade soap opera, but he did not say this to Rosa. He tried to stick to practicalities.

"They can't stay with us indefinitely, Rosa. Even if we wanted them to, we don't have the space."

"They can stay at our place," Rosa said. "That was what we had planned anyway. The house is empty. Let them use it."

"But we don't even know them," Charlie said. "Okay, technically speaking, Mike is a relative, but in reality, we don't know the first thing about him. I don't think it's a good idea to have him staying at the house when you and Whiskey aren't there."

"Oh, Charlie, please. I am too tired to argue with you. Don't make it difficult. Mike can have the spare room, and the girls can have the room next door. Whiskey and I already bought them a bunk bed. It only needs to be—what is the word?—constructed."

"I'm sure it wasn't necessary to buy new furniture, Rosa. They're only here for a month. Why don't I get them an air mattress or something? You can return the bunk beds."

Rosa shook her head. "They are our family, Charlie. They have come all this way to see us. I will not let them sleep on the ground like cavemen. It would make me unhappy."

Charlie knew from experience that there was no point arguing with Rosa when her mind was made up. Besides, if she wanted to cling to the hope that having Mike around might help Whiskey, he didn't want to take that from her. He was clinging to some pretty tenuous hopes himself.

× × ×

The first few days were difficult. Charlie tried to avoid being alone with Mike for any extended period. He knew there must be endless questions Mike wanted to ask, but he felt incapable of providing satisfactory answers. Any conversation beyond the banal that the two of them might get into felt too awkward for Charlie.

Mike obviously sensed Charlie's reticence because he did not push him or attempt to get him alone. When they did talk, he stayed on the surface of things—the weather, his first impressions of Australia, his work, Charlie's work. He did not talk about their relationship or about Whiskey's condition. Those conversations he had with Juliet, perhaps because it was Juliet who had been the one to tell him about Whiskey.

When she picked them up from the airport, she had put the roof down on Whiskey's car, and as soon as they were on the Tullamarine Freeway, the wind catching their voices before the girls could, Juliet had told Mike about the accident. She said to Charlie that she told it straight and fast because she had found it to be the best way. Mike had said nothing, but when Juliet took her eyes off the road to look at him, she saw he was crying.

He was Charlie's half brother, a complete stranger to Juliet.

"What did you do?" Charlie asked her.

"I reached over and held his hand."

× × ×

The day after Mike arrived, he had gone to meet their mother, and according to what he told Juliet, the first meeting had gone "as well as could be expected." A few days later, their mother had rung and asked him to come again and bring the girls.

Charlie couldn't believe how easily his mother had adjusted to Mike's presence in their lives.

"It was a shock when the letter first came," she told Charlie. "I won't deny that. But after I had some time to get used to it, I realized I wanted to see him. When you give away a child, everybody tells you it's best to think of that child as being dead. But you can never think of it as dead. Well, I never could, anyway. I thought about the baby I had given away every day; every day for thirty-odd years I wondered about him, where he'd ended up, what kind of person he'd become. It feels like a gift that he's come back into our lives," she said, "especially now."

Charlie couldn't see it as a gift. He saw it as an added complication in a situation that was already complicated enough.

× × ×

Once Whiskey and Rosa's house had been organized and Mike and the girls went to stay there, Charlie felt better. There was less pressure then to get to know Mike, to talk about feelings, to see if they liked each other, to work out if they would ever think of each other as brothers. As soon as Mike was gone, Charlie liked him more. He had held himself together in the midst of what could only be described as an atrocious mess. On top of that, he had protected Holly and Chloe from the fallout, concocting a G-rated account of why Whiskey and Rosa couldn't see them right away, jollying them up until they were quite convinced their holiday was going to be as much fun as ever, despite the change of plans. In their few days at Charlie and Juliet's, Mike had done everything he could to make the girls feel at home. He had read to them every night from *The Secret Garden*, a book they had begun before they left Canada, and on Sunday morning Mike had made pancakes for everyone—because, according to Holly, they *always* had pancakes on Sundays—complete with a bottle of real Canadian maple syrup, which they had brought to give to Whiskey and Rosa.

Mike had rented a car, but he returned it within a few days, after which, at Rosa's insistence, he drove Whiskey's car instead.

"Juliet told me I was not allowed to drive it, that I must to take taxis to the hospital, so now it is seeking cobwebs in the garage."

Gathering cobwebs, Charlie silently corrected.

"You must drive it, Michael. The girls will like it. When I was a child, I always dreamed to ride in a convertible motorcar. Whiskey would want you to use it."

This last comment clinched the argument. No one wanted to deny Rosa the pleasure of doing something that might please Whiskey. It would have been like denying a final cigarette to a man condemned to death.

After a week or so, a pattern had emerged. Every second day, Mike and the girls did their own thing. Mike took them to see their new grandmother, or they went sightseeing—to the zoo and the science museum, for a cruise on the Yarra, up to the top of the Rialto Towers. On the other days, Mike dropped the girls at Charlie and Juliet's after lunch, and then he went to the hospital to sit with Whiskey so Rosa could go home and sleep for a few hours. Juliet would spend the afternoon with the girls, and they would have dinner together before Mike picked them up and took them back to Whiskey and Rosa's.

This arrangement suited Charlie. Firstly, it relieved him of the pressure to visit Whiskey himself. Since his argument with his father, he'd been avoiding the hospital, embarrassed that his motivations for being there were so transparent. He hoped Mike's presence might make his own absence less noticeable.

Secondly, though Charlie felt uncomfortable with Mike, he enjoyed having the twins around. Too young to really understand the situation, they had a lightness everyone else had lost since Whiskey's accident. When he heard them laughing, Charlie realized no one laughed around him anymore, as if, as the grieving brother, he had entered a realm in which nothing was ever allowed to be funny again, like wearing a T-shirt with the slogan *Don't joke with me—my brother's in a coma*. Holly and Chloe were the only ones who didn't know how to behave. They told him jokes. They asked him to tell them jokes. He only remembered one joke, so he told it again and again.

"What's the difference between a hyena and a flea?" he would ask them.

And even though they knew the answer, they knew it was more fun when Charlie told it. So they would wait without speaking for him to say the punch line: *One howls on the prairie, and the other prowls on the hairy.* And then they would laugh raucously, even though Charlie was certain it couldn't be funny to them.

They sang songs. They were obsessed with Manfred Mann's 1964 classic "Doo Wah Diddy Diddy," which they had on a CD they had brought with them from Canada. They sang it at least ten times a day, arguing every time over the parts—which one of them would sing the proper lyrics and which the gibberish refrain. It reminded Charlie of when he and Whiskey were young and their father bought them the record *Peter Gunn*. Every day they had played it over and over again until their mother called up the stairs that if she had to listen to it one more time, she would break it in half. Then they had taken to humming it instead, squabbling about who would provide the bass line and who the dramatic horn solo.

Charlie was fascinated by the dynamic between the twins. Holly had been born first, Mike had told him, and in their relationships with others, particularly adults, Holly was the spokesperson. But when it was just the two of them playing together, it was often Chloe who made the decisions, defined the parameters of their games, took the best roles. Charlie tried to remember being six years old. Once upon a time, were there ways in which he had taken the lead, made the rules? Had he and Whiskey ever been like Holly and Chloe, each dominant in different ways? Was it just his imagination that Whiskey had always had the upper hand, a convenient fiction he had created which corroborated his other ideas of his brother, himself?

× × ×

Juliet liked having the girls around too. She had discovered that they liked old musicals and they had been making popcorn and having matinees, working their way through the films she had grown up with—*Mary Poppins* and *The Sound of Music*, *Chitty Chitty Bang Bang* and *The Wizard of Oz*. Sometimes Genevieve dropped Oscar off, and they played school or took Chester to the park.

In Quebec, they said, their next-door neighbor had a beagle called Boomer, whom they sometimes played with. They began almost every sentence with the phrase "in Quebec."

In Quebec, we would be at school now; in Quebec, we have underground shopping malls; in Quebec, it's probably snowing.

Charlie teased them that he was learning so much about Quebec that if he ever visited, there would be no surprises left for him at all.

Once Charlie was on school holidays he volunteered to look after the girls some afternoons to give Mike a break. It was one of those afternoons, when Charlie and the girls were watching *Bedknobs and Broomsticks*, when Rosa rang in a state, asking Charlie to go straight to the hospital.

"I think I have catched something," she said anxiously. "I must go straight home."

"I've got the girls," Charlie said. "What about Mum?"

"I have called to her already. She is not at home."

"Have you tried Audrey?"

"She is in Bendigo until tomorrow."

Charlie thought for a minute. Juliet was at the library, working on her screenplay; she wouldn't be back for a couple of hours, and her phone would be switched off. Mike had had some errands to run that afternoon, and Charlie had no way of contacting him.

"I might be making Whiskey sick, Charlie," Rosa said. "I must go directly."

Charlie did not need Rosa to explain to him that Whiskey could not be left alone, that what she feared more than anything was some change in his condition when no one was there, some opportunity to get through to him being lost.

"Hang in there, Rosa," Charlie said. "I'll be there as soon as I can."

He left a quick message on Juliet's voice mail, grabbed some coloring books and pencils, and bundled the girls into the car. *They can sit on the chairs in the corridor*, he thought to himself. *I'll be able to keep an eye on them through the window. Juliet can come and pick them up as soon as she leaves the library. There'll be no need for them to come into the room at all.*

But when they got to the hospital, the girls had other ideas.

"Are we going to meet Uncle Whiskey?" Holly asked excitedly.

"You can't meet him," Charlie said. "He's sleeping."

"Daddy said he was in a coma."

Charlie grimaced. "That's kind of like sleeping. You'll have to wait out here."

"Can't we have a look at him?" Holly persisted.

He's not a fucking museum exhibit, Charlie wanted to say. "He's very sick," he said instead.

"We'll be quiet," Holly said. "We'll be so quiet, we promise. Don't we, Chloe?"

Charlie pressed his face into his hands. How did things get so out of control? What sort of person took two six-year-old girls to see a man in a coma? But he didn't want to stand out in the corridor, arguing about it. Rosa was waiting.

"All right then. You can come in and see him. But don't touch anything. And don't say a word until Rosa's gone."

They all went and washed their hands together in the little basin in the handicap bathroom, and then Charlie took them back to the room.

"Thank god, Charlie," Rosa said through her paper mask. "I thought you never would come." She patted the girls' heads absently. "Don't kiss me. I have got a sore throat, a headache. The aspirin they give me did not help. I don't want Whiskey to catch this from me."

Charlie hugged her. "You go home then. Get into bed. Call Juliet if you need anything—leave a message on her phone, and she can pop in on the way home from the library."

"Sit down then," Charlie said to the girls when she had gone, motioning to two chairs pushed against the wall. He sat down in the chair everyone thought of as Rosa's chair, next to the bed.

"Can we sit next to you, Uncle Charlie?" Holly whispered.

Charlie looked at his brother. *What difference does it make?* he thought. He helped them pull their chairs closer to the bed, and they all sat in silence for a while, taking it in.

"Why does he have those tubes in his nose?" Holly asked eventually, in a dramatic stage whisper. "And in his hand too?"

Charlie took a breath. It was natural for them to have questions. He had asked the exact same questions himself the first time he had gone to the hospital. Usually, they explained all the machines to visitors before they went into the room, looking through the window—it was a trick one of the nurses had told them to lessen the shock. But there hadn't been time to do that for Chloe and Holly. He explained all the tubes and machines as simply as he could, omitting the more gruesome details wherever possible, trying to make it sound less frightening than it was.

"When is he going to wake up?" Chloe asked then.

"We don't know."

The girls looked at him expectantly, as though there must be more to be said.

"We don't know," he said again, "but we hope it will be soon."

"Maybe he'll wake up today," Holly said thoughtfully.

Chloe gasped at this, as though Whiskey were some zombie threatening to rise from the grave. That must be how Whiskey appeared to them, Charlie thought, like some creature from a horror movie.

"Don't worry," Charlie said. "It probably won't be today." But he could see them watching Whiskey as though he might take them by surprise at any moment.

"Uncle Charlie?" Holly whispered after a time.

Charlie still wasn't used to them calling him uncle. He didn't think of them as his nieces. They were his half nieces, he supposed, if such a term existed.

"What?" he asked wearily. They had been there for only ten minutes, and he already felt drained.

"Daddy told us you were identical twins, like me and Chloe."

"That's right."

"But he doesn't look like you."

Charlie looked at Whiskey, tried to see him as Holly might see him, as if he were seeing him for the first time.

"Well, the older you get, the less alike you become," Charlie said, thinking. "But we did look pretty much the same, I suppose, apart from different haircuts and things. Whiskey looks very different now because of the accident."

Holly and Chloe were listening intently, waiting for more.

"He's very pale because he hasn't been outside for a few weeks— and he can't eat normal food, so he's gotten a bit skinny…and they had to shave his head to have a look at the cuts and things…and his face got bruised, you know, when the car…"

"So when he wakes up, will you look the same again? Will you still be identical twins?"

"We'll always be identical twins," Charlie started. And then he stopped. He waited until the feeling that he was going to cry had passed.

"I don't know," he said eventually. He could not believe he had not considered this eventuality, that even if Whiskey recovered, the damage might profoundly change his physical appearance, so that though, genetically speaking, Charlie and Whiskey would still be identical, on the outside they would no longer be exactly the same, or even similar, that a stranger might not even pick them as brothers.

The girls were quiet for a while, and then Holly spoke again. "Why aren't you talking to him?" Holly asked cautiously.

"What do you mean?"

"You're supposed to talk to people in a coma, and it helps them wake up. In Quebec, we saw a film where they did that. Didn't we, Chloe?"

Chloe nodded. "The boy's dad came back to life," she added.

Charlie knew about this theory of course. But he hadn't tried it himself. He hadn't talked directly to Whiskey once since the accident. There was too much to say, and it seemed too late. He would have liked to believe Whiskey could hear him, but he didn't. He couldn't say that to Holly and Chloe.

"Well, Whiskey already knows all about me," he said. "I'm sure he doesn't want to listen to me talking. But you can talk to him if you want to. I bet he'd like to hear all about you."

"But what would we say?"

Charlie thought for a moment. "Introduce yourselves. Tell him what you're doing here."

Chloe looked excited and terrified at the same time, but Holly was already standing up out of her chair, moving closer to the bed.

"Hello, Uncle Whiskey," she said solemnly. "I'm Holly, and this is my sister Chloe."

"Tell him we're twins too," Chloe whispered.

Holly shushed her. "We live in Quebec. I don't know if you know geography, but that's in Canada. Our daddy is your brother," she said, as if still trying to understand this herself. "Our grandma died, and Daddy wanted to spend her money on a holiday to meet you. We don't have any more grandmas or aunties or cousins or anything now." She stood for a moment more without speaking and then sat back in her chair.

"Very nice," Charlie said, unsure of whether this little episode was perfectly acceptable or entirely inappropriate. There were no books written on how to behave when one member of your family was in a coma and your long-lost brother came to visit with his children. Briefly, Charlie imagined such a book. *Death and Adoption: When Worlds Collide.* Anything that made the situation more tolerable for anyone involved must be okay, he decided.

"Do you want to say something, Chloe?" Charlie asked.

Chloe shook her head and didn't move, but after a moment she began to speak, very softly, as though she was saying a prayer.

"Dear Uncle Whiskey," she began, in the manner of the Lord's Prayer. "Thank you for letting us stay at your house. Auntie Rosa bought us a bunk bed. We like Auntie Rosa and Auntie Juliet too, and we love Chester. When we get back to Quebec, Daddy says we might get a dog, and it might even be a Dalmatian. Maybe when you're feeling better, you can come over to Quebec and see our dog."

Charlie closed his eyes. "Amen," he said under his breath. He wished he could say such a prayer.

New Year's Eve. Whiskey has been in a coma for five weeks. Charlie has never felt less like celebrating, dreads the thought of being at a party or in a bar surrounded by people getting drunk. But Rosa says Charlie and Juliet should go out, that Whiskey has always liked New Year's Eve, that they should have a drink for him. So Charlie and Juliet catch the tram down to Carlisle Street to have dinner at their favorite wine bar. They order a drink on Whiskey's behalf, an overpriced French champagne that Charlie says should satisfy Whiskey's expensive taste. But when they raise their glasses to make a toast, Charlie can't find the right words to say. What he thinks he wants, most of the time, is for Whiskey to be returned to them, exactly as he was before the accident. But it feels ridiculous to say this out loud, when he has spent so many years wishing for Whiskey to be a completely different person. Charlie struggles for a phrase that won't come out sounding trite or fraudulent, can't summon a single thing.

Juliet reaches across the table for his hand. "To Whiskey," she says simply, touching her glass to his.

Over dinner, Charlie tells Juliet about the only New Year's Eve he'd spent with Whiskey, other than the millennium party where he and Juliet met. It was not long after Whiskey started in his first copywriting position and had just moved out of their home. He was living with roommates in Fitzroy and had organized a cocktail party for New Year's Eve, hoping to impress his new advertising friends, Charlie supposed. Unfortunately, one of Whiskey's guests had baked a batch of hash cookies that turned out to be slightly more potent than anticipated. At midnight, when they should have been clinking martini glasses and kissing each other, at least half the guests were in the bathrooms or the courtyard or out on the grass verge in front of the house, puking their guts up. Within an hour, anyone who hadn't vomited or passed out had staggered home, and the party was most definitely over. Charlie had woken up on Whiskey's bed, still stoned and already hungover, with dried vomit on his shirt. Whiskey, the young sophisticate, was lying beside him, his face scratched and smeared with dried blood from where he had fallen down the front steps and landed headfirst in a rosebush.

× × ×

Charlie has never felt guilty about Juliet leaving Whiskey for him. He has always justified it by saying that Juliet would have broken up with Whiskey anyway, whether she had met Charlie or not. Juliet had admitted as much herself. Over time, Charlie has come to think of Whiskey's losing Juliet to him as a kind of payback for Charlie's losing Anneliese Spellman when they were still at school; a rebalancing of the scales that had tipped out of Charlie's favor in the weeks leading up to the eleventh-grade ball and remained out of kilter for years afterward.

Since Whiskey's accident though, Charlie has begun to feel guilty about a whole host of things that never bothered him before, Juliet being one of them. Whether or not Juliet would have eventually broken up with Whiskey anyway, whether or not it was Juliet who had asked for *his* number, Juliet who had phoned and asked him to go out—if he had been a better person, a better brother, wouldn't he have said no to her? Charlie has always been adamant that the way Whiskey behaved after finding out about Charlie and Juliet's relationship was absolutely inexcusable. Now he wonders if his anger had perhaps been warranted.

And was it really Whiskey who had unbalanced the scales with Anneliese? After all, she too had been Whiskey's girl first. And in the long run, they had both lost her. Maybe it was Charlie who had unbalanced the scales from the start.

x x x

Charlie and Juliet are in bed long before the old year gives way to the new. When Rosa's call wakes them, Charlie has forgotten all about New Year's Eve.

"Happy New Year!" Rosa says breathlessly. "Whiskey has opened his eyes!"

Charlie looks at the alarm clock. It is only just after midnight. He wonders if he is dreaming. "Are you sure?" he asks.

"Of course I am sure! I am looking at him right now, and they are open. Come down and see for yourself."

Charlie is wide-awake then, pulling his jeans on one-handed while he holds the phone with the other. "When did this happen?" he asks.

"About ten minutes ago," Rosa says excitedly. "I fell to sleep a little, and then when I heard the fireworks, I woke up, and Whiskey was looking at me."

x x x

Charlie is almost afraid to let himself believe what Rosa has told him, what it might mean. But when Charlie and Juliet arrive at the hospital, Whiskey's eyes are still open. Charlie hugs Rosa, picks her up off the floor. He hugs Juliet, laughing, and then sits down abruptly, overwhelmed with relief. When their mother arrives with Audrey, there is more hugging and kissing. Usually, if there are more than two of them at the hospital at once, at least one person will wait in the corridor. But tonight no one wants to wait outside. No one wants to run the risk of missing something. They bring in extra chairs and arrange them on either side of Whiskey's bed. They watch him expectantly, waiting for him to blink, or perhaps turn his head, to squeeze Rosa's hand, wondering what the next sign of arousal might be.

At around three o'clock, Charlie gets up to go to the bathroom. As he passes the nurses' station, he gives the nurse on duty, Magdalena, the thumbs-up signal. She frowns a little, makes a gesture that Charlie can't interpret, somewhere between nodding her head and shaking it.

"You know Whiskey's opened his eyes, don't you?"

Magdalena nods. "Rosa called me in when it happened," she says, looking at Charlie with concern.

"What's wrong?" Charlie asks.

"Nothing's wrong." She hesitates. "It's just that after a period of prolonged unresponsiveness, it's not uncommon for a patient to open their eyes, but it might not be accompanied by any other changes to their condition."

"But surely someone opening their eyes is a sign that they're waking up. Isn't it?"

Magdalena shakes her head. "Not always. I'm sorry, Charlie. I know it's difficult. But it's better if you don't get your hopes up too much at this stage."

"Does Rosa know this?"

"I told her, as soon as it happened. Your mother too when she arrived."

"They didn't say anything."

"It's hard for people to take in," Magdalena says kindly.

Charlie looks at Magdalena, at her plain and honest face. There is no possible reason for her to lie to him. In the last few weeks, Charlie has learned she is one of the best people to go to when he wants the simple facts; he has appreciated her frankness and honesty. But now he doesn't believe her. He can't, because he needs, more than anything, to believe Whiskey is waking up.

ROMEO

It was Whiskey, of course, who had first suggested Marco might be gay. They were in twelfth grade then, and Marco, who was the first friend Charlie made in Australia, had become one of his closest friends.

"You know Marco's a faggot, don't you?" Whiskey had said, coming into Charlie's room one night after Marco had left.

"What?"

"You know, a shirt lifter, a pillow biter."

"For Christ's sake, Whiskey, I know what *faggot* means."

"Calm down, Charlie. I'm just telling you what I've heard."

"Heard from who?"

"No one in particular. It's a known thing."

"Based on what evidence?"

"Jesus, we're not in court, are we? Do you want me to show you a gay porn mag I stole from his schoolbag or something? There's no evidence. It's a vibe you get. I can tell."

"Well, you seem to know a lot about it, Whiskey. Maybe you're the one who's gay."

Whiskey smirked. "How come I've had sex with so many girls then?"

"Says you."

"Ask them yourself if you don't believe me."

"Why would I bother?" Charlie said, irritated that the conversation had swung around so easily to Whiskey's sexual exploits. "I couldn't care less who you've had sex with. Now could you get lost? I have to hand this essay in tomorrow."

Whiskey didn't move. "You've got to admit though," he said, "Marco's a real faggot's name."

"You're such a moron, Whiskey. Marco's an Italian name. Because guess what? His parents are Italian."

"Why can't he just call himself Mark?"

"Why can't you call yourself William? Now could you please piss off?"

"Easy boy," Whiskey said. "Don't shoot the messenger. I'm telling you for your own good. What kind of a brother would I be if I didn't tell you? You'd carry on hanging out with him, and pretty soon everyone would start saying you were a faggot too. You should be thanking me for this information."

"I see. I get it now. Thank you, Whiskey. Thank you so much for telling me this. What a terrible mistake I might have made if you hadn't let me know. What would I do without you? How can I ever express my undying gratitude?"

Whiskey got up. "Have it your way, little brother. It's your funeral."

"Shut the door behind you," Charlie said, turning back to his essay.

"As you wish, sir." Whiskey bowed extravagantly and closed the door.

× × ×

It had taken him a while, but Charlie had eventually had to admit Whiskey was probably right about Marco. It wasn't just that Marco had never had a girlfriend—after all, Charlie hadn't exactly had a lot of luck in that department himself at that time. It was more that Marco hadn't shown any interest in girls whatsoever. When you were sixteen and seventeen, girls were what you talked about, even—or perhaps, especially—the ones you didn't have a chance in hell with. You said this one was cute or that one had great legs, or if you wanted to be cruder, you said this one had a nice ass or that one would go off like a firecracker in the sack. But Marco never said those kinds of things. Once he had become alert to it, Charlie had realized Marco never talked about girls at all. He wouldn't bring it up, and when the conversation swung that way—as it inevitably always did—he went quiet. He neither agreed nor disagreed with his friends' assessments of the girls they knew or wished they knew. If asked directly, he would be noncommittal. "She's okay," he might say or, "She's not my type." Charlie had wondered if Marco's other friends suspected him of being gay. He had tried to think of a way he might bring it up sometime. But he had known he never would. It would have made him too uncomfortable to talk about it.

Once he had allowed himself to believe Marco might be gay, Charlie's first reaction had been of anger. He had been angry with Marco for being different, angry with himself for choosing as a best friend the one guy in their grade who didn't like girls, angry to think he might be tarred with the same brush. He had, of course, also been angry with Whiskey for pointing it out to him and angrier still that he hadn't worked it out for himself. Then he had become afraid. He had been afraid that he himself was gay and he didn't know it yet, afraid that spending too much time with Marco had turned him, afraid that Marco might be interested in him. Years later, he had admitted this to Marco.

"Don't flatter yourself, mate," Marco had said. "You're not my type."

"Why?" Charlie asked indignantly. "What's wrong with me?"

Marco looked at him critically. "You're not exactly what I'd call buff."

"What do you call that then?" Charlie flexed his biceps.

Marco snorted. "It's a good thing you're not gay. You'd never get lucky."

"That's bullshit, and you know it," Charlie said. By then he'd occasionally been to gay clubs with Marco and had attracted a great deal more attention than he ever had from women.

"Want to chow down on my big fat one?" a perfect stranger had said once, standing next to him at the bar. Charlie had choked on his drink.

× × ×

Once they had left school, Marco's sexuality didn't seem to matter anywhere near as much. There was no longer any doubt about it in Charlie's mind, but by then he'd had time to get used to the idea, had gotten over his own issues about it, which in hindsight, he could see had been pretty pathetic to begin with. Over the next few years, there were times—admittedly, usually when Charlie was drunk—when he thought about asking Marco about it, forcing him to confess. But after a while it hadn't seemed important.

As Charlie found out later, Marco was waiting for his dad to die before he came out. He was twenty-two when his dad was diagnosed with cancer. That Christmas, his youngest sister, Rosemary, had taken him aside after lunch.

"I don't know if you're planning on telling anyone or not," she had said, "but if Dad finds out you're gay, it will finish him off."

Marco's other siblings were practically a different generation; they'd all been married for years, living in the suburbs with their kids. It wouldn't have even crossed their minds that Marco wouldn't go down the exact same path they had. But Rosemary was only a few years older than Marco, had friends with younger brothers and sisters who'd gone to school with Marco and Charlie. That must have been how she found out.

At first, Marco told Charlie, he had resented Rosemary for what she said, but a part of him had known she was right. Marco was the youngest of seven children; when he was born, his father was already forty. He was from a different culture, a different era, and the idea of men being with other men was beyond his comprehension. Marco didn't want to be estranged from his father when he died. So he kept his mouth shut. He didn't tell his mother, his brothers, his other sisters, his friends. Three years it took his dad to die, and in all that time, Marco never told a soul.

After his father died, he became what he himself described as a *raving poofter*, picking up men three or four nights a week. Once he had gotten that out of his system, he became like all the other people Charlie knew. He had flings; he had one-night stands; he had boyfriends from time to time. Then he met Guy. Guy was a historian who had spent six years writing and researching an epic five-hundred-thousand-word text on the Second Fleet.

"The *Second* Fleet?" Charlie had asked when he first met him.

Guy had laughed. "That's what everyone says. 'Who could care less about the Second Fleet?'"

Guy was in his early forties, quietly spoken with a surprisingly hearty laugh. He was well read, well traveled, well adjusted. He had a penchant for shaker furniture and cello concertos. He adored Marco. After they had been together for six months, Marco moved in with Guy and his spoiled cat Marmaduke.

Marco had always been particularly sarcastic toward people who were overly gushing about their significant others, but after he met Guy, Charlie began to hear him use phrases like *everything I've been looking for* and eventually *the love of my life*. And Guy, it appeared, felt the same. There was only one thing that marred their happiness, Marco told Charlie over one of their lunches at the Windsor: they couldn't get married.

"It's so unfair," Marco had said. "Guy and I love each other. We want to spend our lives together. We're not hurting anyone else. How can that be wrong? It's no different from any man and woman who want to get married. Imagine if you weren't allowed to marry Juliet. Imagine if it was all you wanted, and you couldn't do it."

Charlie had found such a situation impossible to imagine. He found himself in the opposite position, in which everyone wanted him and Juliet to get married, except Charlie himself.

× × ×

Three or four times a year, Juliet received a magazine called *Fideliter* in the mail, a glossy, full-color publication detailing the latest developments and achievements at her old school. "*Fideliter* was the school motto—the Latin word for *faithfully*," Juliet explained. The school depicted in *Fideliter* bore no relation to Charlie's own experience of school. According to a letter from the principal in one edition, Fintona Girls' School was a school where students were "nurtured and encouraged to explore their talents." If they didn't know what their talents were, they had every opportunity to find out. For the artistically inclined, there was music, drama, and dance. For those who excelled at languages, there were trips to France, Germany, and Japan. There were debating and mock trials, the Duke of Edinburgh Awards Scheme, excursions in a bus with the school logo on the side. As well as hockey, athletics, netball, and basketball, the girls could play soccer and Aussie Rules Football.

"I wish they'd show photos of them in footy shorts," Charlie had said to Juliet when he read that.

In eleventh and twelfth grades, you could also do archery or kickboxing, sailing, ice skating, or tenpin bowling. Every time Charlie read the magazine, they seemed to be celebrating the opening of a state-of-the-art facility—a theater, a technology center, a science wing.

Charlie could not have imagined a school where every one of the students was dressed identically, but the photos were there to prove it. From ages five to eighteen, all the girls wore the same blazers and straw boaters, the same tunics and cardigans, the same shirts and ties and socks and shoes. Juliet had told Charlie there were even regulation underpants available at the uniform shop, although after sixth grade, no one bought those.

Charlie was fascinated by *Fideliter*. Often he read it from cover to cover, which was more than Juliet did. What he liked most about it was the opportunity to imagine Juliet as she had been when she was still at school. He could picture her, in the pages of *Fideliter*, with ankle socks and a high ponytail. He could imagine her in the school play, overly dramatic and wearing too much makeup. He could see her cheering for her friends in the athletics carnival. He felt sentimental about Juliet in a way he never had about his other girlfriends. He wished he had known her as a teenager.

The last two pages of *Fideliter* were devoted to *Old Girls' News*, and these were the pages Juliet paid the most attention to. Some of the news was spectacular. There were ex-students doing postgraduate courses at Oxford, Harvard, and the Sorbonne, a girl who had become a lawyer for the United Nations. But most of the news was ordinary—this girl had gotten married, that one had had a baby, the class of 1983 had enjoyed their twenty-year reunion.

"I can't believe Fiona Warren got married," Juliet would say. "Everyone thought she was a lesbian."

One day, long before Whiskey's accident, when life was still simple, Charlie had come home from indoor soccer to find Juliet crying over her latest issue of *Fideliter*.

"What's wrong?" he asked, thinking she must have read some bad news about an old friend. But Juliet wasn't even looking at the *Old Girls' News*. The heading on the page she had open said *Tenth Grade Drama Camp*.

"They're so young," Juliet said, pointing at the photos.

Charlie looked closer, read the caption: "A dramatic moment in *A Streetcar Named Desire*." He felt confused. "Too young to understand *Streetcar*, do you think?"

Juliet sniffed. "I remember tenth grade drama camp," she said. "We had such a good time. It seems so long ago. I wish I could go back to school."

"What do you mean, Jules? What's really the matter?"

Juliet had turned to the back page and jabbed her finger at a photo of a bridal party. "Everyone's getting married," she said miserably. "I must be the only one left."

× × ×

Charlie did not know how to explain his feelings about marriage to Juliet. He could hardly understand them himself. When Whiskey told Charlie Juliet was the most beautiful girl he'd ever meet, he had been right. She still looked as beautiful to Charlie as she had the night he met her. Charlie thought he would never grow tired of looking at her. When she closed her eyes on the pillow at night, her face wore an expression of great concentration, as though falling asleep was something you had to focus on to achieve, like winning a race or passing an exam. But once she was asleep, she looked perfectly calm. She did not drool or snore or gurgle or twitch. She barely moved. Charlie loved to watch her sleep.

She was graceful. She had good posture, flawless skin. She looked as good to Charlie in jeans and an old T-shirt as she did in a cocktail dress. In public, men always looked twice. She was gracious when she rejected the men who offered to buy her drinks or asked for her phone number. She was thoughtful. She remembered birthdays, including Charlie's mother's, which he did not remember himself. She had passions for things, obsessions: a particular brand of roll-erball pens with purple ink, which she bought in boxes of twelve; an oval eraser, like a rubber pebble, which she never used, because she didn't want to spoil its perfect shape.

She had discovered a website called Future Me, which allowed you to compose emails to be sent to yourself in the future. She wrote emails that would be returned to her in a month, a year, five years. When she received them, she printed them out and stuck them up on her pin-up board.

Dear Future Me, one of them said. *It's two years today since you met Charlie. I hope you're not taking him for granted. Don't ever forget how lucky you are to have met someone like him. If you're ever in doubt, think about how desperate you felt with Ryan, always worrying about what he was going to do next; remember how you cried every day during that last year with Nathan. Charlie's everything you wished for. Be good to him.*

Certainly, there were things about Juliet that Charlie was not mad about. She had, for example, more than forty pairs of shoes, which she insisted on storing in their original boxes and which consequently took up more than one third of their wardrobe. Though she had great enthusiasm for planting new herbs and flowers, it was Charlie who ended up watering them. She had unbearable PMS, for which she claimed the only cure was for Charlie to drive her across town to her favorite Thai restaurant in North Brunswick, a place with plastic chairs and tables, cutlery with a Lufthansa logo on the handles, which must have been bought in a fire sale; a place with bad service and no ambience whatsoever, but which happened to serve what Juliet described as the world's greatest chicken satay. She hated the news and would turn off the radio whenever it came on. Some of these things annoyed Charlie. Sometimes they even argued about them, as all couples do. But none of them were reasons not to marry her.

So what were the reasons? It wasn't that Charlie could think of someone else he would rather spend the rest of his life with. But that was exactly the problem. He didn't think he would spend the rest of his life with Juliet either. He still lived in fear that Juliet was going to leave him, and so he couldn't marry her. Because if break-ups were bad, divorces were ten times worse.

And yet, Charlie had sensed Juliet was getting impatient. He had begun to feel that if he didn't propose to Juliet soon, she would grow tired of waiting and end their relationship. And there was the conundrum. She would leave him if he didn't marry her, and she would probably leave him anyway, even if he did. It had gone round and round in Charlie's head, and though he knew Juliet was waiting, he could not bring himself to ask her.

× × ×

A few months before Whiskey's accident, Charlie had arrived home from work one day, and Juliet had taken him outside to show him the hanging baskets in which the geraniums she had planted had started to bloom.

"I've been thinking," she said, and Charlie thought she was going to say something about the garden: the agave might need repotting, what do you think about moving the camellia into that corner, is it still too early to plant some basil?

"How do you feel about getting married?" is what she actually said.

× × ×

Afterward, Charlie had found another one of her emails, composed two years before. *Dear Future Me*, this one said. *Are you married yet? Engaged, at least? If Charlie hasn't asked you by now, he probably never will, so why don't you go and ask him yourself? Now's as good a time as any—don't worry about the roses and violins, you know Charlie wouldn't be into that anyway. PS Don't be upset if he says no—he's probably just scared.* Charlie felt wretched when he read the email. It hurt him to think she'd already wanted to get married, two years ago, when she wrote the email, that she'd waited all this time, knowing he probably wouldn't ask her, and then she'd asked him herself, knowing he would probably say no.

× × ×

It had been Marco's boyfriend, Guy, who started the Romeo and Juliet jokes.

"'Shall I compare thee to a summer's day?'" he had quoted, bowing low when he and Juliet were first introduced.

Juliet had curtsied, thrilled, and offered her hand to be kissed. "And this must be your Romeo," Guy said, shaking hands with Charlie.

"He's no Romeo," Marco said.

"Why not?" Charlie asked, indignant. "I could be a Romeo."

"You're not exactly renowned for your romantic gestures, mate."

"I'm romantic, aren't I, Jules?" Charlie said uncertainly, looking at her for confirmation.

"Has he ever climbed up to your balcony to declare his undying love?" Guy asked her.

"I don't have a balcony."

"What about drinking poison?" Marco asked.

"It's Juliet who drinks the poison," Guy said. "Romeo stabs himself."

"Would you stab yourself for Juliet?" Marco demanded.

"Would you stab yourself for Guy?" Charlie retorted.

"He asked you first," Juliet said.

Charlie pretended to consider the question. "Maybe if the sword was extremely sharp and I knew it would be over in a flash."

Charlie's romantic ineptitude had become something of a running joke for the four of them. Juliet had always laughed along. Now Charlie wondered if she had ever really thought it funny, if all this time she had been secretly hoping for Charlie to surprise her, to prove Marco wrong. He knew she wasn't asking for much. He wasn't required to risk his life, renounce his family. He felt sick when he thought about what he'd said to her in the garden. *I need to think about it.*

SIERRA

Five years on, Charlie still regretted dropping out of his Diploma of Education because of a personality conflict with one of his tutors. When she failed his major essay, he could have applied for a reexamination; instead, he went to her office and called her names, resulting in a disciplinary letter from the dean of the school. He was too ashamed to appeal the mark and too proud to resubmit the essay, so instead of becoming a qualified teacher, he had had to be content working as a teacher's aide.

After Juliet's marriage proposal, Charlie felt pressure to make some changes in his life that would demonstrate he was growing up, making progress, moving in the right direction. He gave up his job at the primary school to take a "real job," a full-time position with all the trimmings: a salary, paid sick leave and holidays (a privilege Charlie had never yet been afforded in his string of casual jobs), an esoteric title (content development officer), and a box of business cards with his name printed beneath a company logo.

The first surprise of Charlie's new life was that the phrase *working nine to five* was inaccurate, that, in fact, his working hours were from 8:30 to 5:30, not to mention the hour it took him by tram and by train to reach the office and the hour home again. No more walking to work, coming home to have lunch with Juliet. Charlie had joined the drones, standing on a platform at Flinders Street Station at 8:00 a.m. with a glazed look in his eyes.

Charlie's employer was Sierra Education Incorporated, the

brand-new Australian arm of a hugely successful European company that developed and distributed learning aids for geography and social studies. Charlie's job involved developing questions for computer-generated quizzes around key learning areas from the primary school social studies curriculum. It sounded good on paper. And according to the recruitment consultant who found Charlie the position, Sierra Education was *geared for success*, and Charlie was going to make an *integral contribution* to a rate of growth *previously unheard of in Australia*.

So confident was the company in their growth that they took out a lease on an office designed for a hundred employees. When Charlie started, however, there were only ten employees, including himself, and their workstations were lost in the vast, bland space, like tiny islands floating in an unnamed ocean. Charlie had never had a workstation before. The partitions were arranged so when he was sitting at his desk, he couldn't see another soul. He was walled in on three sides, the only opening at his back, so whenever someone came to speak to him, they always took him by surprise. Occasionally people stood up from their ergonomic desk chairs (quality secondhand) to peer over their partitions, like meerkats emerging from their burrows.

Initially Charlie found it depressing to be cut off from the other people in the office, but once he got to know them, he discovered it to be a blessing. The graphic designer, who was the father of six children and called himself a Christian, told racist jokes and commented frequently on the number of *Vietmanese* [sic] moving into his area, *driving decent Aussie families out*. There was an obese IT consultant whose diet consisted solely of Coke, pot noodles, and fun-size chocolate bars, which he ate a bag at a time. Charlie's supervisor was a sexist ultracapitalist named Ray who was studying for his MBA, a qualification he described as a *passport to success*—by which he meant wealth. The only topic on which Charlie and Ray saw eye to eye was the utter ineptitude of the office manager,

Elliott. After less than three weeks in the job, Charlie found himself at a team meeting making a mental list of all the things he found intolerable about his new boss:

- He spoke through his nose.
- He jingled the change in his pockets as he moved about the office.
- He bounced on the balls of his feet when he walked.
- He laughed like a girl.

In a rare moment of wit, Ray joked to Charlie that Elliott's management skills had come from a little-known text titled *The Fascist's Guide to People Management*. Among his other managerial crimes, Elliott was notorious for sending emails to employees who were more than three minutes late, requesting an explanation for their tardiness. As a result, all the Sierrans—as they called themselves—clung desperately to the last minutes of their lunch breaks and left the office at five thirty on the dot. At first, Charlie was appalled by such pettiness, but after a while, he came to see his colleagues' behavior as an appropriate response to a manager who would send a memo complaining about the *excessive* quantity of toilet paper being purchased and asking employees to conserve their use only to what was *absolutely necessary*.

Catching the train in the morning, Charlie dreaded the day ahead. He passed nine hours in a kind of numb stupor, returning home feeling sick about the decision he had made. The worst part was no one else seemed to appreciate the sacrifice he was making. His mother said, "Welcome to the real world, Charlie," when he complained about the long days, and when he joked about the Sierrans to Juliet, she was unsympathetic.

"Don't be so superior, Charlie," she said. "They can't be as bad as all that."

"They're worse, Juliet. You can't even imagine it."

"Well, what were you looking for, Charlie? I don't know what made you take this job in the first place. I thought you loved your job at the school."

"I'm not a proper teacher, Juliet. I'm not even full time. I'm just a teacher's aide. I'm going nowhere. And I'm not getting any younger. I thought this would make you happy."

"Why would your doing a job you hate make me happy?"

"I thought you'd be happy I was being responsible, getting my shit together, you know." Charlie realized he couldn't begin to explain to Juliet the real reasons why he took the job. "I thought I could save some money so we could buy a house," he said desperately.

"We've got a house already."

"But it's your house, Juliet."

"Don't say that. How can you say that? Just because it's in my name, I never think of it as mine; you know that. We've lived here together for five years—to me it's our house."

"It's not the same," Charlie said stubbornly.

Juliet sighed. "You've never talked about buying a house before, Charlie. Why don't you tell me what this is really about?"

"I feel like I can't do anything right for you."

"Why are you saying that? I didn't ask you to take this job. I couldn't understand it at all, but you didn't even want to discuss it with me. You said you'd made up your mind."

"I don't mean that. I don't know what you want anymore."

"Oh, Charlie." She sounded exhausted. "I think you know exactly what I want."

* * *

It takes days for Charlie to accept what Magdalena has told him as the truth, days in which his reluctance to visit Whiskey is overcome by a new hope, in which he sits beside Rosa at Whiskey's bedside for hours at a stretch, watching for a further sign of arousal, allowing himself to imagine how different things are going to be when Whiskey wakes up. One after another, the members of the medical team tell Charlie the same thing, that Whiskey's vital signs are unchanged, his brain activity remains the same, he is still showing no response to the arousal therapy. Eventually Charlie has to admit to himself that he can see no change in Whiskey, that he does not blink or turn his head when people talk to him, that though his eyes are open, it is only a blank stare.

It depresses Charlie to see Whiskey staring into space. The hope that something had shifted, followed by the realization that everything is exactly the same, is more painful than when there was no change at all. Worse than that, there is no consensus among the medical staff about Whiskey's potential for recovery. Charlie knows the statistics. They are always in his mind, keeping him awake at night, like flashing neon signs he can't switch off: 50 percent of coma victims die; one-third are seriously injured for life. *Surely by now*, Charlie thinks, *the medical staff must have worked out which group Whiskey is going to end up in.* But if they have, none of them want to say so.

The CT and MRI scans indicate too much damaged tissue for recovery to be possible. And yet, Angie and Fergal are still scratching Whiskey's feet, blowing whistles in his ears, holding pungent bottles of god knows what under his nose. Grant is still bending and stretching his elbows and knees, his fingers and toes.

Charlie still doesn't completely trust Angie and Fergal; he's never really gotten over their first coma-arousal session with Whiskey. But he likes Grant. He thinks Grant is more likely to give him a straight answer than the doctors are. Charlie has to wait a few days for a physiotherapy session where neither his mother nor Rosa are present to ask the question that has been tormenting him.

He watches Grant rotate Whiskey's good foot from the ankle, first clockwise, then counterclockwise. After a moment, he picks up Whiskey's other foot and begins massaging, working his thumbs into the arches.

"Can you explain to me," Charlie says tentatively, "why you're working to keep Whiskey's body in shape if his brain isn't going to recover?"

"Who told you his brain isn't going to recover?" Grant asks, surprised.

"It's in the neurology reports. It's what the scans show."

Grant nods thoughtfully.

"I'm not having a go at you," Charlie says as Grant levers Whiskey's foot up and down. "I know it's not up to you. But what use is Whiskey's body to him without his brain?"

Grant lays Whiskey's foot back down on the bed. "I can see it might seem pointless, what I'm doing. But as long as there's a chance of recovery, we keep up the therapy."

"But that's exactly my point," Charlie says. "According to the scans, there *is* no chance of recovery."

"The scans don't have all the answers," Grant says carefully. "Even the neurologists will admit as much. It's still anecdotal to suggest that the longer the coma lasts, the less the potential for improvement. At this stage, there's still no real proof of a finite therapeutic window. That's why we keep up the therapy until we know for sure."

Charlie stands up and goes to the window. He doesn't want to lose his temper with Grant, but they are going around in circles.

"Have you got a brother, Grant?" he asks eventually.

"Not a brother, no. But I've got a little sister."

Charlie nods. "I wouldn't wish this on you, not in a million years, but if your sister was in a coma, wouldn't you want someone to tell you where you stood?"

"I would, Charlie. And I wish I could tell you what you need to know. But coma is one of the least predictable medical conditions in the book. Even people with years of experience can still be surprised when it comes to coma patients."

Charlie tries Magdalena next. Over time, he has come to like all the nurses, even those he had at first found brusque or standoffish. But Magdalena remains his favorite. He asks her about what Grant told him.

"Grant's right," Magdalena says. "They won't stop the therapy unless they're absolutely certain Whiskey can't recover."

"But isn't that what all those scans and things tell them?"

"It's not that cut-and-dried, Charlie. You could get a number of neurologists to look over Whiskey's case, and you might get a different diagnosis from each."

"I don't understand that," Charlie says. "They're specialists. It's supposed to be *science*."

"The thing is, Charlie, it's virtually impossible to *prove* there's no potential for recovery, even in the most severe cases. They've done every test on Whiskey they possibly can. But there is no known diagnostic test that can scientifically demonstrate recovery of function will not occur."

"Okay, so the tests can't prove it. But you've worked here a long time. You must have seen cases like this before."

"Well, yes and no. We've had patients with supposedly 'mild' brain injury, who have emerged from comas with substantial problems, which have permanently affected their lives. On the other side of the coin, I've seen patients who've been deemed to be severely injured, who have returned to more or less normal lives."

Charlie sighs. "But someone will have to make a decision eventually, won't they? They can't leave Whiskey in a coma indefinitely."

"I know this is hard for you, Charlie," Magdalena says. "Maybe you should have another chat with one of our counselors." She picks up the phone.

"I just want somebody to tell me the facts," Charlie says, exasperated.

Magdalena balances the receiver on her shoulder, holds up one finger for Charlie to wait. But Charlie doesn't want to wait. He stalks away, up the corridor to Whiskey's room, is standing looking through the window when Magdalena comes to find him.

"Good news," she says. "Thomas has a window between appointments. He's the one you saw when Whiskey started his arousal therapy. You remember him?"

"I remember," Charlie says.

"I've paged him," Magdalena says. "He'll be here in five minutes if you want to talk."

"You didn't have to," Charlie says, suddenly grateful, and sorry for making it her fault.

× × ×

"Good to see you again, Charlie," Thomas says, shaking his hand, sounding like he means it.

They go again into one of the little waiting rooms, sit again across from each other, over the same table stacked with the same magazines.

"Anyone would think I was the patient here," Charlie says, embarrassed he has been identified as in need of counseling not once, but twice. As far as he knows, no one else has needed to have a counselor called—not his mother, or Rosa, certainly not Juliet or Audrey.

"If there's one thing I've learned in this job, Charlie, it's that life-threatening illness doesn't only affect the patients. We're here to talk to anyone who needs us, whether they're hospital inpatients or not. I talk to a lot of family members in these kinds of circumstances."

"I'm not the only basket case you get called out for, then?"

Thomas laughs. "Far from it. I've had people punching holes through walls, you name it. I've seen it all here, and you're holding up pretty well under the circumstances, believe me. So how can I help you today, Charlie?"

Charlie sighs. "I never dreamed it could go on for this long. I need to know now, one way or the other. At least then I could prepare myself."

"Okay," Thomas says. "First, I should tell you it's normal to feel the way you do. It's a very common reaction for anyone who has to deal with a coma that lasts more than a few weeks. I understand you want the truth, that you think someone knows it and is hiding it from you. Unfortunately, the only fact here is no one can tell you, one way or the other, because no one actually knows. The best anyone can do is make an educated guess. And no one wants to do that, because these days, a doctor can't afford to make a mistake."

"Well, they don't have to worry about that with me," Charlie says. "I'm not the litigious type."

"You say that now," Thomas says wryly, "but you never know. You might surprise yourself. So if you want answers in the medical sense, I can't help you with that. But if what you need is to try to prepare yourself for what comes next with Whiskey, whichever way it goes, well then, that's something I can probably help you with."

Charlie thinks for a minute. What Thomas is offering is not exactly what he wanted, but it is better than nothing. "Okay," he says.

"Great," Thomas says. "And you're ready to talk about this right now?"

Charlie nods.

"All right. So we'll talk through the potential outcomes for Whiskey and the ways you might cope with those. And we can do that at whatever pace suits you. We can go through everything today, if you'd rather get it over and done with, or we can take it one piece at a time, if that makes it easier. What I need to know now is, do you want to start with the good news or the bad news?"

Charlie closes his eyes. He knows he should ask for the bad news first; that's the way you always do it. That way the good news helps you get over the bad news. But this is different. Because the bad news has never been so bad. The bad news is his brother will die. And no amount of good news can help him get over that. And though he thought he was ready to consider that possibility, once it was offered to him, he knew he was not.

"I need the good news first, if that's okay."

"Whatever you need is okay, Charlie. It's your call. We'll start with the best-case scenario, and when you're ready—if you're ready—we'll talk about the other possibilities."

Charlie swallows, leans forward in his chair.

"So let's begin by imagining the best possible outcome for Whiskey. What do you think that might be?"

Charlie takes a breath. "I think I told you last time that Whiskey and I didn't get on. *Don't* get on," Charlie corrects himself.

"You mentioned it."

Charlie closes his eyes. He thinks it will be easier to say what he has to say if he isn't looking at Thomas. "I've spent most of the last ten years wishing I had a different kind of brother or wishing Whiskey would change, become the kind of person I could like." He opens his eyes, exhales. "After what's happened, I don't want Whiskey to change," he goes on after a moment. "What I want now is for him to wake up and be exactly the same as he always was, to be able to go back to the life he had, do all the things he used to do. Even if it means we still don't get on, I don't care now. As long as he can do what matters to him."

"What kinds of things matter to him?"

Charlie shrugs. "The sad part is, I don't even know the answer to that." He takes another deep breath, looks away from Thomas. "That's one of the things that's been driving me nuts since the accident, how much I don't know about him. I thought I didn't care."

"But you do."

Charlie nods.

"If you had to guess then," Thomas says, "what do you think might be important to Whiskey?"

"Rosa," Charlie says after a while. "Rosa's important to him."

"Rosa?"

"His wife. I know he loves her—they love each other."

"How do you know that?"

"You can see it."

"How, though?" Thomas persists.

Charlie thinks for a minute. "The way he treats her...the way he is when he's around her. He seems..."

"What?"

"Happy. He seems happy."

"You can tell when he's happy?"

"I guess I can."

"You seem surprised."

Charlie doesn't know what to say. He is surprised.

"It sounds like you know a bit more about him than you thought."

Charlie nods.

"What about you?" Thomas asks. "How do you get on with Rosa?"

"I like her. It took me a while, but I like her a lot."

"Why did it take you a while?"

"They got married on a whim. They hardly knew each other," Charlie says, hating how judgmental it sounds, even as the words come out. "I didn't think it would last. I didn't see the point of getting attached."

"Have you ever acted on a whim, Charlie?" Thomas asks after a moment.

"Of course."

"You don't believe in love at first sight though?"

Charlie sniffs. "I'd like to say no. In theory, I don't. But that's pretty much the way it happened for Juliet and me."

"You knew straightaway?"

"More or less."

Thomas looks at Charlie, says nothing.

"Okay, I get the point." Charlie shifts in his chair. "If it could happen for me, why couldn't I accept that it could happen for Whiskey too?"

"It's worth pondering, don't you think?"

"I guess I didn't cut Whiskey much slack," Charlie says eventually.

"Were you aware of that at the time?"

"I didn't think of it like that before."

"How did you think of it?"

Charlie frowns. "It's hard to remember exactly now. But I think I thought *everyone* cut him too much slack. I thought he could do with a bit of criticism from somewhere."

"So you used to challenge him on things?"

"Well...no. Years and years ago maybe, when we were kids, teenagers. But not for a long time now, not directly anyway."

"Indirectly then?"

"Well, no, not even indirectly," Charlie says, starting to feel uncomfortable with Thomas's line of questioning.

"So if he did something you didn't like or didn't approve of, how would you let him know?"

"I stopped..." Charlie pauses.

"You stopped what?"

"I stopped talking to him." Charlie looks at Thomas and then looks away. Never has his part in things been shown to him so clearly. He puts his head in his hands.

"Charlie?" Thomas says gently.

Charlie can't answer him.

Thomas waits awhile. "Do you want to leave it there for today?" Charlie nods without looking up.

"I've left something for you to read," Thomas says. "I'll check in with you tomorrow, okay?"

"Okay," Charlie says, but he still doesn't lift his head. And for a long time after Thomas is gone, he sits there, shame and remorse heavy in his blood, slowing his heart like a poison.

Thomas has left Charlie a pamphlet titled *Stages of Grief When Facing Terminal Illness*, the same pamphlet that had been tucked for months into the back of the notebook they used to record information about Whiskey's condition. Charlie had never read it. He did not believe a mass-produced leaflet could give him any insight into how he should feel about his brother being in a coma. And besides, didn't grieving come after death, or at least once you knew death was inevitable? Charlie did not believe Whiskey could die; therefore, he did not accept that he might be grieving.

When he finally reads the pamphlet, Charlie feels embarrassed by the extent to which he has conformed to the expected behaviors. Even his denial of the fact that he is grieving turns out to be the first stage of grieving. Denial is apparently *a temporary response to the initial shock*, one of the psyche's protective mechanisms. According to the information in the pamphlet, it is characterized by behavior such as avoiding the patient. Charlie thinks about the number of times he has resisted visiting Whiskey.

"I'm such a cliché," he groans to Thomas the next time they meet.

Thomas is bemused by Charlie's response. "There are no points awarded for *not* going through the grief cycle, Charlie. In fact, if you weren't experiencing any of these emotions or exhibiting these behaviors, we'd have concerns about your psychological state."

"It just seems pathetic to be so predictable. First the denial, then the anger—I'm an absolute textbook case."

"Those are normal responses, Charlie. There's nothing pathetic about them. This information is designed to reassure you that virtually everyone in your situation responds the same way. A lot of people find it helpful to know that the way they're feeling or behaving is a stage they're going through, that they will at some point pass through those feelings and into another stage. It helps them to cope. But if it makes you feel uncomfortable to label them, we can forget about it."

Thomas reaches for the pamphlet. Charlie finds himself grabbing it.

"No," he says. "No. You're right."

Thomas waits.

"It does help to know."

"Which part helps?"

"Knowing everyone goes through the same things, I suppose. I mean, sometimes I've felt like I'm the only person getting angry about it. It's reassuring to think that other people feel angry too. I think I just feel a bit exposed."

"Can you tell me what you mean by that?"

"Well, the third stage, about the bargaining. Reading that was like reading an exact description of my thoughts. It was as though someone had opened me up and looked right inside my head. I feel sort of...foolish that my motivations are so transparent."

"There's nothing foolish about it."

"It's pointless though, isn't it, bargaining?"

"I think that depends what comes out of the process for you. What makes you think it's pointless?"

"Well, if you believed in God, you could say, 'I'll be a better human from now on if you let this person I love pull through.' You might believe that by doing good deeds or being kinder, you could impact God's 'decision' and therefore whether the person you loved would live or die."

"I take it you don't believe in God."

"I don't. So who am I bargaining with? I can say to myself, 'I'll be a better brother if Whiskey lives,' but deep down, I know that being a better brother won't influence the outcome. So it's pointless."

"Is being a better brother pointless?" Thomas asks after a pause.

"What do you mean?"

"I mean, even if you believe God can't influence the outcome for Whiskey, do you think any good can come of you behaving in ways that would make you feel like a better brother?"

Charlie thinks for a minute. "It would make my mom happy. And Rosa, I'm sure. I think Juliet would appreciate it as well."

"Is there anyone else you can think of?"

Charlie frowns. "Well, Audrey, I suppose. Whiskey's friends maybe?"

"What about you, Charlie?" Thomas asks eventually.

"What about me?"

"Do you think it could do you any good, being more the kind of brother you think you should be to Whiskey?"

Charlie looks away from Thomas. How did he not see this for himself?

TANGO

For as long as they had lived together, Charlie and Juliet had always lain in bed and talked before they turned out the light. They had talked about nothing and everything, the minutiae of their daily lives, the things that mattered to them most. Charlie had loved those talks. But ever since Juliet had asked "the question," Charlie had felt that every time they talked, Juliet was waiting for "the answer," and he had begun to fear those times they spent alone together, to dread the thought that the question might rise up again and he would still be unable to meet it. He had felt the question between them always—as if the words were printed on a badge Juliet wore pinned to her clothing—but never more acutely than when they were lying together in bed. Charlie had taken to reading before he went to sleep, saying it was the only chance he ever had for it, that it helped him to wind down from the day. He had thought he was buying time. It took him too long to realize that with that time came distance, a gap between them that would prove much harder to close than it had been to open.

× × ×

After Whiskey's accident, Charlie had felt the tension between himself and Juliet ease. He knew Juliet couldn't expect him to be thinking about marriage while his brother was in a coma. She had been so supportive in those first few weeks, the accident bringing them closer than they'd been for a long time. Then Juliet had begun working at the school, keeping the focus off their relationship.

It had started when the modeling agency she worked for asked her to deliver their grooming and deportment classes. Juliet had wanted to give up modeling ever since Charlie met her, but as she had often told him, writing screenplays didn't pay the bills. So the classes had seemed like a good idea, easy money for something she could do with her eyes closed. But she'd been disturbed by the bitchy competitiveness, the unhealthy attitudes girls as young as nine or ten had about their bodies. The very first week, she told Charlie, she had heard two girls arguing over rice crackers.

"They're ninety-eight percent fat-free," one of them had said.

"They're *carbohydrates*," said the other disgustedly, as though she was naming a disease.

"I'm on the Atkins diet, like Reese Witherspoon," a girl named Imogen had boasted in another class.

Juliet had told the girls they shouldn't be dieting at their age, that it was essential to eat plenty of fruits and vegetables to keep their skin healthy. "Sallow skin doesn't look good in photos," she had added.

"But I don't want to do photographic. I want to do catwalk. You have to be a size two for that."

"You also have to be five-foot-eight," a taller girl called Caitlin said smugly.

"I'm still growing," Imogen said.

"Good luck trying to grow eight inches in two years."

"Why does it have to be within two years?" Juliet asked.

Caitlin had looked at her disdainfully, as if asking such a question made her unqualified to be their teacher. "If you haven't been discovered by the time you're fourteen, you might as well forget it."

After a conversation with an old friend who'd become a high school teacher, Juliet had begun developing her own course for teenage girls, one that focused on health and self-esteem rather than how to maintain a size-two figure or perfect the catwalk strut. Charlie helped her with the course structure and session planning, and when she had finished, she contacted the eighth grade coordinator from her old school and arranged a meeting to present her idea. After a lot of to-ing and fro-ing, it had been approved by the board to be put on trial as part of the health education program the following year.

Over a four-week period, Juliet worked with more than a hundred Fintona students, teaching them about the importance of regular exercise and the dangers of eating disorders, how to look after their hair and skin and apply makeup to enhance their natural features, what kind of clothing flattered what kind of bodies, how to improve their posture. She did not lecture them from the front of the classroom or give them handouts to clip into their binders; she brought in magazines for them to look at—*Teen Vogue*, *Seventeen*, *Cosmopolitan*. They looked through them together and talked about the articles, and Juliet tried to teach them to think for themselves about the real messages they were being given.

She came home from her days at the school exhausted and elated, thrilled by the girls' responses, full of ideas for ways to grow the program. She talked about enrolling for a Diploma of Education, becoming a real teacher. Now that Charlie was no longer working at a school, she had developed a new understanding of the world he had worked in, joking with him about the staff room politics, the strangeness of suddenly finding herself on the other side of the student–teacher dynamic.

Charlie convinced himself that the unanswered question had not been forgotten but put aside, that his reticence had been forgiven, that the rift between them was healed.

Then Darius entered the scene. Through her success at Fintona Girls' School, Juliet had been given a contact at another private girls' school called St. Mary's, a health education coordinator who was looking for new programs. He had asked Juliet to extend the program to run over eight weeks and to expand it to include ninth and tenth grades.

Charlie was suspicious of Darius from the start. He was too keen, too dedicated, too involved. Every time he and Juliet met to work on the program (which seemed to be more often than Charlie thought necessary) Juliet came home talking about how brilliant Darius was, how perceptive and innovative, how charismatic. She described him as *an amazing educator*.

Charlie complained to Marco about her enthusiasm for her new boss. "You've never heard her refer to me as an amazing educator, have you?" he asked.

"You should be happy for Juliet, that she's finally found something she loves doing."

"I *am* happy for her. But this guy's trying to cut my lunch!"

"So what if he is? It takes two to tango."

"I hate that stupid expression," Charlie said. "I don't even know what it means."

"It means, it doesn't matter how much this Darius guy likes Juliet—nothing's going to happen between them unless *she* wants it to. He can't tango alone," he added unnecessarily. "Juliet would have to be willing too."

"All right, I get it," Charlie snapped.

"Come on, Charlie. Juliet's been fighting off other men since the day you met her. What makes this guy any different?"

"Nothing, I suppose," Charlie said. But as soon as she had started the job at St. Mary's, he had felt things shift between them, the ground opening up. They had begun reading in bed again, and this time it had been Juliet's suggestion.

× × ×

As well as being *an amazing educator*, Darius was also, apparently, *a gifted actor*. After they had been working together for a month or so, Darius had invited Juliet to see a play he was performing in. It was the last thing on earth Charlie wanted to do, but it would have been worse to let Juliet go without him.

"I haven't been to the theater for ages," she said on the way there, sounding too enthusiastic for Charlie's taste.

"I wouldn't get too worked up. I'm a bit dubious about these group-devised things."

"You didn't have to come," she reminded him.

If he was honest, Charlie had to admit that the play wasn't too bad. But without a doubt, the best thing about it was finally seeing Darius in the flesh. Darius was what Marco would have called *plug ugly*, except he pronounced it *plurg urgly*, which made it sound even worse. Every time Darius appeared on stage, Charlie added to his mental list of his flaws. To begin with, he was short. Not "of medium height," which is how short men always described them-selves, but downright vertically challenged. And not only short, but also stumpy. He had an enormous, misshapen nose and strange, tufty-looking hair. He resembled, Charlie thought, a donkey. Charlie bet he had a hairy back. Making this mental list pleased Charlie. It pleased him so much that he almost managed to enjoy the play. He reached over and squeezed Juliet's hand.

The thought that Juliet—beautiful Juliet—might be interested in him was absurd. Charlie felt so good he agreed to stay and meet Darius. He left Juliet sitting at a little table in the foyer while he went to get the two of them a drink. It was a typical theater bar, where none of the bottles had been opened in advance, and as soon as the rush came, the bottle opener couldn't be located, and there wasn't enough ice and they were short on change and had to ask every customer if they had something smaller. As a result, every round took three times longer than it should have, but Charlie felt perfectly cheerful throughout the lengthy and painful process. When he finally moved away from the bar with his two flat gin and tonics, without ice, he saw Darius was sitting at the table with Juliet, wearing, of all things, a waistcoat.

The nail in his coffin, Charlie thought to himself. Juliet had a thing about waistcoats. She said they should be worn as part of a three-piece suit or not at all, that to team them up with pants or, worse still, jeans was one of the top-ten fashion crimes of all time. Charlie thought he would make a joke about it to Juliet later. He imagined them laughing together about it. Then he saw Juliet burst out laughing at something Darius had said, and he suddenly noticed how close together they were sitting, and all his smug confidence evaporated. Darius was looking at Juliet as if she was the only woman in the room. This was nothing new to Charlie. He had seen it happen before, hundreds of times. But what made this time different from all the others was this time, Juliet was looking at Darius the same way.

Charlie walked over and put the drinks down on the table.

"There you are," Juliet said, jerking back in her chair. "This is Darius."

"Ah, Darius," Charlie said. "The way Juliet was laughing, I thought she must be talking to Woody Allen."

Juliet frowned.

Darius looked uncomfortable. "Nice to meet you, Charlie." He put out his hand.

Charlie shook it. *Cock blocker*, he thought to himself.

"So what did you think of the play?" Darius asked.

It was a steaming pile of dung, Charlie wanted to say. He shrugged. "It wasn't really my cup of tea, to be honest."

"Fair enough," Darius said pleasantly. "Contemporary theater's not for everyone."

Wanker, Charlie thought. *You wouldn't know contemporary theater if it came up and bit you on the ass.*

"I was very moved by it," Juliet said. "I thought it was very honest."

Darius smiled at her. "I had a feeling that's what you'd think."

How would you know what she'd think, donkey man? You don't even know her. Keep your hairy hooves off her.

"I'm sorry to hear we didn't win you over though, Charlie. I always think there's nothing more painful than sitting through a play you're not enjoying."

Too right, Charlie thought. *Especially when the lead is played by a furry beast masquerading as a man.*

"Charlie doesn't like things that are too emotional," Juliet said apologetically. "They make him uncomfortable."

Darius nodded sympathetically, as though Juliet was shackled to a caveman.

That's right. I'm a shell of a man, Charlie thought. *I've got no feelings at all. That's why I don't mind you two talking about me as if I'm not even here.*

Darius cleared his throat, and Juliet's face went dark. Charlie realized he had spoken aloud.

"Well," Darius said after a moment. "I have some other friends I should catch up with so..."

"Of course," Juliet said. "There must be lots of people waiting to congratulate you."

"See you soon," he said, smiling at Juliet and nodding at Charlie.

Juliet didn't look at Charlie. She picked up her handbag and made for the door.

"What is wrong with you?" she asked when he caught up to her outside the theater. "How could you be so rude? I've never been so humiliated."

"You think that was humiliating for you, do you? Well, how do you think I felt, standing there like a spare prick at a wedding while you two made eyes at each other and talked about what an emotional cripple I am?"

"Don't be ridiculous. You're twisting things. It wasn't like that."

"Don't lie to me, Juliet. If you're going to cheat on me, you could at least show me the respect of being honest about it."

Juliet turned away from him. "Don't shout at me, Charlie. I'm not cheating on you."

"What does that mean? You haven't slept with him yet? You've thought about it though, haven't you?"

Juliet put her head in her hands.

"Tell me, Juliet, you like him, don't you?"

She nodded.

"Are you in love with him?"

"I don't know."

"You don't know? Jesus Christ, Juliet." Charlie felt like he'd been hit from behind. He beat the heels of his hands against his forehead, as if that might help him to understand what was happening.

"Stop it, Charlie." Juliet reached for his hands, but Charlie lurched away from her.

"Don't touch me." He tried to steady himself. "So what about us then? Is this it? Are we finished? Were you planning to tell me anytime soon?"

"I don't know, Charlie. I don't know."

"You don't know much, do you?" Charlie kicked the wall. "I don't believe this," he said and then he started to walk away from her.

"Where are you going?" Her voice was small.

"Why would you care?" Charlie said without turning around.

"Please don't go, Charlie."

But Charlie kept walking. He left the only girl he had ever loved sobbing on a street corner, and he crossed the road without looking, because he felt like he wanted to die.

He thought about going back to the theater and punching Darius, knocking him to the ground and breaking his big, ugly nose. He thought about going to a pub and drinking himself blind. Then he thought about Marco, told himself Marco would be able to make sense of things. Charlie needed to hear that Juliet was right out of order, that he deserved better, that he shouldn't put up with it. Marco was a straight talker. He would say that Darius was a lowlife, a snake in the grass, and that Charlie would be perfectly within his rights to knock his block off. They would share a bottle of scotch, and Charlie would sleep on the couch, and in the morning, Juliet would call there, looking for him, begging for his forgiveness.

It took Charlie almost an hour to walk to Marco's. But when he got there, things didn't go exactly the way he imagined. Marco listened to Charlie's tale of woe, and then he gave it to him with both barrels. He said it was Charlie's own fault that Juliet wanted to leave him, that he had dug his own grave, and if it hadn't been Darius, it would have been someone else.

"For fuck's sake, Marco. My brother's in a coma. My girlfriend wants to leave me. I came here for your support. Some best mate you are." Charlie started to walk off down the driveway, but Marco came after him.

"Don't use Whiskey as your excuse, Charlie. This has nothing to do with him, and you know it. How long is it since Juliet talked to you about getting married? Eight months? Nine months? How long has she been waiting for you to think about it? How much longer do you expect her to wait? Wake up, Charlie. Juliet's the best thing that ever happened to you, and if you lose her, you'll regret it for the rest of your life. And believe me, I'm telling you this because I *am* your best mate."

Charlie stopped walking. "Jesus, Marco, don't tell me this. I don't know what to do."

"There's only one thing to do, Charlie. You've got to go home and beg for her forgiveness. Tell her you want to spend the rest of your life with her. Do whatever it takes." Marco grabbed him suddenly, hugged him. "I love you, mate," he said. "If you mess this up, I'm going to be really disappointed in you. More disappointed than I've ever been."

Charlie nodded numbly.

"I'll call you tomorrow, okay?"

He nodded again.

Marco shut the door, and Charlie started walking. He walked up Kerferd Road, through the cool darkness of Albert Park, meaning to turn homeward at Queens Road, or St. Kilda Road, but finding himself inexplicably staying on Commercial Road until he found himself outside the Alfred Hospital. He took the now-familiar path up to Whiskey's ward, the corridors hushed at this time, quieter than he had ever seen them. At the door to Whiskey's room, he stopped, momentarily surprised to see Rosa through the little window. He pushed open the door, startling her out of sleep.

"Charlie! What are you doing here?"

Charlie kissed her hello. "I came to see Whiskey."

"Now? At two o'clock in the morning? What is wrong?"

"Nothing's wrong, Rosa. I just wanted to have a think about things…and I suppose I thought…this would be a good place." Charlie couldn't believe he had forgotten that Rosa spent all night at the hospital. It struck him how incredibly selfish he had been to show up there in the middle of the night.

"What is going on, Charlie?" Rosa asked, wide-awake now. "Are you drunk? You look terrible. Where is Juliet? Does she know you're here?"

"I'm perfectly sober. Juliet's at home, I suppose. I hope. We had a fight, if you must know."

"You had a fight." Rosa looked at him suspiciously. "Why would you want to fight with Juliet?"

Charlie shrugged. Rosa always took Juliet's side. "I don't *want* to fight with her. Sometimes it happens. You should know that. I bet you and Whiskey fight."

Rosa looked at Whiskey. "Not lately," she said, smiling sadly.

"God, I'm sorry, Rosa, I'm so sorry. I'm upset. I don't know what I'm saying."

"It does not matter, Charlie. I know you do not mean to put your foot inside your mouth. It is true what you are saying. Whiskey and I did fight, because we both were always thinking we were right. If he was awake now, we would still be fighting. But that is another story."

"I don't know what to say. I shouldn't have come."

"Well, you are here now. You might as well tell me the problem."

"It's hard to explain."

"I do not think you are the very first man to have this problem, Charlie."

"You don't even know what it is yet."

"Of course I know what it is. Juliet is upset with you because you make her wait too long for getting married, yes?"

"She told you that?"

Rosa snorted. "She does not need to tell me this. The words are written on to her face, Charlie. It is only you who cannot read them."

"Believe me, Rosa, I can read them perfectly," Charlie said morosely.

"Then why do you not ask her, Charlie? What are you waiting for?"

Charlie thought for a long time. "I don't know, Rosa. I'm scared, I suppose." Admitting it, he felt broken.

"What is there to be scared of?"

"What if it doesn't work? What if she leaves me? I couldn't live without her. I'd rather not get married at all."

Rosa shook her head. "Don't be ridiculous, Charlie. What are you looking for, a guarantee? That is something which only comes with a washing machine, and even then it is only lasting for five years. Do you think Whiskey and I had a guarantee? Of course we did not. We hardly knew each other. There is no guarantee when it comes to marriage."

Charlie looked at Rosa, thought of all those nights since November, when she'd sat in that room, holding Whiskey's hand. He thought of Juliet, waiting, waiting. He thought of how he had left her standing on the street corner, crying. He got up and left the room, walked to the end of the corridor, to the window that overlooked Fawkner Park, pressed his forehead against the cool glass, looked out into the darkness.

"You're right, Rosa," he said when he finally came back. "I've been ridiculous."

"Never mind," Rosa said. "We all are ridiculous sometimes."

"I'm sorry I disturbed you," Charlie said, and he really meant it.

"Don't say sorry to me," Rosa said. "Go home and say sorry to Juliet. That is the most important thing."

Sorry, he thought. It was a good place to start.

UNIFORM

Though it was outside the usual guidelines, in view of the extenuating circumstances, Holly and Chloe had been given permission to enroll for one term at the local primary school. Juliet had gone with Mike to buy their uniforms. In Quebec, they said, they didn't wear school uniforms, and they were thrilled with their red-and-white-checked sundresses, their sweaters bearing the school logo.

Charlie remembered how excited he had been about his first school uniform—dark gray shorts, a lighter shirt, a yellow tie, and a cap. Some time before Whiskey's accident, Juliet had come across a photo of him wearing it, when they were looking through an old album one night at his mother's.

"Their first school photos. I used to have them in a twin frame," Charlie's mother said. "No one could ever tell which was which."

Juliet looked at the two photos again. She picked Charlie without hesitating. "It's a beautiful photo," she said.

"I'll make you a copy, if you want," Charlie's mother said. "I'll do one for Rosa too, of Whiskey."

"How did you know which one was me?" Charlie had asked her later.

"I could tell by your facial expressions," Juliet said. "Whiskey already looked like he'd seen it all before, like nothing could impress him. You looked kind of jumpy and excited, as if being at school was an adventure."

Charlie remembered that feeling well. He envied the twins. He had loved school when he was their age, had loved his work at the primary school for the same reason. Watching the kids cutting and gluing, writing in their "diaries," sharpening their pencils as if their lives depended on it; the hardest decision they ever had to make was who they wanted to sit next to.

He did not know how his own life had ever gotten so complicated.

× × ×

When he arrived home from the hospital the night of the play, Juliet was still awake. Her face was red and swollen, but she didn't cry when she asked Charlie to leave.

Instead, it was Charlie who cried. He cried when she said that it wasn't Darius, that as soon as Charlie had walked away from her, she had known she didn't care about Darius. He cried when she told him she loved him as much as she ever had but she couldn't wait for him anymore.

He cried when he told her he was sorry, that he loved her, that he had made a mistake, that he wanted to marry her after all.

Then it was Juliet's turn. She cried and cried, and Charlie held her, and when she stopped, she said it was too late.

Charlie thought of Marco's advice. He had no pride left because he had done nothing to be proud of. He apologized for all the ways he had hurt her. He begged her to give him another chance.

Again she cried, again he comforted her, again she said no.

"Give me two months," Charlie asked her. "Two months to prove I can change." He pleaded with her until they had both cried themselves dry, and in the end she agreed.

× × ×

Whiskey had been in a coma for six months. With every day that passed, the chance of him coming out of it grew smaller, and if he did come out of it, the chance of permanent damage grew greater.

Charlie had spent all those months trying to find evidence that Whiskey was to blame for their estrangement, looking for justifications for his refusal to forgive Whiskey, excavating the last twenty-five years of their lives in order to come to some kind of definitive conclusion—which of them was guilty, which of them was not. At last he saw that the truth was somewhere between those things, that it wasn't all Whiskey's fault or all his own, that at times they had both done the right thing by each other, and at other times the wrong thing, that they'd both made mistakes and both come good in their own ways over the years and that if Whiskey lived, they'd probably do it all again.

For months, Charlie had been going to see Whiskey at the hospital once a week, feeling like a martyr for doing so. Finally, he understood what Thomas had been trying to show him: that the accident had wiped the slate clean on both sides, that he had another chance to be the kind of brother he wanted to be, that even if Whiskey died, Charlie had the weeks or days or hours until that happened to begin again, to do things differently.

And what about Mike? He had put his life, his daughters' lives, on hold for a year to support a family who had been, only months before, perfect strangers. He had said he wanted to stay until it was over, whichever way it went.

When Mike first made this decision, he had wanted to rent a small flat for himself and the girls, but Rosa wouldn't hear of it. She had said she would be lonely without them, that she couldn't bear to think of coming home alone to that big empty house. So Mike had been taking care of Whiskey's house, cleaning Whiskey's car, mowing Whiskey's lawn. He had been going to the hospital every second day to support Rosa. He had been doing, in short, all the things Charlie should have been doing. And Charlie had resented him for it, felt that Mike's behavior was only serving to show up his own shortcomings.

Once Charlie had started working full-time, he had managed

to avoid Mike almost entirely, telling himself that letting Mike in would be accepting the terms, agreeing to the exchange—one brother for another—it would be like signing Whiskey's death certificate. But that was just an excuse. The night of the play, Charlie saw that he was jealous of Mike as he had been of Whiskey, afraid of being compared and failing to measure up, terrified that he would make the same mistakes all over again because he didn't know any other way.

× × ×

Eight weeks. Charlie began by handing in his notice at Sierra Education.

"Charlie, Charlie, Charlie, what are you doing to me?" Ray said when Charlie gave him the letter. "There is a glorious future around the corner. And you're a part of that, my man, a major part."

"My brother's in a coma, Ray; you know that. There's a chance he's going to die. I need to spend some time with him. My girlfriend's going to leave me if I don't get my shit together. And I hate this job."

It was the first time Charlie had ever seen Ray speechless, and it gave him courage.

"Four weeks' notice then, if that's the way you want it. Your loss, Charlie," Ray said eventually.

"I'm not staying here another four weeks, Ray," Charlie said.

Ray looked at his monitor, as if a solution might appear there. "I suppose we could get away with two, as you haven't been here long."

"I want to leave today."

"Today?" Ray laughed without humor. "Well, I'd like to say yes, Charlie; you know I would. If it was up to me, it would be different, but we have policies and procedures—"

"I know," Charlie interrupted. "I've read them. All of them. I'm sure I'd be eligible for compassionate leave."

"Compassionate leave? Well, we don't give that out at the drop of a hat, Charlie. It's reserved for extreme circumstances."

"My brother's in a coma," Charlie said again, as if Ray hadn't understood.

Ray looked back at his monitor. "You win, Charlie. Compassionate leave it is."

And at eleven o'clock that morning, Charlie commuted out of zone two for the last time, with a check for a month's severance pay in his pocket.

× × ×

The following week, Charlie found a job at a café to tide him over until the start of the next school year, when he might be able to get another teacher's aide position. On the days when he wasn't working, he went to see Whiskey. Sometimes he went in the mornings and sat with Rosa or took her seat by the bed while she went to get a coffee. Sometimes he went in the afternoons when Rosa was at home sleeping and Mike was in her place.

In the beginning, Mike didn't say too much. He told Charlie about growing up in Canada, about the "sugar shacks" where they made their own maple syrup, about learning to pee his name into the snow. Charlie tried to think of things Mike might want to know, funny stories, things from their childhood. He told him about Bravo, about Whiskey getting caned for *Delta of Venus*, about the voyage to Australia.

Mike taught Charlie to play backgammon. They played across the end of Whiskey's bed, and Charlie found that when their eyes were on their pieces, there wasn't much he couldn't say, which was how, in less than a month, Mike went from knowing almost nothing about this family he had adopted, to knowing just about everything there was to know. He knew about the India debacle, their parents' divorce, the reasons why Charlie had refused to be a sperm donor for Whiskey and Rosa. He also knew why Charlie and Whiskey had finally stopped talking. Charlie told Mike how, after Whiskey found out about Charlie and Juliet, he had fed his mother all sorts of vicious lies about Juliet, how Charlie's mother, who was unaware of Whiskey's hidden agenda, believed every word Whiskey said and refused to let Juliet in the house or even to meet her. Charlie even told Mike the other part of the story, the part he had never told before, and of which he was so ashamed—that after Whiskey got over his anger, he had tried, more than once, to apologize, and Charlie had refused to accept his apology.

Charlie knew Mike had ignored the advice of every one of his friends who had urged him to *let sleeping dogs lie*, had told him, without exception, to use his inheritance as a deposit on a house. He knew how devastated Mike had been when Sarina left him with a *Dear John* letter when the twins were only three months old, how in the six years since, she'd never once been to visit the girls or even phoned them, that all they got was a postcard every now and then. He knew Mike felt that without Charlie and Whiskey and their mother, he and the girls would be alone in the world.

And by the time they had told each other all these things, it was impossible for Charlie not to think of Mike—if not as his brother—at least as his friend.

× × ×

Winning Juliet back was the hardest part. She had finished up the term at St. Mary's and declined the invitation to continue the following semester, so Charlie didn't have to worry about Darius anymore. But he felt the pressure of the two-month time frame acutely, thought of it like a ticking bomb in a movie, with a countdown timer displaying the minutes and seconds remaining until everyone was blown to smithereens. For Charlie, it was not minutes and seconds, but weeks and days. It wasn't as simple as taking the back off and poking around inside to work out whether the red wire or the green wire should be cut. There would be no explosions if he didn't make things right, and it wouldn't be limbs that were lost. But it would be just as devastating; the time was just as precious.

Charlie had heard about self-help books in which you were encouraged to wake up in the morning and think, *Today is the first day of the rest of my life!* But that is not what Charlie had thought when he woke up the day after the play. What he thought was, *Today is the first day of what might be my last two months with Juliet.* He had to make it count, make every day count.

He went out and bought a bunch of pink and orange tulips, had them extravagantly wrapped in tissue and silk ribbon. Juliet thanked him and arranged them in a vase, but she did not say they were beautiful or hesitate over where to put them. Two days later, Charlie bought her irises, left them on the bench when he went out, with a note saying *Love Charlie x*. When he came home, the irises were in a vase on the dining table, but Juliet didn't mention them. Two days after that, a day he thought of as the fifth day, he bought her antique lilies. She looked pained when he gave them to her.

"Charlie," she said, and then stopped.

Charlie thought she was going to say she shouldn't have agreed to the two months, that she couldn't do it. He leaned against the bench to stop his legs shaking.

"We've only got two vases," she said. "And they're both full."

On another day, this might have been funny. They would have laughed together about it, stuck some of the flowers into a bucket. But it was only the fifth day, and nothing was funny.

Charlie tried anyway, even as he was waiting for the blow to fall. "I'll get another vase," he said.

Juliet smiled a little, but it was a small, sad, awkward smile. "It's not that, Charlie." She looked away from him. "You don't have to keep buying me flowers."

She paused, and Charlie could see her casting about for the right words. She was trying to spare him. He didn't deserve it, but that was her way.

"You said you were sorry," she said eventually. "There's no need to try so hard. It's making me…nervous."

She didn't mean nervous. She meant sad. Charlie was making her sad.

"Let's just try to get on with things," she said. "Act normal. Okay?"

But Charlie didn't know what normal was anymore. They kissed each other hello and good-bye, they ate meals together, they slept in the same bed. But they made love without speaking, and afterward, Juliet spent a long time in the bathroom, blowing her nose, slept with her face turned away from Charlie on the pillow.

× × ×

Charlie and Juliet usually had dinner at Charlie's mother's every second Thursday. Elaine had initiated the dinners a year or so before, hoping to get him and Whiskey talking, Charlie supposed. After the lies Whiskey had told his mother about Juliet, Charlie thought she should understand that it would take more than two hours over a couple weeks to sort out their differences, but Juliet, who still did not know the real reason behind their rift, had asked him to go to the dinners and do his best. So they had gone. Charlie had talked to Rosa, Whiskey had talked to Juliet, and Charlie and Whiskey had perfected the art of sitting together at a table and completely ignoring each other.

After Whiskey's accident, they had kept the dinners up, the three of them for a while, and sometimes Mike and the girls too.

The dinner at his mother's fell in the second week of what Charlie came to think of as his probation.

"Do you still want to go?" he asked Juliet that morning.

"There's no reason not to," Juliet said. "It would look funny if we didn't." She hesitated. "I'd rather you didn't tell your mum about the…situation though. Better to wait until we've made a decision," she said carefully.

When they arrived at dinner, Charlie's mother looked pleased with herself.

"I've got something for you," she said, giving Juliet a book-size parcel.

Juliet unwrapped it in the kitchen, with the two of them watching. It was the photo of Charlie in his first school uniform, in a wooden frame. She looked at it without speaking.

"Sorry it's taken me so long," Elaine said. "I meant to copy it months ago, after you first saw it, but then Whiskey had his accident..." She looked at Juliet uncertainly, waiting for her to say something. "It was the one you wanted, wasn't it?"

Juliet nodded. Charlie could see she was trying hard not to cry.

"Thank you," she said eventually, but her voice was barely audible. She smiled awkwardly, at no one in particular, and excused herself to go to the bathroom.

"What was all that about?"

Charlie swallowed. "I suppose she's thinking about Rosa," he said quickly, "and the photo you were going to copy for her."

"I know she feels for Rosa. But you two have still got each other. You should be happy about that."

Charlie tried to smile but found himself only capable of a grimace.

× × ×

Though Juliet had asked him not to tell his mother, she hadn't asked him not to talk about it with anyone else. Charlie told first Mike and then Marco about the incident with the flowers. There was a time when he would rather have died than share such a confidence. But if there was one thing Charlie had learned in the last year it was that there was nothing to be gained by hiding feelings, keeping secrets.

Mike told Charlie just to be himself, that Juliet would see all the changes he was making in his life, would know he had changed.

Marco said it was about more than just showing Juliet he had changed; he also had to prove he loved her, prove he had meant it when he said he wanted to marry her.

"But that's what the flowers were for," Charlie protested. "How can I prove it if I'm not allowed to *try too hard*?"

"Of course you have to try hard," Marco said. "You have to try harder than you've ever tried at anything before. But you have to do it without appearing to try at all. The art of fighting without fighting."

"But what does that mean?" Charlie asked. "What can I actually do?"

"You'll have to get creative. No more flowers, no candlelit dinners. You have to be cunning like a fox."

"I don't know how to do that," Charlie said desperately.

"Well, I don't know," Marco said. "Juliet's your girlfriend. You should know what pleases her. You'll think of something."

× × ×

At first Charlie couldn't think of anything much. He turned his socks the right way around before he threw them in the wash, made sure he emptied the kitchen trash *before* it was overflowing, fixed the broken door handle on the cupboard in the study. He had to resist the urge to cook every night and clean up as well. That wouldn't have been *normal*. Normal was that they took turns, and whoever cooked was spared the washing up. But Charlie went to extra trouble with the meals he made, tried some new recipes, cooked some of Juliet's favorites.

He remembered it was Mike's birthday and suggested they host a dinner for their mother, Audrey, Mike, and the girls. He enlarged and framed a photo of Holly and Chloe in their uniforms that he had taken on their first day at school so that when Juliet asked him if he had any ideas for a present, he could say he had already taken care of it.

He and Juliet ate at the restaurants they had always eaten at, saw movies, caught up with friends, took Chester for walks in Alma Park. They did the things they had always done, but they were going through the motions. They didn't laugh together. They didn't really talk. Juliet had closed herself against him, and he couldn't

find a way back in. It reminded Charlie of his own parents' relationship, and Charlie understood for the first time how his father
might have felt being married to his mother, always waiting for
the blow to fall.

Four weeks passed like this. The halfway mark came and went.
Charlie began to doubt the advice Mike and Marco had given him,
but he didn't know who else to ask. One afternoon, sitting alone
with Whiskey at the hospital, he tried to imagine what Whiskey
would do if he found himself in Charlie's position. He thought
about it for a long time, and eventually he hatched a plan.

Despite the bank's promises to the contrary, it took five business
days to get a loan approved, a week more to choose the ring, and
then another to have it made. By then there were only six days left
in Charlie and Juliet's agreement. The following Friday would be
exactly two months since the night of the play. But Charlie couldn't
wait another six days to know what Juliet wanted. The bomb was
ticking. It was do or die. He had to cut one of the wires, even if it
was the wrong one.

He arranged the deliveries for the Monday when he knew Juliet
would be home all day. The first flowers—poppies—were to be
delivered at nine o'clock with a note from Charlie saying just
I love you. The second flowers were arranged to arrive at ten—
ranunculus, with a card that said *I still love you*. At eleven, the courier was to deliver the parcels from David Jones—five vases of all
shapes and sizes, individually gift wrapped. At twelve, a barbershop
quartet would ring the doorbell and serenade Juliet with "Always
on My Mind" before presenting her with a bunch of daffodils.

At one, the yellow irises would arrive—*Did I mention that I love
you?*; at two, the oriental lilies—*I'm nothing without you*; at three,
the gladioli—*I know I'm trying too hard, but I can't help myself*; and at
four, the roses—*I meant it when I said I wanted to marry you*.

At five o'clock, Charlie arrived home from work. He was shaking
when he rang the doorbell. Juliet opened the door cautiously.

Charlie waited for her to say something, but she turned away and walked back toward the kitchen.

So this was how it ended. He and Juliet were finished, which meant that already, this was no longer his home, that he should wait to be invited before following her into the kitchen. Charlie stood inside the front door, turned the ring box over in his pocket, wondering what to do. He could walk out now, come back to collect his things, and say good-bye to Chester at a time when he knew she wouldn't be there. But as he considered this option, he heard Whiskey's voice in his head. *Don't be so gutless, Charlie. You can do better than that. You've been with Juliet for five years. If it has to end, end it properly.*

Charlie didn't know why, after all these years, he had suddenly started taking his brother's advice. He couldn't explain it. But he shut the door and went down the hallway into the kitchen. The flowers were in a bucket of water by the sink, the vases on the benchtop, all but one still in their gift wrapping. Juliet was standing in front of the window, already in tears. She took a clean tea towel out of a drawer and pressed it against her eyes.

"I wish you hadn't, Charlie," she began, gesturing toward the gifts.

She was right, of course. It was a ridiculous idea; he could see it now.

"I already told you I didn't want flowers. You can't change a relationship with flowers, Charlie, not with all the flowers in the world." She shook her head. "Surely you know me better than to think this would change my feelings. I don't understand it. I can't even begin to think of what would make you do something like this. It's like something Whiskey would do."

Charlie laughed, a short bitter laugh. "It's funny you should say that."

"What's funny about it?"

"It was Whiskey's idea, in a way."

Juliet looked at Charlie strangely. "What do you mean?"

Charlie hesitated. Probably it would sound crazy, but what did it matter now? The thing that mattered to him most was lost. There was nothing else to lose.

"I mean, I wondered what Whiskey would do if he was in my position. I sort of asked him."

"I don't understand. You talked to Whiskey?"

"Well, no, I didn't *talk* to him, of course, not in the normal sense of the word. I just sat and thought about it, and after a while it seemed like I could hear his voice in my head. He was saying, 'You've got to surprise her. Do something flamboyant, something over-the-top romantic, something she'd never expect from you.' It was like he was answering my question." Charlie shrugged, feeling embarrassed by how weak it sounded.

Juliet was staring at him. "You went to the hospital to have this conversation?"

"Well, yes. I mean, no. I didn't go there specifically to have this conversation, if you could even call it a conversation. I was just there, and this is what I was thinking about."

"What do you mean, you were *just there*?"

Charlie sighed. He didn't want to do this with Juliet, this archaeological excavation of all their problems, to dig up every last bone and brush it off, to arrange them into some kind of shape. "It doesn't matter," he said.

"It does matter, Charlie. Please."

"I don't know what you're asking exactly. What do you want to know?"

"I don't understand what made you go to the hospital and talk to Whiskey about this."

"I don't really understand it myself, to be honest, Juliet. In the past, I never would have taken Whiskey's advice, especially about relationships. But I'd run out of ideas. I'd asked Marco, I'd asked Mike..."

"You asked Mike?"

"I'm sorry. I know you didn't want other people to know about it. But I had to talk to someone."

"But why Mike of all people? You barely know him."

Charlie felt upset by this. He felt that in the past few weeks he was really beginning to know Mike.

"Is that what he feels?" Charlie asked Juliet. "That we barely know each other? Is that what he said to you?"

"Of course not. We've never discussed his relationship with you. He's too tactful for that."

"Then why would you say we barely know each other?"

"I'm stating the facts, Charlie. He came over here to meet you, and you didn't want anything to do with him."

"I know I was like that in the beginning. I'm not proud of it. You don't need to rub my face in it. I needed a bit of time to get used to it. Mike understands that. It's totally different now."

"How is it different, Charlie? Since when have things changed so much that you would choose to talk to him about our relationship?"

"Since the hospital, I suppose."

"What happened at the hospital?"

Charlie felt like he was on trial. He couldn't understand why Juliet was so fixated on the fact that he had talked to Mike about their relationship. In the overall scheme of things, he thought there were far worse things he had done. But maybe those things were too difficult to talk about. If this was the thing Juliet wanted to take issue with, perhaps it was her right to do so. Perhaps he deserved it.

"Nothing happened," he said. "We started talking, that's all."

"You went to the hospital and talked to Mike?"

"Yes, of course. Many times."

"Many times?"

"Well, you know, two or three times a week."

"I don't understand, Charlie. You're telling me you go to the hospital two or three times a week and talk to Mike?"

Charlie shrugged. "Sometimes I talk to Mike, sometimes to Rosa. Sometimes it's just me and Whiskey."

"But what are you doing there?"

"What am I doing there? I don't know. Sitting and thinking mostly."

"But you go there to see Whiskey?"

"Who else would I go there to see? What are you getting at?"

"I didn't know," Juliet said quietly.

"Didn't know what?"

"I didn't know you'd been going to see Whiskey at the hospital."

"You didn't know?"

She shook her head.

"What do you think I do all day when I'm not working?"

"I didn't know."

"Why didn't you ask me?"

"Why didn't you tell me?" she said defensively.

"I assumed you knew, I guess. I thought maybe Mike or Rosa would have said something."

"So how long has this been going on?"

"A couple of months, I guess. Since I finished at Sierra. What difference does it make?"

"What do you mean, what difference does it make?"

"I'd rather just get this over with, Juliet. I don't want to argue with you. This stuff has got nothing to do with us."

"I can't believe you're saying that, Charlie. It's got everything to do with us. Ever since I met you, you've had these issues with Whiskey, and you've never wanted to deal with them or even talk about them. You just turned away and tried to pretend he didn't exist. That's the way you respond to every problem, in all your relationships. There's some part of you that switches off when things get difficult. And I didn't think you could change, Charlie, I thought you'd gotten too set in your ways. To me, it seems like your relationship with Whiskey is at the heart of it. If you can fix that, maybe we can fix things between us too."

"I wouldn't say I've fixed it, Juliet," Charlie said. "Whiskey's still in a coma. Going to visit him a few times doesn't exactly wipe the slate clean. It probably won't make any difference."

"Don't think like that, Charlie," Juliet said. She moved closer to him. "The fact that you'd go to see Whiskey willingly, the fact that you'd talk to him, ask his advice, I think it makes a world of difference. Even if you don't believe Whiskey knows—and I like to believe he does—don't you think it makes a difference to Rosa that you would make that effort, to your mother? It makes a difference to me."

"How, though?"

"Because it says to me that you're willing to change, that you've already changed. It gives me hope that we could work things out, if you wanted."

Charlie had thought it was over, and that thought had dried up all the hope in him. It felt painful to have Juliet standing so close to him and to think that he might never touch her again. He moved away from her. "It feels too late," he said.

Juliet moved closer. She took his hand. "If it's not too late for you and Whiskey, it's not too late for us either. Don't you think we could give it another go?"

Charlie shook his head. "I've been walking on eggshells for two months. I can't live like this anymore. All this wait and see, with Whiskey and now with you. I can't do it."

Juliet started to cry again, pressed the tea towel into her face until she'd composed herself. "I know these last few weeks must have been unbearable for you. I've been so unforgiving. I said I'd give us a chance, but I wasn't really. I'm sorry for that, Charlie, I really am. But I feel different now. I don't want us to end. I don't know what I'd do without you, Charlie."

It would be Charlie, not Juliet, who would really be lost if they ended. Beautiful Juliet. She wouldn't need to worry. She would have suitors queuing up around the block. She would meet someone handsome and charming, infinitely easier to deal with than Charlie, someone without any comatose or long-lost siblings, someone who could really love her as she deserved to be loved.

"You'd be better off without me, Jules. You'd meet someone else."

Juliet pressed his hand. "I don't want anyone else. I want us."

"Do you really think it can work, after everything that's happened?"

She nodded.

Charlie couldn't believe it. He pulled Juliet into him and held her and held her and held her. He didn't understand it, he couldn't think of what he had done to deserve it, but somehow he had been given another chance—one last chance to make things right.

And maybe, just maybe, he would get it right this time.

* * *

It is a few days before Charlie feels capable of facing Thomas again. In those days, the implications of Whiskey's situation, which have for a long time seemed extraordinarily complicated, come to seem quite simple, for Charlie at least. The best-case scenario means Charlie has to face up to the part he has played in the breakdown of his relationship with Whiskey, and work to change it. In the worst-case scenario—the one in which Whiskey dies—Charlie still has to face up to the part he's played, but in that scenario, there is no opportunity to make amends.

It's common when someone dies, Thomas tells him, for people to have misgivings about things they did or didn't do while that person was alive. Even people who had mostly harmonious relationships with the deceased can feel guilt or regret, sometimes for things that happened years earlier, things that have long since been forgiven and forgotten. Those who are religiously inclined might share these regrets with a priest—speaking them aloud brings relief, and the priest can offer absolution.

"What if you don't believe in confession?" Charlie asks.

"Those who don't believe in confession—in the strictly religious sense—often unconsciously find someone else to confess to, usually the person they perceive as being closest to the person who has died. In your case, this would be..."

"Rosa," Charlie says without even needing to think about it.

"Subconsciously, you might think Rosa can offer absolution on behalf of Whiskey. But she can't. By confessing to Rosa, you'd be giving yourself the relief of speaking these things aloud. But at the same time, you'd be passing the burden on to Rosa."

"Then who should I confess to?"

Thomas doesn't answer this question.

"I have to say whatever I need to now, while Whiskey's still alive," Charlie says eventually.

"It would be better, don't you think?"

"What if he can't hear me?"

"As you know, there's a lot of evidence to suggest that people in comas can hear. In Whiskey's case, we may never know. But try thinking of it like this: What if he *can* hear you and you don't say it?"

"So if he can hear me and he wakes up…"

"Then you'll have a head start with sorting things out."

"And if he wakes up but he hasn't heard me?"

"Then you've had a practice run."

"The glass is always half-full with you, isn't it?" Charlie says.

"I don't think miserable bastards are in high demand as counselors," Thomas says mildly. "So when do you think you might talk to Whiskey?" he asks.

"I suppose it doesn't matter exactly when. As long as I do it before…before it's too late."

"I'm sure you've considered this," Thomas says after a pause, "but you might not get any advance warning."

"You mean it might happen suddenly?"

Thomas nods.

"I just want to wait until…I feel more ready."

"Do you think you'll ever be truly ready?"

"Probably not."

"I've got a theory," Thomas says, "that there are some things in life we never feel ready for, that it's only by doing them that we become ready."

VICTOR

After Whiskey's accident, a social worker at the hospital had told Rosa, Charlie, Mike, and their mother about Coma Support. Charlie remembered it, because it was Boxing Day, though it was not like any other Boxing Day he had known. When Whiskey had been in a coma for four weeks, the social worker had told them then, there was only a small possibility of him making a full recovery. Coma Support was a charitable organization where they could receive counseling from qualified therapists and meet the family members of other coma victims who might be facing similar challenges. At that stage, Charlie had not been interested in counseling. He had no desire whatsoever to share his feelings about Whiskey with a complete stranger or, worse still, a room full of strangers. Back then, Charlie had wanted to know what was meant by a *small possibility*. He had wanted to understand what constituted a *full recovery*, what a *partial recovery* entailed.

After he was given the answers to these questions, he had wished he hadn't asked. It would have been easier to get through those weeks and months since then without the knowledge that Whiskey's chance of a complete recovery was 15 percent, that there was, therefore, an 85 percent chance the coma would affect his physical, mental, or behavioral functioning, that he might have problems with understanding or communicating, that his social or emotional skills might be impaired, that he might suffer from depression or anxiety or have difficulty maintaining personal relationships. Hearing this, Charlie had begun to understand just how much he was asking. Because he had wanted so much more than just for Whiskey to wake up. He had wanted him to defy all the statistics, to wake up and still be Whiskey. And after only four weeks, the chance of that had already been so very, very small it had seemed almost impossible to bear.

× × ×

Charlie's mother was the only one who had taken advantage of the services offered at Coma Support. She had made a decision that she did not want to attend the group sessions, she told Charlie, once she understood that she would come into contact with people there whose family members had never recovered from comas or those whose loved ones had emerged as different people. Charlie did not need his mother to explain that, in the beginning, she was not yet ready to accept either of these possibilities for Whiskey. She had opted instead for weekly one-on-one counseling with a psychologist named Victor.

Victor had recommended books for her to read, one of which she had passed on to Charlie, titled *Living with Coma: The Cycle of Hope and Despair*. Charlie hadn't even opened the book. Just reading the title felt overwhelming to him. Once he had come home from work to find Juliet reading it, making notes in her pointy handwriting on a scrap of paper. Later, he had found the page down the side of the couch when he was looking for the remote control. *Family members and friends may wish to make amends for perceived misdeeds and suffer because they are unable to*, she had written. Charlie screwed the paper up and threw it away.

After six months, Charlie's mother had told him she had started attending the group sessions at Coma Support. Once or twice, she had asked Charlie to go with her, but he had said he was seeing Thomas, and she had not pressed him. Now eight months had passed, and she made a special request, not only of Charlie, but of

Juliet and Mike as well, that they come with her to speak to Victor. Since they all accepted that there always had to be someone with Whiskey at the hospital, even now that the chance of a change in his condition was remote, it was understood that Rosa would not come to meet Victor. But Charlie's mother said, for all of them, Victor had something to say that they all needed to hear.

× × ×

Charlie and Juliet picked up Mike on the way. They were all silent in the car. Charlie tried to imagine what pearls of wisdom awaited them, what sage advice of Victor's seemed so valuable that their mother wanted them all to hear it. He was dubious that a person who had never been in their position could have anything enlightening to say about it. Juliet said if it was important to their mother, they should go.

The address Charlie's mother had given him was that of a grand old house in Camberwell, set back from the road, with a driveway bordered by dense rhododendron bushes. They climbed the stairs, followed the signs for Coma Support down a long, narrow hallway. His mother was already there, sitting with a man who could only be Victor, in a room with molded plastic chairs and a sign on the door saying *Group Therapy*. When Charlie's mother introduced them, Victor made a point of shaking hands with each of them before ushering them into chairs. Charlie sat opposite the window, with a view of the driveway, the rhododendrons. He noticed a book on the coffee table in the center of the circle of chairs: *Clutching at Straws: The Tyranny of Hope in the Face of Terminal Illness.*

Victor had the bland, unassuming manner Charlie expected of a counselor. Physically, he made no impression at all: neither tall nor short, without glasses, a beard, or any other distinguishing features. Later, Charlie would not be able to recall the color of his eyes or hair, the clothes he was wearing. There was nothing about him that made him stand out from any other middle-aged man, except for a shuffling, pigeon-toed walk Charlie noticed when Victor got up to shut the window. When he began to speak, he had, not quite a stutter, but a way of nibbling the edges off his words before he managed to spit them out that gave his speech a sense of hesitation.

It was this apparent lack of confidence in his own words that made Victor's point—when he finally arrived at it—all the more shocking and unexpected. He began, predictably enough, by discussing the emotional states a family member of a coma victim could expect to experience. He spoke of anger and denial, depression and guilt, the confusion that hope could bring to the equation. He quoted Emily Dickinson—*Hope is the thing with feathers that perches in the soul*—a line from a poem Charlie recognized from his studies in American literature. Victor did not acknowledge the quote, Charlie noticed, probably hoping to pass it off as his own.

Charlie thought about his hopes for Whiskey, the hopes Rosa, his mother, and Mike had shared with him. In the beginning, they had all hoped for the same thing: that Whiskey would wake from his coma in hours or days, completely unscathed save for the physical wounds from his accident. As the months passed and the likelihood of Whiskey making a perfect comeback became ever slimmer, they had hoped variously that any damage sustained might be physical rather than mental, that his fine motor skills might be impaired, but not his sense of humor, that though he might be confined to a wheelchair, he would still be able to do the work he loved. Or, they had hoped if his memory was damaged—if, for example, he could not make new memories—that he would be able to retrieve the memories he had already stored in his mind, that at the very least, Whiskey would remember who they were, what they meant to him. Charlie was the only one who did not hope for this last thing, though he never said so, not even to Juliet. Sometimes, Charlie hoped for the opposite, that Whiskey would wake with no memories of Charlie at all, not a single recollection of their messy, tangled history. He would be told Charlie was his identical twin brother, and looking at old photos, he would accept that it was true. Then Charlie would create a new history for the two of them, manufacture new memories in which, prior to Whiskey's accident, indeed throughout their lives, they had been the best of friends.

Charlie understood what Victor meant when he spoke of hope being tied to unrealistic expectations and unfounded beliefs. But he began to feel uncomfortable when Victor said that while they probably thought of it as what was sustaining them, it was actually holding them back, preventing them from apprehending and accepting the reality of Whiskey's situation. And then he said the words that snatched the air out of Charlie's lungs.

"The best thing you can do for William now, and indeed for yourselves, is to let go of your hope, to grant William his freedom. That's why your mother wanted you to come here today. So we can begin to talk about the possibility of turning off William's life support."

Charlie looked at his mother in disbelief, waiting for her to cry out against Victor's words. But she did not. She sat perfectly still, her eyes on Victor's face, avoiding Charlie's eyes.

"I realize this may come as a surprise to you at first," Victor said, each of the words getting caught in his teeth before being dislodged. "But I think once you get over the shock, you'll see, as Elaine has come to see, that this would be an act of mercy and the best possible decision you could make, both for your own sakes, and for William's."

"What about Rosa?" Juliet asked. "Surely this would be Rosa's decision, if it was anyone's?"

"In a legal sense, you're absolutely right. But this is a decision too great for one person to take responsibility for, a burden that can be lightened by being shared. If you can be united about this as a family, you can work together to help Rosa make the decision that's best for William."

"But Rosa's a Catholic," Juliet persisted. "She would never agree to this—it wouldn't matter what we said."

"Juliet's right," Mike said. "Rosa believes this is in God's hands."

"Let's not worry about Rosa right now," Victor said. "It would be more helpful to work through your own emotions at this stage. Once you've reached some clarity in your own feelings, you'll be in a better position to think about how to approach Rosa."

There was a stunned silence. Victor took the opportunity to suggest that they might start by thinking about how they wanted to say good-bye, what, if anything, they wanted to say before they *let William go*. He said it might help to start talking about his funeral, about what sort of ceremony might be a fitting way to honor his life and death, about what he might have wanted; that they might even start thinking about what they would say at the funeral—if they wanted to speak—how best to describe the person they had known and loved.

Charlie looked at Mike, who seemed to be bracing himself against Victor's words, pushing against the floor, against the back of his chair, his face red with the exertion. Charlie did not need to look at Juliet to know she was crying. He wanted to reach out for her, to touch her, to hold on to something he could trust in, but he found he could not move, that his blood had turned to lead.

It was Juliet who broke the spell. "I don't think we should even be talking about this. I'm sure it's not what Rosa would want."

"It's very thoughtful of you to say that, Juliet," Victor said obse-quiously. "And I know you mean well. But Rosa is in no position, emotionally speaking, to make this decision."

"With all due respect," Mike said, "you've never even met Rosa. What do you think gives you the right to make a judgment about her emotional state, her ability to make a decision like this?"

In the eight months Charlie had known Mike, he had never heard him raise his voice. Seeing him on the verge of losing his temper, defending the wife of a brother he had never met, Charlie felt a rush of love for him that roused him from his stupor.

"I can't believe you brought us here to listen to this," he said to his mother.

"I know it's a shock," she said. "When Victor first suggested it to me, I felt exactly the same as you do now."

"You can't have felt the way I do," Charlie flared, "or you wouldn't have come back. You certainly wouldn't have invited the rest of us here to rope us into your sick plans."

"Let's all try to calm down," Victor said. "It's natural that you feel upset right now, Charlie, but it won't help to get angry. Your mother's told me a great deal about your relationship with William. I can understand that you feel you've got a lot to lose by turning off William's life support—the chance to make amends, to heal the rift. Try to think beyond what's best for you to what's best for William. Turning off the machines is the most wonderful gift you can give your brother now, the kindest act—a way of forgiving and being forgiven that will bring peace to you as much as to him."

Charlie rose abruptly from his chair and turned on Victor. "How dare you!" he bellowed. "How dare you presume to tell us what we should feel, what we should do, what's best for us!" He kicked at the legs of the chair, sent it dancing back against the wall. "You don't know us, you don't know Rosa, and you certainly don't know Whiskey. You call this support, do you? Persuading your clients to kill off the people they love? What's in it for you? Some kind of kickback for saving insurance companies' money? A commission for every machine you switch off? What you're saying is bullshit. It's total fucking bullshit."

Juliet stood up, put her hand on Charlie's shoulder. She looked at Mike. He stood up.

"It's too much," Mike said. "I'm sorry, Elaine." He didn't call her Mum because, as he had told Charlie, he still thought of the woman he had buried in Canada as his mother. Charlie could not even bring himself to look at her as he left the room.

× × ×

Charlie's mother called that night, the next day, and the day after, but Charlie would not speak to her. He spoke to Mike every day—learned she had been calling Mike too. And though, like Charlie, Mike had at first not wanted to hear her justify what Victor had said, eventually he had given in. Charlie wondered if Mike felt he had more to lose by shutting Elaine out, if the suggestion Victor had made was less abhorrent to him because he didn't know Whiskey, or if perhaps he was just a more forgiving person, more inclined to give someone a chance to explain themselves. Whatever the reason, Mike had agreed to meet Elaine, to hear her feelings, and somehow, in the process, he had come to see her point of view.

"Whatever Mum said to you, I don't want to know," Charlie said to Mike when they met.

"I'm not going to fight with you over this, Charlie," Mike said. "Whatever you decide, I'll stand by you. Because even though, by blood, Whiskey's my brother, I'll never have the same bond with him, the same claim to him that you have. I know it's not my decision to make. And I'm not going to try to persuade you. It's just that some of the things your mother said made sense to me, and I thought if you had a chance to think it over, it might make sense to you too."

"Killing my own brother could never make sense to me."

"That's how I thought of it at first," Mike said, "that we would be killing him. Hearing what Victor had to say made me sick to my stomach. But after I talked to your mother, I saw it differently. I saw that in a way, doing what Victor suggested would be the opposite of killing him. We would be saving him."

"How do you get to that?"

"Everything I've heard about Whiskey makes me think he was a person who ran at life full tilt, that he met whatever came to him head-on, squeezed the juice out of it. Now he's been lying in a hospital bed for months on end without moving or speaking or even breathing for himself, and I don't even know him, but I can't help feeling that's what would be killing him."

"Is that what my mother thinks?"

Mike nodded. "She said that in the beginning she didn't even want to entertain the idea of letting Whiskey go. But she couldn't stop herself from thinking about what Victor had said, and after she got over her anger, she came to see the truth in Victor's words. That being kept alive by machines couldn't possibly be what Whiskey would want, what he would choose, if he was able to choose. She said that eventually she had to admit to herself that it was only for herself that she wanted to keep him alive."

For a long time after Mike had finished speaking, neither he nor Charlie moved. It got dark outside, but Charlie made no attempt to get up and turn on the lamp. He felt glad of the darkness, the silence.

What Charlie's sessions with Thomas had helped him to understand was that in between the best- and worst-case scenarios was a realm in which virtually anything was possible. Because Whiskey's injuries were not limited to one area of his brain, it was almost impossible for the doctors to predict how the damage might affect him. To satisfy Charlie's need to know, Thomas had given him a list of some of the most common problems resulting from brain injury and extended coma states. The list ranged from physical impairments, such as loss of muscle coordination, to problems with thinking skills, communication, and social skills.

Charlie had considered each item on Thomas's list in terms of how it would affect Whiskey's ability to resume the life he'd had before his accident. Beginning with the physical impairments, Charlie thought it seemed reasonably likely that Whiskey might never surf or snowboard again. At a more basic level, it was possible he might not be able to drive the car he had loved, that he may not even be able to walk. Those thoughts alone seemed terrible to Charlie. But Thomas had explained that the cognitive, behavioral, and personality defects were often more disabling than any residual physical defects.

Charlie had attempted to picture Whiskey leading a life in which he could no longer do the work that had been so central to who he was, in which a loss of emotional control alienated his many friends. Thomas had told Charlie about the *difficult stranger* syndrome, in which the person you knew and loved seemed to have been replaced by a person you did not know and found difficult to love. Charlie had tried to imagine Whiskey suffering from depression, lethargy, anxiety, his unpredictable moods and erratic behavior gradually eroding his intimacy with Rosa, with everyone who loved him.

When he gave Charlie the list, Thomas had cautioned him to remember that Whiskey would almost certainly not be affected by everything listed and that some of the problems may be only mildly disabling. But Charlie had found it impossible to retain this perspective. Once he had allowed himself to imagine it, he could not rid himself of this picture in which Whiskey could do none of the things he loved. Worse, Charlie could not shake the thought that the only way to make amends for his mistakes in the past was to stick by Whiskey in his new life, long after everyone else had given up on him; that eventually, Charlie alone would carry the burden of the life of isolation and frustration Whiskey was condemned to lead.

What scared Charlie the most about what had happened at Coma Support was that there was some part of him that responded to what Victor had suggested. For a long time—perhaps too long—Charlie had allowed himself to hope that Whiskey would return to them intact, that he would be one of those miracle cases of late-night made-for-TV movies—*based on a true story*—a case that went against all the predictions of medical science, defied all the statistics. After all, Charlie had reasoned, wouldn't it be just like Whiskey to prove everybody wrong? Hadn't their grandmother always said Whiskey was born under a lucky sign, that someone was looking out for him, that he had nine lives like a cat?

Even now, despite everything he had learned about coma

recovery, there were still days when Charlie entertained these hopes, convinced himself that it was possible. But as Whiskey's coma wore on, those days came less and less often. In time, Charlie's vain hopes had been replaced by a new hope, a different kind of hope entirely, one Charlie could not share with anyone, did not even want to admit to himself. Though he knew it was cowardly, though he despised himself for it, the time had come when Charlie had begun to hope Whiskey would not wake, that he would simply fade away from them so they could preserve the memories of the person he had been. The real reason Charlie hadn't talked to his mother was because he was terrified of how little it would take to persuade him that letting Whiskey go was for the best.

"Do you think Mum's right?" he asked Mike after what seemed like hours.

Mike thought for a long time before he answered Charlie. "I want to know my brother, the person I came here to meet. But maybe that person, the person you know as Whiskey, is already gone. And maybe it's only my own selfishness that wants to keep him hanging on by a thread, day after day. I don't know what Whiskey would want. All I know is that if it were me, I would rather be dead than live like that."

Lately, when Charlie sat beside Whiskey's hospital bed, he could hardly remember the contempt he had felt for his brother for so long. What he remembered was a feeling twenty years older, a feeling he'd had before he was old enough to have feelings. It was the feeling of Whiskey being his best friend, the person he loved more than anyone else in the world.

Charlie tried to stand up but found himself on the floor, kneeling on all fours. "I know you're right," he tried to say to Mike, but he couldn't get the words out. He beat the carpet with his fist. "I want him to live!" he screamed. "I want him to live!"

Mike pulled Charlie up off the floor, put his arms around him, and they stood, two men who had been strangers for most of their lives, brothers now, holding each other until their sobbing subsided.

× × ×

It was Marco's idea to ask Thomas to mediate between Charlie and his mother. "You went to see her counselor," Marco said. "Surely it's not unreasonable to ask her to come to yours."

"I can do it, of course," Thomas said. "But I'd like to make sure we're on the same page with regard to what *mediation* means."

"I know what mediation means," Charlie said, insulted.

"I know you know, in theory. But I want to make it absolutely plain that I won't be going to bat for you. I'm not going to take sides. I'll be there to assist you and your mother in coming to a resolution you both feel comfortable with. My role is to help both of you talk and listen so you can understand each other's position."

"I already know her position. That asshole Victor made it perfectly clear."

"I know you're angry with your mother," Thomas said evenly, "and I certainly don't think she and Victor approached things the best way. But try not to think of her as the enemy. This is not a matter of wrong and right. Your mother's struggling to weigh up what's best for Whiskey, what's best for the whole family, as you are. It would be better for everyone concerned, yourself included, if you would at least listen to what she has to say."

"I don't want to hear it."

"Don't you think she has a right to explain?"

"No."

Thomas was quiet for a moment. "Is your mind totally made up about not switching off the life support?" he asked eventually.

Charlie nodded.

"Well then, where is the harm in letting your mother tell you the reasons behind her thinking?"

"I'm not going to reconsider."

"I'm not asking you to reconsider. But you and your mother—and Rosa too, of course—need to come to a decision about Whiskey that you can all feel at peace with. In order to do that, you're going to need to talk to your mother and to listen to what she has to say."

"Switching off Whiskey's life support is not an option," Charlie repeated.

"All right," Thomas said patiently. "Let's try looking at this from a different angle. Can you tell me the reasons why you're not prepared to do what Victor suggested?"

"Because I want my brother to live!"

"I understand that, Charlie. And I'm sure that at some level that's what your mother wants too. But there's a very strong ethical argument that it's better for a person to die with comfort and dignity than to be kept alive with no quality of life."

"Do you think I don't know that?" Charlie said, barely controlling his anger.

"So when you say you want Whiskey to live, do you mean regardless of the quality of his life?"

"Of course I don't mean that. You're twisting my words."

"I'm just trying to understand. How do you feel about the quality of his life right now?"

Charlie stood up. "He's in a coma, for fuck's sake. He's got no quality of life. You know that as well as I do. What are you getting at?"

"Take it easy, Charlie," Thomas said calmly. "I'm trying to help you get some clarity about the reasons behind your decision so that when you come to talk this over with your mother, you can help her to see it from your point of view."

Charlie sat back down.

Thomas waited a moment or two, and then he continued. "When you say you want Whiskey to live, you need to be clear about what you mean by *living*, what kind of quality of life would be the minimum you could accept for Whiskey."

Charlie nodded, and Thomas went on.

"Have you thought, for example, how much longer you would be prepared for Whiskey to remain in a coma with no change in his condition?"

"If I thought he was going to stay in a coma, then I would say my mum was right, that we should switch off the machines," Charlie said, calmer now.

"But you don't think he's going to remain in a coma?"

Charlie shook his head.

"What makes you think that?"

Charlie shrugged. "It's a feeling I have."

"What do you mean? Like a hunch?"

"No, not a hunch."

"Is it something one of the medical team said?"

"No."

"What then?"

"I can't explain it to you."

"Why?"

Charlie stood up again, went to the window. "It sounds stupid," he said quietly.

"Try me," Thomas said, his patience seemingly endless.

Charlie kept his back to Thomas. "You know that thing they say about identical twins?" he said after a long silence.

"What thing?"

"About them being telepathic."

"Yes, I've heard that. Do you feel you and Whiskey have something like that?"

Charlie turned abruptly and sat back down. "No," he said. "It's bullshit. Forget I mentioned it."

They sat in silence for a while.

"Did you and Whiskey ever have a special way of communicating—when you were closer, when you were kids?"

"Not unless you count walkie-talkies."

"Walkie-talkies?"

"Our aunt bought us some. A long time ago. But we just played games with them. We've never had a special way of communicating."

"What kind of games did you play?"

"The kind of games any nine-year-olds play," Charlie said. "Cops and robbers, that sort of thing."

"Were you close then?"

Charlie nodded slowly. "Inseparable."

Thomas was quiet for a moment. "What did you say to each other, with the walkie-talkies?" he asked after a while.

"I don't remember," Charlie said. He had a pain in his chest. No, not a pain: an ache.

"Can you try to remember something? Anything."

"We used to use the phonetic alphabet."

"What's that?" Thomas asked.

"You know, *Alpha, Bravo, Charlie*. They use it over two-way radio systems, to spell out words."

"Oh yes, I've heard of that. *Foxtrot. Tango*. Aren't they in there?"

"That's right."

"How did you come to use that?"

"This friend of my dad's taught us. An American guy, used to be in the air force. We were obsessed by the alphabet. That's how Whiskey got his name."

"What do you mean?"

"Well, *Charlie*, that's the word for the letter *C*. So my name was already in the alphabet. But William—that's his real name—he wanted an alphabet name too. The word for *W* was *Whiskey*. So that's what I started calling him."

"And he still goes by that name now."

Charlie nodded.

"Does everyone call him that?"

"Pretty much. Apart from my mum."

"So for more than twenty years, he's called himself by the nickname you gave him. That must feel special for you."

Charlie shrugged. "I think he just thought it was a cool-sounding name."

"I'd say there's a bit more to it than that."

"So what about this mediation then?" Charlie asked after a pause.

"To be perfectly honest, Charlie, if you can't articulate your reasons for your own decision, and you're not willing to listen to your mother, I don't think there's much point in having a mediation."

"I know how it must sound," Charlie said. "But would you do it for me anyway?"

"Of course I'll do it," he said.

× × ×

The mediation meeting lasted less than ten minutes.

"Do you know how they do it?" Charlie asked his mother as soon as the introductions had been made.

"Victor says…" she began, and then she corrected herself. "I've been told it's very humane, that William won't feel any pain." She looked at Thomas for confirmation.

"That's right," he said. "They'll give him morphine—he won't feel a thing."

"They take out the feeding tubes," Charlie said, as if Thomas hadn't even spoken. "They'll take out the tubes, and he'll die of starvation and dehydration."

Charlie's mother paled. "Is that true?" she asked Thomas.

Thomas nodded.

Elaine pressed her hands against her eyes. Charlie could see her shaking. "It's too much to put this decision in our hands," she said, not to Charlie but to Thomas. "It's impossible to know what's right. It's too much," she repeated.

"I know it must be very difficult for you, Mrs. Ferns. It might help you to hear how Charlie feels about it."

"Yes," she said, gathering herself. "That's what I came to hear." She looked at Charlie.

Charlie stood up and went to the window, his back to Thomas and his mother.

"Charlie," Thomas prompted after a while.

"I had a dream," Charlie said suddenly. "Whiskey was calling out to me."

"What did he say?" Charlie's mother asked, her voice so small Charlie could barely hear her.

"Just my name," Charlie said. "He called out my name. Everyone was there, but no one else could hear him. He was out of sight, like in a cave or something. But I could hear his voice. I knew it was him."

"When did you dream this?"

"Last night," Charlie said. "The night before. The night before that…"

Charlie heard his mother stand up. "You have it every night?" she whispered.

Charlie nodded.

"When did it start?" Thomas asked.

"The day we came to Victor." Charlie turned around.

"Poor William," his mother said in that tiny voice, and Charlie could see she was still shaking. She took a step toward him. "Poor William," she said again, and then she swayed a little and fell forward just as Charlie moved toward her. Though Thomas was already out of his chair, it was Charlie who caught her. He took her weight and held on to her, and as they stood there together, she said, "You're right, Charlie. We can't turn the machines off. We've got to hold on to him. We've got to hold on."

WHISKEY

A couple of days after the mediation with his mother, Thomas phoned Charlie and asked if they could meet again.

"I didn't want to say this before the issue of Whiskey's life support had been resolved," Thomas said carefully, "but I've thought a lot about your meeting with Victor, and although I think his approach was flawed, to say the least, I think one of his suggestions perhaps had some merit."

"I doubt that very much," Charlie said.

"Hear me out, Charlie," Thomas persisted. "We've talked very little about the possibility of Whiskey dying, but we both know the statistics. Even if you choose to keep Whiskey on life support for the time being, there's still a possibility that his condition may deteriorate. I think Victor's recommendation that you start thinking about the funeral is a good one. It will be painful for you, but thinking about the funeral is a way of practicing acceptance, of allowing the possibility that this is something you may have to accept eventually. It's a good place to begin."

"I'm not ready for that."

"It doesn't have to be all at once. Is there one small thing you could consider, something you might like to say about Whiskey, for instance?"

"I suppose I could give it a try," Charlie said.

× × ×

Charlie was fairly certain that if the worst did happen, neither Rosa nor his mother would be fit to speak at Whiskey's funeral. Mike too was out of the running. Charlie knew what Mike would say if he asked, that he hadn't actually met Whiskey, that he was completely unqualified to speak about him, that most of Whiskey's friends did not even know who Mike was, and it was too complicated to explain. There was a reasonable chance Bill would not return from England, and Charlie knew that even if he did come, he could not be relied upon to make a speech. Therefore, it would fall to Charlie to speak about Whiskey on behalf of the family, to convey something meaningful about his life, to give those who came to acknowledge his life and death something to take away, something humorous, something poignant, something comforting. Here was Charlie's punishment for failing to make things right with Whiskey: known to most of Whiskey's friends and acquaintances as the brother Whiskey didn't get along with, it was nevertheless he who was left with the painful, impossible task of summing up Whiskey's life.

Charlie did not feel up to it. The very first night he allowed himself to imagine the funeral he had a terrible nightmare. In the dream, the funeral was taking place in the church in the village in which they had grown up. The organist was ready, the choir standing behind Charlie in their blue robes. Whiskey was in an open casket, wearing a light brown suit with a blue shirt and a yellow silk tie embroidered with a map of South America. The church was full in a way Charlie had never seen it, every pew crammed with people. There were friends from grade school, still only eight or nine years old, high school friends and teachers, advertising colleagues. Some of the mourners were dressed for the funeral, the women in dark dresses and coats, the men in somber suits and ties. Many of their school friends were wearing their school uniforms—shorts and short-sleeved shirts—despite the cold in the church. One pew was filled with Whiskey's model ex-girlfriends, dressed as if for the

Spring Racing Carnival in frilly outfits and silly hats with feathers and flowers.

From where he stood, Charlie could see everyone. He was standing, not at the lectern, where members of the congregation usually stood to give readings, but in the pulpit, where only the priest ever stood. Looking down at the sea of faces made him dizzy, so he focused on his notes, began to read the words he had written to honor Whiskey's life.

Almost as soon as he began to speak, he heard a murmuring in the church. The mourners began to shift uncomfortably on the hard, wooden seats, to lean toward the people sitting beside them and whisper under their breath. Charlie tried to ignore the muttering, but as he continued to read, it grew more insistent. Distracted, he lost his place in his notes, and in that pause, he distinctly heard a voice say, "He doesn't even know Whiskey!" In the silence that followed this comment, someone else interjected, "They never got along."

"He's been jealous of Whiskey all his life," a third voice said. Then everyone started speaking at once, defending Whiskey, accusing Charlie, calling him a traitor, a fraud.

Charlie woke up sweating and shaking.

"What's wrong?" Juliet asked, putting her hand on his arm, drawing him out of the church, back into their bedroom. "Was it a nightmare?" she asked, switching on the lamp.

Charlie nodded.

"What happened?"

He closed his eyes, saw the congregation again before him. "I can't remember," he lied. "It's gone already."

"That's good," she said, switching off the lamp, curling around him. "Just a bad dream," she said, already nearly asleep again.

Charlie wished it were true.

× × ×

"I don't know what to say about him," Charlie confided to Marco when they met up at the pub that weekend. "How would you describe him, if you had to say something?"

"I'm sure my perspective wouldn't be of much interest to anyone. I don't know a tenth of what you know about him."

"I need some help here," Charlie said.

"Well, most of what I know about Whiskey comes from you anyway," Marco said. "Apart from when we were in high school, when I was a bit scared of him, if I'm honest. He was on to me, long before anyone else was—used to make snide comments about me being gay. I lived in terror of being exposed then, and I think he knew that, and it gave him a kind of power over me. For what it's worth, my impression is that he was full of shit when he was younger, but he seemed to get over all that in the last few years, especially after he met Rosa. He seemed to be a lucky scoundrel though. It seemed like everything fell into his lap. Until this, of course."

Charlie thought about what Marco had said. "Do you really think he was lucky?"

Marco shrugged. "Who knows? Probably not. I hardly knew him really. Why?"

"I don't know," Charlie said. It was what he'd always told himself, that Whiskey had never had to try as hard. But since the accident, he'd started to wonder if it was just an excuse he'd made because Whiskey was more successful. Whiskey had gotten his first job as a copywriter when he was twenty. While Charlie was still messing around at college, repeating courses he could easily have passed the first time, Whiskey was already being headhunted by a better advertising agency.

"I always told myself he was lucky," Charlie said. "But maybe he was just more talented than I was."

"Maybe he just knew what he wanted."

"But he knew how to get it too. Perhaps that was part of his talent. It couldn't have all been luck, could it?"

"I'm not sure what you're asking me, Charlie."

Charlie sighed. "I'm not sure myself. I've been so jealous of him."

"It's been a long time since you've had reason to be jealous of Whiskey."

Charlie shrugged. "Some habits are hard to break."

It was only now that Whiskey was in a situation no one could envy, now that just by being able to breathe and eat and talk for himself, Charlie had everything Whiskey could ever really want, that Charlie could see things clearly.

"I've been so wrong about him, Marco. I've been jealous of him for so long, I don't have any idea who he really was."

"Don't doubt yourself so much," Marco said. "Go back to the beginning. You know who he was."

× × ×

Charlie thought no one would know the beginning as well as his mother. So he asked her, to try to help him remember.

"It was a shock having twins," she said, filling up the kettle. "One newborn baby is hard enough, but two!" She rolled her eyes. "Your dad was pretty much useless, as you'd expect, although in that day and age, he was no exception to the rule. Went and played rugby a couple of hours after you were born. The midwife was disgusted."

Charlie's mother gave him his cup of tea, sat at the kitchen table opposite him with her own. Charlie couldn't count the number of times they had sat like that, talking, but he didn't know if he had ever heard this story before.

"You didn't look identical to begin with," she said, pushing the biscuit tin across the table. "William was completely bald, and you had a great mop of hair like a toupee. Lots of people bought you matching outfits, but I never dressed you the same. I had this notion that I wanted you to form your own identities. Still, once you started to look the same, people thought it was a great novelty. I used to have this double stroller, and as soon as you were old enough to clutch things, one of you would always be gripping onto the other." She smiled at the memory of this. Charlie wondered if he should be writing it down.

"You used to turn your face away and close your eyes when strangers held you, whereas William would smile and gurgle on demand, even when he was only a few months old."

She started to cry as she recalled these things, but she didn't stop talking. She pulled a tissue from the box on top of the sideboard, blew her nose, and kept going, wiping away the tears as she spoke.

"You shared a room," she said. "You had your own cribs, but when William got big enough, he used to climb out of his and get into yours. They were supposed to be clamberproof, but I'd come in most mornings and find him lying next to you. His name was the first word you said, before even *Mum*. You called him *Wim*.

"When you were toddlers, you were inseparable. Even when you were surrounded by other kids, you'd always be playing together. If anyone picked on you, he used to give them a good thump. You made up all the games though. William always had to play what *you* wanted. You could outtalk him, and you'd never back down—you were stubborn like that."

Charlie was surprised by these stories. He couldn't remember it for himself, of course, but he thought he remembered his mother telling it differently before, that in the stories he had heard previously, Whiskey had always been the boss.

"He couldn't wait to go to school, whereas I think you'd have been happy staying at home forever, playing with your LEGOs and your plastic soldiers," Charlie's mother went on. "On the first day, William ran off without even saying good-bye, and you wouldn't get out of the car. Then when you got used to it, you loved it and he hated it. You used to come home and tell me what you'd learned, and William would tell me jokes he'd heard and stories from the playground. In first grade, he cracked his head open falling off the monkey bars. I nearly had a heart attack when the nurse rang me."

Elaine shook her head, pressed the tissue against her eyes. "After that, it seemed like every time he left the house he'd come back with something broken. You probably can't remember," she said to Charlie, "but I lost count of the times we had to rush him to the hospital."

"I remember," Charlie said.

"He turned my hair gray by the time I was thirty. He'd try anything, always take a dare, nothing scared him, and that terrified me. And then when he got bigger, he was always in trouble at school. I was forever walloping him or sending him to his room without any dinner." She stopped speaking, lost in thought, seemed to have forgotten Charlie was there.

"We thought he'd never amount to anything, your father and I. But he proved us all wrong, didn't he? He's had a successful career, found himself a lovely wife. He had to do his settling down in his own time, that was all. He's been a good husband to Rosa, hasn't broken a bone since that snowboarding accident, what was that, eight years ago?" She laughed mirthlessly, the thread of the story she'd been telling Charlie lost. "Eight years without breaking a bone—we should ring the *Guinness Book of World Records!*" She started to laugh again, and then Charlie saw she was crying, really crying this time.

He stood up and went around the table to hug her, but she pushed him away.

"You've got no idea what it's like for me, Charlie," she said, suddenly angry. "We were so hard on him. We didn't believe in him. Can you imagine how that makes me feel?"

"Come on, Mum," Charlie said helplessly. "Whiskey knows you're proud of him."

But she wasn't listening.

"Do you know the worst part, Charlie, the reason why I've been going to see Victor every week for eight bloody months? The worst part is that I used to wish he was like you. I used to wish that instead of a broken-boned daredevil I'd had another boy just like you. And when I sit with him now at the hospital, all I can think about is whether he knows that. Whether he knows that his own mother couldn't just love him for who he was. I want to tell him I'm sorry, that I was wrong about him, that I wouldn't change a hair on his head. But I can never tell him now. He'll go to his grave thinking you were my favorite, and I can never forgive myself for that."

Charlie could not believe what he was hearing. All these years of thinking Whiskey had been his parents' favorite; to find out now it had been the other way around all along, it changed everything. Charlie could hardly take it in.

His mother had her face in her hands, shaking and crying. Charlie tried again to put his arms around her, and this time she let him, sobbed into him until his shirt was soaked through.

Ever since the accident, Charlie had been so consumed by thinking about his own problems with Whiskey it had never crossed his mind that others too might have regrets, that his mother and father, even Rosa, might have spent the last eight months feeling as guilty as he did, continually rehashing the past, wishing they had done things differently. Hearing his mother express the same feelings that had tormented him, Charlie had a sudden flash of clarity about the pointlessness of it.

"Don't think about it like that. It doesn't matter anymore, Mum," he said. "We've all made mistakes. But there's no point going over it all now. Whiskey wouldn't want us to do that. He knows you love him. That's all that matters."

And speaking the words, Charlie knew them to be true.

X-RAY

Charlie was already awake when the phone rang. For days he'd been waking in the space between night and morning, in that haunted hour when it was no longer dark but not yet light, when time seemed to stand still. He'd been waking and lying and thinking about Whiskey's funeral. At first, he had thought mostly about the logistics: where the service and the wake would be held, how many people might attend, what food and drinks should be served. It had taken him a few days to allow himself to think about the part of Whiskey's funeral that scared him the most: his own speech. In particular, he had spent a lot of time wondering how to address the issue of his estrangement from Whiskey.

Initially he had decided it was better not to mention it at all. Then he changed his mind. If he wanted his speech to do justice to Whiskey's life—and he did—he had to start by acknowledging the mistakes he had made, the ways in which he had been wrong about his brother.

Charlie had never had to make a speech before, not in any formal sense. He had never been a prize winner, or even a best man. But he did not need experience to know that this was the most difficult and important speech he would ever have to make. He would not insult Whiskey with some half-baked collection of clichés. For once in his life, Charlie would do his very best, for himself as well as for Whiskey.

He had not written anything down. He knew that once he had found the right words, he would not forget them. So far, what he had was this:

> Right after Whiskey's accident, I remember thinking that if he died, I would not know which songs to play for his funeral. But it turned out I did know. And though there are plenty of things about Whiskey I don't know, that I wish I knew, that I'll never now have the chance to find out, what I've learned in the months since Whiskey's accident is that I know a lot more about my brother than I thought I did.

The phone rang as Charlie was thinking about his next line. Even as he lay planning the speech, he hoped he would never have to use it. The sound of the phone ringing stopped his heart. He didn't know what time it was, but he knew it was early, that a phone call at that time could only be about Whiskey.

"Charlie?" Juliet murmured.

Charlie didn't answer her, didn't move.

"Charlie?" she said again groggily, reaching to turn on the bedside lamp. "Do you want me to answer it?" she asked, sitting up.

The phone stopped ringing. Then from another room, they heard his mobile begin to ring.

"We better see who it is," Juliet said. She disappeared, following the phone's inane ringtone, came back with it still ringing.

"It's Rosa," she said looking at the screen. "Do you want me to talk to her?"

Charlie shook his head. Juliet sat down next to him on the bed. The call went to voice mail.

Charlie closed his eyes. For a long time he had avoided thinking about this moment, when Rosa or his mother would call to say, "It's over. We've lost him. He's gone." Lately, with a lot of help from Thomas, Charlie had been trying to prepare himself for this. But now

ANNABEL SMITH

that it was upon him, Charlie knew he wasn't ready for it at all, that
he wasn't even close to being ready, that in fact, nothing could prepare him for his brother's death. He felt terrified, more frightened
than he had ever been. If he hadn't been lying down, he was certain
he would have passed out.

"Did you hear me, Charlie?" he heard Juliet say. He opened his
eyes and looked at her.

"Rosa's left a message," she said gently. "Do you want me to listen
to it?"

Charlie nodded, the slightest of movements, as though stillness
could prevent the inevitable. Juliet dialed his voice mail, frowning
as she held the phone to her ear. Charlie knew she too was expecting the worst. He was afraid to look at her, afraid to look away.

"Rosa said Whiskey moved," Juliet said slowly.

"What do you mean, *moved*?"

"I don't know. But it sounds like good news, doesn't it? Let's ring
back and find out."

"Wait a minute," Charlie said. "I need a minute. Are you sure
that's what she said?"

"Positive. She sounded really happy. Do you want me to play you
the message?"

Charlie shook his head. "I thought it was going to be bad news."

"I know," Juliet said. "I thought the same. Let's ring Rosa, and you
can talk to her, put your mind at rest."

She dialed the number and gave the phone back to him.

Rosa answered at once. "Charlie! Thank goodness. Did you listen
to my message? He moved, Charlie, Whiskey moved! He's coming
back to us at last!"

Charlie felt shocked by Rosa's excitement. He was lagging
behind, still getting over the dread that had tightened around his
heart before Juliet listened to the message.

"What happened?"

"He squeezed my hand!" Rosa said triumphantly.

"Are you sure?"

"I am absolutely sure," she said impatiently, and Charlie could hear the old Rosa in her voice, the spark he had almost forgotten.

"Should we come over?"

"Of course, Charlie, of course! Your mother is already on her way."

"What did she say?" Juliet asked as he hung up.

"She said Whiskey squeezed her hand."

"I can't believe it! After all this time!"

Juliet hugged Charlie, elated. Charlie found himself unable to respond.

"What's wrong, Charlie?" she asked, pulling away. "Did Rosa say something else?"

He shook his head.

"What then? Aren't you happy? Whiskey's waking up!"

"We don't know that yet," Charlie said hesitantly. He remembered the drive to the hospital on New Year's Day, after Whiskey opened his eyes; the way they had all sat around Whiskey's bed for hours on end, hardly daring to take their eyes off him for fear they might miss something. It had taken them days to admit to themselves what the medical staff had told them right away, that opening his eyes didn't mean Whiskey was coming out of his coma, that it might not mean anything at all. Charlie couldn't bear to go through it all again: the hope, the disappointment.

"It's possible Rosa might have made a mistake," he said to Juliet. "Let's wait and see what the doctors say."

× × ×

Charlie's mother was already sitting with Rosa beside Whiskey's bed when Charlie and Juliet arrived.

"Isn't it wonderful?" she said, standing up to greet them.

"I can hardly believe it," Juliet said, hugging her and Rosa exuberantly. "Does Mike know?"

"He'll come as soon as he's dropped the girls off at school."

"Have there been any other signs?" Charlie asked, bending down to kiss Rosa hello.

"Not yet," she said. Charlie could see her holding Whiskey's hand tightly.

"What did the doctors say?" he asked.

"They haven't been here yet," Rosa said dismissively.

"Why not?"

Rosa didn't answer.

"The nurse said they won't call a doctor unless there are further signs," Charlie's mother said after a pause.

"Who said that?"

"Robina."

"She wouldn't call a doctor?" Charlie was incredulous.

"Apparently she told Rosa it might only have been a reflex."

Charlie looked at Rosa. "A reflex? Is that possible, Rosa?"

"For goodness' sake, Charlie, not you as well!" Rosa snapped. "For the last nine months I have done nothing but sit here and hold Whiskey's hand. Do you think I do not know what a reflex feels like?"

"Sorry, Rosa," Charlie said. "I just don't want to…"

Juliet looked at him warningly. "Maybe Charlie could talk to Robina," she suggested.

Rosa shrugged.

"Do you want me to come with you?" Juliet asked him.

"No," Charlie said. "You stay here. I won't be long."

Out in the corridor, he leaned against the wall. The atmosphere in Whiskey's room was too charged, too intense. It was difficult not to get swept up in Rosa's excitement. It wasn't impossible she had felt something. It might have been true. But it had been the early hours of the morning; she must have been tired; wasn't it as likely that she had imagined it? Or been half asleep and dreamed it? Charlie wished Mike was there. He needed someone to help him keep a grip on himself.

He found Robina in the supplies cupboard.

"Hello, Charlie," she said. "I thought I might see you this morning."

"Is it true what Rosa said?" Charlie asked her.

"Which part?"

"That you won't call a doctor."

"It's not that I won't call a doctor," Robina said gently. "It's just that sometimes, with coma patients, someone might think they've seen something or felt something, and it turns out to be a false alarm. Now we've checked Whiskey's monitor, and his vital signs are unchanged. But if Rosa was right—if she did feel something, and if it was a genuine sign of arousal—there's a good chance there'll be further signs. So it's not that I won't call a doctor. But I'd like to see further evidence of arousal before I do that. Do you understand?"

Charlie nodded.

"I know it must be terribly hard on you, Charlie," Robina said sympathetically. "You want it so much to be true. And we do too. But it's better not to get your hopes up at this stage, just in case."

Charlie nodded again and turned to head back to Whiskey's room. Halfway there, he changed his mind, went back to the supplies cupboard.

"If Rosa *was* right, though," he said, "when would we know? How soon would there be another sign?"

"The rate of recovery varies a lot," Robina said. "It's difficult to predict the speed at which a patient will emerge from a coma."

"But could you give me a rough idea? I mean, if there are no further signs today, would that prove Rosa was wrong?"

"I'm very hesitant to put a time frame on these things, Charlie, because there are always exceptions to the rule. But if you want some kind of norm to work by, it would be reasonable to say that if there's been no further signs of arousal in the next thirty-six to forty-eight hours, it would probably indicate that Rosa was mistaken."

Forty-eight hours. Charlie nodded grimly. "Thank you."

× × ×

Try not to get your hopes up, Robina had said. And Charlie did try. But as the long, slow minutes gave way to hours, he lost his resolve. He felt hope surging through him like adrenaline, making him fidget and sweat. Looking around that tiny room, he saw it on every face. He understood then the phrase he had seen in the title of Victor's book—*the tyranny of hope*. It was like a habit you couldn't kick, a false friend who kept you clinging on long after you should have let go.

Late that afternoon, standing up to stretch, Charlie felt tense and shaky, utterly drained. His own body odor smelled strange to him. He and Juliet had been sitting beside Whiskey for almost eleven hours, his mother a little longer, Rosa a great deal more. Mike had been and gone, leaving reluctantly just before three to pick up the girls from school. All day they had survived on the strong tea and biscuits the catering staff brought around on trolleys. Charlie suddenly realized how hungry he was.

"I need to eat," he said. "We all do."

It was while Charlie was at the hospital cafeteria, waiting for their toasted sandwiches, that Whiskey moved again. But it didn't matter that Charlie missed it. Because Rosa and his mother and Juliet all saw it, and they couldn't all have imagined it.

All day the room had been quiet, but after Charlie came back from the cafeteria, they couldn't stop talking. Charlie heard the account of how Whiskey had bent and straightened his index finger, first from Juliet, then from his mother, and last from Rosa. None of them had anything to add to the other versions. But each of them needed to describe it for themselves. Charlie didn't mind. He could have listened to it recounted a dozen times. When they phoned Mike to tell him the news, he too seemed to need to have it repeated. He spoke first to Rosa, then to Elaine, then to Rosa again. Next they called Audrey, who was getting over the flu and could not come for fear of passing the virus to Whiskey. By then Charlie had heard the story so many times, he had gotten over his disappointment at missing it. By then he felt sure Whiskey would move again, and this time he would be there to witness it.

He didn't have to wait long. It was only a few hours later that he saw Whiskey slowly flex the fingers in his left hand, relax, and then flex them again. Charlie shrieked with excitement. He jumped up and hugged Juliet, his mother, Rosa. He sat down and thanked the god he did not believe in. Then he put his face in his hands and sobbed. When he had composed himself, they phoned Mike again and then Audrey, and this time it was Charlie who had the privilege of recounting the story.

By morning, Whiskey had moved several more times. Each time, there were four witnesses, and though she saw none of the movements herself, the night nurse was convinced enough to record the movements on Whiskey's chart.

The doctor came first thing the next morning. She frowned as she read the chart, checked Whiskey's monitor.

"Did you open his eyes this morning?"

"He opened them himself," Rosa said.

"What do you think, Dr. Marinovich?" Charlie's mother asked anxiously.

The doctor smiled unexpectedly. "Call me Sanja." She looked at Whiskey. "It certainly sounds very positive," she said, still smiling. "We'll need to send William for tests to find out more, but at this stage the signs are very good."

After she left, Magdalena came into the room. She'd been on shift for two hours, and though she was trying to be matter-of-fact, Charlie knew that she too was excited about the change in Whiskey's condition.

"I know you feel like celebrating," she said, "but you should all go home and get some rest."

"I couldn't possibly sleep!" Rosa exclaimed.

"Take a tablet if you have to," Magdalena said sternly. "Whiskey will be gone for tests for most of the day, so you won't miss anything, I promise you. I don't want to see any of you back here before four, okay?"

"Will you make sure she sleeps?" Magdalena asked Charlie's mother.

Elaine nodded. "I think I'll need a tablet myself," she said. "I'm wound up like a spring."

× × ×

When Whiskey was first admitted to the hospital, all those months before, it had seemed to Charlie that he had undergone virtually every test known to medical science. They had rolled him in and out of the X-ray machines so many times, Charlie had feared that if the accident itself hadn't permanently damaged Whiskey's brain, the amount of radiation flooding his head would finish the job. But once Whiskey's condition had stabilized, all the testing had stopped.

As soon as Whiskey started to move, it was like the beginning all over again. When Charlie and Juliet returned to the hospital later that afternoon, Whiskey was in the X-ray suite. Mike was outside, watching through a glass panel. He had been at the hospital all day while the others caught up on sleep, sitting with Whiskey between tests.

"Any news?" Charlie asked him.

"Nothing yet. They say they won't know until they look at the results of all the tests together, and compare them against the earlier ones. But he's still moving."

"You've seen it?" Juliet asked excitedly.

"No. But the nurses told me they've had to retake some of the X-rays because of the movement."

"Where are the girls?" Juliet asked.

"I arranged for them to stay at a friend's place."

"So you can stay tonight?"

"You bet. I'm hoping to be here when he comes around. That's what I came all this way for in the first place—to meet this guy. And you, of course," he added, grinning at Charlie.

Charlie grinned back. "Where are Mum and Rosa?" he asked. "Not still sleeping?"

"Hardly. They've been back an hour or so. They got a ticking off from Magdalena, I believe." Mike laughed. "They're at the café now—they didn't want to watch the tests."

Charlie nodded. Some of the X-ray machines had tiny chambers into which Whiskey had to be rolled on a gurney, and Rosa, who was claustrophobic, couldn't stand to watch.

"What are they doing now?" Juliet asked, looking through the window.

"I think they said an EEG. It doesn't look too pleasant."

"It's just recording his brain waves," Charlie reassured Mike. "What other tests have they done?"

"I don't know all the names," Mike said. "They did one where they injected dye into his blood. They said it would help them distinguish damaged tissue from healthy tissue."

Charlie tried to recall what he had learned about the tests immediately after the accident. "A CT?" he asked.

Mike frowned. "That doesn't sound right. It was something magnetic."

"Magnetic resonance imaging?"

"MRI, that's the one," Mike said.

"How many more to go?"

"This is the last one for today."

"Looks like they're finishing up," Juliet said.

The three of them watched in silence as the electrodes were unplugged, the paste cleaned from Whiskey's scalp. As the orderly wheeled Whiskey out, Charlie noticed his eyes were closed.

"Have they given him something to make him sleep?" he asked, alarmed.

"Not that I know of," the orderly said.

"Is it normal for him to be asleep after all that?"

"You'd have to ask the doctor," the orderly said apologetically.

Charlie watched tensely as Whiskey was wheeled away.

Juliet put her arm around him. Mike knocked on the window to attract someone's attention.

A nurse came out to see them.

"Did everything go okay?" Charlie asked her.

"I'm afraid we won't have the results until tomorrow."

"I don't mean that," Charlie said. "Whiskey looks really out of it."

"We wondered if you might have given him something to make him sleep," Mike added.

"He's probably worn out after all the testing," the nurse said.

"Surely he wouldn't be able to sleep with you poking around at his head like that," Charlie said.

"There's no discomfort to the patient when the electrodes are removed," the nurse said reassuringly. "The testing can be very tiring for patients, even if they seem unaware of what's going on. It's nothing to worry about."

"He looked shocking," Charlie snapped. "Don't tell me it's nothing to worry about."

Mike put his hand on Charlie's shoulder. "This is a very tense time for us," he said to the nurse, "and we're a little uneasy about the way Whiskey looked."

"I'll ask Dr. Chang to come out." They watched through the window of the suite as she spoke to him, waited while the doctor carefully washed and dried his hands.

"Why don't you let me do the talking?" Mike said to Charlie.

Charlie nodded. He didn't want to make another scene, have a counselor called.

The doctor finally emerged, shook hands with each of them. "Emma tells me you're concerned about William."

"We are a little," Mike said. "The thing is, for quite a few months now, he's had his eyes open, except at night, when we've closed them, so it was unexpected to see his eyes closed. And we're certainly not trying to tell you how to do your job, it's just that we know you don't see Whiskey every day like we do, so you might not know it's not normal for him to have his eyes closed."

"Is there a chance that the tests you've done could have caused him to regress?" Juliet asked.

The doctor shook his head. "I understand your concern," he said, "but there's nothing we've done that would affect William's condition, either positively or negatively. It's absolutely normal for a patient in William's state to sleep deeply after a day of testing. In fact, it's a good sign, because a return of sleeping and waking cycles is an indicator of coma arousal."

"Are you quite sure that's all it would be?" Mike pressed him.

"Whiskey's been monitored all day, as normal," the doctor said patiently, "but if you like, I can call across and have the ward nurses double-check everything."

"We'd appreciate that," Mike said, shaking hands with the doctor again.

Charlie felt ashamed of his outburst. He remembered how Mike's arrival in Melbourne had felt like the last straw. Now he wondered how he would have gotten through the long months since Whiskey's accident without him.

× × ×

Though it had not yet been confirmed in any official medical sense, once Whiskey began to show signs of emerging from his coma, Charlie's mother had suggested they set some ground rules that might help Whiskey in his transition back to consciousness. Charlie suspected the suggestions had come from Victor, whom he knew she still saw, but the ideas seemed sensible, so he did not question them.

The first suggestion was that Whiskey should never be left alone, that there should always be at least one member of the family sitting with him. This suggestion was based on the assumption that Whiskey would recognize his mother, his brother, his wife: of course, they all knew Whiskey's brain may have been damaged in such a way that he might not recognize any of them. But to know this, theoretically, was different to behaving as though it might be a reality. So they had all agreed to this first suggestion. It made sense to every one of them that seeing a familiar face might alleviate Whiskey's distress at being confronted with so much that was unfamiliar. But it did raise the issue of what to do about Mike.

Though it had seemed impossible to imagine when he first arrived, in the months since Whiskey's accident, everyone had come to feel that Mike was part of the family. No one wanted to insult him by suggesting otherwise. And yet, Charlie could not help thinking that to Whiskey, Mike would not be familiar. Even if Whiskey recognized the rest of his family—which was, in itself, a long shot—it seemed ridiculous to hope that he might recognize a person he had seen only in photos, spoken to on the phone a handful of times, a person whose existence he had been aware of for only a matter of months.

"Do you think there's any chance Whiskey would remember the plans he made for Mike to visit?" Charlie asked Juliet when they had a moment alone together.

Juliet took a long time to answer. "I don't really know anything about the brain," she said, "or about the way memory works, and I hate to say this, but before the accident, the idea of Mike being your brother was still so new, so tenuous really, it seems unlikely to me that Whiskey would remember anything about him at all."

When Charlie talked it over with his mother, it turned out she'd had the exact same conversation with Rosa. They all felt that to present Mike as part of the family might be very confusing for Whiskey.

"What do you think we should do?" Charlie asked his mother.

"We'll just have to tell Mike the truth."

Charlie pulled a face.

"We have to put William's needs first," his mother said. "Mike will understand."

"Do you want to tell him?" Charlie asked her, though he already knew what her answer would be.

"I think it would be better coming from you. You're closest to him."

Charlie knew his mother was right. He waited for an opportunity to talk to Mike about it. But by the time that opportunity presented itself, Mike had already worked it out for himself.

"I've been thinking about Whiskey coming to," he said to Charlie, "and I think for now, it might be better to introduce me as a friend of yours. It's not exactly a lie. And it's much less complicated than the truth."

Charlie wondered, not for the first time, where Mike had gotten his common sense. Given that he seemed to have so little himself, he thought it must have come from Mike's adoptive parents.

On the day after Whiskey's tests, Charlie, Juliet, Mike, Rosa, Elaine, and Audrey were all at the hospital when Dr. Marinovich came to deliver the results. It went without saying that they could not discuss Whiskey's condition in front of him, nor could they all go outside at once. Someone had to remain with Whiskey and wait to hear the news. Charlie volunteered.

"I'll stay with you," Juliet said reluctantly.

"You go with Rosa," Mike said to her. "I'll wait with Charlie."

Except for Mike and Audrey, they had all seen Whiskey move, some of them more than once. In the moment, they had all per-ceived the movement to be voluntary, to be evidence that Whiskey was returning to them. And yet, there was a part of Charlie that still did not dare to believe it could be true, a part of him that wondered if, in their desperation, they might have only imagined Whiskey moving, shared in some collective hallucination, as a group of weary travelers might see the same oasis in what was only a barren desert.

As the women left the room, Charlie once again felt fear and hope doing battle within him. He wanted to stand by the door, to watch through the small, square window as the news was delivered, but he was not confident his legs would hold him. He dropped into the chair beside Mike, sick with anxiety.

A minute passed, the longest in history.

"I can't bear it," Mike said eventually. He went to the window.

"Can you see anything?" Charlie asked.

"It's good news!" Mike exclaimed.

"How do you know?"

"I can tell by their faces. It's definitely good news."

"Are you sure?"

"I'm absolutely sure!"

Charlie had expected to feel elation, to want to jump up and down, whooping and hollering. But when Mike pulled him out of his chair and hugged him, Charlie didn't make a sound. There was nothing to say. He had everything he wanted, and the relief was overwhelming.

* * *

In the week that followed, Charlie spent every possible moment at the hospital. He saw Whiskey open his eyes in the morning, and close them at night, saw him move his arms, his legs, his head. When the machines that had kept Whiskey alive for all those months were at last unplugged and wheeled from the room, Charlie and his mother opened a bottle of champagne and toasted their great fortune.

As soon as Whiskey's transfer to the rehabilitation facility had been arranged, the psychologist who had been assigned to Whiskey's case asked Charlie to come in for a chat.

"I'm responsible for Whiskey's emotional well-being while he's at Rosehill," Dr. Parvati said, "and I know family and friends play a critical part in that. I'm speaking to all Whiskey's close family members to let them know how they can contribute to Whiskey's recovery. I understand you've been a regular visitor to your brother at the hospital, but there might be certain things we do differently here, and I'd like to take you through some of our guidelines, if you don't mind."

"If it will help Whiskey," Charlie said.

Dr. Parvati nodded. "I'd like you to put yourself, for a moment, in Whiskey's shoes. Try to envision waking up one day in an unfamiliar room, with no memory of how you came to be there. You can't move or speak, and you don't know why. Strangers are coming and going at all hours of the day and night. Among the strangers are people who are familiar to you, but you can't quite place them. As you can imagine, Whiskey is probably feeling shocked, confused, frightened, disorientated. My job is to minimize those feelings, make him feel as safe and comfortable as possible on his recovery journey. In light of this, the first of our guidelines is that at this stage, you don't mention either the accident or the coma."

"Why is that?"

"Because Whiskey may not yet understand that these things have happened to him."

Charlie nodded.

"The other thing we recommend is that, for now, you don't refer to the past."

"What do you mean? Surely you're not suggesting we can't mention anything about his life before the accident?" Charlie was incredulous.

"I know that seems extreme," Dr. Parvati said, "and it's not forever. But yes, for now we ask you not to speak of Whiskey's past at all."

"Well, what on earth do we talk about with him?"

"Keep things in the present. Talk about your day, about his day. We'd like to get him grounded in the here and now before we attempt to stimulate his memory."

"But surely we want him to remember."

"Absolutely, we do. Don't think we won't be stimulating Whiskey's memory—that's an essential part of the rehabilitation program. But memory is a delicate thing. Even for those of us who work with it every day, there is much we don't understand. Whiskey must be allowed to recall things at his own pace. I know that can be difficult. I understand that you might feel desperate to know if Whiskey recognizes you, but pushing a patient to recall things from the past can put emotional pressure on them, which can be counterproductive. You have to try to put his needs first. Apathy, fatigue, and depression are common responses in post-coma patients—we need to do everything we can to keep Whiskey positive."

x x x

Charlie came to Rosehill most days, after he had finished his shift at the café. Sitting in on a session with the occupational therapist, he watched as Whiskey was guided again and again through the motions of picking up a small, oblong block. After a time, Charlie found himself growing agitated by the process and he was relieved when Mike arrived. He stepped outside, and they watched for a while through the window.

"He's never going to learn it," Charlie said dejectedly. "Carl's shown him dozens of times, and he isn't getting any closer."

"I thought the same," Mike admitted. "I asked Carl at what point he would give up, accept that Whiskey wasn't going to get something."

"What did he say?"

"He used a good analogy to explain what he's trying to do. He told me to think of the brain as a mechanism for delivering messages—like a postal system. He said if a courier was delivering a parcel within this system, usually they would deliver their parcel by the quickest, most efficient route. But, if for some reason this route was closed to them, they would have to find an alternative route. They might make a wrong turn, have to retrace their steps a few times. But if they persevered, eventually they would reach their destination and deliver the parcel."

"But what does that mean for Whiskey?"

"Apparently, if the usual pathway along which a message travels is damaged, there is still a possibility for the message to get through. Every time Carl shows Whiskey how to pick up that block, his brain is trying to find a way to get that message to the muscles in his arm, his hand. So far, it looks like that message has been lost every time, before it manages to reach its destination. But if he keeps trying, eventually Whiskey's brain might find the right path, get the message through. Carl said though it might appear that Whiskey isn't getting any closer to picking up the block, his brain might actually be getting very close."

"I wish someone had explained it to me like that before," Charlie said.

x x x

After he had been at Rosehill for a couple of months, Whiskey was assigned a speech therapist, a tiny birdlike woman, the only person Charlie had ever heard pronounce the *H* in Whiskey. Though any real communication took place through a system of hand signals, Whiskey was moaning and mumbling, squinting and frowning, and straining into the mirror Lucinda held up for him, trying to make his mouth move like hers.

"He's doing well, isn't he?" Charlie asked Lucinda after one of the sessions.

"He's responding well to the therapy, yes," Lucinda said carefully.

"How soon do you think he might start talking?"

Lucinda seemed surprised by Charlie's question.

"Not whole sentences or anything," Charlie clarified. "I know that takes time, but a few words perhaps…"

Lucinda was looking at Charlie with concern. "You obviously care for your brother very much, Charlie," she said gently, "and I don't want you to get the wrong idea, because after what Whiskey's been through, he's doing very well indeed. But coma arousal is a slow process, and Whiskey is a long way off from talking, a very long way."

"But he's responding to everything you do," Charlie protested.

"It's true that in relation to the state Whiskey has been in, his responses represent a huge leap—please don't think I underestimate that," Lucinda said. "But most of what you're seeing from Whiskey at the moment are reflexes, innate responses we're born with, and as such, they are only the first stage of coma arousal."

"So what's the next stage?" Charlie asked. He wished Juliet was with him, or Mike.

"The second stage is what we call perceptivity, which refers to learned or conscious responses. Talking is, of course, a learned response. In fact, most aspects of communication—gestures, body language—are learned. After a prolonged coma, many aspects of perceptivity need to be relearned."

"And how long does that usually take?"

"Have you been shown the results of Whiskey's tests?" Lucinda asked carefully.

Charlie saw the pity in her face, and it carved a pit out of his stomach.

"The biggest concern is the damage to the cerebellum, at the back of Whiskey's brain," she said. "The damage to that area is most likely what's preventing Whiskey from walking. But it's also affecting his fine motor skills. Once we've learned it, we take it for granted, but talking is actually an extraordinarily complex process. Every sound we make requires a precise arrangement of the lips and teeth and tongue. It requires the synchronization of a range of muscles that would usually be coordinated by the cerebellum. In addition, Whiskey has sustained damage to the temporal lobe, which houses our memory for words and names. It's possible..." she started, then trailed off.

"Go on," Charlie said, though a part of him did not want her to.

"We'll do our very best, of course. But taking into account the damage to these two areas, there is a very real possibility that talking is one skill Whiskey may never be able to relearn."

× × ×

Charlie had thought he would be able to manage without Thomas once Whiskey came out of the coma. But it had been almost a year since Whiskey's accident, and after his conversation with Lucinda, every time he saw Whiskey, part of him asked, *What if this is as far as his recovery goes? What if this is all that's going to be returned to us?*

Surgeons, neurologists, psychologists, nurses—the staff at Rosehill had all told Charlie the same thing—that after nine months in a coma, Whiskey's recovery would be slow and arduous, that he might be in rehab for as long as he had been in the hospital. No matter how many times he'd heard this, and from how many different sources, Charlie had refused to believe it. Whiskey's bones had set, his wounds healed. He had been disconnected from every one of the machines that had come to seem like a part of him, discharged from the hospital they had feared he would never leave. Charlie was convinced that recovering from the accident, surfacing from the depths of the coma, had been Whiskey's greatest challenge.

He had been clinging to the fact that Whiskey's frontal lobe—the part of the brain that was responsible for personality and emotions—was undamaged, which meant, theoretically, that Whiskey would still be Whiskey. And when he was away from him, Charlie found it easy to remember Whiskey as he was before the accident, to imagine he could become that person again. But after a while, Charlie found it increasingly difficult to reconcile this image with the Whiskey he visited at Rosehill.

After weeks of Marco badgering him, Charlie made another appointment with Thomas. Thomas reminded Charlie about the cycle of grief.

"We don't experience grief only in the face of death, Charlie. We also mourn other losses. It's reasonable to expect that you're going to experience grief about some of the things Whiskey has lost, especially the loss of aspects of his character, which you believe made him who he was."

"I'm not grieving," Charlie said.

"You're in denial about the reality of Whiskey's condition. That sounds like grieving to me."

"I'm not in denial," Charlie said.

"If you're telling yourself that Whiskey should already be walking and talking, that in a matter of weeks he'll be back at home, the same old person he used to be, believe me, Charlie, that's denial.

Whiskey's recovery is going to take time. It may be months before the full extent of the brain damage becomes clear. He might never be the person he once was. You need to forget about the old Whiskey, and start getting to know the new Whiskey. Ultimately, you're going to have to accept him for whoever he is now."

YANKEE

Every Saturday throughout Charlie's childhood, his father had gone to the betting shop to put some money on the horses. Now and again he had some luck and came home from the betting shop with more money than he went with. Occasionally he won a trifecta. Charlie did not know what a trifecta was, only that it usually meant a visit to the toy shop, where he and Whiskey were invited to choose anything they wanted.

The most memorable moment in Bill's gambling career took place the year after Charlie and Whiskey finished school when Bill bet on four different horses to win or be placed in four different races, and every one of his horses came in. According to their father, this kind of bet was called a Yankee, and the odds of winning it were smaller than minuscule. Charlie wasn't the slightest bit interested in horse racing, but he remembered the name of the bet; even the names of the horses stuck with him: You Little Dizzle, Prim and Proper, Cool in Springtime, and Maple Leaf Rag. He remembered because his father's Yankee bought him his first car.

Charlie hadn't thought about his father's win for years. It was Marco who reminded him when they finally caught up for a beer, and Charlie recounted the events that had taken place in the weeks after Whiskey woke from his coma.

"Sounds like all your horses have come in at once," Marco said.

× × ×

The offer came at the end of the first week of January. The following week, Charlie arranged a meeting with his old boss, the principal at St. Kilda Primary School.

"How lovely to see you, Charlie," Deirdre said enthusiastically. "How's life treating you?"

"It turns out I wasn't cut out for climbing the corporate ladder," Charlie admitted.

"Well, I can't say I'm surprised," Deirdre said. "But you have to give these things a go. A bit of trial and error never hurt anybody. So what next?"

"No more mucking around," Charlie said. "I'm going to do what I should have done a long time ago. I've been offered a place in the Diploma of Education at Monash University, and I'm going to take it. This time next year I'll be a real teacher. Finally."

"That's wonderful news," Deirdre said sincerely. "We need more young men like you in the profession. If we had a suitable opening, I'd have no hesitation in giving you a job."

"Really?"

"Don't sound so surprised, Charlie. You're a natural. I've seen how much your students adore you, especially the bigger boys. It's great for them to have a positive role model."

Charlie was touched. He had never thought of himself as a role model. "Thank you," he said.

"My pleasure," Deirdre said. "But tell me, did you just come to share the good news, or is there something else I can do for you?"

"Actually, there is something else."

"Fire away then."

"I know I can't have my old job back," Charlie said. "I know Mary's doing that now. But I wondered if there was…anything else I might be able to do?"

Deirdre tapped her fingers on a stack of papers on top of her desk. "As a matter of fact," she said, "I've had funding approved for two new students—one intellectually disabled boy in fifth grade, and a second-grade girl with learning difficulties. I'll need an integration aide to work with them. It's one-on-one work, mostly within the classroom—more challenging than what you were doing before, but certainly within your capabilities. Would that interest you?"

"Definitely," Charlie said.

"The only thing is, it's not many hours—I'd have to check, but it's possibly only eight, twelve at the most."

"That would be perfect for me with college," Charlie said.

"Well, great! That's settled. It was lucky timing actually, because I was about to advertise."

"That's it?" Charlie asked. "Don't I need an official interview or something?"

"Consider this your interview," Deirdre said, smiling. "Come and see me the week before term starts, and we'll sort out the details."

Charlie stood up. "Thank you so much," he said. He felt a little stunned by how quickly things had happened.

"Thank *you*, Charlie," Deirdre said. "It'll be great to have you back on board."

Charlie's first horse had come in.

× × ×

The second horse was Mike. He called while Charlie was in the car.

"What do you think about meeting me at the Royston?" Mike asked.

"I'm on my way to see Whiskey," Charlie said.

"Me too. I thought maybe we could grab a beer first."

"*Before* we see Whiskey?" Charlie asked. Sometimes, if Whiskey was tired, they left early and went for a beer at the pub around the corner. But they had never gone for a drink beforehand.

"If you don't mind. I've got some news. I don't want to tell you at Rosehill."

"Okay," Charlie said reluctantly. He was suspicious of the kind of news that needed a special one-on-one engagement to be told. He'd had enough of that to last a lifetime.

"So what's up?" he asked Mike before their beers had even been poured.

Mike laughed. "Let's at least sit down first. Not all news is bad news, Charlie."

"I know."

"Well, mine is good news anyway. At least I hope you'll think so. The girls and I got our permanent residency."

Charlie was astonished. "Do you know for sure?"

"One hundred percent. I found out this morning."

Charlie couldn't take it in. He had known about the application of course—Mike had asked every member of the family to write a letter testifying to the nature of their relationship with him and the girls. Charlie and Juliet had printed out photos and labeled them, awkwardly elucidating their complicated connections: *Holly and Chloe with Aunt Juliet (Michael's half brother's partner),* etc. Mike and the girls had been to interviews, had had physicals, filled out endless paperwork. And then for months nothing happened. Whenever Mike inquired, the Department of Immigration told him the application was *still being processed.* Charlie had stopped asking about it. He had thought they would be refused permanent residency, and he didn't want to think about what that meant for them, or for himself. The news that their application had been successful came as quite a surprise.

"What did Mum say?" Charlie asked, still trying to take it in.

"She doesn't know yet."

"Rosa?"

"I wanted to tell you first."

"You're really going to live here permanently?"

"We'd like to, if you guys will have us."

Charlie was overcome. He took a long drink of his beer. "Of course we'll have you," he said eventually. "We should celebrate," he added.

Mike raised his glass to Charlie's. "We are."

Charlie laughed. "This is such good news," he said, finally

recovering himself. "Juliet will be so happy. Can I call her? Or do you want to tell her yourself?"

"If it's okay, I'd like to tell Whiskey first."

"Yes!" Charlie said. "Great idea." It was absolutely right that he should be the next to know. After all, if it hadn't been for Whiskey, Mike would never have come.

× × ×

The third horse was Juliet. Charlie was at Rosehill with Mike when Juliet phoned him.

"How long do you think you'll be?" she asked.

"I only just got here. Why?"

Juliet never checked up on him.

She paused. "There's something I want to talk to you about. But there's no rush. We'll talk when you get home."

"Is everything okay?"

She laughed. "Absolutely."

"What is it then?"

"I don't want to tell you on the phone."

"Why not? Are you sure there's nothing wrong?"

"There's honestly nothing wrong. But I can't tell you now. You'll understand when you get here."

"That was weird," Charlie said to Mike after he hung up. And then, remembering himself, he said to Whiskey, "That was my girlfriend, Juliet."

"Is everything okay?" Mike asked.

"I don't know," Charlie said. "She didn't sound upset, but she said she needed to talk about something."

"Did she give you a hint?"

"None at all."

"Do you need to leave right away?"

"She said not to. But I'm worried now. I'll come again tomorrow afternoon," he said to Whiskey apologetically.

Whiskey smiled. Charlie stopped for a moment to enjoy it. Whiskey had relearned so many things since he'd moved from the hospital to Rosehill. But after so many months of seeing Whiskey's face without expression, the novelty of seeing Whiskey smile still hadn't worn off for Charlie.

When he got home, Juliet opened the front door before he had time to get the key in the lock. She kissed Charlie, wrapped her arms around him, but Charlie pulled away. "What's the matter?" he asked.

"Nothing's the matter, I told you that."

"Why did you call me then? I rushed back here."

"I told you not to rush. Don't worry so much, Charlie."

"I am worried. It must have been something important."

"It is important. But it's nothing bad."

"Come on, Jules. I don't like guessing games."

"Don't be a stick in the mud, Charlie. Can't I have a little fun?"

"Not at my expense," Charlie said irritably. "Why don't you just tell me?"

"I found something today," she said, smiling mysteriously.

"What kind of something?"

"Something pretty."

"What's happened to you?" Charlie asked. He'd never seen her act so stupidly. "Are you drunk?"

"I'm perfectly sober."

"Are you going to tell me what you found?"

"Maybe you could tell me."

"How can I tell you? I don't have any idea what you're talking about."

"Well, I'll give you a clue. I found it in your wardrobe."

"Found what?"

"In your sock drawer, to be precise."

Charlie swallowed. "You found *that*?"

Juliet nodded, suddenly serious.

He looked at her carefully, trying to read her expression. Things had been so good between them since that day when they had come close to breaking up. But Charlie had botched the first proposal so badly he still hadn't worked up the confidence to have another shot at it.

"What do you think?" he asked. He felt shaky.

"It's beautiful."

"Not the ring. I mean, what do you think about…us?"

"Is that your marriage proposal?" Juliet asked him.

"No," Charlie said. "Yes. I don't know." When he had rehearsed this moment in his head, he had planned to say something profound, something romantic. "Does it fit you?" he asked, confused.

"I don't know," Juliet said seriously.

"Haven't you tried it on?"

Juliet shook her head.

"Why not?" he asked desperately.

"I was waiting for you to put it on my finger," she said to him.

"Is that true?"

She nodded.

"You want to wear it?"

"Very much."

"So you want to be my…wife?" Charlie had trouble getting the word out.

"Is *that* your marriage proposal?" Juliet teased.

Charlie laughed now, relieved. "I think that's as close as you're going to get."

"Ask me again," Juliet said.

"Would you like to be my wife?" Charlie asked her. He couldn't keep the smile from his face.

"Yes, please."

"Is that your acceptance?"

"It's as close as you're going to get."

"Say it again then."

"I'd like to be your wife, Charlie," Juliet said.

Charlie wasn't much for poetry, but he thought it was one of the loveliest sentences he had ever heard.

"Are you sure?" he asked.

"Of course I'm sure."

Charlie held her beautiful face in his hands and kissed her.

"I suppose we should do the ring thing then," he said. And then remembering, he asked sheepishly, "Where is it?"

"In my pocket."

"Ideally, it would have been in *my* pocket," he said, but it didn't matter.

"There you are then," Juliet said. She pushed the box into the pocket of his jeans.

Charlie took the box out of his pocket and opened the lid. "Do you really think it's beautiful?" he asked her.

"I really do."

He took her left hand and pushed the ring onto her finger. It fit perfectly. She held out her hand. "Do you think it suits me?"

"Do *you* think it suits you?" Charlie asked. He wanted so much for her to like it.

"I love it because you chose it," Juliet said. "*And* I think it's beautiful."

"Are you really going to be my wife?" Charlie asked, suddenly overwhelmed by what had unfolded.

"I really am," Juliet said.

× × ×

The last horse in Charlie's Yankee was Whiskey.

Since Charlie had gone back to college, he'd been dropping in to see Whiskey before class. One morning, Charlie and Juliet were at Rosehill particularly early, before Whiskey was even awake. They sat without talking until he began to stir. Charlie waited for Whiskey to look at him before he spoke.

"Hi, Whiskey, it's me, Charlie—your brother."

They knew the damage to Whiskey's temporal lobe had affected his memory for words and names. Introducing themselves each time they saw Whiskey was a way of jogging his memory and was also supposed to alleviate any anxiety he might feel if he failed to recognize someone. Charlie had felt foolish at first, introducing himself to his own brother, but they all did it, even Rosa, and after six months, Charlie didn't even think about it anymore.

"This is my girlfriend, Juliet," he said after a moment. He still couldn't get used to the word *fiancée*.

"Hi, Whiskey," Juliet said, squeezing his hand. "You've had a nice long sleep. It's overcast and humid—a typical summer day!" she said cheerfully, opening the blinds.

Whiskey blinked. His eyes followed her as she went over to the calendar they had hung on the wall. "It's March fourteenth today," she said. "It's a Wednesday. Meredith will be here to do your physiotherapy this morning, and later on your wife, Rosa, will be back, and your mother."

She sat back down, smiled at Whiskey. Charlie reached over and took her hand.

The door opened.

"Here's your breakfast," Juliet said, taking the tray and bringing it over to Whiskey's bed.

Charlie adjusted the bed, raising it slowly so as not to startle Whiskey.

"All right, what have we got here?" Juliet said, looking at the tray. "Would you like some yogurt and fruit?"

Whiskey tapped his finger twice for *yes*.

After Whiskey had been fed, Juliet went to get herself a coffee. "Do you want to listen to some music?" Charlie asked when she was gone.

Whiskey tapped twice.

Charlie took a CD out of his bag. It was a compilation he had made for Whiskey, of music they had liked as boys. He hadn't been able to find any of their original seven-inch singles, not in Whiskey's collection, nor his own. They had long been lost or broken, he supposed, or thrown out in one of their mother's famous purges. But with a lot of help from Marco, Charlie had managed to download most of the songs he was looking for from the Internet. Charlie had been carrying the CD around with him for several days, taking it to Rosehill and home again, waiting for the right opportunity, wanting to be alone with Whiskey when he played it for the first time.

The opening track was the *Peter Gunn* theme. Charlie thought about the first time they had heard it, when they were seven or eight years old, and their dad brought it home from the pub. Bill had done this once or twice before—coughed up fifty pence for records that had lost their currency on the jukebox. The last one had been Art Garfunkel's "Bright Eyes," which Charlie and Whiskey didn't like and never played. The record they'd been waiting for was Joe Dolce's "Shaddap You Face." So they were disappointed when their father brought home "Peter Gunn," a song they had never heard of. But their disappointment didn't last long. With its sinister bass line and sudden crescendos, listening to the record made them feel like spies, like villains. Hearing the horn solo again, Charlie still felt the thrill of it. But when he looked at Whiskey, his eyes were closed. Twenty-five years on, the pull of memory was so strong for Charlie; it cut him to think his brother didn't feel it at all.

Heavy-hearted, he turned the CD off without even waiting for the song to end. But as soon as the music stopped, Whiskey opened his eyes, tapped his finger several times on the bed. Charlie had never seen him make this gesture before.

"Do you want it back on?" he asked. Whiskey tapped twice.

Charlie got up and started the CD again. A minute or so into "Peter Gunn," Whiskey looked straight at Charlie and repeated the gesture he had made before, tapping his finger several times in quick succession. For months they had been using the same code, in which one tap meant *no*, two meant *yes*. Charlie did not know what these repeated taps meant.

"Would you rather I turned it off?" he asked, wondering if he had misinterpreted Whiskey before.

But Whiskey tapped once decisively. Charlie tried hard to think about what Whiskey might want. He felt panicked that he did not understand. He wished now that he had played the CD when Juliet was there. He tried to calm himself, to think it through from Whiskey's point of view.

"Do you want some different music?" he asked. Another single tap.

"Do you want me to turn it up?" he asked desperately. He was sure it couldn't be that, but he had run out of ideas.

Whiskey tapped twice.

"You want it louder?" Charlie asked. He couldn't believe it.

Two more taps. Charlie jumped out of his chair and turned up the stereo. "How's that?" he asked.

Whiskey tapped several times. "More?" Charlie asked, incredulous. Whiskey kept tapping.

Charlie laughed. He turned the stereo as loud as it would go. Then he stood by Whiskey's bed, held his brother's hand, and danced a strange, awkward dance of elation as the tears ran down his face.

ZULU

I can't believe the girls are turning eight," Juliet said on their way
to the twins' party at Whiskey and Rosa's. "I keep thinking
about the day they arrived, when I went to pick them up from the
airport, and they were sitting there sucking their thumbs, like two
little lost lambs."

"How old were Holly and Chloe in those days?" Oscar demanded
from the backseat. *In those days* was his latest expression.

"They must have only just turned six."

"And how old was I?"

"You were three."

"Now I'm four," Oscar said. "Turning five," he added, in case his
first point had not been understood.

"Thank goodness you're early," Rosa said, coming out to meet
them. "We haven't done the balloons."

"I'm very good at blowing up balloons," Oscar announced.

"Well, that's wonderful. But we also need someone to tie them.
Whiskey always used to do it, but it's too…" She gestured rapidly
with her fingers. "What's that word?"

"Fiddly?" Charlie offered.

"Yes. Too fiddly for him now."

"I can tie them," Charlie said. "Oscar, you can be the chief blower."

"Let me carry something," Rosa said, taking the cake from Juliet.
She peeked into the box. "Oh, that's beautiful."

"It's a butterfly," Oscar pointed out.

"Oscar helped me choose it," Juliet said.

"Yes, and we got those candles that when you blow them out, they come back again, as a surprise for Holly and Chloe!"

"That sounds like fun," Rosa said.

Charlie's mother and Aunt Audrey were in the living room with Whiskey, putting up streamers.

"Here's Charlie and Juliet," Elaine said.

"Hello," Whiskey said slowly.

Charlie bent down to hug him.

"Hi, Whiskey. This is my nephew, Oscar," Juliet said.

Oscar came closer to Whiskey's wheelchair. "I saw you in the hospital," he said. "But you didn't see me. You were asleep."

Charlie looked at Juliet. It was almost two years since Whiskey's accident, but they still tried to avoid talking about it, as it sometimes upset Whiskey.

Whiskey looked at Oscar for a moment. "I *did* see you," he said eventually, in his slow way. "I was only pretending to be asleep."

Charlie smiled. It seemed like a miracle to him that despite everything that had been lost from inside Whiskey's head, his sense of humor was still intact.

"Can I go for a ride in your wheelchair?" Oscar asked Whiskey.

"No, Oscar," Juliet said quickly. "Whiskey needs his wheelchair. It's not a toy."

"I could take you for a ride on my lap," Whiskey volunteered.

Oscar beamed.

Then they heard a horn toot from outside.

"They're here!" Rosa said, rushing to turn off the light. Charlie's mother lit the candles. They started singing "Happy Birthday" as Holly and Chloe burst through the door.

"I remember that song," Whiskey said afterward, thoughtfully.

"That's the song we always sing for someone's birthday," Elaine said.

Whiskey frowned as he always did when he was trying to place something in his memory.

"All right now, time for the presents!" Rosa announced, clapping her hands.

"Daddy bought us a Barbie town house," Holly said.

"We didn't bring it," Chloe added.

"Because it was too big to even carry!" Holly finished.

Oscar wanted to give his present first. Charlie had taken him to choose a gift, and he had browsed without shame in the Barbie section of the toy shop before selecting a hot-pink sports car. Charlie's mother gave the twins a miniature beauty parlor, where they could style each other's hair and paint their nails. From Rosa and Whiskey, they had new backpacks, and from Juliet and Charlie, secret diaries with little keys on golden strings. When all the presents had been unwrapped, the paper discarded on the floor, Charlie put another present on the table.

"This one's from me and Whiskey," he said.

Whiskey looked at him, confused.

"I chose it on behalf of both of us," Charlie added for Whiskey's benefit.

The twins tore open the paper.

"What is it?" Holly asked, opening the box.

"They're walkie-talkies," Charlie said.

Whiskey looked up. Charlie could see him mouthing the word, trying to fit the sound of it with his memory of the object.

"But what are they for?" Chloe asked.

"So you can talk to each other when you're not together. Whiskey and I used to have them when we were your age. Do you remember, Whiskey?" Charlie asked casually.

Whiskey picked up one of the boxes to have a look. "I remember," he said slowly.

"But what would we say?" Holly asked.

"There's a whole alphabet you can use," Charlie said. "I'll teach it to you later if you like."

"How does it go, Uncle Charlie?" Chloe asked.

"Alpha, Bravo," Charlie began. He could see Whiskey's eyes on him. "Charlie, Delta, Echo."

"That doesn't even make sense!" Holly said.

"Foxtrot," Whiskey said suddenly.

Everybody looked at Whiskey, but only Charlie knew it was the correct word.

"Golf," Charlie said, looking at him.

"Hotel," Whiskey replied, frowning deeply.

The girls giggled.

"What are you talking about?" Rosa asked.

"India, Juliet," Charlie went on, smiling at Whiskey.

"Kilo," Whiskey said after a moment. He seemed about to say something else, and then he stopped. Charlie kept looking at him.

"Lima," he prompted. Three words were enough—more than enough, but why not try for more?

"Mouse?" Whiskey tried.

"Mike," Charlie corrected him, grinning at Mike.

"November," Whiskey said very quietly, nodding his head.

"Why are you crying, Uncle Whiskey?" Chloe asked.

"What is it, my darling? Are you in pain?"

"I'm fine," Whiskey said. "There's no pain. It's a strange feeling"—he looked at Charlie—"as if everything had started all over again."

Whiskey was still crying when he said this, still looking at Charlie, the tears rolling down his face, which despite everything, was still the same as Charlie's face.

"I'm going to call the hospital," Rosa said.

Whiskey took her hand. "There's no need, Rosa," he said gently. Hers was the first name he had learned.

"Are you sure, William?" their mother asked.

"Honestly, Mum. I feel as strong as a…what is the word?" He looked at Charlie. "A Zulu." He laughed.

Charlie laughed with him.

"What's a Zulu?" Oscar asked.

"The Zulu were an African tribe," Charlie's mother said, looking at her sons, their partners, her grandchildren.

"They were brave and fearless," Juliet said.

"They were warriors," said Mike. "Warriors who fought for their tribe."

"They would have died for their tribe," Charlie said, looking at Whiskey.

And looking back at him, Whiskey said, "It's the last letter. The last letter of the two-way alphabet."

READING GROUP GUIDE

1. *Whiskey & Charlie* is structured around the two-way alphabet. How does the author use the two-way alphabet as a narrative device within the story?

2. What are Charlie's perceptions of his brother, and how do they change over the course of the novel?

3. Do you relate to Charlie's feelings about Whiskey? Have you had a time where you felt resentful or jealous of a sibling? How did you resolve those feelings?

4. In what ways does Whiskey's accident force Charlie to grow up? Is there a defining moment in Charlie's maturation?

5. How has Whiskey's accident affected the other members of their family?

6. Suppose that Charlie had been the one in a coma rather than Whiskey. How do you think Whiskey would have handled that situation? What are some regrets he may have had about their relationship?

7. Charlie loves Juliet yet is afraid to marry her. What stops Charlie from proposing to Juliet or from accepting her proposal? And what finally makes him change his mind?

8. How does the counseling Charlie receives in the hospital help him to resolve the issues in his life? How might things have worked out differently if he had received that kind of help earlier?

9. How does Charlie's relationship with Whiskey affect his relationships with others around him, including his mother, his father, and Juliet?

10. What role does Rosa play in the novel, as a relative newcomer to the family and in the dynamic between Whiskey and Charlie?

11. What role do you think Mike plays in the story? How does his arrival further complicate Charlie's feelings about Whiskey?

12. For most of the novel, it is unknown whether Whiskey will recover from his accident. What are some issues related to quality of life and euthanasia that arise in this story?

13. Does *Whiskey & Charlie* have a happy ending?

A CONVERSATION WITH THE AUTHOR

Whiskey & Charlie deals with the complexities of sibling relationships. What was your inspiration for writing it?

In an interview for *The Paris Review*, Jonathan Franzen describes the discovery that his best writing was about "something as trivial as an ordinary family dinner." I think the term "dysfunctional family" is something of a tautology—all families are dysfunctional in some way, which makes family life very rich with dramatic possibilities. What led me toward exploring this particular aspect of family life was my father having a falling out with his only brother, which resulted in them not speaking for a decade. I wanted to understand how two people who had grown up together could reach a point where they didn't speak for ten years, so, at some level, I think I wrote the book to answer that question.

Whiskey & Charlie is structured around the phonetic alphabet, with one chapter for each letter. Why did you choose that structure, and did it pose any problems?

I'd seen other writers experiment with structural motifs and had been attracted to trying it, but I had never come across anything I'd thought I could use in that way. Then a friend taught me the radio alphabet, and I went around reciting it to myself for a couple of weeks while I committed it to memory, and this was at the exact time when I was beginning to write the first scenes of the novel that became *Whiskey & Charlie*, and I thought, why not build a book around this?

It was a great springboard for giving me ideas about episodes in the twins' lives. But it also posed some challenges. Any of the chapters with names (Charlie, Juliet, Oscar) were simple—they became character names. But Yankee kept me awake at night. For a long time, I had no idea how I was going to work that in. Others posed problems in terms of chronology. X-ray, for instance, was an easy idea to work in, given that Whiskey was hospitalized, but I really wanted that information to appear earlier in the novel. I had to do some tricky maneuvering, like using flashbacks, to make some of the chapters work.

Retrospectively, there seemed to have been a logic to it all along because it became, at its heart, a book about communication, specifically a two-way communication, and the structure seemed to make perfect sense.

What research did you have to do for *Whiskey & Charlie*, and how did you go about it?

I had to understand comas, both in a medical sense and in terms of its impact on family and friends. For a long time, I wasn't sure whether Whiskey would recover from the coma. So I needed to know for how long someone could plausibly remain in a coma, what kind of therapy they would receive, and other health threats they might face while in a comatose state. In case Whiskey woke up, I researched recovery, rehabilitation, and the physical and mental implications of long-term comas. In the event he would not recover, I explored right-to-life issues and the euthanasia process. The last thing I wanted was for readers to pick holes in the science. So I gathered statistics, diagrams of the brain, explanations of testing procedures and diagnostic tools, etc. I don't really have a science brain, so it was pretty heavy-duty reading for me!

I used medical and anecdotal sources and came across some amazing recovery stories—and many heartbreaking accounts without happy endings. There are lots of forums on the Internet for the loved ones of comatose patients, and they were an excellent source of material. People contribute advice about things they've learned along the way, tips on what helps them get through; some just need an outlet to share their stories with others who understand what they're going through.

In addition to information that had dramatic possibilities, I gathered details that would help to make the story feel real, especially to readers who might have some knowledge of coma, all of which were collated into a giant tome I printed out and carried around with me for months on end. I was very happy to retire it when the book was complete.

Like the title characters of your novel, you were born in England and moved to Australia as a teenager. How autobiographical is *Whiskey & Charlie*?

There are elements that are loosely autobiographical: my family did emigrate from the UK to Australia in the 1980s, though we came by plane, and ended up in Perth rather than Melbourne. The feelings of alienation that Charlie experiences at his new school were very much my own. The anecdotes of the voyage to Australia are based on my husband's family's emigration by boat in the 1970s. There are a few specific scenes that are based on my own experiences—our dog being hit by a car, the costume competition in the village fete, and the character of Oscar is a sort of amalgam of my two oldest nephews. But the main characters and their experiences are entirely fictional.

Which character do you feel most closely connected to?

I think there are tiny fragments of me in almost every character—I am forthright like Rosa, romantic like Juliet, impulsive like Whiskey. But the character I most identify with in this novel is Charlie. I think everyone has times in their life where they're not moving in the direction they want to, where they're not doing the things they need to do, where they're lost and floundering—and I have a lot of compassion for Charlie as he goes through this process. I feel proud of him when his self-awareness grows and he begins to make changes. I feel for him as a parent feels for his or her own child!

Did you always want to be a writer, or did you start off in a different career?

I always enjoyed writing stories at school and certainly always loved reading, but when I was a child, my burning ambition was to be an actress. My mum told me it was very difficult to be successful and that I would probably have to do some other work to make ends meet. So I gave that up…and eventually ended up in a profession with exactly the same prospects! I have worked as a corporate trainer and as a teacher of English as a Second Language to support myself financially while I write.

What's your writing process like?

My writing process is completely organic. I just show up at the page and see what comes out. This has been the way I've written all my novels so far. I love the surprise of discovering what my unconscious has cooked up while I wasn't looking. I write in my home office while my son is at school. The writing "zone" is an elusive space! Some days I sit down and it surrounds me, sealing me inside. Most days it's not that easy. I have to creep up on it from behind or chase it around until it gives up in exhaustion and finally lets me in. Occasionally it eludes me entirely.

What do you love most about writing?

One of my favorite things about being a writer is hearing from readers: when I receive an email from someone telling me how much my book has resonated with them, it really makes my day and reminds me what it's really all about—connecting with book lovers.

At what point do you show your work to others? Is it something you'd encourage all writers to do?

I was part of a writing trio while writing *Whiskey & Charlie*, so I started showing drafts to them almost from the start. I found it really helpful to have feedback at an early stage, when I was still uncertain about the voice, the style, and whether the story was appealing or compelling to readers. Once I got on a roll with it, I had more confidence and felt less in need of ongoing feedback. After finishing the first draft, I sought more feedback, from a wider circle. I think it's critical to have perceptive readers, whose feedback you trust, to look at your work. If you can find the right people, they can support you when you lose faith in yourself, brainstorm a way through issues in the text, and notice things you can no longer see because you're too immersed in the work. I have no doubt that the feedback I received made my book stronger and more satisfying to read.

Who are your favorite writers? Why?

I love Jennifer Egan for her wry humor and psychological perceptiveness, Louise Erdrich for the vividness of her prose and her incredible insight into human nature, and Ann Patchett for creating relationships so intimate I feel like I'm part of them. I love Margaret Atwood's world-building and sense of playfulness, Haruki Murakami's wild imagination, Justin Cronin's ability to make my heart almost stop with suspense, and Maria Semple's gift for creating the most hilarious and improbable scenarios.

What would be your advice to new writers?

- Read widely and deeply. Talk about books, and take them apart to see how they work.
- Write as much and as often as you can, and be patient. Allow yourself time to develop and find your own voice.
- Join or form a writing group. The process of critiquing

and being critiqued will improve your writing like nothing else I can think of.

- Subscribe to writing journals. One day you'll be ready to submit your stories to them. They rely on subscriptions to survive, and without them, you'll have no markets for your work.

- Support local independent bookshops. Online stores won't give you the time of day until your books start to sell in the tens of thousands, whereas local bookshops will hand sell your novels when you're a complete unknown. Don't let them go out of business!

ACKNOWLEDGMENTS

I would like to begin by thanking Georgia Richter and all the folks at Fremantle Press for helping *Whiskey and Charlie* to come into the world. I am hugely grateful to Shana Drehs for her enthusiasm about bringing the novel to a U.S. audience and to Anna Michels and the editorial team at Sourcebooks for their careful and sensitive editing and for being willing to preserve the Australianisms that give the novel its flavor. I am deeply indebted to my fellow writers Amanda Curtin and Robyn Mundy, who gave detailed and insightful advice on numerous drafts over a period of several years. My first draft "guinea pigs" were Swifty, Kathryn Porter (aka Little Katie Hardcore), Lucinda Pullinger, Jim Gill, and last but not least, my mum—thank you all for your feedback and encouragement. I am, as always, enormously grateful to Richard Rossiter, who told me things I needed to know but didn't want to hear, asked me some hard questions, including the memorable "Why is Charlie such a dickhead?" and who gave me the incredible gift of the time and space to finish my final draft in his magical writing loft. Finally, my gratitude goes to my amazing husband, Duckers, for his love and support.

I acknowledge the following sources for the quotes that appear herein:

"She was moist and trembling," p. 25: Anaïs Nin, *Delta of Venus* (New York: Pocket Books, 1991).

"History is nothing," p. 40: Milan Kundera, *The Joke* (London: Faber & Faber, 1992).

"Hope is the thing with feathers," p. 258: Emily Dickinson, "Hope," *The Poems of Emily Dickinson*, ed. R. W. Franklin (Cambridge, MA: Harvard University Press, 1999).

ABOUT THE AUTHOR

Photo by Justine Monk

Annabel Smith is the author of *A New Map of the Universe* and the interactive digital novel/app *The Ark*. She holds a PhD in writing and is on the editorial board at Margaret River Press. She lives in Perth, Australia, with her husband and son.

Check out her website: *annabelsmith.com*